T0247789

FIRST
FROST

By Craig Johnson

The Longmire Series

Also by Craig Johnson

Stand-alone E-stories

CRAIG JOHNSON

FIRST FROST

VIKING

VIKING
An imprint of Penguin Random House LLC
penguinrandomhouse.com

Copyright © 2024 by Craig Johnson
Penguin Random House supports copyright. Copyright fuels creativity,
encourages diverse voices, promotes free speech, and creates a vibrant culture.
Thank you for buying an authorized edition of this book and for complying with
copyright laws by not reproducing, scanning, or distributing any part of it in any
form without permission. You are supporting writers and allowing Penguin
Random House to continue to publish books for every reader.

LIBRARY OF CONGRESS CATALOGING-IN-PUBLICATION DATA
Names: Johnson, Craig, 1961- author.
Title: First frost / Craig Johnson.
Description: New York: Viking, 2024. | Series: The Longmire series
Identifiers: LCCN 2023052664 (print) | LCCN 2023052665 (ebook) |
ISBN 9780593830673 (hardcover) | ISBN 9780593830680 (ebook)
Subjects: LCGFT: Detective and mystery fiction. | Novels.
Classification: LCC PS3610.O325 F57 2024 (print) |
LCC PS3610.O325 (ebook) | DDC 813/.6—dc23/eng/20231121
LC record available at https://lccn.loc.gov/2023052664
LC ebook record available at https://lccn.loc.gov/2023052665

Printed in the United States of America
1st Printing

Netflix is a registered trademark of Netflix Inc. All rights reserved.
The series Longmire™ is copyrighted by Warner Bros. Entertainment Inc.

This is a work of fiction. Names, characters, places, and incidents
either are the product of the author's imagination or are used fictitiously,
and any resemblance to actual persons, living or dead, businesses,
companies, events, or locales is entirely coincidental.

For Ben Petrone, who paved the way.

Through wind, hail or frost my living's made.

—FRANÇOIS VILLON

Acknowledgments

I was talking to my good friend Michael Crutchley, one of the youngest elected sheriffs in Texas at one time, and he told me that true cowboys should switch from their palm leaf hats to their wool felt ones at the first frost. The title fits this particular book because both Walt and Henry are most likely facing the first frost of their lives when they graduate from college, lose their deferments, and in 1964 read the writing on the wall and enlist.

Throughout the story that is attached to Vic's discovery of a surfboard in the basement of Walt's house, we get to hear the saga of an epic road trip starting from the beaches of Point Dume in Malibu, California, with the final destination being Fort Polk, Louisiana, for Henry and Parris Island, South Carolina, for Walt. Though they're not driving a Corvette convertible but the half-ton pickup Walt was bequeathed from the family ranch, the boys, in their early twenties and at the peak of their physical prowess after playing college football for the past four years, head out on the Mother Road, Route 66.

The question, of course, is how far they will get before they get into trouble—the answer being, not very.

I've always been intrigued by the internment camp at Heart Mountain over the Bighorns from the ranch, and I used to stop in there long before it was a Historic Landmark. I think it's highly laudable what's been done there, but I think it might've made an even greater impact when I saw it all those years ago when you could drive right up to the ramshackle buildings with the windows broken out and the doors hanging off the hinges, the ever-present Wyoming wind sandblasting through those aged structures, as if attempting to erase what was one of the darkest moments in American history.

A good friend's father had been the superintendent of the camp, and I'm always on the hunt for an intriguing story, so I asked her if there had ever been any criminal activity. She smiled and said yes, that there had been. She also said that there had been a thriving and helpful smuggling operation made up of local ranchers, who had heard that the detainees needed sewing, art, or other supplies, and so would sneak them into the camp. As Walt Longmire says in *First Frost,* "Kinda gives you hope for humanity."

First Frost isn't the first time I've ventured into Walt's past and is not likely to be the last, because I find it interesting to discover the sheriff's history and grow closer to the man who he becomes and why. Besides, whoever thought that Longmire had a surfboard? Everybody knows that Walt's too big to surf.

When you head out looking for the big waves or attempt to write a novel like this one, you need to make sure you're in good company, and I can't think of any better than Gail "Hang Ten" Hochman and her wingperson, Marianne "Men in Grey Suits" Merola.

The mayor of Surf City, however, has to be Brian "Big Kahuna" Tart, and when it comes to applying the surf wax, the queen of sheen is Jenn "Big Wednesday" Houghton.

If you want to catch a wave, I always follow Sara "The Duke" Delozier and Yuleza "Goofy Foot" Negron down the pipeline.

When I'm hanging ten, I rely on Johnathan "Wipeout" Lay and Michael "Cutback" Brown to fish me out, but when it's time for a surfin' safari, I hang loose with Christine "Cowabunga" Choi, Alex "Big Wave" Cruz-Jimenez, and Molly "The Shred" Fessenden.

A big shaka shout-out to Eric "Hang-Loose" Wechter and Francesca "Gidget" Drago—where would I be without you?

Last, but certainly not least, the little surfer girl in my life when I'm looking for the warmth of the sun is Judy "Wahine-Kai" Johnson, the siren of the surf.

FIRST
FROST

1

"You're too big to surf."

I took another sip of my Rainier, smiled, and then looked up at the ten-foot surfboard stuffed in the floor joists of my cabin's little-known basement. "I didn't used to be."

Victoria Moretti balanced on the stepladder and stroked a hand over the board, detecting the little scuffs, dents, and scars on the otherwise remarkably smooth varnished surface. "It's a monster."

"The Monolith, as Henry used to call it." I sat on the concrete steps that led down from the Bilco doors into the cellar. "They used to be even bigger back in the day, in Hawaii—the Duke boards."

"The Duke, you mean John Wayne?"

I smiled. "No, Kahanamoku, kind of the father of surfing."

She shook her head. "So, you mean to tell me that when you went to college in California you actually surfed?" When I smiled at her she pushed up, lifting one end of the longboard. "It's heavy."

"About a hundred pounds, stout for the day. It's a Bob Simmons sandwich model, one of his early designs, but it's still got the twin fins."

"Who's Bob Simmons?"

"Another surfing legend."

"And he sold you the board?"

"No, he died back in '54 so I never met him. The smaller, more maneuverable boards were all the rage in the 60s and those big boards were going for a song—I bought that one for thirty bucks and strapped it to the top of a Country Squire station wagon on the Pacific Coast Highway near the Santa Monica Pier."

Pushing her thick, dark hair back from her face and tarnished-gold eyes, she ran her fingers over the fins as if the board might swim away. "You hauled this thing all the way back from Southern California?"

"Not exactly."

"Then what?"

I took another sip of my beer. "It's a long story."

She stared at me for a moment before carefully climbing down the ladder to stroll over and take the beer from my hand. With a final look she lifted the Rainier and downed the whole thing, then handed me back the empty can, but only after crushing it. "You've got to stop saying that."

"What?"

"That long story shit."

"Sorry, I guess I'm kind of distracted." I tossed the crumpled can into the trash by the steps, pulled another one from the sixer by my boots, and offered it to her. "Frosty beverage?"

She sat on the hard steps beside me and took the beer and then pointed toward the surfboard, specifically at the ragged gouge in the front edge. "We'll start small; tell me about that dent in the front there."

I snorted.

"What?"

"That actually is a long story."

She torqued open the can and looked at me with the electrified eyes, transmitting the thought that if my lips didn't start moving pretty quickly my goose was cooked. When I didn't say anything, she stood, turned, and walked up the steps out into the blazing sunlight above.

We'd been living together for over a month, something that neither of us had been used to for quite some time. I'd never thought of my cabin as being small, but with my undersheriff's oversize personality the space was becoming something of a problem. She'd thought that making a home gym out of the little-used basement might help her blow off some steam and maybe inspire me to get into shape, hence what had become known as "the great purge."

I looked around the dim space at the plastic tubs and beer crates that held portions of my life I'd hardly remembered. I called my daughter as a reinforcement, but her response had been that if there were anything down there, she had lived without it for the last twenty years, so she'd be satisfied to continue as such.

My good friend Henry Standing Bear had had a similar response and said I should simply rent a truck, load everything in, and haul it to the dump.

So far, I hadn't been able to do it.

So far, I hadn't even been able to open a single box.

It was almost as if I was afraid of the things I would find there. At this fragile point in my relationship with Vic, I wasn't sure I could sustain throwing away the life I'd had before. Martha had passed almost ten years ago, but if I were to risk opening even one of those boxes, it was possible that decades could disappear in the blink of a dimly lit eye.

I sat there for a moment more and then grabbed myself another beer. I lumbered up the steps after her and turned off the light. It was a gorgeous July morning with the meadowlarks singing and a slight breeze from the mountains keeping it cool. I closed the basement's cellar doors to keep any wayward animals out, and rounded the tiny cabin to find her seated on one of the rocking chairs on the front porch.

I stopped at the bottom of the steps. "Pax Romana?"

"What the fuck is that supposed to mean?"

I lifted two fingers. "Peace, little Roman."

She sipped her Rainier. "Sure, whatever."

I hoisted myself up onto the porch and stepped over Dog as he raised his big, bucket head to check on me and then went back to snoring. I seated myself in the opposite rocker, opened the beer, and took a sip. "I'm sorry."

"It's okay, honest. You're just not ready to go through all that stuff."

"I'm not so sure I ever will be."

"Well, then, there's that." She sat studying me. "Is there anything else?"

"Maybe."

"Like what?"

I took another sip of my beer and thought about the week ahead. "This preliminary hearing tomorrow."

"What about it?"

I breathed a laugh. "I haven't done one in twenty years."

"You didn't do anything wrong."

"I guess I'm worried that I'm out of practice."

"Just tell the truth, and you'll be fine."

I stared at her.

"Prolly." She smiled, reached her can out, and we tipped the edges in a toast. "Now, the gouge in your surfboard?"

FRIDAY, MAY 22, 1964

"You too big to surf, mon."

Looking at the chop waves rolling in past Point Dume near Malibu as the sun got shouldered out by the grim-looking clouds above the vast Pacific Ocean, I leaned my back against the still warm wall of Marvelous Marv's Snack Bar and let the heat there relax my sore muscles, a trick I'd learned from Henry. "What do you know, Marv? You don't surf."

Marvelous Marv was a transplant from Jamaica, having given up his island paradise for the California coast and specifically Malibu

Point. His snack bar was an on-again, off-again operation in a partially crumbling structure of cement block on Pirate's Cove Beach that everybody was pretty sure he'd acquired because the previous owner had abandoned it. Truth be told nobody knew his real name, but Marvelous Marv was painted on the side of the weathered white building in a sweeping turquoise script, so the name had stuck. With dreadlocks and a crocheted hat, he served up cold drinks, chips, ice cream when it wasn't too hot—and from what I was to understand, the finest Lamb's Breath marijuana ever smoked by man. Personally, I'd tried the stuff once but had gotten nothing more than a headache and went back to beer.

I turned toward the ocean, aware that in four years it hadn't lost any of its fascination for me. Maybe because when the wind blew across the grasslands of the high plains the whole world felt alive, and the same could be said about the Pacific. The thing about the ocean was that it never was the same; whether it was the north swell or the rip curls off the point, it was always different. I guess that over time, I never again saw the sea as an adversary but rather as an intimate companion.

"Ain't nobody should be surfin' today, mon." He turned and raised the volume on the tiny transistor radio behind him, bringing in the throaty voice of Richie Barrett singing about "Some Other Guy," one of the Cheyenne Nation's favorites. He looked up at the darkening skies and then at the chop of the waves and at the checkered flag that the local meteorologist had placed on top of the rock cairn at the point, signaling danger to the many fishing vessels that hugged the coast rounding the point.

"Hey Marv, when did that boat go down last year?"

"About nine months ago, mon. The *Siesta Royale*, working boat, she took eight souls wit her." Marvelous crossed himself and stared down at the scaly, painted surface of the counter that spanned the only window at the snack bar. "Hey, mon, why don you buy a candy bar or somethin'? I got Baby Ruth."

"Not hungry."

He nodded, giving up on the sale and looking out to the sea. "Where that good-lookin' girl you hang wit?"

"Rachael?" I pointed to two fearless individuals who waited on a set not too far out, biding their time in the rising storm to catch just one more maxed-out curl onto the beach. "Over there with Henry."

Marv shook his head. "That Bear, mon—he crazy."

I thought about the celebratory trips the Cheyenne Nation and I had taken down to Tijuana and how many drunken brawls we'd barely escaped with our lives. "Sometimes, yep."

"How long he been surfin'?"

I thought about when the Bear had come down from Berkeley. "About a month now. He finished up early, and to be honest I think they were happy to get rid of him—he majored in political science, but I think he spent more time at protests and sit-ins than he did in class."

"Protesting the war?"

"Yep, but it looks like he's going to be a part of it anyway."

He nodded. "You good on dat ol' board—simple, old-fashioned style, drawing long lines with perfect balance, big man—but dat Bear, he look like he been doin' it all his life."

I sighed. "Yep, he's kind of a natural athlete."

Sensing my feeling of inadequacy, Marv threw me a bone. "Hey, congratulations on that fruit bowl you won, mon."

"Rose Bowl."

"Ya . . . Dat a big deal, mon?"

"I guess."

"You gonna play more dat football?"

"No, both Henry and I graduated and lost our deferment, so we enlisted."

He slid down the heavy sunglasses on his nose and looked at me. "Enlisted?"

"Yep, before we could get drafted."

He shoved the glasses up with a middle finger and looked back out at the threatening ocean, where Rachael and the Bear finally caught what looked to be a premium wave as it feathered, the crests throwing spray as the swells steepened. They had a hard time finding the line, when suddenly the wave looked bigger and more frightening. "Day got dat football up in Canada too."

I nodded, pressing my back harder against the blocks and sliding up to a standing position so I could watch them better. "No, but that won't be the direction we'll be going."

"Mexico?"

The long-period glassy and gray swell lifted them as they stood on their boards. "No, Henry is supposed to go to Fort Polk—someplace called Tiger Land in Louisiana—and I'm supposed to go to Parris Island in South Carolina for some reason." I watched as the questioning look returned to his face and figured I'd cut it off at the pass. "If you're a marine in the western part of the states you go to Twentynine Palms down the road here, and if you're from the eastern part of the country you go to Parris Island in South Carolina."

"But . . . Ain't you a cowboy, mon?"

My two closest friends were silhouettes now, backlit by the one glimmer of the gray sun that threw a single shard of mercury light between the closing clouds. Their boards carved like dark blades, slashing and gliding beneath their balanced feet as Rachael effortlessly cut back behind the Bear. "I am, but for some reason they want me to report to Parris Island, so we've got a road trip ahead of us starting tomorrow."

He shrugged. "Dat should be fun."

It was the perfect wave to finish the season, a gift sent by the sea gods with glowing hooks and tall shoulders, a day of glory on Big Wednesday. "Yep, kind of a last hurrah."

"How long dat trip take?"

"Four or five days in my ranch truck."

"You need some money?"

I turned to look at him, aware that in the four years I'd known him I'd never heard him offer a loan to anybody. "No . . . No, I think we're good, but thanks, Marv."

We both watched as Henry and Rachael made the beach and stumbled onto the sand of the all but empty stretch. Usually, the Pit, as we called it, was full of the surfing royalty, but with the weather being the way it was, the majority had decided to give the middle of the week a pass. Giving each other a high five, they turned to wave at Marv and me, and I waved back, relieved that they'd made it to shore and that they'd gotten one last magnificent sunset ride.

Rachael had been born here in Southern California, and, of course, Henry, even though a native of the high plains, had taken to the sport like surf wax. As my college years had gone by, I'd found myself spending more and more time at the beach, trapped between two worlds, one on land and the other the ocean. I guess it wasn't such an abnormality in that nine times out of ten when you asked somebody from my home state what branch of the service they'd been in, they'd generally say the navy.

That explained part of the thrall, a kid from a landlocked state who till four years ago had never even seen the ocean. During football season my time was pretty much not my own, but in the offseason I'd find myself loading up my board, the Monolith, as Henry called it, and heading up the Pacific Coast Highway in the ranch truck my parents had bequeathed me. Sometimes I camped, sometimes I slept in the bed of the two-tone half-ton, and sometimes I'd spring for a cheap motel, where Rachael and I would ride our own waves.

I'd first met Rachael Weisman in a literature class where we'd squared off on Dostoevsky's *Crime and Punishment*; I'd say it was a spectacular treatise on morality and she'd say it was the most moribund and depressing declination of a novel she'd ever read. I'd never met anybody that used the words *moribund* and *declination* in the same sentence, and we never agreed on the subject of Dostoevsky, but we'd both respected each other's ardor concerning the written word.

We'd slept together that weekend and had been a couple for nearly the last three years. I'd even brought her back to Wyoming, where my parents had fallen madly in love with her. But things had changed since I'd enlisted.

I'd told her I wasn't comfortable extending the relationship into my military service, and that I didn't want her to be stuck with a guy she would be lucky to see in the next four years, if at all. She'd argued that we were already a couple and that allowing something arbitrary like the Vietnam War to break us up just seemed stupid.

My response that the Vietnam War was about to become anything but arbitrary for me was not met with a great deal of benevolence.

"Did you see that ride?"

The two of them leaned their boards in the driftwood rack next to mine at the end of the derelict snack bar. Rachael shook her tawny-brown hair, the curls catching the last glimpse of the sun as the clouds took final command and the winds picked up. "Fabulous."

She smiled, her hazel eyes flashing as she shook an unfolded towel in an attempt to dry off. "It was, wasn't it?"

Smiling, Henry took her board and straightened it in the rack. "Did you see her?"

"I did." Gesturing toward the water, I shook my head. "I think the two of you made it by the skin of your teeth." The waves were now slamming the beachhead, sounding like cannon fire. "We better get the truck loaded up and get out of here before they close the bridge at Malibu."

I turned to deliver a final farewell to Marvelous Marv when I saw him leaning out the window across the counter and looking out to sea, his sunglasses snatched from his face.

Automatically turning back to the ocean, I could see one of the fish-for-hire boats bobbing around the point, lying on its side as the big swell attempted to crash it onto the rocks.

Both Henry and Rachael followed our gaze as she stepped forward, facing the rain that swept over us. "What do they think they're doing . . . ?!"

A spray struck at us as we watched the tiny boat bob upright, teetering on the crest at nearly a 45-degree angle only to be slammed by another wave and flipped so far as to dip a mast tip into the previous wave. "Probably got caught out in the storm. They are trying to make it around the point and get either to Santa Monica or Marina Del Ray."

"They are going to go over." Just as the words left the Bear's lips, another monstrous groundswell slammed into the tiny fishing boat as lightning struck the horizon with the in-rushing storm.

The boat managed to slide down the other side of the wave, safe for only a moment as another wall of deep water walloped the thing like a convoy of semitrucks. The plate glass of the cabin shattered as the mast collapsed and the rigging was carried overboard. You could see people being swept over the side, with a few holding on to the railing, screaming for their lives as they plummeted into the ocean.

You couldn't hear the sound of the motor, even when the wind died down for a second, meaning the boat was defenseless against the onslaught of waves that continued pounding it until another one, a good thirty feet high, assaulted it again, this time rolling the boat completely over from starboard to port.

I don't remember grabbing my big board from the rack, but I do remember running with it over my head as I dug my feet into the sand and ran for the point. I was almost there when I could feel something gaining on me and hoped it wasn't a wave coming in at an odd angle.

Henry.

He'd grabbed his own board and was running past me toward

the point, probably faster than he'd ever carried a football for UC Berkeley.

His hair was whipping in the high-knot wind as he got to the farthest point out. When he reached the water, he flipped the board like a poker chip and slammed onto it, submerging through one of the disembodying waves before reemerging on the other side like a U-boat, then paddling in a direct line for the wreckage of the small vessel out a hundred yards.

I dove in, feeling the wave pull me to the side as I turtled, then grabbed the edge of the surfboard and flipped over before straightening into the next swell where I was smothered in water and blackness.

It was hard to see which way to go as the waves allowed a visibility of only about twenty feet, but I caught sight of the Bear as he paddled to the top of a wave before disappearing over the other side.

Figuring that he had a better idea of where he was going, I corrected my angle and caught a break as the next wave slipped off. I was nowhere near the natural athlete that Henry was, but after fighting in the trenches of college football and pushing those blocking sleds for the last four years, I was bigger and stronger than I'd ever been, and so I began digging my hands like a paddleboat into the surf.

My left shoulder ached where a defensive lineman from Wisconsin had dislocated it during our stint in Pasadena, but it held, and through my surf-blinded eyes I could see I was gaining on the Bear.

Another wave hit me and buried me underwater, but I held on to the board and kicked forward, dragging it upward till I breeched out of the water with it like a wooden whale.

I could see debris in the water, heard somebody screaming to my right, and then nothing. Paddling that way, I got blindsided by another wave, then felt something brush by me. It was a gamble in that I could've been grabbing hold of a piece of the mast, which would most likely tangle up and drag me to bottom, but I closed my hand around whatever it was and felt fabric and skin.

Yanking it up, I could feel the cumbersome weight of a body and threw the man across the board. Panic-stricken, the guy coughed and attempted to move, but I yelled for him to stay still and hold on to the board.

Between the swells I could see two more individuals in the water: one caught in the lines and another who was clinging to the side of the hull. Directing the board, I grabbed the arm of the one tangled in the rigging and pulled him upward next to the first man. I unwound the line from his leg and then used the overturned boat as cover to get closer to the man now sliding down the hull and into the darkness.

Turning the board, I reached out and gripped the collar of his shirt just as another mammoth wave struck the boat, lifting it above and beside us a good twenty feet. "Well, hell . . ."

The swell was strong, but it hadn't crested, giving us a heck of a ride, but at least it didn't turn the damn thing over and slap us to the bottom of the ocean. The point of my board rammed into the propeller before sweeping us clear, and I pulled the third man up and onto the board, figuring I had to get these three back to dry ground, because there wasn't room for anybody else.

Staying to the left, I rode one of the smaller sets, then dragged my board forward toward the shallow water.

Rachael and Marv, having joined us in the knee-deep water along with two others, grabbed the three bodies off my board one by one and began pulling them onto the beach. Content that they were safe, I yanked the Monolith up and started back into the roaring surf.

Rachael screamed after me. "What are you doing?!"

Partially swiveling my head, I bellowed. "Henry's still out there!"

I turned back and was immediately trounced by an incoming wave, but I dug my legs in and stood my ground with the board point buried in the sand along with my feet. When the ocean was done with me for a moment, I snatched the board and made it into the next wave, imitating the Bear's method of entry and piercing the next wall of water.

Blowing through the other side, I wiped my eyes and could see the bright white of the boat's hull through the next swell, looming like some bloated monstrous jellyfish, and dug into the water again. Pulling great handfuls of salt water, I drove over the next wave, barely beating the crest, and then wallowed down the other side.

I could see someone hanging from the railing who had been torn from the boat, so I circled to the right trying to get there, but the topside hull lifted once again just as I reached a hand out. I saw the fingers slipping from the rail as another wave smacked the side of the fiberglass hull like thunder, and I wasn't sure how the thing hadn't been crushed inward.

If I tried to go around the hull, I'd probably lose them, and over the top wasn't going to be possible in these conditions. With the lashing rain, the blowing surf, and the relentless waves, it was almost like being underwater anyway.

So, slamming all two hundred and fifty pounds onto the board, I drove it under the hull of the sinking boat and kicked with everything I had, catching the ridge with my feet in order to shoot downward. The big board fought me every inch of the way, banging me against the smooth surface of the hull as another wave lifted us up and I used the opportunity to continue kicking.

The board tried to turn sideways on me, but I held fast and thought I could see something ahead in the water, something that looked like flowers.

Flowers?

Just then, I remembered that the Bear had been wearing a pair of old-man baggies with a blue and yellow floral pattern. There was no way I was going to get to him if I held on to the board, so I took a desperate gamble and let it go, watching as it shot upward, abandoning me.

Diving to the left where I'd seen the pattern, I thought about that last gasp of breath I'd sucked in about forty seconds ago and just hoped I had enough air to last. Looking to the left, I couldn't see anything but figured that down was the only way he could've gone.

Digging in the water like I was in a coal mine, I realized that if I got much deeper there would be no light at all and I'd never find him.

I furiously dug, and it was then that I saw a flash of that same flower pattern even farther to my left and slowly descending. Diving deeper, I straightened like a knife blade reaching a hand out, and then grabbed toward the direction of the pattern but missed. Feeling that something had slipped through my fingers, I grabbed again, but this time I got it.

Hair.

I wrapped it in my fingers to make sure I wouldn't pull loose and then lifted, having felt the thump of a body against my shoulder. I turned and slipped an arm around it and then kicked toward the luminescent hull of the overturned boat and the available light.

Allowing the rolling current to assist me in getting to the surface, I could feel my lungs screaming for breath, telling me it was okay and that I should just inhale.

Ignoring my lying lungs, I held fast and finally burst through the surface only to bash my head against something. Slumping to the side, I pulled the Cheyenne Nation from the water and spotted my board, which had tangled in the gear spillage, banging against the overturned deck of the boat.

I heaved him onto the board just as another swell lifted us and threw us against the wooden planking before we dropped again like unwanted flotsam but certainly not jetsam. Placing my feet against the cabin, I pushed us to the left and dragged the surfboard along with me to best keep the Bear splayed across its surface.

I thought about checking him, but there wasn't anything I could do except to fight for our lives and try to get him to solid land. Pulling more leftward, I was able to clear the stern section of the fishing boat and kickaway from the damn thing in hopes of lessoning its opportunity to crush us.

As luck would have it, the next swell steepened but then passed both us and the wreckage to the right, sending it back toward us as if trying to get one more shot before we got away.

"Well, hell . . ."

The propellers were headed straight at us, and though they weren't turning, they still looked plenty sharp. Pulling the board away, I held it and Henry at arm's length just hoping he wouldn't slip off. The stern came down on top of me instead, but I was able to put my shoulder into the rudder as it slapped me away, but not before reading the name of the boat: *EL ESPECTRO.*

Momentarily losing my grip on the board, I was forced under but scrambled to get back to it, knowing that the only thing that was going to keep the Bear on that board and enable any chance of survival was me.

Finally, bouncing a hand off his leg, I swam upward and grabbed the board again, which shifted Henry along its flat surface. Then I kicked us away from the rudder, hoping that we were finally free of it.

I thought we'd made it when the exact same wave slipped to the right, dumping the aft section on us again, but this time I wasn't so lucky and something very large, heavy, and unforgiving slammed against my shoulder, driving me down.

Almost blacking out, I just hung there in the water, suspended between heaven and earth, my lungs whispering what little air they held, telling me again that I had tried, that it was okay, that I could let go.

The pain in my head rang like pealing bells, and for a moment it was all I could do to not inhale two lungsful of seawater. Stretching my jaw in hopes of straightening my head, I shook, but that only made it worse. Blinking my eyes, I couldn't see anything but darkness and was startled back to awareness by the thought that if that damn boat hit me again I was done for.

Rolling to the side, I could see the shadow above me, the darkened shape that had to be my board with Henry on it.

Gritting my teeth and tasting the salt that was either the sea or blood, I swam, lifting myself from the would-be watery grave and bursting through the surface once more. Pulling Henry's body to the center of the board again, I swung around to find that the boat had shifted its bow toward the shore, and we were clear.

Attempting to stay in the spot where the swells had shouldered off and hoping we had a chance of making shore despite the waves that were crashing constantly on us, I was able to maneuver to where they began kicking us toward the beach that seemed so very far away.

Paddling, I reached out and lifted the Bear's face, but his eyes were closed, and he didn't respond. I felt an iciness and tried to get us to shore faster, but I could only go so fast, even with the cresting swell that pushed us forward.

I finally got to a depth where I could feel the bottom, so I trudged, dragging the board with me. I fought to stay on my feet until somebody pushed me aside and took the Monolith.

I stayed on my hands and knees after falling, the waves still pushing me forward, at last settling for crawling in the wet sand and water. I made it a good twenty feet, escaping the last clutches of the Pacific Ocean before finally slumping to my side to feel if my shoulder had dislocated again.

I blinked so that I could see more than an arm's length away. The board lay between us, and I reached out a hand, steadying it as it worried the beach.

It was an odd tableau, a strange vision of an intimate act seemingly out of place.

I blinked again, moving my shoulder to provide a little more support for my head, but then gave up as I had no energy left.

I lay there looking at what appeared to be a kiss. Maybe it was a kiss, or maybe it was a mermaid having finished the job of pulling the two of us from the sea. She sat with her tail curled up under her, her face pressed against the man's in a rhythmic grace as she held his head, his raven hair stretched out and spread onto the sand like tree roots.

Mesmerized, I just watched through half-closed lids and became aware that I was shaking. All I could do was curl up a little as I kept my eyes on the two of them.

There was a sudden movement as she pulled her face from his and he coughed violently before turning his head and throwing up a stomachful of churning seawater. He coughed some more before dry heaving again and then lay there, breathing.

My focus had been drawn away, but when I looked back up, the mermaid had become a land-based creature and had stepped over him and onto my board with two legs before kneeling and reaching down to take my face in her hands. The hazel eyes peered through the rain-laden curls.

Rachael looked down at me. "Are you all right?"

I cleared my throat and then did a little coughing of my own. "No, I think my shoulder is partially dislocated and I'm dead."

She laughed. "I think you survived, but I'm not sure how."

I watched as she sat, half turning to place a hand on the Bear's back as he continued to retch.

"I think he made it too, thanks to you." She reached out and ran her fingers along my hairline. "Looks like you got conked." She leaned in and looked closer. "Yeah, pretty good one—what, you find a shark out there to wrestle with?"

"It . . . it was that damned boat." Reaching down, I pulled and turned my arm as a medico on the sidelines of the Rose Bowl had shown me, relocating the socket with a grisly crunch. "Did it sink?"

She shuddered and glanced back out to sea. "Yeah, finally."

"Did we get everybody?"

"I don't think so, one made it to shore, and you got three." She shrugged a head at Henry. "He hauled two more before going MIA." There was some commotion behind her. "The EMTs are here along with some reporter and a photographer."

"How did they get here so fast?"

"They were on the PCH taking pictures of the storm when they saw all the hubbub down here on the point." She smiled. "The cops are here too."

"Cops?"

"Yeah, they found waterproof packets of some kind of wholesale heroin. It's all over the beach."

"Good grief."

"I had to explain to the cops that we weren't involved and that we were just trying to help fish these morons out of the drink. I tried to get Marv to help, but he vacated as soon as the cops showed up."

"Probably wise on his part." The Cheyenne Nation had made it up onto his elbow and peeked at me from around Rachael. "I . . . I think I drowned."

"We both did, but today the sea decided to give up its dead, at least a percentage of them."

Rachael looked behind her. "The cops want to get a statement from you guys, but they're willing to wait until after the EMTs get a look at you."

Over her shoulder, I watched as the medical attendants worked on the survivors, loading them onto gurneys and carrying them away, the Los Angeles County Sheriff's Department in long slickers looking on. "Any way we can get out of that?"

She shook her head. "I doubt it, but why?"

Henry coughed again. "People and stuff." He flopped over onto his back. "Stuff gets you into people, people get you into stuff."

Rachael glanced around. "We can try, but I don't think we'll make it."

She reached a hand out to me, but I pointed toward Henry. "Get him, I think I can make it."

We'd just started to stand when I noticed the galoshes near my bare feet and raised my face to find a tall, lean individual in a hooded slicker with a name tag that read TANEN looking at me.

"Going somewhere?"

I reared up to my full height and looked down at him. "We thought we'd get out of the rain and get ourselves patched up, if you don't mind?" To emphasize my point, I smeared some of the blood from my head and flung it to the sides with my fingers.

He smiled. "Okay, but don't go far."

"I don't think we're capable." Turning, I took the Bear's other arm and threw it over my shoulder as I lifted, Rachael taking the other as best she could.

He watched us limp off toward the cliffs. "The medical units have vans set up on Cliffside Drive."

"Got it."

By the time we got to the switchback on the trail, we could see the revolving lights of the emergency vehicles. "Do you think they think we're involved with this contraband boat?"

Rachael nodded. "They seemed pretty adamant about talking to you guys."

"What, we look like drug smugglers?"

She nodded at Henry. "He does."

I regarded my lifelong friend. "Yep, I guess he does at that."

"Thank you." He nodded toward a bench. "I think I need to sit down for a moment."

We did as he asked, and I had to admit that even when sitting there in the pouring rain, it felt good to rest.

"Are we still planning on leaving tomorrow morning?"

"We have to, I'm sure it's going to take at least four and a half days plus the time you wanted to spend in Oklahoma with your relatives . . ." I lowered my head to look at him. "Are you okay?"

"Yes, just a little waterlogged."

"You'll feel better after a night's sleep."

"Hmm." He glanced down the trail where one of the rubber-cloaked deputies appeared to be carrying my surfboard. "Hey, isn't that the Monolith?"

I held out a hand. "Excuse me, but that's mine."

The deputy with the name tag REEVES stopped and looked down at me. "Well, it's evidence now."

"Evidence of what, that we were surfing?"

He stared at me for a few moments. "When we're done with it you can pick it up at the courthouse, downtown."

"Oh, come on, man . . ."

"Tough titty."

He started off again, but a voice called to him from back down the trail. "Paul, hold on."

We watched as the other deputy who I'd spoken with on the beach came up and reached a hand out for my board. "I'll take that."

"Yes, sir." The one deputy handed the board over and then turned and started back toward the beach. "Your show."

"Yes, it is, Deputy Reeves." As Tanen watched the deputy go, he called after him. "And grab us a few blankets down there!"

The deputy mock saluted, and I looked at Tanen. "Are you really taking my board?"

He leaned it toward himself, examining the chunk taken out of the front. "Must've been rough out there."

"It was."

He studied me for a moment, the rain dripping from the hood of his black slicker as I caught a glance of his six-point uniform cap and the gold cap piece with his badge number.

One.

"I'll make you a deal—these two can go ahead up to the medical vans, and you stay here with me for a few minutes to talk and we'll call that a statement."

"Sure."

Rachael squared off with him. "Look, I don't think you realize what these dudes—"

I pulled at her shoulder. "You go on ahead and get Henry patched up, and I'll be along in a minute."

She gave him one last defiant look and then turned to meet my eyes for a moment, then we both helped Henry get on his feet so they could start up the trail.

Watching them go, I addressed the commanding officer. "How can I help you, Sheriff?"

"You're a little big to be a surfer, aren't you?"

"So everybody tells me."

He glanced back at the primordial ocean. "'If you would know the age of the earth, look upon the sea in a storm—'"

I finished the line for him. "'The grayness of the whole immense surface, the wind furrows upon the faces of the waves, the great masses of foam, tossed about and waving, like matted white locks, give the sea in a gale an appearance of hoary age, lusterless, dull, without gleams, as though it had been created before light itself.'"

He turned back to me, only half his face visible in the hood. "English major?"

"Yep, as a matter of fact."

He choked a laugh and then gestured toward the water like an old salt. "You swam out there twice to save some guys you didn't know?"

"The first time, then I went back for my buddy."

"But you didn't know that boat or anybody on it?"

"Nope."

"Then why did you do it?"

I stared at him. "Because it was the right thing to do."

He studied me like a rare specimen. "Where are you from, son?"

"Somewhere else."

He smiled, continuing to scrutinize me. "And what brings you to the City of Angels?"

"One of your universities invited me down here to play offensive tackle."

"That where you learned your Conrad?"

"No, that was from my father."

"Which university?"

"University of Southern California."

He nodded, preoccupied. "Been there long?"

"Four years."

"Well, I'm going to need to see some identification, and I'm assuming you don't have that on you?"

"No."

The deputy, Reeves, showed up with a blanket and handed it to Tanen. "Everything okay, Chief?"

"Yeah, we're good." He handed me the blanket and then gestured up the hill with a parody of a German accent. *"Come along und ve vill get you back vit your friends und you can show me your papers."*

I pulled the army surplus around me and picked my way up the trail and toward the emergency vehicles as he was kind enough to carry my surfboard. "I understand the boat that got sunk was carrying a lot of drugs?"

"Heroin, 10 mg hypodermic tablets—thousands of them in each waterproof packet we were able to retrieve."

"And you think we were a part of that?"

He said nothing but stared at the ground as we walked along the sodden path.

"I mean if that was the case, don't you think we would've been gathering up the drugs rather than diving in there and risking our lives to save the drowning people?"

"As a matter of fact, I do." He stopped and turned to look at me.

"I'm just curious if you saw or heard anything that might tell us from whom and where this stuff might've come."

"No, we were kind of busy." I thought about it. "The boat's name was *El Espectro*."

"Hmm . . ."

We continued walking. "So, only one guy died?"

"According to the survivor who made it to shore, but he disappeared."

We made another switchback, and I could see Henry and Rachael inside one of the vans as the Bear was attended to. Stopping, I pulled the passenger side door of my truck open and flipped down the glove box, retrieving my license and handing it to him.

He leaned the board against the quarter panel of my truck and read. "Wyoming."

"Yep."

"Walt Longmire."

"Yep to that too."

"And where do you live here in California, Walt Longmire?"

"Near USC, 1131 West Thirty-fifth Street, second floor behind the post office."

He handed the card back but continued to examine me. "You know, not a lot of people would jump in that ocean and attempt to do what you did."

Tossing the license back into the truck, I shut the door. "Yep, most are smarter than that."

"Got any plans after college, son?"

"A few."

He pulled a card from inside his slicker and handed it to me. "This is a police benevolent society pass with my name on it; kind of a get out of jail card. You keep it—we could use men like you."

I stared at the printed name and title: Los Angeles County, Sheriff Ned Tanen. "I'll keep it in mind."

"Well, be careful."

"What's that supposed to mean?"

He slid his hands into the pockets of his slicker. "Somebody lost millions of dollars down there, and in my experience with those kinds of people, they don't take such things lightly."

Lifting the surfboard, I placed it in the bed of my truck. "I told you; we had nothing to do with all that."

"Oh, I believe you, but it's possible whoever made that stuff won't. You see, in my experience with the drug trade there are three major commodities: drugs, money, and if those two go wrong—blame." He began walking away only to turn and add. "By the way, I'm going to need you to not leave town—you weren't planning on going anywhere, were you, son?"

"No . . ." Turning back from my truck I laid an arm on the bed and then tightened the blanket around me, taking a few seconds to finish my response. "No, sir."

2

"So, wait, you started the great road trip of your life as a fugitive from justice?" She was fighting to tie my tie, which, like surfing, was something else I hadn't done in years.

"Well, not exactly . . ." Frustrated, Vic pulled me to one of the kitchen chairs and pushed me down to sit. Then, as she circled around to my back, she reached around to tie my tie in a more natural position. "You were asked to not leave town."

"Technically, but I had an appointment with another organization."

Flipping the tail over and wrapping it through the knot, she then came back in front of me and tightened it. "And who was that?"

"The United States Marine Corps."

Vic snugged the tie a bit tighter. "You know what I mean."

"It was before I was in law enforcement, and I didn't think it was that big of a deal. We weren't involved in anything, and I figured I'd just call Tanen, the sheriff, at the phone number on the card in a few days."

She snugged the tie with another tug. "That's not what he meant, and you know it."

I stood in an attempt to keep from being strangled. "I suppose so, but we were kind of pressed for time."

"I'm sure the Marine Corps would've understood."

I slipped my aged blazer on. "Boy, I can tell you've never been in the armed services." Picking up my hat, I headed toward the door with Dog following as my undersheriff joined us, and I took the time to really look at her. "You're wearing a dress."

She curtseyed. "I am."

It was a lightweight, navy summer job, conservative, with a slight flounce past the hips and a décolletage that revealed just enough without revealing too much. "Let me be the first one today to tell you that you look absolutely stunning."

She gathered a small purse hanging from the chair near the door. "I know."

I opened the door and followed her and Dog out. "And a purse?"

"Gotta have somewhere to put my gun."

Closing the door, I walked out and opened the suicide doors, one for Dog and one for her. "Let's not shoot anybody at the hearing, shall we?"

She shrugged as I closed the doors. "We'll see how it goes."

Climbing in and backing out, I swung the three-quarter ton around and headed for town as she slipped off her heels and placed her feet on the dash like she always did. "So, why were you in such a hurry to go off to war?"

I drove, thinking of that time so long ago. "I was but Henry wasn't, he was feeling kind of ambivalent about the whole thing but had family in Oklahoma that he wanted to see, and I didn't know how long that was going to take."

"The Bear has family in Oklahoma?"

Driving, I glanced at her. "The Southern Cheyenne Reservation."

"Wait, there are *two* Cheyenne reservations?"

"Yep. In 1830 a large group of the Tsistsistas, or Human Beings, elected to take the federal government up on an offer of some land on the upper Arkansas River near Bent's Old Fort. Later the government tried to collect them all together in Oklahoma, but that didn't end very well. So now there are two Cheyenne reservations, one in Montana and the other in Oklahoma."

"Does he have a lot of family down there?"

"Did. That's the thing about the Cheyenne, they've got family everywhere."

Her eyes went back to the road, but her movements were languid and dangerous. "So, tell me about this Rachael Weisman."

I smiled but said nothing.

She didn't turn her head, but I could tell she was studying me with her peripheral vision. "What?"

"I knew you were going to ask me about her."

"So . . . ?"

"Why is she important, she was a woman I dated a lifetime ago, multiple lifetimes ago."

She shrugged. "She was important to you at one time, so I'm naturally curious."

I said nothing.

"So?"

"So, what?"

"How important was she?"

"At the time, pretty important."

"You and your wife weren't a thing?"

"Not at that time, no. When I went off to college, Martha called it quits."

She shifted, placing her feet in my lap and reaching back to pet Dog. "Pretty smart on her part."

"Why is that?"

She threaded her fingers into her hair and studying me like a lab rat. "I take it she wasn't going to school there, so the two of you were going your separate ways in a bold new world. If she really loved you, then she'd have to let you go and see if you came back to her. Otherwise, she'd have been holding on to you and nobody responds well to that, especially when you're young and have your whole life ahead of you."

"If you love something set it free?"

"Yeah, that always works . . ." She snorted. "Anyway, it was the smart move, else you'd have made a run for it." She repositioned her feet in my lap to get my attention. "So, about Rachael Weisman . . . ?"

"What do you want to know?"

"She was beautiful?"

"Yep."

"As beautiful as me?"

"In a different way."

"That was a good answer."

"Thank you."

"Jewish, I'm assuming?"

"Yep."

"What did her mother and father do?"

"He was with the public defender's office there in Los Angeles, and her mother was a cardiologist at Cedars-Sinai Medical Center."

"She was rich."

"Half rich; the other half was socially responsible."

Vic made a face. "She didn't want to go on this road trip with you guys?"

"Yep, she did."

"And you told her no?"

"Yep."

"Wow. You were even a worse hard-ass then than you are now?"

"I guess."

"You ever see her again?"

I glanced over at her. "Once."

SATURDAY, MAY 23, 1964

Attempting to stand upright, I pulled my face from hers, but she kept her arms around my neck, holding my face only a few inches away in a bid for intimacy on the busy street. "Fly, that way we can spend a few more days together."

"I can't, I promised Henry."

She stood there in her one-piece bathing suit, cutoffs, and Japanese zori sandals. "He understands."

I tipped the battered palm leaf cowboy hat I'd picked up in Mexico back on my head, stretching my heavy arms in the blue chambray shirt. "And how do you know that?"

"I asked him." I shook my head, slipping from her arms but not entirely as she rested her palms on my chest. "He says he'll take the truck and sell it in Louisiana and send you the money."

"No, we made plans."

She backed up and sat on the retainer wall outside my apartment building, curling her legs into her cutoff jeans and squinting at me in the bright Southern California sun. "I'm offering you another week with me."

"I'm aware of that, and I'm also aware of how much I'm going to kick myself for not taking you up on it."

We both watched as Henry exited the duplex. He was wearing a leather Greek fisherman's cap, leather sandals, and a jean jacket with more patches than a NASCAR racer. He carried his duffel out to the truck in the driveway, tossing his luggage into the back with all my stuff. "Hey, did I hear you offered to leave me behind?"

He came over pulling the John Lennon wannabe hat down low over his eyes. "Nothing personal."

Rachael tugged at my shirt. "How about I fly to Oklahoma City and meet you?"

"No."

"How about I fly into Savannah and meet you?"

"No."

"Saigon?"

Reaching my hand out I pulled her up and snugged her in under my arm and kissed the top of her head. "Especially no."

"Don't go." She looked at me with the hazel eyes, the color that made me feel like sand was squeezing between my toes and my heart was standing still. "We'll just go find a place on the beach down in Mexico, Baja someplace. Remember that little stone cottage on the beach near Boca del Salado? We could just fish and live off the sea."

I stuffed my hands in my jeans. "You can't fish."

"I'll learn." She stepped back. "I'm serious, Walt . . . Don't go."

We stood there with the emotional chasm between us as a Plymouth Savoy, black and white with twin cherries separated by a large chrome siren on top, eased along the curb beside us like a decorated panda.

Henry lifted the bill of his cap along with an eyebrow and turned, moving back toward the ranch truck. "Uh-oh."

We watched as the deputy from yesterday got out, now dressed in green slacks, a short sleeve khaki shirt, and an eight-point hat. Smiling, he straightened his duty belt but kept his hand on his sidearm as he came around the front of the car. "I knew I recognized you from somewhere."

I cleared my throat. "Deputy Reeves."

"Mr. Longmire." He stepped onto the curb and cocked his head at me as he gestured over his shoulder toward the campus. "Offensive tackle at USC this last year, right?"

"Yep."

"You won the Rose Bowl."

"I had some help."

"Hell of a game." He placed his hands on his hips and drew himself up to his full height. "What are you, six-four?"

"Five."

"I was a strong safety with the Cal Poly Mustangs in San Luis Obispo in '58—we were 9-1 and 4-1 in conference play."

"Who was the 1?"

He deflated a little. "Fresno State. We tied it up by the end of the season, but they won it 'cause they beat us in the regular head-to-head."

We watched as Rachael disentangled herself from me and joined the Bear at the truck. "Bummer."

"Yeah."

"So, how can I help you, Deputy?"

He took his sunglasses off and hung them on the pen opening in his pocket. "Me? Nothing."

I nodded and then waited a moment before asking. "Just here to make gridiron talk?"

"Oh, I'm also confirming your address for the sheriff." He reached out and punched my shoulder. "You don't have a listed number."

"I don't have a phone."

He pulled out a spiral notepad and pen. "Dude, how do you live without a phone?"

"Quite well, actually. If I could just get rid of the US Mail all my problems would be solved."

"1131 West Thirty-fifth, second floor." After scribbling down the address, he looked at the battered duplex that had seen better days. "It's a dump."

"All I could afford."

He glanced at Henry and Rachael, talking beside the loaded truck. "Going somewhere?"

"Just moving some stuff." Shucking my hands into my jeans, I glanced around. "Look, Deputy . . ."

He moved to the side, choosing to stand between me and my friends. "You know that was something out there, all those drugs."

"Yep, I guess so."

He folded up the notepad and tucked it and the pen away. "Street value of close to four million dollars."

"Wow!"

"Yeah, the boat finally washed ashore, and it looks like they were trying to scuttle her. Probably figured they were going to get caught with the stuff, so they decided to just sink it."

I looked at the sidewalk and my bare feet. "Did you happen to get anything from the guys on board?"

"Nah, they don't seem to know shit. One interesting thing did happen, though . . ."

"What's that?"

"We finally found the guy who made it to shore, this Alex Ballard that the *El Espectro* was actually registered to in Half Moon Bay near San Francisco."

"Really?"

"Yeah, they found him face down in a furrow in a kale field up in Ventura County with three bullets in the back of his head. Man, that ain't how I want to go . . ."

"Me either."

"Yeah, I hate kale." He stared at me. "That was a joke."

"Oh."

We stood there for an uncomfortable moment and then he went around his car, where he stopped and looked at me from over the expansive hood. "You know, it would be a real feather in my cap if you were to tell me something that I could tell the sheriff when I got back to the station."

"Concerning?"

"Anything. I'm just trying to work my way up the ladder, and if you thought of anything else that might be of interest, I'd love to hear it."

I shrugged. "I pretty much told Sheriff Tanen everything yesterday."

"Nothing else comes to mind?"

"No."

He nodded and opened the door of his unit before stretching a hand across the top of the car and drumming his fingers on the warm sheet metal. "Wyoming, huh?"

"Yep."

"You a real cowboy?"

I pulled my disreputable hat down. "My family run cattle, yep."

"I got a question for you." He gestured toward my head. "There are two kinds of cowboy hats, the straw ones like you've got on and the fabric ones?"

"Fur felt, usually beaver."

"Really?"

I dipped my head, looking at him from under the brim. "Your question?"

"How do you know when to switch?"

"I beg your pardon?"

He leaned against the drip railing of the car and rested his chin on his forearm. "What time of year do you switch from the one you're wearing to the fur one?"

"First frost."

"Really?"

"Yep."

"Hell, I'd only get to wear my hat a month and a half here in SoCal." He started to get in the car but stopped. "And the other way?"

"Excuse me?"

"When do you go to the straw one?"

I thought about it. "When it gets hot."

"I hadn't noticed, has it gotten hot, Mr. Longmire?" He nodded, glancing around. "Let's hope it doesn't get too hot, shall we?"

I watched as he climbed the rest of the way in, started the Plymouth, pulled it into gear, and then, spinning a U-turn, cruised away in the school of traffic like a killer whale.

Henry and Rachael came over after Deputy Reeves had gone, the Bear hanging an arm on my shoulder. "What was that about?"

"I'm not exactly sure." Turning, I carefully placed a hand around Rachael's back. "We've got to get going, we were supposed to leave early this morning."

Henry was kind enough to move off again as she reached out and took his hand, giving it a squeeze. "You're going to miss surfing with me, you barbarian."

He smiled back at her. "I think you are right."

We both watched him walk away, and then she turned to me. "And you, you're going to miss a lot more than that."

"More than you know." I lowered my face and kissed her, lingering there for a moment before straightening and moving toward the truck where the Bear had already climbed into the passenger side and closed the door.

Walking down the sidewalk I looked up at the duplex and thought about the great times I'd had there for the last four years of my life, and then I looked across the street at the campus of the university that had changed my life. I'm not sure what I would've done if I'd stayed back in Wyoming, unsure of what I would've become. But somehow the time I'd spent in college had expanded my horizons and had set me on a path on which there might not be any turns.

At the truck, I turned to look back at Rachael, feeling the same way about her. There might not be a return to who and what we'd been, but I'd carry a little bit of her with me for the rest of my life. "I'll—"

She stood there on the sidewalk, watching me with her arms folded. "Don't."

"I was just going to say that I'll call . . ."

"Don't." She shook her head. "Just don't."

I stood there watching as she turned and walked up the sidewalk, an image I would also carry with me for the rest of my life.

After climbing in, I hit the starter on the ranch truck and shifted into reverse, then gripped the giant garnet of a suicide knob and backed out onto the street, looking around for Reeves just to make sure nobody was witnessing our departure. Shifting into second to avoid the super-low granny gear, I drove forward and took a right, following the surface streets to the on-ramp of the I-15 that would lead to I-40 that we'd be on for at least 2,473 miles.

The Cheyenne Nation was silent, studying the Texaco road map and popping his fingers on the edge of the paper as I gained speed and merged into traffic. Folding the map, he tucked it into the glove box and leaned over the windowsill, allowing his hair to swirl in the cab. "Hey, did I thank you for saving my life?"

"Actually, I think it was more Rachael."

"Oh." He said nothing more. Instead, he adjusted the vent window and then reached over and picked up a thick paperback that I hadn't noticed lying on the seat between us. *Crime and Punishment?*

I laughed and shook my head. "Her idea of a joke."

"A little light summer reading?"

"I guess."

He casually flung the book out the window, where it fluttered like a shot bird for an instant and then disappeared.

"Did you just throw Dostoevsky out the window?"

"I did."

"Do you mind if I ask why?"

He fiddled with the window some more. "You are morose enough without us dragging Dostoevsky across the country along with us."

Considering going back for the book, I glanced out the rear window. "That was a gift."

"I believe . . ." He reached across the cab, pulled the leather fishing cap over his face, and slumped down in the seat, muttering. "And correct me if I am wrong—it was commentary."

Interstate 40 was only six years old, but the Mother Road it replaced is still one of the most storied paths on the face of the earth at least since 1926. Bobby Troup wrote the song "Route 66" on a road trip across the country, even rattling off locations along the way, but for some reason left out Albuquerque—maybe because it was hard to find something that rhymed with it. Then Nat King Cole and his trio got their kicks and rode it to number three in 1946.

There is even a TV show currently on CBS about two guys driving across the country in a Corvette convertible; but in the ranch truck, as far as we'd gotten that first day was somewhere near the pop-hit-maligned Albuquerque—at least I thought that's where we were. Interstate 40 replaced most of the original road, but there were spots where the remnants rolled along in the desert frontage beside the interstate highway. I took those side roads when I could, happy to lose time when that's all we had for the next four days and possibly for the last time in our lives.

The Bear slept the majority of that first day, periodically rousing himself, sitting up and looking around to question where we were. After being told, he'd collapse back into the seat and would soon be snoozing again.

I didn't mind. I had a lot of thinking to do.

We had plenty of money due to a fund that Sheriff Lucian Connally and his friends back at the VFW in Durant had strung together—more than two thousand dollars to be exact. At thirty cents and thirteen miles a gallon, we'd have more than enough for the trip with hotels and as much food as we could pack in.

I wasn't completely sure why the old sheriff had sent us the money other than an altercation we'd had with him and our assistance when the movie actor Robert Taylor had come to our town and rode in the county fair and rodeo parade.

My mother and father had tried to send me funding as well, but I'd told them we had plenty. Henry's parents had tried to do the same, but he'd threatened to forward the money to the Students for a Democratic Society or the American Deserters' Committee.

I wasn't quite sure why the Bear was with me as I drove through the night and not somewhere up in Canada or Switzerland for that matter. He protested against the war even back in Montana, but here he was heading toward Fort Polk and then most certainly Southeast Asia. He was the best friend I had in the entire world, but sometimes I couldn't help but view him as something of a stranger.

I thought we were somewhere near the unrhymable Albuquerque, but the landscape had grown darker and there certainly didn't seem to be any lights from a large metropolitan area anywhere on the horizon, just the two-lane blacktop that had petered out a few miles ago and not much else.

I'd taken the frontage road, but I think I might've accidentally taken a few other turns, and now here we were in what might be the middle of nowhere—and when a guy from Wyoming refers to a place as the middle of nowhere that truly means the epicenter of nowhere. Seeing something in the road, I swerved to find a drop-off into an irrigation ditch but locked the brakes up to slide to a stop, and only after dropping off the edge of the concrete with a resounding crunch.

The Bear pried himself from the dash and looked at me. "What in the otherwise flaming hell . . . ?"

"It was a dog."

He stared at me. "A dog?"

Pulling the handle, I pushed open the door to look out at the floating dust in the headlights and watched as the animal in question limped from the road, taking the time to give me one last glance before disappearing into the darkness. "It was a coyote."

Stumbling out the other side, he eased away from the viaduct, came around the bed, and looked at me. "A coyote?"

"Yep."

He stretched and then looked around in the darkness. "Where are we?"

I had a look around myself. "Good question."

"Why are we not on the highway?"

"I took a shortcut that the guy at the filling station in Needles told me about."

"So, we are still in California."

"Arizona." Turning, I gazed about in the darkness. "I think."

"Was there a sign?"

"Not that I'm aware of, but it's possible I missed it in the dark." Walking around the front of the truck, I knelt and even in the darkness could see that the damage was substantial. "Well, that's not good."

The Bear came around and looked over my shoulder. "Damage report?"

I pointed. "The one wheel is turned the wrong way, so I'd suspect it's a tie-rod end."

"And that is bad?"

I stood and looked around. "Out here with no tools or replacement parts—pretty bad, yep."

"So, we start walking?"

"I guess so." Glancing back at the truck, I asked. "You think we should bring our stuff with us or lock it in the cab?"

"Who would steal it?" The Cheyenne Nation laughed, spinning around with his arms wide and walking ahead. "Here, coyote . . . Here, pretty coyote."

Shrugging, I started to follow but became aware that the temperature was dropping. Returning to the truck, I reached into the open window and pulled out Henry's old sherpa-lined Wrangler with all the patches, including the giant peace sign on the back, and my horsehide highwayman, slipping it on as I followed.

About a quarter mile up the gravel road, I found him standing at a T, looking in the direction of the darkness as I handed him his jacket. "Find your buddy, the coyote?"

He pulled on his jacket and then fumbled in one of the pockets, pulling out a Zippo and then lighting it, allowing me to see a hand-painted sign that read BONE VALLEY.

"Well, we know where we are now."

He slipped the lighter back into his pocket. "Wherever that is."

I followed along, flipping the collar of my jacket up. "Where do you think we are?"

He shook his head. "Somewhere west of either Phoenix or Prescott, according to where you took the so-called shortcut."

Walking along, I strained my eyes ahead. "I don't see any lights in that direction."

He checked his wristwatch. "They are probably asleep in Bone Valley, as is customary at this time of night."

"Are you being a smart-ass for a reason?"

He shrugged. "It is customary when you are being a dumbass."

"I didn't wreck the truck on purpose." I glanced around at the desolate landscape. "Anyway, it isn't everybody who gets to go to Bone Valley, you know."

He stopped again, rubbing his shoulder before looking at the side of the road with his hands on his hips. "And I can see why." Following his gaze, I made out the remains of an eight-foot chain-link fence and a weathered sign that read NO TRESSPASSING—GOVERNMENT PROPERTY.

"You think this is downtown Bone Valley?"

"I certainly hope not." He turned and continued walking as I tagged along, and we noticed a looming structure to our right. "Is that a gun tower?"

"It appears to be."

The fence was slack in a few spots, almost dipping to the ground. "A prison, maybe?"

"It is in remarkably dilapidated shape—perhaps abandoned."

Soon the fence ended, and we continued walking over a rise, finally able to see a few structures ahead on either side of the road. "Bone Valley proper?"

"Let us see."

Over the hill and in a slight desert depression in front of the foothills of the mountains to the east, there was a collection of buildings hunkered at a crossroads, gathered together almost as if there was safety in numbers.

"We must be near Prescott; there are no mountains east or west of Phoenix."

We continued down the gravel road, and the buildings became more discernible in the partial moonlight, and I could make out a church and a couple of storefronts and, amazingly enough, a tiny, oblong box service station with a portico that sheltered a single pump that had EVERSON'S LAST CHANCE GAS on it.

When we got there, we could see a tow truck parked in one of the stalls with a model suspiciously similar to mine. "I think we're saved."

The Cheyenne Nation wandered toward the corner and looked in all directions at the few scattered buildings in the distance. "There does not appear to be anyone around, and I do not see a five-star hotel."

"We'll just have to rough it for the night."

He walked back over. "The temperature is dropping."

"Yep." I gestured toward the spired structure. "We could check the church and see if it's unlocked; we could sleep in the pews."

Unimpressed with my idea he passed me, approaching the sales portion of the service station, cupping his hands around his eyes and peering inside through the glass door. "There is a light in the back."

"It was probably just left on."

"There is also some noise." He reached down, pushing on the bar at the center of the door. The heavy glass swung open, and he turned to look at me as the tiny bells attached to the door rang quietly.

"You're going to get us killed." Smiling, he entered the establishment as I hung there at the door, looking up at the GO GATES . . . GET ACTION! illuminated clock over the door that read 1:20 a.m. We listened to the sporadic popping noise and the hiss of industrial gas in the room beyond. "Welding, somebody is back there welding."

Moving past the oil racks, he walked to the counter and then leaned to one side to look through the partially open door. The crackling and popping of the gas unit stopped and the tools clattered on what sounded to be a metal worktable.

I whispered. "Henry, let's wait outside—you're likely to scare them to death."

He ignored me and stepped into the room. He pushed the wooden door with the PRIVATE sign on it farther open and stopped, not moving a muscle.

Inching closer, I could see his back in the next room and whispered again. "What are you doing?"

"Nothing, I am doing nothing."

"Then what are you . . . ?"

He slowly began raising his hands. "I am doing nothing because there is a shotgun pointed at my face right now."

Moving to the right, I could see an individual in a welding cap, visor, and grimy suede apron, with even his welding gloves still on, holding what appeared to be an old Montgomery Ward 20-gauge pump—the end of the barrel no more than six inches from my friend's face.

I made myself known by easing in the doorway and lifting my own hands. "Hey friend, easy there . . ."

He shifted the muzzle toward me and, in a flash, the Bear stepped forward and hooked his hand around the barrel, pushing it down and away as he reached with the other hand and snatched the breechblock, rolling it away just as the thing went off.

The blast blew a hole in the wall beside me as I ducked the other way, knocking over the oil rack and then pressing myself against the door face as Henry took the butt of the shotgun and seemed to tap the gun-wielding welder in the forehead, whereupon he fell backward like a poleaxed steer.

"Is that the way that was supposed to work?"

He jacked the forestock, pumping the shells onto the concrete floor where the welder lay. "Not exactly."

Moving forward, I pushed past Henry and then kneeled down to pull the visor from the victim. "You could've gotten me killed."

Having emptied the shotgun, he leaned it against the wall beside the door. "It was a risk I was willing to take."

"Thanks." Setting the visor on the floor beside him, I tapped the older man's face in an attempt to bring him to. "I can't believe he could even see us with this thing on." He began moaning, and I bent down and raised him up by his shoulders. "Hey, are you okay?"

The Bear took the other side, and we picked up the welder, half carrying him into the more public section of the service station and then sitting him in one of the chairs by the large, glass window. Henry kneeled in front of him, steadying him with a hand. "Mr., are you okay?"

He coughed and then brought a hand up to his wrinkled face, feeling the bump that was growing in the center of his forehead. "What happened?"

"You tried to shoot us."

His face rose and his eyes grew wide as he stared at the Cheyenne Nation. "Don't kill me . . ."

The Bear looked up. "That was not the plan, was it?"

I placed a hand on the man's bony shoulder. "No, that wasn't the plan, no."

"Who are you?"

He tried to stand, but I held him in the chair. "Just a couple of pilgrims on the road to Damascus, friend. My name is Walt Longmire, and this is my friend Henry Standing Bear—our truck broke down on the road a few miles out and we're looking for someone to fix it."

Pulling off the welding gloves, he sat them in the seat beside him. "You're not cops, are you?"

Henry and I looked at each other. "No."

He tried to stand again, and this time I let him. "Well then, you two need to get out of here."

"Why would you ask if we were cops?" He didn't answer, so I

tried another line. "Do we look like cops? I know we don't particularly look like it, but we've got money."

"I don't want your money." He glanced around. "Where's my shotgun?"

Henry stood and then gestured toward the doorway leading into the back room. "Around the corner there but be careful because I emptied the rounds onto the floor."

"Why'd you do that?"

The Bear laughed. "You tried to shoot us once; I was just making sure that you did not get a chance to do it again."

He moved in that direction. "That's what you hippies get for breaking into a man's place of business."

"I am assuming you are Mr. Everson?" Henry followed him. "The door was open, and as my friend explained, we are looking for a mechanic."

The man picked up the shotgun and turned to look at us. "There's nobody around here that can do that kind of thing, so the two of you need to shove off."

"Well, Mr. Everson, if this truly is the last chance of gas, where do you advise us to go? I've got a truck out there with a busted tie-rod end, sitting halfway in a culvert, and other than that tow truck you've got in that bay out there, I don't see any way of getting it back on the road."

Rubbing his head again, he took out a pack of cigarettes and lit a Lucky, taking a puff and then looking at me through one squinting eye. "Son, where is it that you're headed?"

I gestured toward Henry. "He's headed for Louisiana, and I'm going on to South Carolina."

"How'd you end up here?"

"I think I might've taken a few wrong turns."

"Well, I reckon so." He looked between the two of us. "I know I'm gonna regret this . . ." He tucked the shotgun under the counter and stripped off the suede apron before snatching a set of keys from a rack on the wall and walking toward the door that led to the service bays. "C'mon and show me where your truck is, and we'll try and get it fixed by morning, but then you two need to get out of here as fast as you can."

We followed him into the bay and climbed into the passenger side as he raised the garage door and then climbed in himself, firing up the tow truck and backing out before turning and straightening the wheels enough to head down the road.

As we climbed a slight hill, I couldn't help but ask. "Is everybody in Bone Valley as welcoming as you, Mr. Everson?"

He glanced at me, then plucked the cigarette still lodged in the corner of his mouth from his lips and tossed it out the window like a curveball. "No."

Henry and I smiled at each other as we drove alongside the swooping chain-link fence and the ominous guard tower. "Mr. Everson, do you mind if I ask what that compound might be?"

"Nope, don't mind if you ask." He glanced at the Bear, but then his eyes returned to the road. "But my goddamned name ain't Everson."

3

"Sheriff, did you know it was Tom Rondelle you'd shot through the door?"

I straightened in the wooden witness chair, feeling like the thirteen-year-old blazer I was wearing was a straitjacket. Pulling on the knot that Vic had tied this morning at my throat, I thought about when the tie had been bought and was pretty sure it had been when my daughter, Cady, the Greatest Legal Mind of Our Time, had graduated from law school. "Um, no. Not really."

"Are you in the habit of shooting unknown people through doors in your profession, Sheriff Longmire?"

"Not customarily, but when they shoot through the door at me first, then I have a tendency to not really care."

Scott Snowden, the adjudicator they'd brought in from California, suppressed a chuckle and then spoke. "Answer the question, Sheriff."

I glanced around the courtroom that used to be Verne Selby's prowling grounds and wondered how the old judge was doing down in Yuma, where he'd retired—probably frying like bacon. "I thought I did."

"I'll withdraw the question, Your Honor." The young man from Cheyenne with the fashionable haircut adjusted his glasses and looked at his notes lying on the shining surface of the oak table. "But you've done an awful lot of shooting during your tenure as the sheriff of Absaroka County, haven't you?"

Judi Cole, my defense attorney, adjusted her glasses and pulled a lock of red hair behind one ear before raising the same hand. "Objection, your honor. It's been established that Sheriff Longmire is one of the most decorated and venerated law enforcement officers in the state."

Snowden leaned forward, giving the prosecutor a sharp look. "Mr. Whinstone, we can do without the snide remarks."

"Sorry, Your Honor." He glanced back at me. "You'd met Tom Rondelle before, is that correct?

"In Joe's office."

"The Joe in question would be Attorney General Joe Meyer?"

"Yep."

"And what kind of meeting was that?"

I shrugged, repositioning my cowboy hat on my knee. "I'm not sure I understand the question."

"Was it a cordial meeting?"

"No, I don't think you could describe it as such."

"Did you or did you not threaten to throw the board director of the Wyoming State Treasury through the window of the second story office?"

"I may have."

He checked his notes again, picking up a pencil and tapping the stack of papers for effect. "In fact, you did."

"Yep, I did."

"Do you recall what the conversation was about?"

"I think he was attempting to delay the investigation of the rifle I'd found in the mountains."

"Your grandfather's rifle?"

"Yep."

"The one that was used to kill Bill Sutherland, the accountant for the state of Wyoming."

"Yep."

"And possibly involved with the disappearance of Misters Grafton and Carr, two other men in the employ of the State Treasurer's Department?"

"I can't comment on that."

"Can't or won't?"

"I'm not commenting on the disappearance of those two men because there's no evidence to give any indication as to what might've happened to them."

"Oh now, come on, Sheriff?" He laughed. "Your grandfather Lloyd Longmire killed all three of those men."

"I'd like to see any proof you have." He dropped the pencil, folded his arms over his chest, and smiled at me.

"Sheriff, if you don't mind my saying, I don't think you're taking this hearing very seriously."

I said nothing, which, when there was a stenographer in the room, was always a safe bet.

"Are you?"

"Am I what?"

He sighed. "Taking this hearing seriously?"

I stared at him for a good, long while. "Young man, have you ever killed anyone?"

He stood there, staring back at me. "No, Sheriff, I haven't."

"Then you don't know what it's like, do you?"

"No, sir, thankfully I don't."

"Well, I have, and I can tell you from personal experience that it's not something that you can ever undertake without a great deal of seriousness. It's the only act that you can't make reparation for—once you take a life, you can't ever give it back, it's gone forever. I shot that man, and I'm going to carry that with me till the day I die."

He looked at his notes again. "Are you going to carry all of them with you, Sheriff?"

For some reason I thought about Fort Pratt, Montana. "Yes, I believe I will."

"Are you aware that the weapon Mr. Rondelle was carrying was not his own?"

"No, I was not aware of that, but it really didn't make any difference."

"No difference?"

"No, he was armed, and he fired it at me—in my mind that's all that mattered."

"I see." He stepped around the corner of the table and approached. "Are you aware that Mr. Rondelle was not particularly familiar with any form of firearm; that he had no formal training, or that he had possibly never held a gun before in his life?"

"He did that night."

"Why do you suppose that is?"

"I honestly wouldn't know."

"Is it possible that he was forced to go toward that door and fire that gun by Mike Regis?"

"You'd have to ask Regis about that."

"Well now, that would be difficult because he was also killed that night, wasn't he?"

"I didn't kill him."

"He would be one of the few you didn't kill that night, wouldn't he?"

Snowden's voice was low. "Counselor."

"Is it possible, Sheriff?"

"I doubt it, the relationship between Rondelle and Regis struck me as master and man."

His eyebrows bunched. "Excuse me?"

"Mike Regis was under Tom Rondelle's employ as far as I know."

"Would you be surprised to know that Mr. Rondelle was deeply in debt to the Regis family for certain unsecured loans that family had made to him and business concerns of his?"

"Not particularly."

"And why is that?"

"Because I don't especially care. Those men were there, armed to the teeth, and prepared to do whatever it took to keep this hidden mineral fund quiet."

Whinstone didn't seem to want to follow that line of questioning and returned to the table. "The investigation by the Division of Criminal Investigation found that either of the two bullets that struck Tom Rondelle could've been the cause of his death. Any particular reason why you felt compelled to fire twice with your sidearm . . ." He checked the notes again. "A 1911 .45 ACP?"

"I wanted to make sure whoever was shooting through that door wasn't going to be shooting anymore."

"Is that .45 of yours a standard sidearm here in Wyoming?"

"Not particularly."

"Then why do you carry it?"

"It's what I'm used to, since Vietnam and a little before."

"It's a very powerful weapon, isn't it?"

"Nowhere near as powerful as those combat rifles they were carrying."

Snowden's voice sounded again. "Answer the question."

"I suppose."

"Do you think of yourself as a cowboy, Sheriff?"

"No."

"No?"

"No, I'm a sheriff."

"But you wear the hat, right? You wear the boots with the big iron on your hip? C'mon, Sheriff, you think of yourself as a cowboy."

Judi threw up her hands. "Your Honor, is this going somewhere?"

Whinstone spread his hands in absolution, allowing them to fall to his sides as he sat. "No more questions, Your Honor."

The judge sat forward, picking up his wristwatch from the surface of his desk and glancing at all of us. "Folks, it's approaching one o'clock and my stomach is drowning a lot of you out. Would all parties be open to the idea of recessing for lunch and then recommencing at two?"

———

Vic was waiting for me on the stair landing, leaning on the railing in her summer dress and looking out the courthouse window. "I didn't see any bodies fall, so I guess it went well?"

Tipping my hat back, I hooked a finger in my collar, loosened my tie, and sat on the top step. "I have no idea."

She turned and slipped a lipstick from her purse to reapply to her lips. "Well, you didn't come out in handcuffs, that's a plus." Replacing the lipstick, she snapped the thing shut and came over, sitting on the step with me. "What's wrong?"

"Nothing."

She bumped her shoulder into mine. "C'mon."

"I've devoted my whole life to law enforcement, and I'm not so sure it's turned out the way I hoped it would."

She laughed. "You're fucking kidding, right?"

I stared at the steps leading to the courthouse proper below.

"Nobody's life in law enforcement has turned out the way they hoped it would . . . ever."

"Nobody?"

"Nobody I ever met, and I come from an entire family full of cops." She wrapped an arm around mine and pulled me toward her. "Walt, you've done some really incredible things in your life, righted a lot of wrongs, and helped a shit ton of people—so ease up."

I nodded, taking my hat off and running my hands around the edge of the brim as I rotated it. "Yep, but how many lives have I ruined in the process, and how many rights have I wronged?"

About that time Judge Snowden, his assistant, and the stenographer appeared. Chatting in the antechamber and then seeing our side of the stairs blocked, they moved to the left to be able to descend those steps.

"Hey, Snowden—you beating up on my boss?"

He paused, turning toward us across the open space, and raised his hands, looking all the world like a print ad for *Justice Today!* "He's comporting himself quite well, Officer Moretti." Lowering his hands, he started down the steps. "But you know I'm not allowed to discuss these proceedings." He gave one more roguish smile and then continued with his retinue in tow.

"He's a handsome devil, isn't he?"

"Whatever." She stood, watching them go and then extended a hand. "C'mon, we've got a lunch date."

I took the hand and allowed her to pull me up. "With whom?"

"Your old surfing buddy."

Exiting the courthouse from the back, we took the shortcut down the hill and through the alley and then turned right toward the Busy Bee Café where Henry Standing Bear, tossing fish food from the bubblegum dispenser, stood overlooking Clear Creek.

He looked at us. "Hey, kids." He tossed the last of the trout treats into the sparkling water, and we shook hands. "What are you doing in town?"

He glanced at Vic. "I was offered a free lunch."

"There's no such thing as a free lunch."

Vic moved toward our venerable café. "C'mon, I'm buying."

I glanced at the Bear. "I stand corrected."

Following her, we took a seat by the window. I studied the creek and watched as a few ducks held their own against the middle current, the smaller trout studiously avoiding them as Vic questioned Henry. "So, I hear you guys were surfing ho-daddies?"

Henry glanced at me and then smiled at Vic. "He is too big to surf."

"So I hear, but I found evidence in his basement."

"Ah, the Monolith." He picked up a menu. "What else have you discovered?"

"Bone Valley?"

He took a very long time to respond but finally smiled the

paper-cut grin. "That far, huh?" He nodded, his attention going back to his menu. "There is still a long way to go concerning that particular trip."

The owner/operator Dorothy arrived, taking the plates, glasses, and refuse before mopping off the surface of the table and pulling a pencil from behind her ear. "Okay, you three. What'll it be?"

I handed her my menu. "What's the *unusual* special today?"

She stared at me. "Are you in one of your moods?"

"What's the last thing you think I'd order?"

Dorothy glanced around at the crowded café. "Walter, I'm kind of busy here . . ."

"I'm serious. Of all the things on the menu, what would be a surprise?"

She studied me a moment more and then turned to the others. "You two?"

Henry handed her his. "The unusual."

Vic provided hers. "Make it three." She watched the chief cook and bottle washer depart and then asked, "I wonder what we ordered?"

"Time will tell." He glanced at me. "So, he is telling you of our great exodus from California?"

"You didn't get very far."

"Not on the first day, no."

"Fugitives from justice."

"He told you that part too?"

"He did."

The Bear shrugged. "It was our salad years."

"Did you keep your surfboard?"

"No. As I recall I gave it away."

Dorothy arrived with glasses of water. "Gave away what?"

Henry sipped his. "My surfboard—Walt still has his."

She shot me a look and called over her shoulder as she departed. "You're too big to surf."

SATURDAY, MAY 23, 1964

"Maybe so, but I do."

The mechanic with the angular face connected the cables to my truck's differential and then stared at the surfboard before going back to the tow, adjusting the tension with the controls on the side and then pulling my truck slowly from the culvert.

It dragged the wayward right front tire until I kicked at it, straightening it out and enabling it to roll forward. "Tie-rod end?"

He lit another cigarette and drew a breath in, thinking. "Possibly, or possibly a kingpin."

"How hard is that to replace?"

"Not real hard, if you got the part."

"Do you have the parts?"

"No." He hoisted the back end of my truck into the air and then started toward the cab before looking at the two of us. "Well, c'mon, then."

We joined him in the cab and got seated as he started off, pulling my disabled truck back toward Bone Valley's tiny hamlet. We made the turn from the frontage road, or what I thought was the frontage road, and then tooled along beside the haphazard fence when I saw a sign I hadn't noticed before.

It was lying in the ditch beside the fence and had flipped up with the passing breeze and flipped over to warn us.

—STOP!—
AREA LIMITS
For Persons of Japanese Ancestry
Residing in This Relocation Center
SENTRY ON DUTY

"Bone Valley was a Japanese internment camp?"

The man didn't answer and drove on grimly.

Henry and I looked at each other again before Henry's gaze went back to the guard tower. "Have you ever been to the one at Heart Mountain?"

I thought about the camp three hours west of the home county and the few times we'd driven by it on our way to high school football games. I'd remembered it being a great deal like this one, desolate and forbidding. "Only to drive by."

"I went there once. I was with my father, and we were curious—at least I was. I asked him about it, and he said that we could stop. It was pretty run down when I saw it, maybe six years ago."

The man pulled up to the service station and then lowered my truck and backed it into the stall with expert ease. Henry and I climbed out and stood there as he disconnected the cables and reeled them into the tow before pulling it out, blocking the entry, and closing the stall door. "C'mon inside."

We did as he said, following him through the shop and into the work area, where he disappeared into the pit under my truck.

"As I remember, Heart Mountain was in pretty rough shape."

He lip-pointed toward the one at the edge of town. "Not as bad as this one." He walked toward the thin window at the top of the garage door and peered into the darkness. "I remember asking my father why it is they did not put all the Germans and Italians in camps, and he said it was because the Japanese looked different. I asked him if we looked different." He turned to look at me. "He said—indeed we do."

"It's the tie-rod end, all right. Broken . . ."

I kneeled and could see him fighting with something. "And you don't have the part?"

He hung his hands over the damaged suspension and looked up at me. "Is this a '60 model?"

"I believe so."

"My tow truck is a '59, but it's possible that I can strip the tie-rod end off it and get you two out of here."

"Well, that'd be great."

He started fussing with the part again. "Don't get your hopes up too high. This here is a half-ton and my tow is a full-ton—might not fit."

"Well, then we'd have to wait for a part?"

"The hell you will."

Rising back up, I noticed Henry was still looking out the window. "I'm assuming you heard all that?"

"I did." He turned and walked toward me. "So, we have a couple of hours to kill?"

"Or they kill us?"

He smiled. "I think I will take a walk."

"Okay." I glanced back under the truck where the mechanic was swearing at what I assumed was the tie-rod end. "I guess I better stick around here, just in case he needs help."

I watched as the Bear walked back through the shop portion of the station, opened the door, walked toward the road, and then took a left toward the internment camp just as I knew he would.

The older man reappeared from under the truck and was walking up the concrete steps to confront me with a greasy piece of hardware in two pieces, the rounded end with a locknut and grease fitting and a stem that appeared much the worse for wear. "Shot to hell."

He walked past me and back to the shop again. "I'm gonna try and weld it."

"Great."

He pushed open the door that read PRIVATE, where we'd found him. "But I wouldn't hold my breath if I were you . . ."

"Right." I started to follow. "Can I help, Mr. . . . ?"

"Sure, get the hell out of here and from underfoot." He called over his shoulder. "Pickens, my name is Donnie Pickens."

I looked at the row of chairs in the waiting room, figured they would support about half of me, and so decided to see if I could catch

Henry. Pushing open the door, I looked down the empty road and saw nothing. Seeing the small gathering of buildings in the other direction, I decided to reconnoiter that way instead.

I passed first by the church but then noticed there was a heavy chain run through the door handles, secured with a brass padlock. Weeds had grown up around the place, with tumbleweed lodged under the stairs. The windows weren't broken, but it looked as though the church had been abandoned for quite some time.

Continuing, I could see that one of the buildings was a post-office dry-goods store by the words on the sign: EVERSON MERCAN-TILE. There was another building; comical looking, with a sign and two large columns out front that dwarfed the rest of the diminutive structure: EVERSON BANK. There was also a run-down looking bar/café with an extravagant longhorn skull and a sign that at least said something other than Everson: THE ASTORIA. And in smaller letters that read CA-34—maybe we were still in California after all.

There were a few other buildings in varied states of disrepair, and a few outlying houses in the distance, and one or two pump jacks, or nodding donkeys, as we called them back in Wyoming, but not much else.

I walked over to the Everson Mercantile and stepped up onto the dry, warped wood of the walkway to peer into the dark windows. There was a moderate number of provisions, but I doubted there was a tie-rod end for a '60 half-ton.

The sign on the door said they opened at eight o' clock, and who knew, maybe the café did too.

My stomach rumbled and I thought about the vending machines back at the service station and about maybe drinking a root beer—and a Mallo Cup didn't sound half bad.

I'd just started down the length of the boardwalk when I saw a strange sight behind the church. Somebody was kneeling beside the fence that surrounded a small cemetery, fussing with something.

I stopped at the edge of the walkway to study them, aware that there was something strange about their size but also about the way they held their head.

Making my way down the two steps I began to cross the street but didn't want to scare the living daylights out of whoever it was, so I stopped there and raised a hand. "Hello . . . ?"

The figure started and then turned to me, and I have to admit that I was more than a little surprised to see a devil face gazing back, red-complected with a large nose, gaping, fanged mouth, and a full set of horns.

The intimidation factor was undercut by the fact that the individual was only about four and a half feet tall and wearing a dress along with a mask of some kind. "I didn't mean to startle you . . ."

She stared at me through the mask a moment longer and then began backing away down the length of the fence.

"No, wait." She ran like a jackrabbit, and I took a few steps out into the road. "I don't mean to . . ." I stood there in the middle of the street, watching her circumnavigate the fenced area of the cemetery, dodge behind the church, and disappear.

Walking the rest of the way across, I stood near where she had been kneeling and could see a loose bouquet of wildflowers, one that she must have left lying on the ground.

I stooped down to study the flowers but then, hearing a vehicle in the distance, turned to see a truck headed from the mountains to the east and toward town. It was only about a mile away as I started walking toward the crossroads, stopping and watching as the truck approached.

The headlights struck me along with a spotlight, and I stood still, watching as it slowed, but then the driver clicked on the high beams.

Bringing an arm up to my face to shield my eyes, I waited as the vehicle stopped in the center of the intersection, and I listened as a door opened and closed, a deep voice calling out, "Who in the hell are you?"

Lowering my arm, I could see the outline of a large individual, larger than me. "Howdy. The name's Walt Longmire, I'm getting my truck fixed over at the service station."

He moved closer. "Says who?"

"Excuse me?"

He moved even closer, and I could see the broadness of his face and that he was wearing a hard hat. "Ain't no excuse for you . . ."

I watched, incredulous as he set up as if for a punch, but figured that couldn't really be the case, and then paid the price as his ham-of-a-left-fist caught my jaw and grazed my nose. It was a good punch, but like all punches to my face it felt like little more than a nuisance. Maybe it was because I'd been beaten up by the best of the Athletic Association of Western Universities for the last four years. Or maybe it was because of the inherent hardness of my head, but I snapped back quicker than he could come around for another shot and brought my own fist into the back of his head, sending him and his hard hat sprawling into the dirt.

He attempted to catch himself with a stretched-out hand but slipped and rolled to one side and came back up at me. I thought he'd missed his mark, but when the dirt and pebbles struck my face, I figured what he was up to just a tad too late.

As I shied away, trying to get the grit out of my eyes, the next punch struck my midsection and lifted both of my feet off the ground. Happy that I hadn't already had that root beer and candy bar, I kept my balance, grunted, and stepped in closer, bringing my head up fast and listening to the sound like the crushing of an egg carton.

Clutching his nose, he stumbled back into the street. I took a breath and followed as he pulled his hands from his face and put up his dukes.

"Haven't you had enough?"

He swung with his left again, but this time it was a clean miss, due I'm sure from the amount of blood pouring from his face, and I timed it so that as he went by, I buried my right into his kidney and watched him fall to his knees facing the other way.

I stood there for a moment more and then reached out in front of him so that he could hopefully see it. "Here, let me give you a hand . . . ?"

It took a moment, but he finally took my grip but then turned, catching me with his left, right in the sweet spot under my chin.

Now, I have been hit hard before but nothing like this. Well, maybe once when I hadn't been paying attention while my father had shod a big blond draft mule that caught me in the ribs when I was twelve. The result was much the same, with me sailing and stumbling backward and over the fence in front of the church, landing like two tons of manure in a one-ton bag. Stretching my jaw, I started to stand, but he'd leaped over the fence and was on me before I could get up. He got a few more blows in the trunk of my body before I was able to get an arm around him and sling him toward the steps of the church like a wayward defensive back, but when he turned at me this time, I caught him with a right hook in the side of his head straight out of the Bighorns and watched as his knees gave in and he fell like an imploded building.

Standing there breathing, I felt a few loose teeth with the tip of my tongue and wiped my mouth, unsurprised to find more than a little blood there. I thought about spitting the blood onto the back of his CPO jacket but instead stepped over the broken fence into the street. "Nice town you've got here."

Taking a few more meandering steps out of the beam of the headlights, I looked at the vehicle he was driving, an oil rig maintenance truck with a boxed flatbed loaded down with the tools of the trade.

The firm on the side read EVERSON OIL.

"So, are you an Everson too?" I nursed my jaw and then walked back toward the church steps, this time not offering to help him but at least going to the trouble of picking up his green hard hat and tossing it in the scrub grass beside him.

Kneeling down, I stayed an arm's reach away. "So, are you *the* Everson?" Not getting any response, I reached out and pulled on his work boot as he moaned. "Well, whoever you are at least you're alive . . ."

I didn't finish the statement, the words lodging in my throat as the image of the devil face appeared under the porch of the church, caught in the headlights from the truck as I moved slightly to the left.

"Wow . . ." I could see the mask much closer now and in greater detail.

It was some kind of Kabuki mask, like the kind I'd seen hanging in Japanese restaurants back in Little Tokyo in Los Angeles while in college.

"Howdy." Stooped there, I waved at the figure, letting my hand drop. "I didn't mean to scare you."

The face moved a bit, now half-sheltered from the light by my shadow as she crouched back.

"You know, hiding underneath a church might not be the best place for a devil." I glanced up at the locked doors. "But then again . . ."

When I looked back, she was gone.

Moving in closer, I tried to look under the porch of the church, but in the limited light I couldn't see much of anything. I could go over to Everson's truck and probably find a flashlight, but what was I doing out here besides hunting for lost children and going all twelve rounds with a colossal roughneck?

Crawling back out, I stared at the man lying on the ground and figured I couldn't really leave him there. Unlatching the gate to the small fence that surrounded the front of the churchyard, I took him by his boots and dragged him into the street, finally getting a good look at him.

He was big, bigger than me but he was older, maybe in his forties. He wasn't in as good a shape as I was, but he had the look of one of those country bruisers that you saw lurking in the corners of bars and roadhouses just waiting for a victim. His nose had been spread across his face by my blow, and as my father used to say—he could now give directions without taking his hands out of his pockets.

Weighing a proper ton, it took a little while for me to drag him over to his truck, but I finally got him there, propping him up against a tire where I read the name spiraled across the left breast of his coveralls—LESTER. I yanked open the driver's side door and came back around, dead jerking him up to his feet and sloping him over one of my shoulders. I trudged around the door and leveraging him onto the bench seat, which was covered with trash, a packing blanket, and a smaller man crouched against the far door and staring at me through thick Coke bottle-bottom lenses. He was holding a cheap-looking .32 semiautomatic pistol, which was pointed at my head.

Slowly raising my hands, I tried to speak as reassuringly as I could. "Easy, there . . ."

He didn't move other than the actual shaking, and I could see he was terrified out of his mind, making him just as deadly as if he'd been an Ian Fleming character, and maybe more so. "You beat him."

"Yep, I did, but if you were here for the whole thing it was kind of close and Lester here didn't give me much of a choice."

Licking the spit from his lip, he repeated himself. "You beat him."

"Yep, but I didn't start it, really." I lowered my hands, but he gestured with the handgun, and I quickly raised them again.

"I ain't never seen anybody beat Lester."

I nodded toward the body between us. "He's big, and he's a southpaw, which puts a lot of people he's fighting at a disadvantage." I gestured with my shoulders. "Hey, look, can I lower my hands?"

"You ain't got a gun?"

"A what? A gun? No."

He gestured with the pistol again, and I slowly lowered my hands. "Do you mind pointing that thing somewhere else? I've seen more people get shot by accident than on purpose."

He adjusted his own hard hat. "Are you a cop?"

"What?" I thought about asking him if they were doing something illegal but quickly scrapped that idea. "No, I'm not. Look, do you want to help me get him the rest of the way in the truck and then you can do whatever you want with him?"

He seemed unsure but stuffed the pistol into his coat pocket and reached behind him, opening the door and carefully sliding out. As I pushed, he pulled, and we were able to get the giant into the cab enough so that somebody could actually sit in the driver's side and operate the vehicle.

I watched as he closed the passenger side door and came around, now holding the pistol again. "Back away."

"Hey, I'm not looking for trouble here."

"Maybe so, but you might'a found it anyway, okay?" He looked past me to where you could see the lights on at the service station. "What're you doing here?"

"My truck broke down, and my buddy and I were lucky enough to find that place open."

He moved around the door and climbed in, keeping the pistol on me. "Yeah, well that's his problem."

"Why is it a problem?"

He pulled the door closed. "When the Judge finds out about you being here it's going to be a problem, okay?"

I nodded toward the body beside him on the seat. "Is that your father, the judge?"

"Him?" He laughed. "No, Lester just works for my poppa, like everybody else around these parts."

"So, you're an Everson?"

"Yeah, Parker Everson."

I glanced around. "Your dad own the town?"

"Pretty much."

"Even the bar?"

He ground the truck to life, finally lowering the pistol. "Especially the bar."

I tucked my hands into my jeans just to reassure him that I wasn't going to lunge for the truck and studied him, coming to the conclusion that he was probably in his forties. "It doesn't have your name on it." I glanced around again. "The only thing that doesn't . . ."

"It's named after my brother's ship, the one who died in World War Two, okay?"

"The *Astoria*?"

"Yeah."

He started to pull out, but I raised a hand. "Hey, do you know anything about a girl in a dress wearing a Kabuki mask—looks like the devil?"

He stared at me for a moment and then pushed his thick glasses back up on his crooked nose with a forefinger. "You saw her too?"

"Yep." He didn't say anything, so I asked. "Why did you just cross yourself?"

He whistled through his teeth. "Bad things happen when she shows up."

"Does she live here?"

"Who knows?" He tried to pull out again. "The best thing you can do is just forget about her, okay?"

I stepped forward, even being so bold as to place a hand on the sill of the side window. "But she's a kid, you can't just leave her out here running around the streets at night."

"Hardly anybody's ever seen her, so do yourself a favor and forget you even saw her, okay?"

I made a face. "Say, what kind of town is this?"

"The kind of town you should forget about, okay?"

"No, not okay."

He stared at me. "Look, I'm trying to help you, but you've got to help yourself. Now when you get your truck fixed, you and your friend need to get in it and vamoose the heck out of here."

I stepped back, shrugging. "As soon as he gets back, we'll see . . ."

"Where'd he go?"

I threw a thumb over my shoulder, indicating south. "He walked down toward the old internment camp."

The guy's voice rose, and he looked genuinely concerned. "What's he doing down there?"

I glanced toward that direction. "He's a student of history, especially social history."

"You need to go get him before he gets hurt."

"Who's going to hurt him?"

He started to pull out again but paused for a moment to look at the body in the cab with him and then back at me. He slipped off his hard hat and ruffled his wayward blondish-gray hair, smiling at me with his horse teeth. "You know something? I don't think anybody's ever beat Lester at all."

The sun crawled a little higher, and I watched him swing the truck around and speed back up the road as I stood there smearing a little blood from the corner of my mouth with the back of my hand, muttering to myself. "It happens to everybody, eventually."

4

As we ate our collection of BLTs, Vic, the youngster of the group, posed a question. "So, these internment camps, they were mostly out west?"

I rested my sandwich on my plate and thought about it. "Shortly after the bombing of Pearl Harbor, which resulted in this country's entrance into World War II . . . You've heard about World War Two?"

She continued eating her sandwich and eyeing me with an arched brow. "If you're going to be an asshole, I'll just go read about it in a book or watch a documentary on YouTube."

"What's YouTube?"

"See, you don't know everything either."

The Bear interrupted, possibly not able to stand anymore. "Executive Order 9066, one of the most atrocious violations of civil rights in the country's history, certainly that of the twentieth century."

"It was supposed to be an anti-espionage act, taking all the people of Japanese ancestry from the West Coast and placing them in these inland relocation camps."

"Not just people of Japanese ancestry but American citizens." The Bear glanced at me. "Six days' notice to decide what you could carry with you for the rest of your life and what you had to simply sell or leave on the sidewalk, untold amounts of goods and assets were seized or left behind."

Vic pulled a piece of bacon from her sandwich and held it up like a talking stick. "But these weren't concentration camps like what the Nazis had, were they?"

"No, there wasn't any slave labor or systematic extermination of a people . . . But over one thousand six hundred people were killed due to inadequate health care and environmental stress, and some were actually shot."

She munched on her bacon talking stick. "Why just the Japanese? I mean, I'm Italian, and I don't think they corralled my people back in Philadelphia?"

Henry glanced at me. "The Japanese looked different."

I took a sip of my tea. "I don't think you can overstate the anti-Japanese sentiment on the West Coast immediately following the period after Pearl Harbor. Ships were sunk, hundreds of aircraft were destroyed, and over two thousand Americans were killed. Only a couple of hours after the attack on Oahu, Hawaii, the FBI rounded up more than twelve hundred Japanese American community and religious leaders, incarcerating them and freezing their assets. All in all, one hundred twenty thousand people were confined."

She sat back in her chair. "Here in the West?"

"Inland California, Idaho, Utah, Arizona, Arkansas, and right here in Wyoming."

"Where in Wyoming?"

"Heart Mountain, right over the Bighorns outside Cody. Not to make excuses, but it was a different time . . . We could always get Lucian over here to give you his impression."

"I can guess." She shook her head, thinking about the old Doolittle Raider. "What happened to all those people when the war was finally over?"

Henry grunted. "Twenty-five dollars and a one-way ticket when the camps closed."

"Almost all went back to the communities where they'd been before the war. You have to remember that the camps were in some pretty remote areas, and these were mostly city people."

I moved over toward the counter with the check and stood in front of the brass cash register as Dorothy came out. "What's all this World War Two talk going on over there?"

I pulled some cash from my wallet. "Just old war stories . . ."

"Heart Mountain?"

I gave her the bills. "A place very much like it."

"I had a friend who was one of the guards over at Heart Mountain. He came up 4-F because of his asthma, so he volunteered to go over there."

"Did he say what it was like?"

"Hard, he said it was hard on the internees in that they were used to a temperate climate and hadn't even had time to bring the kind of clothes they would need for a Wyoming winter." She punched the numbers into the cash register and then caught the tray as it shot out. Counting my change, she handed it to me. "He said there was a certain quality of criminal activity."

I was surprised. "Such as?"

"People smuggling things into the Japanese." She shoved the cash tray shut. "If people found out that a certain internee was an artist, they'd smuggle art supplies to them, instruments for musicians, books, that type of thing . . ."

I dropped a five in the tip jar. "Kinda gives you hope for humanity, doesn't it?"

SUNDAY, MAY 24, 1964

Dabbing the blood from the corner of my mouth with the continuous towel dispenser, I pulled on it again, but it didn't move, causing me to wonder what kind of bacteria I'd just introduced into my system.

I looked at my face in the cracked, filthy mirror, especially at the swelling jaw. Raising two fingers at my image, I made a peace sign. "Make love not war."

Pushing the bathroom door open, I walked out into the early morning and back around to the front of the service station, ducking my head down in my coat, pulling my hat on a little tighter, and breathing into my hands and rubbing them together. Behind me, I could see the sun just starting to peep over the cardboard cutout of the mountains to the east and I walked by the window of the service station. I saw that Henry Standing Bear was seated on one of the client chairs beside the hole in the wall and was reading from a battered paperback copy of *The Complete Poems of François Villon*.

He looked up at me as I pushed open the glass door, the bell tinkling just above my head. "Rough night?"

"Obviously a little rougher than yours . . ." I sat in the chair opposite him beside the oil can rack, listening to the hammering going on in the stall behind me. "I don't get to read Dostoevsky, but you get to read medieval French poetry?"

He smiled. "I have discovered that existence in Bone Valley lacks a literary largesse."

I felt my jaw. "You can say that again."

"I found this in the camp." He gestured with the paperback. "Did you know that Villon killed a man in a tavern brawl, knifed him in the groin?"

"Well, that's romantic."

"He spent a lot of time in and out of the prisons of Paris until he was finally banished and then disappeared . . . Probably hanged."

"Or lost another knife fight." I nodded back down the road toward the ruins of the government camp. "Is there much down there?"

"Surprisingly, yes." He closed the book. "The buildings are in remarkable shape, probably to do with the dry, desert environs—but there is something more."

"Like what?"

He placed the book in his lap. "There are plates and dinnerware on the tables, clothes still hung in closets . . ." He gestured with the paperback. "Books lying open or with bookmarks only halfway through."

"As if they were evacuated?"

He looked up at me. "As if they suddenly vanished from the face of the earth."

"Odd."

"That would be the catchphrase for this town, yes." He leaned forward. "Amazingly, you found someone to fight in this thriving metropolis?"

I nodded toward the intersection. "Some roughneck by the name of Lester, who I guess didn't like my looks, and I met an Everson."

"An Everson?"

"Everything in the town has the judge's name on it, except for the bar over here that's called the Astoria CA-34."

"CA as in armored cruiser?"

I stared at him. "Now, how did you know that?"

"You forget, my father was in the Navy."

"Oh, right." I stretched my legs out on the green-flecked linoleum. "Evidently, Judge Everson had a son who was killed onboard a ship called the *Astoria* back in World War Two."

"You met the father?"

"No, another son in his forties."

"Is he the one who beat you up?"

"No, the son's name is Parker. Lester is the one I went five rounds with—and no, he didn't beat me up."

"You fought Lester?" We both turned to see Pickens standing in the doorway to the stall, wiping his hands on a shop towel. "Well, mister, you must'a run because there ain't nobody that tussled with Lester and come out looking as good as you."

I felt my jaw. "Oh, he packs a punch with that left; I'll give you that."

The mechanic's face grew a little more serious. "Honest, you fought Lester?"

"Yep. I wasn't particularly in favor of it, but he didn't give me much choice in the matter."

"He's that way." He walked past us and peered over the Bear and through the window in the exact direction in which the roughnecks had retreated and where the sun continued to rise. "They still in town?"

"No, he and the Everson fellow retreated in the direction you're looking."

"Parker Everson was with Lester?"

"Yep, glasses and a crooked nose? He pointed a gun at me, but we didn't get properly introduced."

His voice vibrated against the glass. "How long ago was that?"

"I don't know, maybe forty minutes ago."

"They'll be coming soon."

"Who?"

"Judge Everson, and the rest."

"So?"

He turned to look at me. "You better be gone by then."

"Well, how's my truck?"

"The tie-rod off my tow is too big, so I'll have to try and weld the one you got."

"Okay."

"No, not okay." They're gonna be back here in no time and you two need to get gone."

The Cheyenne Nation and I looked at each other. "Well, we won't get far without our truck."

"Suit yourself, but I wanna get paid for my labor before they get here."

"What?"

"You pay me now, 'cause you won't be able to later."

I stood. "What do I owe you?"

"Forty-seven dollars and thirty-three cents."

Pulling my wallet from my pocket, I plucked out a few bills. "That's pretty exact."

"I ain't no thief."

I handed him a ten and two twenties. "Here, keep the change."

He was about to say more, but something caught his eye as he looked over my shoulder to where a dark-haired girl in a weathered blue and white letterman's jacket walked by, waving at us but continuing.

Henry stood and looked after the young woman. "Who is that?"

With a worried look on his face, Pickens glanced up at the square Gates clock behind the counter that read 6:55 a.m. "Noriko. She's on her way to the café."

"Well, I have to admit that I am getting a little peckish." The Bear stretched and started toward the door. "Come on, we can have breakfast while we wait for the Everson gang to arrive."

I watched as he pushed open the door, and I shrugged at Pickens before following the Bear out into the cool, clear air of the high desert. "Hey Henry, wait up."

He paused at the corner to turn and look at me.

"Do you remember that Japanese restaurant we used to eat in back in Little Tokyo in the historic district?"

"Hayami's?" He looked at me, puzzled. "Yes?"

"There were Kabuki masks on the walls, including a red one that looked like a devil with horns and this big, gaping mouth."

He started across the street. "Hannya mask. Worn in Noh theater and during Shinto kagura——'angry woman face,' as I recall."

"Angry woman face?"

"Yes, not Kabuki but Noh theater. The mask you describe depicts the vengeful female spirit on the verge of becoming a demoness." He stared at me. "Do you mind if I ask why it is at this juncture that you decided to ask me about this?"

I glanced about. "There's one running around out here."

He also glanced about, looking somewhat suspect. "A Japanese demoness, here in Bone Valley?"

"Well, a mask with a kid attached to it."

He studied me. "Are you sure you were not hit hard on the head during the fight?"

"I'm telling you that there was a girl out here running around with one of those masks on. She was placing wildflowers along the fence by the cemetery over there. I guess I scared her off but then saw her again under the church."

He glanced in that direction at the dilapidated, spired structure. "*Under* the church?"

"Well, under the porch."

He shook his head at me, continuing across the street. "You know, sometimes I believe you lead a much richer and varied imagination than I could ever suspect."

Stooping down I peered under the church in hopes of seeing her but then started after the Bear. "Hey, wait up . . ."

I had a sneaking suspicion that the establishment the Astoria CA-34 in Bone Valley had been here much longer than the war in the Pacific. Except for the checkered tablecloths and the tiny vases with wildflowers in them, we might've stepped onto the set of an old John Ford Western.

The bar was small but impressive and well stocked with a flip-up counter at one end that stopped where a set of swinging doors must've led to the kitchen. There were photographs on the wall, a number of them of a young man not dissimilar to the one I'd met in the truck earlier, but without the glasses and with a straighter nose. There were also photos of what I assumed to be the actual *Astoria CA-34*, including a rather crude painting of the ship on the wall behind the bar. There were fringed flags, certificates of honor, and even a life preserver with the vessel's name, USS *Astoria CA-34*, stenciled upon it.

"I think this place would be more at home in San Diego or Hawaii." We stood there for a moment and then closed the door, just as the same dark-haired woman we saw earlier, Noriko, entered from the kitchen with a coffeepot in hand. "Howdy."

She stopped, and I thought for a moment she might run for it.

"Is that coffee, because we sure would love some?"

She didn't move.

I slipped off my hat and dipped my head. "My name is Walt Long-mire, and this is my friend Henry Standing Bear."

The Bear also dipped his head but first took off the fisherman's cap. "How do you do?"

I took the time to get a closer look at her and figured her to be about our age, and even from this distance could see she was at least part Asian. "Is it okay if we sit down? We'd love some coffee and something to eat if you're serving?"

She stammered out the words. "The coffee is ready, but I've got to get the stove going . . ."

I moved over and pulled out a chair, sitting with my back against the wall and flipping over one of the mugs on the table. "That's fine. Can I take that from you?"

"No, no, that's all right." Stepping around Henry but keeping her eye on him the whole time, she flipped another mug and then filled them both.

It was possible she was our age, but she looked younger. Her hair was dark and cut at the nape of her neck, accenting the strong jaw-line, and she was gorgeous. "Our truck broke down and we're get-ting it fixed across the road . . ."

The dark eyes glanced at me. "The only thing we have ready would be some day-old biscuits and gravy as soon as I get it warmed up."

I sipped my coffee and immediately felt every loose part of my teeth. "Sounds good to me."

Henry smiled at her again as she retreated past him, going back toward the kitchen. "I am sorry, but we did not catch your name?"

She paused for a moment, and I could tell she was considering whether or not she was going to serve it up. "Noriko, my name is Noriko."

The Bear bowed just a bit in a respectful manner. "*Hajimemashite, Noriko.*"

He looked after her and then sat, picking up his own mug and sipping his coffee. "My, things are looking up here in Bone Valley."

"I happen to know that you only know six phrases in Japanese."

"Yes, and that is one of them." He pulled out the volume of French poetry and opened it, skimming through the verses. "This demon, did it have a white face or a red one?"

"What demon?"

"The one living under the church."

"Oh, the mask—it was definitely red, why?"

"White demon face means high born, whereas red demon face means low born."

"Well, she's living under a church . . ."

He looked up at me. "And it was a child?"

"Or a small person, yes. A girl."

"How could you tell?"

"She was wearing a dress."

He sipped his coffee. "This is a strange town."

"Yes, it is." I nodded toward the kitchen where we could hear preparations being made. "How about you ask your newfound friend about it?"

"I may."

On cue, Noriko reappeared in the swinging doors carrying two plates stacked with biscuits and smothered in red-eye gravy and sided with a few slabs of ham. She slid them onto the table along with napkin-wrapped silverware. "Here you go."

I gazed at the feast, my stomach now in full gurgle. "If this is what you throw together at a moment's notice, we'll be back for lunch and dinner."

She smiled at me, but her attention was drawn to the Bear. "You're Native?"

He smiled, placing the book to the side and unrolling his utensils. "Native to what?"

She smiled again, but this time covering it with a hand. "You're not Apache or Navajo?"

He smoothed the paper napkin on his knee. "Cheyenne. My friend and I are from Wyoming and Montana, respectively."

We watched as she made a mental map. "Is it cold up there?"

"Colder than here. You have never been?"

"No, I've been to Prescott a couple of times and Phoenix, once."

"But you live here?"

"Yes."

"Seems kind of lonely."

She blinked once and then swallowed. "It can be . . ."

"May I ask you a question?"

Her eyes widened a bit as she glanced at him. "Sure."

"My friend here says he saw a child running around the street out here last night, wearing a mask. From what he described to me, a kagura Hannya mask."

She stared at him for a long while. "There are no children here."

"None, really?" He picked up his cutlery and began sawing at his ham steak. "My friend here is usually very good at noticing things like that."

"There are no children here." She reached over, taking a salt and pepper shaker and placing them on our table. "You should eat your food before it gets cold."

We both watched her go and then began eating. "That was really something; smooth the way you handled her."

"Just getting started."

I rolled my eyes and then looked out the window where my attention was drawn to two trucks sliding to a stop outside on the dirt road, the roiling dust all but clouding them out as they slid to a stop.

One was the vehicle I'd seen this morning, and the other was a crew cab, the same sky blue with the Everson brand on the door. "Well, hell . . ."

The Bear raised up in his seat, watching as at least a half dozen workmen piled out of the two trucks and clambered onto the board-walk toward the door of the bar/café. "I guess we better hurry our breakfast."

Henry continued eating as the group burst through the door. The first through was an older man, deeply tanned with close-cropped silver hair and a light-colored cowboy hat perched on the back of his head. He was trim and powerfully built, carrying himself like the leader as the others crowded around him like a pack.

"Howdy, Judge Everson."

He stopped at our table, folding his arms. "I know you?"

I noticed Parker Everson and the ogre who I'd battled with earlier loitering in the back, the large man looking a bit worse for wear with toilet paper rolled up and plugging both nostrils. "I don't think so, but I've met your son and some of your men here."

He stepped in closer, resting his hands on the chair in front of him. "What are you doing in my town?"

I took another bite of my biscuits and gravy, allowing myself to chew before answering. "Why, just enjoying the gracious hospitality of the place."

"You some kind of smart-ass?"

I glanced at the Bear. "Am I some kind of smart-ass?"

Henry shrugged between bites. "No, he is a genuine smart-ass."

His gaze stayed on the Cheyenne Nation. "And what're you?"

I pointed at my friend with a bite of ham impaled on my fork. "He's more of smart-ass-in-training, but he's working on it."

Everson turned and looked at his men with a kind of wonder-ment and then pulled the chair out, turning it and straddling the seat as he leaned forward. "Which one of you was it who hauled off and beat the shit out of Lester here?"

Lester interrupted in a deep but nasally voice, speaking through the toilet paper in his nose as he stepped forward. "He didn't beat me Mr.—"

"Shut up, Lester."

The giant moved back. "Yes, sir."

Parker spoke up. "Poppa?"

Everson ignored him as his gaze drifted back and forth between us. "I'm trying to figure out if there's more to you two than meets the eye." He leaned in, inspecting both of us. "We're getting ready for a war. How come two able-bodied boys such as yourselves haven't stepped up to serve your country?"

I glanced at Henry and then echoed my voice off the table as he continued eating. "That would be our business and not yours." Finishing off my ham steak and starting on the last of my biscuits, I lowered my silverware and sat back in my chair. "Judge, our truck broke down, and we're just getting it fixed across the road here, and then we'll likely be on our way."

Shaking his head, he leaned back in his own chair. "Yeah, I'm gonna have a word with Donnie Pickens about that."

I shook my head. "Mr. Pickens is doing his best to get us out of here, and that's all. Isn't that what you want, to get us out of here?"

"That I do."

Over his shoulder, I watched as Noriko entered from the kitchen but then stood there with her head down. "Mind if I ask why it is you want us out of here so badly?"

Everson studied me as Henry picked up the Villon book and opened to a page, silently reading to himself. "We haven't had the best interactions with outside people coming into our part of the world for decades."

"Does any of this have to do with the old internment camp down the road?"

"Started with that."

"That was twenty years ago, what in the world . . . ?"

He nodded toward the primitive painting on the wall behind the bar. "You see that painting, son?" He didn't wait for an answer. "That is the USS *Astoria* and that proud ship fought in the Battle of the Coral Sea, the Battle of Midway, and Battle of Savo Island near Guadalcanal, where she was sunk by a sneak Jap attack that sacrificed the lives of 219 noble souls, one of whom was my elder son, Andrew."

"Well, I'm sorry for your loss, Judge . . ."

"And then them sorry bastards put that camp full of slant-eyed sons-a-bitches right here in my town."

I started to say something, but then stopped as the older man stood, straddling the chair as Henry cleared his throat and began reading aloud:

> "You lost men deaf to reason
> Unnatural, fallen from knowledge
> Emptied of sense, filled with unreason
> Deluded fools stuffed with ignorance."

The older man stood there, for all intents and purposes, dumbstruck. "Breakfast is over, boys."

The Bear lowered the book and went back to carving off chunks of biscuits and gravy with his fork. "I am not through eating."

"The hell you're not." Everson reached across the table and started to pull the Bear's plate away, and you would've had to have known what was going to happen if you were to see it at all.

I knew the hand was going to come out like a rattlesnake in full strike, and I knew the grip that latched on to the judge's arm would be just like that same rattlesnake and watched as it yanked him from his awkward position and placed him beside Henry as his hat and chair fell to the floor and the full length of a stag-handled Bowie knife came up under his chin like a straight razor.

There was no movement and no sound except for the frightening blade scraping the underneath of the older man's Adam's apple as the Bear held him there.

Lester and one of the other men started to move, but Henry tightened the blade on Everson's throat, causing his head to tilt back alongside the Bear's face.

The older man lifted a hand, just barely. "Don't."

They stood still.

I forked another bite and chewed, looking at the judge. "Like I said, my friend here is kind of a smart-ass in training, but as a badass I'd have to say he's a fully graduated, real deal." Taking another bite and chewing as I rested the utensils on my empty plate, I propped my elbows on the table, making a combined fist to rest my chin. "We're not looking for any trouble, Judge, but we're not looking to put up with any either. Now, why don't you take a seat and have some breakfast, or you and your men can just go on about your day?"

We stayed like that for what seemed like a couple of eternities, and then he made a curt nod.

Henry slipped the knife away just as magically as it had appeared. He then pulled Everson up into a standing position and returned to eating his food.

The older man stepped away, first looking at his henchmen and then turning back to look at us, his face a lively shade of crimson. He reached down to pick up his hat and dusted it off before returning it to his head and starting toward the door as the others made way. He placed his hand on the handle and stared at the floor a moment before raising a hand and pointing a long finger at us. "You're gonna rue the day you came into my town."

He yanked the door open and strode out with the others following, but not before they all gave us the stink eye.

Throwing an arm over the back of my chair and gazing through the plate glass window, I watched as the pack climbed into the pair of trucks and roared away. "Well, he's got us there. I've done nothing but rue coming to this town since I got here. How 'bout you?"

He turned in his seat and raised his mug. "I beg your pardon, Noriko, but could I get some more coffee, please?"

The young woman, who had been frozen by the door up to now, reached onto the bar and brought over the stainless pot with a little trepidation before refilling Henry's mug. When she finished with him, she turned toward me, and I also proffered my mug. "Sorry about the ruckus."

"I've never heard anybody speak to the judge like that."

"Seems like he's about due." I took a sip of my coffee. "I apologize for the remarks he made."

She looked genuinely puzzled. "What remarks?"

"About Asian people."

"Oh." She shrugged. "He just says those things . . ."

The Bear finished his breakfast, wiping his mouth with his napkin and handing her his empty plate. "He owns this establishment?"

Taking Henry's plate and then mine, Noriko stacked it on top of his. "He owns everything."

Henry studied her. "Excuse me for asking, but with bigotries like his, how is it he employs you?"

"That's easy." She smiled and then started back for the kitchen. "I'm his granddaughter."

"You know, the longer we're here, the weirder this town gets." Walking back toward the service station, Henry stopped at the corner, looking at the heavy chains looped around the door handles of the locked-up church as I paused in the middle of the street. "What?"

"I find it odd that even in a town like this one, the church is closed."

"Everson probably couldn't find a way to put his name on it." I crossed the rest of the way and then turned back to look at him. "Don't."

He looked at me, pulling a handful of dark hair from his face as the condensation of his breath whipped away. "What?"

"Get involved."

He adjusted his cap and then shoved his hands into his pockets. "I do not know what you are talking about."

"People and stuff—people get you into stuff and then stuff gets you into people."

"I am just curious."

"We have less than a week before you have to report to Fort Polk and I have to be on Parris Island."

He stood there, refusing to cross the road, just staring at the ground. "So?"

"So, you are thinking about getting involved."

"I am curious." He spread his hands. "Are you not?"

"Not enough to stick around—I have enough on my plate right now." I continued to study him. "It's the girl, Noriko, right?"

"There is also the child in the mask."

"You never even saw her."

"Perhaps I want to."

"Henry . . ."

"I do not like bullies, and neither do you."

"As I said, we've got a previous engagement with the United States Armed Forces."

He stood there for a moment more and then walked across the road and past me. "And why did you not want to tell him we had enlisted?"

"It's none of his business."

"Like Bone Valley?"

He kept walking toward the service station, as I called after him. "Exactly."

I followed, catching the glass door as we both entered the shop, waiting as the mechanic, Pickens finished on the phone and hung it up, staring at us. "The damn thing won't weld, so I had to order you another one."

"Is this going to cost me another forty-seven dollars and thirty-three cents?"

He ignored me. "My guy says he can run it over here from Iron Springs but to not hold my breath—says he'll definitely get it here by tomorrow."

"So, we're stuck here for another day, at least?"

Pickens nodded. "I reckon."

"How about we take your tow truck and run over to Iron Springs and get the part?"

"The way that truck is geared it would take you two hours, and besides, that gas is running at thirty cents a gallon and you'd end up paying for your tie-rod twice."

"Doesn't sound so bad."

"Why not hit your buddy the judge up for a ride; maybe he'll accommodate you?"

"I kind of doubt it."

The Bear glanced back at me as I flicked my eyes at him and then he continued studying the book of poetry, which he started to read aloud.

> "I am François which is my cross
> Born in Paris near Pontoise
> From a fathom of rope my neck
> Will learn the weight of my ass."

He closed the book and looked out onto the desolate street where the cold morning sun did nothing to enhance the aesthetic. "Fate, it would appear, has taken a hand."

5

Judi Cole sat at the other table in the courtroom, shook her head, and then slowly stood, walking toward me and then standing in front of my chair clutching an elbow and adjusting her glasses. "Hi, Sheriff, how're you doing?"

"I've had better days." I liked Judi, she was one of the finest defense attorneys in the county, and she didn't suffer fools easily—many had tried but they generally ended coming up short on the litigious stick.

"I bet." She looked down at her shoes, rubbing the toe of one across the worn municipal carpet. "Why do you suppose a man like Tom Rondelle was there at your grandfather's ranch that night?"

"Mike Regis said that he wanted Rondelle to have skin in the game."

"I see." She covered a smile with her hand. "And you think Mike Regis wanted Tom Rondelle to be committed in the situation of covering up the Sovereign Wealth Fund?"

"His exact statement was that they'd never done anything quite like killing a sheriff, so he wanted Rondelle there to make sure they all had a hand in it to keep anybody from getting the idea of throwing everybody else under the bus."

She nodded, glancing at Prosecutor Whinstone. "To be clear, Tom Rondelle was the only person you shot that night?"

"Yes."

"Could you have killed the young man, Jordan Heller?"

"I suppose."

"You overpowered him."

"I did."

"But you didn't kill him, why? He was actively hunting you, wasn't he?"

"It wasn't necessary."

"And Maxim Sidarov?"

"It wasn't necessary to kill him either."

She walked back to the table and scooped up her own notes. "What about the driver, Phillip Lane?"

"The one in the tunnel?"

"Yes."

"I didn't know his name." I thought about it. "I didn't really have any choice. I was unarmed at the time, and the only thing I could think to do was kick loose the coal car, and he didn't get out of the way in time."

"Was he armed?"

"Yep, everybody in the place was armed except me, except for the icepick I was carrying."

She glanced at me and then checked her notes. "Everyone was armed, including Treasury Agent Ruth One Heart."

I nodded. "She had her sidearm, a 9 mm."

"And you were not aware she was a federal agent until she helped with your escape after you'd been drugged and handcuffed by Mr. Heller?"

"That's correct."

"And after making that escape, you sent her to try and get rein-forcements?"

"Yep."

"But she was captured in attempting to do that?"

"Unfortunately, yes."

"And Agent One Heart was the one who eventually shot and killed Mike Regis?"

I adjusted my hat on my knee again. "Yep."

"After Regis had fired at you multiple times?"

"Yep."

"Could you have also shot Mike Regis after Agent One Heart?"

"Sure."

"Why didn't you?"

"Once again, it wasn't necessary—he was dead, he just didn't know it."

"There were two other ancillary victims in this case, am I correct?" She consulted her notes. "A gentleman by the name of Jules Beldon and a young woman, Trisha Knox?"

Whinstone waved a hand. "Objection, your honor. We'll be dealing with Mr. Beldon and Ms. Knox in another hearing."

Snowden sat back in his chair, bridging his fingertips. "Ms. Cole?"

"Your honor, I'm just trying to establish that with all the killing that was going on in this Wild West of a weekend, my client showed amazing restraint."

"I think we're all getting that, Ms. Cole, but I don't think that as wide reaching as this hearing is that we need to introduce any more elements at this time."

"Yes, Your Honor."

I sat there in the oak chair thinking about how many occupants' lives had been changed while here and listened to the traffic out below on Main Street. If I concentrated hard enough, I could meld the sound of the rubber tires on the concrete just enough so that they formed one sweep of sound, almost like waves.

There's no part of the world that changes more constantly than a coastline; the perpetual battle, negotiation, or intercourse between land and sea.

SUNDAY, MAY 24, 1964

With nothing else to do, we'd wandered down to the camp where Henry had been exploring before. As he'd said, there were a surprising number of buildings still standing, with only a few on the perimeters having succumbed to wind and weather. The ones nearest the road were like that, looking as if they'd gotten tired of living in the desert and decided to just lie down and take a nap.

On closer inspection, it seemed as if a couple of the communal buildings and at least one barrack toward the center had actually burned, probably a result of faulty wiring or vandalism. With Judge Everson's attitude, I was surprised that there was anything at all left of the place.

Henry had found a desk in one of the centralized buildings, a school that still held some bookshelves and a chalkboard, and I imagined he'd also found the volume of Villon's poetry there.

There were corrugated irrigation pipes filled with cement, holding large rough-cut poles that supported the rafters, and two-by-eights that made up the outside and inside surface. It's possible the stuff had fallen away, but there was no insulation, and I wondered how cold it must get in winter.

The floors were rough planking, and stock must've been allowed in or had broken in at one point because there was fossilized cow shit anointing different spots like a checkerboard.

"I'm tired; I don't suppose you saw any cots or anything?"

He looked up from his book. "Not in this building, but there are others. You are welcome to use the desk if you would like."

I studied the dust-covered hard surface. "It doesn't look very comfortable."

He glanced at it. "No, it does not."

"You're just going to stay here?"

"There is not much else to look at, just more crumbling buildings."

"And cow shit?"

He nodded and went back to his book, a hole in the roof providing a perfect skylight. "Some are in remarkably good shape, as if the inhabitants had left in a great rush."

I nodded and decided to go out and poke around. Other than a few windows, the only openings were at the ends of the buildings, so I went out the other side and looked down the row of identical barrack bunkhouses stretching to the east. There were about a dozen of them, which seemed small in comparison to photographs I'd seen of Heart Mountain back in Wyoming, where I seemed to remember hundreds of buildings that had housed over ten thousand evacuees.

"Why would they build a camp this small?"

Startled by my own voice, I noticed a tall, brick stack beside one of the buildings, likely a boiler facility to heat the radiators that were prevalent in the period. Walking in that direction, I watched as a jackrabbit shot out from under one of the buildings and disappeared under another as I mumbled to myself. "I bet there are rattlesnakes galore around here."

"There are."

Startled again, I glanced in the direction of the voice. "Hello?"

"Over here."

I turned toward the voice and could see that it was Noriko, the young woman from the café. She was smoking a cigarette and sitting on a flight of steps in the letterman's jacket. "Hello."

I walked toward her, stopping a little away. "Taking a break?"

She smiled. "Not much business after you left."

I glanced around. "This is an odd place."

"You can say that again."

"Pardon me for asking, but was this camp not finished? I mean, it's so small in comparison to the others I've seen."

"What others have you seen?"

"Heart Mountain up in Wyoming had over a hundred structures, and this one only has a half dozen."

She took a puff of her cigarette and looked down the rows of buildings in a fit of muse. "This was not a regular camp."

"Then what was it?"

"Malcontents, at least that's what my mother used to call it: Camp Malcontent." She smiled. "The prisoners who were difficult or problematic or political—they would ship them here. Kind of a basket for all the bad eggs."

"Your mom was a bad egg?"

"The worst; she was political."

"I see." Walking a little closer, I looked over her shoulder and into the interior of the building behind her. "What's this?"

"The dance hall—it's where my mother met my father."

"I'm assuming that would've been Andrew Everson, Judge Everson's son?"

"My father, yes."

"Sounds like an interesting story."

She shrugged, stubbing the butt out on the wooden tread. "He came home on leave and met my mother here, where they fell in love." She spread her arms, smiling in unquestionable existence. "And here I am."

"But you never met him?"

"No, or at least I don't recall. They say he came home again, but I was just born, so I don't remember him. Then his ship was sunk . . ."

I thought about the young woman, working in a place named for the ship on which her father had died. "Your mother stayed here after the war?"

"Yes, because of me." She stood. "After all, I'm half Everson."

"That seems to mean a lot in this town."

She stepped down from the warped and cupped wooden steps. "For some."

"You want to take a walk?"

"I have to get back to the café."

I nodded. "Well, we'll probably be back over for dinner."

"No lunch?"

"We don't want to particularly overstay our welcome."

She glanced around. "It doesn't look as if we're going to be having much of a midday rush . . ."

"Then you may see us."

She started to head toward the road but then stopped and looked back at me. "You need to be careful."

"Excuse me?"

"With my grandfather—he can be a dangerous man, and he has nothing to lose."

"He has a great deal to lose, if you ask me."

She nodded. "Things maybe, but there's nothing left that he loves, and that makes him dangerous."

"Doesn't he love you?" She didn't answer. "Noriko, what happened here? I mean, there's only one reason someone like your grandfather tries to keep a place this guarded—something happened, something bad. What was it?"

She stared at me.

"What's going on?" I glanced around. "I mean, if it was something during wartime that was over twenty years ago . . ."

Her gaze went to the ground, and I watched as she walked back toward the road, an incongruous sight in the oversize letterman's jacket, the skirt that reached her knees, and the untied work boots. She climbed over the drooping fence and turned right, heading back toward town or what there was of it.

I walked down the center of the complex between the rows of buildings finally coming to an end where there was an open area marked off as some kind of all-purpose, freshly graded football field complete with a scoreboard that had also decided to lie down and have a rest.

I was just about to head back when I heard something—a wavering, mournful kind of cry that keened with the wind but then died away. I stood there for a moment more and then started off when I heard it again.

I stopped again to listen.

I was sure that it was high-pitched melodic singing in Japanese, at least to my ears.

Trying to get an idea of where the music might be coming from, I focused on the last building to my left. Walking in that direction, I was sure I heard the singing and that it wasn't my imagination.

When I got to the building in question, I stopped. Although alien to me, the voice singing the song was mesmerizing.

I stepped onto the first tread, reached up, and pushed one of the doors, but discovered the set was chained together with the other one on the inside. Inadvertently making a clunking noise, I listened but the singing had abruptly stopped.

Pushing the doors open as much as the chain would allow, I could see light at about the midpoint of the building. There were no holes in the roof, so the illumination must've been coming from something inside.

I decided to circle the building, finding that a second set of doors were also chained shut. I looked around and determined there wasn't anybody to object to my doing it, so I blasted a cowboy boot into the doors, a kick that knocked the set off their rusted hinges. I watched as they flew inward and landed flat on the floor.

I inspected as the dust settled, but there was still no movement inside.

Taking a step into the darkness, I walked forward, looking around, and then worked my way toward the center of the building and the area I'd seen from the other side.

To my amazement, however, I could make out a crate turned on its side with hundreds of candles that had melted to the floor. There were also two fresh tapers, their flames wavering like living things as a soft breeze entered the shotgun length of the building where I'd kicked down the doors. Along with the candles there were a number of items—some broken alabaster figurines, ornamental rocks, twigs, incense sticks, singing bowls, and jam jars with a few sprigs of fresh wildflowers in them, as well as a very old katana, or samurai sword.

I kneeled down to study the sword, which was razor-sharp. There was also a small piece of paper at the center of what had to be some kind of altar, and there was a photo with very small printing. On closer inspection, I could see it was an identification card from the United States War Relocation Authority claiming Indefinite Leave.

The small, square, black and white photo was of a slight woman identified as Mae Mayko Oda, who was in a black blouse with a white collar. It gave her residence as Seattle, with a transfer destination of Santa Anita, California, along with a listing of special conditions and restrictions signed by the project director's name, which had faded away.

There was also a spent cartridge from what looked to be a .32 caliber round.

I stared at the assortment of things and then stood again, turning in all directions, finally seeing a trail in the dust that led straight away to the other side of the building where I had also noticed an opening in the floor.

Kneeling down, I peered underneath, and I have to admit that I was surprised to see a comical devil face looking back at me from the shadows.

She was far enough away that there was no possibility I could reach her, even if I tried. "Howdy."

The face, the only part that was visible, didn't move.

"I heard your singing, at least I assume it was you. The song was beautiful . . . What was it?"

She didn't move.

"I didn't mean to frighten you; I don't usually kick doors down."

Still nothing.

"I'll put the doors back up. I didn't mean to do any damage, but I was curious."

Nothing.

"Hey, are you all right?" I waved my hand, but she still didn't move, so I lay flat on the floor and reached farther in, finally feeling the mask with my fingertips and pulling it from the nail where it hung underneath the floor.

Drawing it nearer, I noticed it was different from the one that I'd seen on the girl before. This one was white as opposed to the red one, and I thought about what Henry had said about the red one depicting a lowborn woman while the white one indicated a highborn.

"I'm sitting here talking to a mask."

I stared at the artifact, this time made of a kind of pottery, an object hand-painted, delicate, and easily damaged. Standing, I turned and looked at the shrine for Mae Mayko Oda. Someone must have gone to a great deal of effort to keep such a thing safe over the years.

"Boo."

He turned to look at me as I stood there with the mask over my face. "Is it Halloween—we have been here that long?"

I sat on the edge of the desk with his boots and slipped off the mask, then handed it to him. "Here, in case you still don't believe me."

"This is the same mask you saw on the supposed child in the street early this morning?"

"With a variation in color, yep."

Laying his book aside, he studied it. "Definitely Hannya, used in Noh theater."

I was annoyed by his breadth of knowledge. "So, how do you know so much about this stuff?"

"I had a class in Berkeley concerning Asian theater—that is where people sometimes learn things, in these things called classes."

"Oh."

"It is used in Noh or Kyōgen plays as well as during kagura performance of Shinto ritual dance." He held it up to the light. "The

Hannya mask portrays the souls of women who have become demons through obsessions or jealousy, something like the Buddhist portrayal of the hungry ghost. The wearer is said to be not only demonic but sad and tormented." He moved the thing at different angles. "You see, the emotions of the wearer can be manipulated by the degree and angle of stage light upon the mask."

"Huh."

He handed it back to me. "You should return it."

"Why?"

"Someone was obviously using it to protect something."

"Like a shrine or an altar?"

His curiosity peeked, and he glanced up at me. "Exactly. Did you find such a thing?"

"I did, in one of the buildings farther back. A shrine to a Mae Mayko Oda."

"And who is she?"

"I don't know, but her identity card is front and center on a rather extravagant display back there in another one of the bunkhouse buildings."

He nodded. "Care to show me?"

"Sure." Carefully holding the mask, I got up from the desk and started for the door at the far end. Henry picked up his book and followed. "I also ran into your waitress friend from back in the café."

"Noriko?"

I nodded. "She was taking a break from the restaurant and had a warning for us."

"And what was that?"

"That her grandfather is not one to be trifled with."

"I understood him to be giving us the same message." He followed me down the steps into the warming sunshine. "Anything else?"

"She's expecting us for lunch."

"Well, we do not want to disappoint her."

We'd just started toward the back of the compound when I saw a metallic-blue convertible pull up at the edge of the road and stop. We watched as a dark-haired man who sat on the back of the seat scanned the area.

"What do you suppose he wants?"

"I do not know, but if he is looking for a warm welcome, he has come to the wrong town." Henry started off, and I stood there a moment before following.

The Bear had circled around the building. He took a quick look at the doors lying on the floor and then back at me.

"They were locked."

Shaking his head, he entered the building, and I followed him as we approached the altar in the center. The Cheyenne Nation was careful to skirt the rug but then kneeled down and looked at the arrangement.

"Pretty intricate, huh? Check out that sword."

He nodded. "Yamashiro-school katana blade." He even went so far as to touch the tip. "Kissaki point."

"You learn that in a class too?"

He stood. "It is a Buddhist shrine to the dead."

I drew closer to get another look. "But why the identification card of the woman?"

"You do not understand, it is a personal shrine that one has in their home; an offering to a specific ancestor."

"Always an ancestor?"

"To my knowledge, yes."

I glanced around in the gloom. "Did Noriko give us her maiden name?"

"No."

"She was pretty adamant about being an Everson when I talked to her just awhile ago."

He leaned to one side, still studying the mask in my hands. "The cartridge is strange."

"Not the type of thing you normally see?"

"No."

"Is this where you found Noriko?"

"No, but someone's been here since I was here last."

"How can you tell?"

"There's another candle." I pointed at the shrine and the relatively freshly lit taper to the left. "That one wasn't here thirty minutes ago."

Henry clutched his chin and studied the altar. "You are sure it was not Noriko you saw in the mask this morning?"

"No, no way—female but smaller than her, childlike." I glanced around again, focusing on the hole in the floor behind us. "This has to be the girl I saw early this morning. She must belong to someone around here; she can't just be feral . . ."

"She cannot? I walked toward the hole and peered into the darkness beneath the floor, then carefully rehung the mask on the nail where it had been. "When I saw the kid in the mask this morning, she was at the outskirts of the churchyard, the cemetery, and was placing bunches of wildflowers beside the road."

"Unhallowed ground."

"Unconsecrated?"

"Why else?"

"You think somebody is actually buried there?"

"Or here, who knows?" He gestured toward the altar. "With the amount of the wax accumulated, I think we can safely say that this has been here . . . perhaps years."

"How many?"

"I do not know, but something happened here, and I cannot help but think that Judge Everson had something to do with it."

"Well then, we should report it to the authorities."

He barked a laugh.

"What?"

"Are you truly that naive? We have dealt with the authorities before, and all they are going to say is that it is all very interesting but where is your proof?"

"True. We've got a number of interesting circumstances, but nothing to lead us to a conclusion.

He nodded and looked at the wide planks of the weathered floor. "You are proposing an investigation?"

"I am."

"Even though neither of us has had any experience in such things?"

"I've read a lot of Donald Westlake and John D. MacDonald."

"I do not think that particularly counts."

"Sure, it does." We both turned toward the smooth but unfamiliar voice and the backlit shadow in the doorway about sixty feet away. "Some of my best ideas for an investigation come from mystery novels."

"And who are you?"

"Michael Tanaka, private investigator." Henry and I looked at each other as the fiftysomething man approached. "Yeah, I know . . . It sounds a lot more dramatic than it really is. I spend most of my time taking clandestine photos of divorced couples cheating on each other." He stuck a hand out to Henry. "You can just call me Mike."

The Bear shook his hand. "I am Henry, Mike, and this is my friend Walt."

We shook, and he stared at the shrine. "So, what brings you two to the most welcoming town in Arizona?"

"We're in Arizona?"

He smiled, running a hand over his silvered crewcut. "What the hell, are you guys that lost?"

"Nope, just broke down. My truck took a hit in the tie-rod, and we're waiting on a part."

"Judge Everson allowed that?"

"Begrudgingly." I studied his expensive shoes, khaki slacks, golf shirt, and windbreaker. "We saw you pull up. What brings you to Bone Valley?"

"An investigation, actually." He pulled out a pack of Luckys and bumped one up, taking it in his teeth as he offered the pack toward us. When we both shook our heads, he produced a lighter and lit the end of the cigarette, taking a puff and pocketing the combustibles as I noted a snub-nosed revolver tucked into a holster at his armpit. "A missing persons case, a newspaperman working as a stringer for *The Arizona Republic*."

"And where's that?"

"Phoenix."

"That where you're out of?"

"As of late."

"You sound like one of those novels."

"Damned charming, isn't it?" Winking at us, Tanaka took a drag and smiled, "You meet the judge?"

"We have."

"He's something, isn't he?"

"That's one way of putting it. What's the missing reporter's name?"

"Alan Yoshida."

"Japanese?

He spread his hands. "Isn't everybody around these parts?"

"Are you?"

"Like a transistor radio."

Deciding that I needed a little air, I started walking toward the open door. "Mike, if you don't mind me asking and even if you do, what's the dope on this place? I heard it was the camp for disgruntled internees during World War Two?"

He nodded as we walked along. "You ever hear of the Tokyo Twelve?"

I glanced at Henry, who shook his head, and then back at the man. "No."

"Well, you're a little young . . ." He stopped at the opening and looked down at the collapsed doors. "There was a movement in the camps during wartime, and my buddy Alan was doing a feature piece on it when he disappeared a year ago."

"What kind of movement?"

"A Selective Service–resistance kind of thing—I mean, imagine these poor bastards. Many of them American citizens, American born, scooped up by the FBI all along the West Coast, forced to sell anything they couldn't carry and thrown into what they called relocation centers in horse stalls before they got shipped off to the ass end of nowhere. Then, to make things even worse, they designate all the able-bodied individuals as 4C, "enemy aliens," then listed them as 4-F, "disabled and unfit for military service," because—who the hell knows why—and then, as a final insult, call on them to surrender to a draft and sign the War Relocation Act to be willing to serve in combat duty and foreswear previous allegiance to the emperor of Japan. Well now, many of those folks couldn't tell the difference between Michinomiya Hirohito and Jack Benny for goodness' sake."

"They wouldn't sign?"

"Hell no, they figured it was some kind of trap, they'd never sworn allegiance to some emperor, but if they signed that thing it could then be misconstrued as admitting that they had. You gotta remember that we were fighting guys who were rounding people up and putting them in camps, and here they were having the same thing done to them, and who knew how that was going to end."

"And this place?"

"Bone Valley Internment Camp, where they were going to lodge the worst of the so-called worst before shipping them off to maximum security prisons until the war was over."

"And the Tokyo Twelve?"

Tanaka took the last drag of his cigarette and then flicked it out into the sand. "Disappeared."

I moved down the steps and then turned to look at him. "What do you mean 'disappeared'?"

He blew into a hand, spreading his fingers with a breath. "Poof, gone overnight without a trace."

"Wasn't there any investigation?"

"You gotta remember, kid, it was wartime, and nobody cared about a bunch of draft-dodging traitors or rotten apples." He laughed, joining me in the sunny warmth. "There was one of the Twelve, Mae Mayko Oda, who said that if she was going to die for democracy, she'd like to see a bit of it first."

Henry gestured behind him. "The woman whose ID is on the altar?"

Mike nodded. "Yeah, I'm guessing Noriko is the one doing the extravagant shrine—have you met her?"

"The one working at the café/bar?"

"Yeah, that's her, Mae was her mother."

"The one who had the affair with Everson's son, she was an activist?"

"Affair, hell, they were married." He walked past me toward the playing field behind us and pulled out another cigarette and lit it. "Strange bedfellows, huh?"

"It couldn't be the girl in the mask?"

He turned to look at me. "The what?"

Henry moved down the steps, positioning himself between us. "My friend thinks he saw a child in a mask earlier this morning, but I am thinking that he might have been a little hung over."

Tanaka studied me and then looked back at the Bear. "No, as far as I know there aren't any kids around here and haven't been for years."

The Cheyenne Nation studied him in turn. "Since Noriko?"

"Yeah." Tanaka thought about it. "She's the crack in the judge's racist armor. He treated her like his own, at least until she got old enough to see what he was really like."

"Why does she stay?"

He shook his head. "I honestly don't know."

"Another question." I walked out to face him. "How long have you been on this investigation?"

He turned to look at me, the glamour shot smile in full display. "About four years now."

"Who's paying you?"

"Nobody." He chuckled. "I mean, someone was in the beginning. A Kara Hayami. Owned a laundromat outside of Palo Alto, her son was one of the Twelve."

"Owned a laundromat?"

"She passed away three years ago."

"And where does Alan Yoshida fit into all this?"

"He was my partner back in San Francisco before he retired."

"Retired from what?"

"You ask a lot of questions." He laughed. "San Francisco PD, we were detectives—I went into the PI thing, and he went to work as an investigative journalist."

"So, he's why you stick with it?"

He nodded, pulling out another cigarette but then pushing it back into the pack. "My wife says I smoke too much."

"From the small time I've known you, I can tell you she's right."

He deposited the pack back into his jacket. "Alan was smart, way smarter than me, and I refuse to believe that he just walked off into the desert or ran off with some blond to Barstow."

"Now you really sound like one of those novels."

"Maybe so, but there's a lot of truth there, especially about the kind of devotion you have to a comrade in arms—like the military."

"You serve?"

"We both served in the all-Nisei 442nd Infantry Regimental Combat Team." The smile again. "Hill 140 in Castellina, near Tuscany, and the Vosges Mountains in Bruyères, France—we chased Nazis all up Italy and into the fatherland. You should've seen their faces when us so-called Japs took 'em prisoner." He glanced at Henry and then back at me, giving us a good once-over. "You guys enlist?"

My turn to smile. "Say, you are a cop." I threw a thumb toward Henry. "I'm on my way to Parris Island, and he's on his way to Fort Polk."

Tanaka raised a fist at the Cheyenne Nation. "Every man a tiger."

The Bear stared at him. "I do not know what that means."

"You will."

"So, how often have you been here?"

"I try to come up here every couple of months or so. It's a long shot since Alan's car was found over in Prescott, burned to a husk. There's nothing to connect him to this place other than the newspaper piece I know he was writing."

"What does Judge Everson say?"

The private investigator chuckled again. "He says he talked to Alan once back in October of last year, but that was it—says he got in his car and drove away."

"Do you believe him?"

He turned and looked out at the field. "I don't know. I guess that's why I'm here, like a ghost with a gun."

"Is that why the judge doesn't monkey around with you?"

"Oh, he's got guns, but if he is involved in Alan going missing, then he's too smart to do something to me."

"There seem to be a lot of ghosts around here."

"Yeah." He pulled out a pair of sunglasses and slipped them on. "I was born in Hawaii, and they didn't intern us." He took a few more steps and then looked all around the camp. "I'm not so sure how I would've reacted to them carting me and my family off to a place like this." He turned back to us. "The Tokyo Twelve, they raised some interesting legal questions concerning whether the inmates were being detained by the government, and if they were, were they subject to conscription? If the answer to the first question was yes, then the second had to be no."

Henry's voice rumbled behind us. "What do you say?"

"I say insane asylums, jails, penitentiaries, and reformatories . . . The day after you were discharged the superintendent or warden was required to complete your registration card and send it in to the Selective Service."

"Kind of like when we graduated and would eventually lose our deferment?"

Tanaka's eyes followed the swooping fence line. "Something like that, but you were never really charged, now, were you?"

"Meaning?"

"These people were never really discharged." He pointed up at one of the nearest towers, still an ominous structure looming above us. "All I know is that those guns . . ." He turned to look at us, the structure reflected in the dark lenses of his sunglasses. "They were pointing inward."

6

"I have got a shipment coming to the bar, so I am afraid I will have to take my leave." The Bear stood on the sidewalk, making to go in the opposite direction of Vic and me.

"Don't you have people who can do that in the summertime?"

"I do, but strangely enough the deliveries always seem to come up a few bottles short."

"It's a nefarious business you're in."

"I am not the one in a preliminary hearing right now—nice tie, by the way." He watched as Vic moved over and studied the goods behind the glass in one of the storefronts on Main Street, giving us a little space. "Speaking of, how are things going?"

"Okay, I guess. I haven't done one of these things for about twenty years."

"Be careful."

"What's that supposed to mean?"

"Times have changed and the things that used to get you out of the frying pan can now deposit you squarely into the fire."

"Right."

"How is your friend Judge Snowden?"

"Fine. I think he considers this hearing to be as big of a crock as I do."

"Has he told you that?"

"Not in person, no. I mean, he really can't discuss the case with me concerning an OIS hearing . . ."

"OIS?"

"Officer-involved shooting."

"Is this protocol new?"

"Relatively. I mean, they used to just do it internally with the attorney general's office, but I guess they want these things to be more transparent and open to the public."

"Has any of the public or the press shown up?"

"Not at this point, but it doesn't mean they won't. I'd imagine the press is holding off until the prosecution decides whether it was a wrongful shooting on my part."

"Is that not a stretch?"

"I keep getting reminded by everyone that the man I shot was cursorily in charge of one of the largest financial support funds for Wyoming and comes from a very powerful family. Besides, they've still got other witnesses to depose, including a federal treasury agent and the attorney general of the state, both of whom are on my side."

"So, you are not worried?"

"No."

Vic moved down the sidewalk as Henry paused to allow some folks by before asking the next question. "Then why is your daughter, the assistant attorney general, worried?"

"She is?"

"Yes. She called me last night, concerned that you might not be taking this hearing as seriously as you should be."

I shrugged. "I'm complying, what more does she want me to do?"

"I am not sure, but seeing as how she is the hired hand underneath your biggest gun, perhaps you should be careful."

"I'll try."

He studied my face. "You will try?"

"What do you want me to do, Henry? Throw myself onto the

mercy of the court?" He gave me one last look before turning and walking away, and I thought about calling after him but decided against it.

"What was that all about?"

I looked down as my undersheriff crossed her arms, watching in perfect profile as the Bear walked away. "It would appear that my daughter is worried about me."

"Why wouldn't she be?" Vic turned her face back to me, threading her fingers through her black hair, her gold eyes focusing. "Aren't we all?"

"What's that supposed to mean?"

She smiled the carnivorous smile, which revealed the one canine tooth just a bit longer than all the others. "Walt, in a bar brawl, in a gunfight, in just about anything, we all have the utmost faith in your abilities to handle yourself. But in a courtroom . . ."

We both watched as Henry made an illegal U-turn on Main and then drifted by in the vintage T-bird and tooted the horn, waving as he drove away.

Vic turned back and looked at me as I stared at her. "What?"

SUNDAY, MAY 24, 1964

We walked back to the road with Tanaka and admired his flashy, metallic-blue car. "The PI business must be pretty good."

He shrugged. "My wife's."

"The one who says you smoke too much?"

I looked at the sleek lines of the relatively new Corvette. "You should do what she says."

The Bear stepped back, looking at the sports car. "'61?"

"'62 Horizon Blue, same as the one in that TV show."

Henry frowned. "TV show?"

"*Route 66*, but the show is in black and white, so who knows what color it is." Tanaka nodded. "My wife, Betty, works at the Chevrolet dealership in Phoenix." He ran a hand over the quarter panel of the Corvette. "Do you know how often you can actually use a convertible in Arizona?"

"Nope."

"About two weeks: one in the spring and another in the fall. I about froze my ass off driving up here this morning."

"Hey, we'll trade you a half-ton with a busted tie-rod end over at Everson's Last Chance Service Station."

"Pickens, he's a grumpy old guy, isn't he?" He opened the door and slid in. "Anyway, I'm not so sure the two of you would fit."

I glanced at Henry, standing by the passenger-side door. "You could be Buz Murdock and I could be Tod Stiles." He stared at me blankly, so I explained. "The two guys in the TV show."

"Which one owned the car?"

"Stiles."

He muttered. "Figures."

I walked toward the front, looking at the misbegotten town over the hill. "So, what's on the agenda now?"

"I'll go ask around again and see if I can get a rise out of anybody or cross up their stories."

"Shouldn't be too difficult." I reached up and felt the swelling on my jawline. "I had a real knock-down-drag-out with one early this morning."

He smiled, shaking his head. "Lester?"

"Yep I think it was Lester."

"You're lucky that's all you got out of it; he's Everson's muscle."

I rested an arm on the top of the windshield. "If it was Lester you tangled with, be careful, he's tough as pig iron, and he carries a grudge, and he'll be looking to get another crack at you."

Henry stuffed his hands into his patch-covered jean jacket. "We will be gone before that happens."

Mike nodded and then hit the starter as the car growled to life, and then he took a moment to look thoughtful. "Good luck over there, guys, and remember if the enemy is in range—so are you."

The Bear raised a fist. "Draft beer, not people."

We watched as he laughed, adjusting his sunglasses and pulling out, drifting onto the asphalt with a rear-end swivel and then disappearing over the rise in a bark of rubber and a roar of exhaust. "Seems like a nice guy."

"If he had had a sensible car, he could have given us a lift."

We started walking. "Why didn't you want me to tell him about the girl in the mask?"

"Until we know how she fits into all of this, it might be best to shield her from all parties."

"So, you do believe she exists?"

"You do." As we made the rise, we could see one of Everson's trucks stopped on the road, pointed our way, the driver's head sticking out the window as he spoke with Mike, who was headed in the other direction in the opposite lane.

"Looks like a confab."

Noticing it was Lester in the driver's seat of the club cab, I was glad Tanaka was armed.

As we grew closer, Mike pulled out and headed into town as Lester drove our way. He swerved before pulling to a stop in front of us and hung out of the window to grumble. "Get in the truck."

"Excuse me?"

He pulled a toothpick from his lacerated mouth. "I said, get in the truck, tough guy. The judge wants to see you."

"Maybe I don't want to see him. I've got a date with a cheeseburger and fries over at the Astoria."

He stared at me for a long moment as I smiled. "Get in the truck, and don't make me have to climb out and make you."

"That didn't work out so well for you the last time, Lester."

He didn't move.

"I see that you got the toilet paper out of your nose."

Yanking the handle, he kicked the door open and climbed out—and I'd forgotten how big he actually was as I glanced at Henry. "You want this round?"

He raised his hands and backed away. "No, you seem to have the situation well in hand."

"Thanks." I turned to square off with the oil rig worker but instead reacquainted myself with his left fist. Once again, it felt as if I'd been kicked by a recalcitrant mule, my head following my jaw as it snapped to my left.

I struggled a bit to stay on my feet, but by the time he got ready to swing again, I slipped under it and buried one of my own fists into his gut, lifting him a good two inches off the pavement.

The air came out of him like a breeching whale, and I thought we were pretty much through until his elbow came down on the back of my neck and dropped me on all fours.

I shook my head and tried to get up, but it was about then that he drop-kicked me, and I swear I could hear a rib breaking under the skin.

I watched his boots as he walked around me and figured he was positioning himself for a kick on my other side, so I launched off the ground, remembering all the time in the last four years I'd spent hitting those four-hundred-pound pushing sleds.

Lester didn't weigh four hundred pounds, and because nobody was around to call holding, I ignored the pain in my side and carried him across the pavement into a narrow ditch. He tried to brace his arms behind him to lessen the impact, but all he accomplished was trapping his arms at his sides as I speared him into the ground and landed on top of him.

Consciously avoiding his nose because I wasn't sure if it would shatter and kill him, I swung an uppercut into his chin, listening to his teeth clack together and then watching his eyes roll back in his head.

Sitting on his chest, I took a couple of breaths, feeling the twinge in one rib in particular. "Ouch."

"Are you hurt?"

I glanced up to see the Bear standing on the road, looking down at us. "A lot you care."

"I was waiting for the critical split second to assist you."

I struggled to stand, holding my side and straddling Lester as I tried to catch my breath, which appeared to be eluding me. "And you don't think when he stove my right side in with his steel-toed work boot, that might've been the moment?"

He gestured toward the motionless man. "You appear to have been triumphant."

Trailing a foot over Lester, I reached a hand out and the Bear pulled me up the hill. "I don't think I can stick around this place if I have to go a couple of rounds a day with this guy."

As I finally caught up with my breath, he stared at the big man. "What are we going to do with him?"

"Leave him for the rattlesnakes and coyotes." I took another moment to breathe and then started back down the ditch. "Come on."

Something akin to lifting a yearling cow, we hauled him back up the bank, where Henry made a suggestion. "The back of the club cab?"

I sniffed at him. "I think the bed is good enough." We carried him around, unceremoniously dropping him into the bed and shoving his legs in enough to close the tailgate. "What now?"

The Bear gestured toward the cab of the work truck. "We have a ride."

As we walked back toward the front, I held the driver's side door open and looked at him through the cab as he opened his own door. "So, where to?"

"Everson?"

"Well, if we were going to do that we could've just gotten into the truck when he asked."

Sidling in, he closed his door, kicking some debris aside to make room for his feet. "I did not like his attitude."

I rubbed my ribs and climbed in. "Yep, well, I wasn't crazy about it either." Starting the truck, I shifted her into gear and did a U-turn, heading back into town. "We don't know where Judge Everson lives."

"How hard can it be to find?" He took in all the open space. "I think we go to the only crossroads and take a right at the Last Chance Service Station, and head toward the mountains.

Turning the corner, we could see the private investigator's Vette parked at the Astoria, where my stomach wished we were heading. Nursing the rib, I fought with the manual steering as we headed east, roiling up a cloud of dust as we drove.

Slumping in the seat, the Bear once again pulled the fisherman's cap down over his eyes and settled against the door for a long summer's nap. "I am sure we will find it."

He was right.

It was an oddly designed place, sitting on top of a row of eight garage doors with stone columns leading up to a large dark-wood deck that ran the length of the light-colored stone building. The main structure had chimneys on either side, one of them smoking, and flat roofs with large panoramic windows that looked out over the valley below. Surrounded by pinyon pines, you couldn't see it from the road, but the house commanded a view of everything, including the tiny town in the distance.

Parking the truck in the large turnaround, we climbed out and Henry glanced in the back at Lester. "He is still out."

"Glass jaw, not the best attribute for muscle." We walked to the edge of the drive, taking in the scenery, displayed in sharp contrast by the late-afternoon sun. "I guess the oil business is doing well enough."

The Bear nodded. "That or being a judge."

"Can I help you?"

We turned to find the son Parker standing at the edge of the deck and armed.

"Your dad wanted to see us?"

He shifted the 12-gauge pump to his shoulder. "Says who?"

I gestured toward the unconscious man in the bed of the truck. "Lester, there."

Leaning a little to one side, he adjusted his thick glasses and examined the giant. "What's wrong with him?"

"I guess he's tired."

The younger Everson glanced between Lester and me, unsure if he really wanted any more answers. "You can come up . . ." He glanced at the Bear. "But he has to stay here. Dad don't allow his kind in the house, okay?"

"No, not okay." I looked at the Bear. "What, college educated?"

Parker turned, disappearing inside as his voice trailed off. "You know what I mean."

Henry shrugged and drifted back to where we'd been standing. "See if you can get me a Coke."

"What are you going to do?"

"Prowl around a bit."

I started toward the steps. "Don't get shot, the US government has plans for you."

"To get shot."

"Well . . ." I raised my eyebrows. "Maybe."

"I will do my best."

Climbing the stairs, I looked around at the empty deck and the door behind where Parker had gone in, figuring that was a direction that I should take. Looking through the glass door, I could see a fireplace with the older man sitting in a chair.

Pushing the door open, I stepped inside and glanced around at the old-school opulence: dark mahogany paneling, thick shag carpets, and questionable artwork.

He said nothing at first, sitting there staring at the fire as if hypnotized by the meager flames. "You lied to me."

I centered my attention on Everson as he rose from his chair and circled behind it and headed toward a bar that consisted of highly lacquered oak barrels and a black-leather surface. "Excuse me?"

He fished ice out of a bucket, replenished his tumbler, and then produced another. "Drink?"

I looked around for his son, but we appeared to be alone. "No, thanks."

"C'mon, this is how I make up, by offering you a drink."

I thought about it. "Got any root beer?"

He paused for a moment in a look of puzzlement. "No, I don't believe I do."

"A Coke?"

He filled his glass with an amber liquid from a cut-glass decanter and then studied me. "A Coke?"

"If you would, please."

He fumbled behind the bar, finally looking at me again as I moved around the room taking in the oil-on-velvet framed surroundings along with the ship model on the mantelpiece, which I recognized as the heavy cruiser USS *Astoria*. "I've got tonic water, will that do?"

"Sure."

He paused. "You want lemon with that?"

"Nope, I'm no longer fighting scurvy."

He slid the glass across the bar, and I took it. "Little umbrella?"

"I'll pass." I took a sip. "This isn't exactly the reception I was expecting, Judge."

He sipped, tipping his hat back as he rested both elbows on the bar and grinned, not a particularly friendly smile. "Made some calls about you and your friend."

"Find anything out?"

He came around the corner of the bar and took a lean against it, then stirred his drink with his forefinger. "You're both scheduled to report for induction in about a week."

I sipped the tonic water some more and moved toward the center of the room. "Sounds about right."

"So, you weren't lying about passing through."

"Do most people stay? I mean, considering the warm welcome . . ."

He licked the finger he'd used to stir the drink. "I guess we're kind of salty around here, but we've come by it honestly. Speaking of, where's Lester?"

I gestured with my glass toward the windows. "Down there in the bed of his truck; cargo."

"Well, there certainly is more to you than meets the eye." His face came up to look at me. "Football hero."

"I don't know about *hero* . . ."

"Me either, never had a taste for such foolishness; sometimes that's what happens when you grow up hard."

I glanced around the place at the vaulted ceiling and antler chandeliers, and of all things a noose hanging from one of the rafters. "Looks like you did pretty well for yourself."

"The key phrase in that statement is *for yourself*. I did all this by myself."

"Including the two sons?"

He moved from the bar and was walking over to the fireplace where he pulled a poker from a stand and adjusted the smoldering logs. "We're not going to discuss that."

"So you decide what we're going to talk about?"

"My house, my rules."

"Your town too?"

He hung the iron back on the stand. "I'm glad you noticed."

"Where does your jurisdiction end exactly?"

"On some points of conversation, it doesn't." We stood there looking at each other until he turned to look at the fire he'd reignited. "I worked as a circuit-court judge in this state for nigh on thirty-four years and my word is law around these parts." He stared at me for a long while. "I'll cut to the chase: I think you and your friend are draft dodgers. Why else would you be here in the middle of nowhere?"

"First off, there isn't any draft just yet." I laughed, much to his dismay. "Anyway, we'd be heading in the wrong direction now, wouldn't we?"

"You could be going to Mexico."

"From Southern California by way of northern Arizona?"

He crossed and sat in the chair where I'd found him when I came in, still looking at the fire. "The point being, that while you're here I can make a lot of trouble for you."

"All right, now I'll cut to the chase: Why?"

"I don't like strangers asking a lot of questions in my town."

"Like Mike Tanaka?"

He looked up at me and laughed. "You know, I've known PI Mike for quite a while now, and I think I can say without fear of correction that his allegiances lie with whomever it is that pays him."

"Do you pay him?"

He shook his head. "What have I got to pay him for?"

"The whereabouts of Alan Yoshida?"

He laughed, shaking his head. "Met the man once when he was here nosing around the camp trying to make up some kind of story, but after that I never saw him again." He sipped his drink. "I think you think there's a lot more going on around here than there truly is."

"Then why is everybody around here running so scared?" I glanced at the rafters, at the noose. "That's an odd thing to have hanging in your rumpus room."

"It's there as a reminder." He regarded the grisly thing. "They used to call it a Jack Ketch's knot after one of the first hangmen to use the modern version back in England in the seventeenth century. It had a number of names—the Scaffold knot, Gallows knot, and the Newgate knot . . . It was probably the first time that a knot had been constructed for the specific use of execution." Continuing to look up, he stood and moved toward the mantel. "The number of coils is for friction, making it difficult to remove once it gets put around your neck. Thirteen turns, and there's a lot of deliberation as to why there are thirteen, but the consensus is that whatever luck got that thing put around your neck was bad."

"Bad luck, huh?"

"Perhaps, but I figure it had more to do with being substantial enough to break your neck. Otherwise, you just strangle somebody to death and that's just plain unprofessional."

I sipped my tonic water. "Sounds like you've had experience."

Ignoring my statement, he continued. "There's a Wild West show they have down near Tucson and some damn fool climbed up on a hitching rail and put one around his neck and slipped and fell—killed him deader than Kelsey's nuts." He turned and walked away from me, looking out the windows and gesturing to his own neck. "They used to weigh and measure you to make sure they did the job right, meaning a hangman's fracture of the C2 vertebra just below the skull. Usually, those hanged will shit and piss themselves and their eyes and tongue bug out . . . They say some of 'em even have a heartbeat twenty minutes afterward." He turned to look at me. "And in answer to your question, there is not a single person I passed a death sentence on whose execution I did not witness."

"Is that usually part of the job?"

"No, but it ought to be. I officiated the last hanging in the state of Arizona back in 1934 when I was still riding the bench. Woman by the name of Eva Dunn killed a rancher acquaintance of mine, and they caught her after she ran off with all his money up in New York State. They shipped her back, and she got the rope, but they misjudged the drop and pulled her head clean off—the reason the state switched over to lethal gas."

"You sound disappointed in that decision."

"There's no history to gas, no humanity to it."

I swirled the ice in my glass. "As I recall, there are hanging references in ancient Greece. Jocasta kills herself with a noose in Sophocles's *Oedipus Rex*, and the group hanging in Homer's *Odyssey*. Then there's the Bible of course and Judas."

"You know, I have a feeling there may be more to you than meets the eye, young man." He returned to the area in front of the fireplace, then studied me. "This country was birthed in violence, and I believe that noose is not a relic but the perfect symbol of that violence." He looked back at the fire. "I'd like to get a promise from you."

"And what's that?"

"That when you get your truck fixed, you and your friend will be headed out, no more questions asked."

I walked back over to the bar and set my glass down. "I'll think about it."

"You better do more than think."

I crossed over in front of him. "What happened here, Judge? What is it that's so bad that you've been keeping this secret for a quarter of a century?"

His eyes came up to mine. "It's none of your or anybody else's business—move on."

"You know, the problem with small-town secrets is that they're never really secrets for very long."

"I think you better go now."

"I will, but I'm not going far." I walked back toward the door I'd come in but stopped and turned to look at him with my hand on the knob. "It's going to break, whatever it is. There are just too many people interested in what happened, whatever it was."

Turning the knob, I stepped outside and walked to the end of the deck, again admiring the view. After that, I noticed that Lester was no longer in the back of the truck and hoped that he'd left the keys so that we didn't have to walk all the way back to town.

My next thought was Henry and whether he was having a confrontation with the man mountain and Parker the son. I was relieved to see him to my right, seated on a bench at the far end of the deck near the stairs, once again reading Villon. "Where's Lester?"

"The slumbering giant awakened and stumbled off." After a

moment, he lowered his book and glanced at the truck. "Did you bring me a Coke?"

"No, all he had was tonic water." I walked over and stood there with him, once again enjoying the view. "How about Parker, is he around?"

"I do not know." He closed the book. "Why?"

"We need to get a ride back into town, and I'd rather not steal the truck."

"Why, we have done it before."

"No, that was a body delivery—"

"I'll drive you two back into town." I leaned forward, looking for the source of the voice and finding it under the deck beside one of the garage doors where Parker appeared, moving out to where we could see him. I noticed he was no longer carrying the shotgun. "Howdy."

"You'll give us a ride?"

"Sure." He glanced around. "But we should get going before Lester finds out you're still here or there will be trouble again, okay?"

"Is he the one that broke your nose?"

He rubbed the feature, self-consciously. "No, that was Poppa."

"Your father, the judge?"

"Yeah."

Henry and I shook our heads as we started down the steps to meet Parker at the base. "So, this Lester guy . . . How many times do you have to kick his ass before he gets the picture?"

He led the way toward the truck. "I think it's a new experience for him."

The Bear laughed.

Parker stopped at the door, looking at the two of us through the thick spectacles. "What?"

Henry smiled. "That was funny."

"It was?"

"Yes."

We climbed into the club cab of the truck—I took the back seat and hung over between them, watching as the middle-aged man started the engine and then quickly swung us around and back down the drive. "Parker, do you mind if I ask you a question?"

"What's that?"

"When you're not pointing a gun at us, are you the only sane person in town?"

"Huh." He smiled. "Does it seem like that?"

"A little."

The Bear shifted in his seat to look at me. "How did the conversation with Everson the Elder go?"

"He says that if we don't get out of here, he's going to hand us over to the authorities as draft dodgers."

Parker glanced at the two of us as he drove through the trees and down the mountain. "Are you guys really running away from the war?"

"No."

Henry looked out the windshield. "Maybe."

Ignoring him, I explained. "We're on our way to induction back east."

"You're on your way now?"

"Due to report in less than a week, both of us."

He sighed as he drove, sawing the wheel on the switchbacks. "I tried to enlist with my brother, Andrew, during the war, but they wouldn't take me because of my bad eyesight."

"So, you were here throughout?"

"Yeah."

"What was that like?"

Staring at us, he made a noise in his throat. "It wasn't easy, especially after the *Astoria*, Andrew's ship, got sunk."

"But he and Mae Mayko Oda met here, right?"

"Before that, yeah." He nodded his head. "Dad wasn't really happy about that either . . ."

"I bet." Watching him, I asked the next question. "You ever hear of the Tokyo Twelve?"

He took a few seconds to respond. "No."

"Really, from what I'm to understand they were interned here at the camp."

"I was kinda young, and Dad kept me away from there, especially after Andrew died. He said nothing good could come from associating with those people."

"What about Mae, I'm assuming she was still here when she had Noriko."

"Yeah."

"Then what happened?"

Driving straight, he drove out of the tree line at the foothills and continued toward the desolate town as the sun set dead ahead. "To what?"

"To her, to Noriko's mother, Mae?"

"She left."

"I don't understand, she had the baby and then she just abandoned it with your father?"

"They had an agreement."

"What kind of agreement?"

"I don't know, but I think Dad gave her some money and she went back to wherever she was from—Seattle, I think."

"That doesn't make any sense. A woman with those kinds of convictions wouldn't just abandon her child, no matter what the price."

Parker drove on as the sun edged the horizon, slowly shaving itself away. "She was strange."

"You met her?"

"A couple of times, yeah."

"Strange, how?"

"She was quiet, I mean, really quiet, and she wrote poetry and stuff." He smiled. "She liked to drive."

I sat back in the seat. "What was your brother like?"

He snorted a laugh. "Everything I'm not."

"In what way?"

"He had his own way of doing things, and he and Dad hardly ever saw eye to eye." He glanced back at me. "Till you came along, Andrew was the only one who would stand up to the judge, and he did it a lot. He read a lot and I guess that's how he and Mae met."

"Reading?"

He nodded. "They met at a dance held at the camp. Dad didn't like it, but Andrew went anyway. He met Mae and I think they danced a bit but mostly discussed books and stuff. Andrew started smuggling books to her every day when he was on leave. I guess one thing led to another and they ran out of books to talk about . . ."

Henry laughed again.

Parker glanced at him. "What?"

"That was funny."

"It was?"

The Bear sat up. "Parker, I think you might be one of those natural comedians who has no idea that he is funny."

"Nobody thinks I'm funny."

I looked around as we pulled up to the village crossroad. "I don't think anybody around here has much of a sense of humor."

Turning around in the center of the road, he pulled into the service station, where my truck now sat in the parking lot, repaired, I assumed.

"Well, like Lazarus having risen from the junkyard." He parked the truck and then got out with us as I looked in the passenger window where the keys hung from the switch. "I guess you don't have to worry about folks stealing vehicles around here?"

"Not much." He rested an arm on the lip of the bed. "You guys are headed out?"

"Yep, nothing much holding us here now."

"Take me with you?"

I turned to look at him. "Excuse me?"

"I don't care where; I just want to get out of this place. I've wanted to get out of this place my whole life, but I never had a chance. If I could just hitch a ride with you guys . . . I've got money."

Henry and I stared at him. "Parker, you're a grown man, you don't need us—you can just climb back into that truck and head out."

He looked at the ground, his head hung. "It's Dad's truck."

"So, you've probably been working for him long enough that he owes you a truck, at least." He said nothing, so I continued. "You can't go where we're going."

"Just take me with you and you can drop me off somewhere."

"I don't think your dad is going to like that either. He's already wanting to hang us up and kidnapping might enter into it if we let you go with us."

"Please, I think you're my last chance to get out of here."

The Bear stepped forward, getting the man's attention. "Why is it you are so desperate to leave this place, Mr. Everson?"

"Bad things happen here, and I'm through with bad things—I just wanna go."

"Bad things like what?"

A moment passed and then the tone of his voice changed as he turned his head toward me. "Are you going to take me with you?"

"I don't see how we can."

He nodded his head once and then walked back to his truck, almost as if something had thrown a switch in him. Henry and I watched him climb into the truck, start it up and turn the wheel, driving away. "You get the feeling he's been told that before?"

"I do." The Bear glanced over at the service station, where there were no lights and the place appeared locked up tight. "Good thing you paid Mr. Pickens."

"Yep."

I looked in the back just to confirm that besides my surfboard, our bags were tucked up against the bulkhead. "Looks like everything is in here." I pulled open the passenger side door. "We can get a few hours in before we have to stop again."

Henry glanced around at the church, the mercantile, and the bar/café where the private investigator's Corvette sat parked. "Or we could head over and have dinner with Mike and possibly see what is what . . ."

"We should go now."

"Walt, there is a child running around the streets with a demon mask on."

"So, you do believe me."

He took a few steps toward the gas pumps. "I believe there is something wrong in this place."

"Yes, there is and for quite some time now, and it is none of our business. Are you sure you're not just putting off the inevitable?"

"Possibly."

I swung my arms out and turned back to him. "And when will you be making that decision?"

"When I decide if this war is moral enough for me to sacrifice my life to it."

"Moral enough?" I stood there looking at him. "There's no such thing as morality in war. That's an oxymoron; there's no moral war."

He smiled, obviously enjoying himself. "Then what is there?"

"Service—doing what's expected of you."

"Expected by whom?"

"Yourself." I leaned in the driver's side window to look at him. "It's not our choice, but it's our time."

"You do not think that is an overly simplified view of the situation?"

"It was how I was brought up, and you were too."

"Then let us go."

I took a moment to think about it. "Now you're talking."

He climbed in, shutting the door behind him and settling into the seat, once again reaching out and pulling his cap down and placing it over his face as he slumped against the door, the book of Villon poetry in his lap again.

"You're stealing the book?"

"The fortunes of war. We can get a few hours on the road."

Opening the door, I climbed in and turned the ignition as the truck leaped to internally combusted life. "A few hours driving or sleeping?"

His voice was muffled under the hat. "Yes."

Pulling out, I stopped at the only crossroads and looked longingly at the bar/café, all the time trying to ignore my grumbling stomach. I took a left, switched on the lights, and drove over the rise and by the chain-link fences of the internment camp, all the time thinking about the strange things we'd been party to in the last twenty-four hours.

Suddenly, the same child in the demon mask was standing in the middle of the street as I swerved and locked up the brakes.

7

"Are you feeding our squirrels?"

"I am."

I sat on the bench under the rustling cottonwoods that sheltered the area behind the courthouse, a place I had sat more times than I could accurately count in the decades I'd spent as sheriff. "You know, we had a pigeon problem with this building back in the fifties. It got to be such a mess with the pigeon shit, the previous sheriff hired a fella with a pellet gun to shoot them until there was an uproar from the Daughters of the American Revolution. Seems they didn't enjoy sitting out here while the maintenance man, Jules Beldon, took target practice."

Judge Snowden looked back at the courthouse, his briefcase open at his feet. "What did they do?"

"Well, Lucian, my old boss, told Jules to get rid of the pigeons—that he didn't care how he did it, but just don't shoot them. Things were quiet the next day or so, but then it got to be a full-scale pigeon Armageddon again with the things falling out of the sky all over the place. It seems Beldon had started sprinkling poison on the ledges of the building, and you couldn't walk by the place without getting hit in the head with a dead pigeon. I remember Jules out here with a wheelbarrow, a broom, a shovel, and wearing an old air-raid helmet for protection. He scooped them up for days."

The Californian sat back on the bench and looked around at the lack of pigeons. "That's horrible—so, what do they do now?"

"Bring a falconer in from over in Big Horn who has a Harris's Hawk and red tail that he turns loose. We get a dead pigeon every once in a while, but it isn't raining them down on us like hail on high."

He glanced down at the small bag of peanuts in his hands. "I'm just feeding the squirrels."

"Those are cooked. Right?"

"What?"

I leaned over, looking at the Planters bag. "Those are roasted, so they're okay. Raw peanuts are bad for squirrels, nutritionally speaking."

He stared at me.

"What?"

"Honest to God, I never know what's going to come out of your mouth."

"Neither does your young prosecutor . . . Is that going to be a problem?"

"You know I can't discuss matters off the record concerning the hearing."

"I was just making conversation."

"I think this bag of peanuts has been in my attaché case since 1978." He studied me for a moment more and then tossed another peanut onto the lawn as a large, red squirrel with one ear bounded from around the tree and retrieved it. He started to head back toward the trunk but, realizing he wasn't being pursued, stopped, and began eating the nut. "He's the big dog around these parts?"

"I don't know, I'm not on a first-name basis with the squirrels."

"Well, he is." He tipped his ivory-colored cowboy hat back and watched the squirrel. "He's always the first one down and over here, although I think he's got competition lately."

"That how he lost the ear?"

"I'm guessing." He waited until the squirrel finished and then tossed him another. "You know, the Japanese have a saying, *shikata ga nai* or *gaman suru* . . ." He glanced over and saw the look on my face. "Something wrong?"

"No, I just . . . I've been thinking about the Japanese a lot lately."

"In what way?"

"Oh, Vic found an old surfboard of mine, and it reminded me of a road trip Henry and I took a long time ago—another life."

"A surfboard?"

"Yep, back when I played football at USC."

"You're too big to surf."

"Didn't used to be."

"A road trip?"

"Prelude to an all-expense-paid vacation to exotic and sunny Southeast Asia courtesy of the United States government."

"Ah." He tossed another peanut, and the red squirrel suddenly had company looking down from the trunk of the tree only a little way away as two others watched him eat. "And what does this road trip have to do with the Japanese?"

"Ever heard of Bone Valley, Arizona?"

"Nope."

"No reason you should have, but there was one of those internment camps there like the one we had over at Heart Mountain—I'll tell you about it sometime."

He studied me. "You know, there was an old judge in my territory of the Northern District of California, Louis E. Goodman, who dismissed the charges against the draft resisters at Tule Lake Relocation Center up near the Oregon border. He said that to prosecute these people was shocking to his conscience and a violation of due process."

"They actually won?"

He nodded. "The federal government didn't appeal his decision. He was the only judge to ever try and help those people."

"So they didn't go to prison like the rest?"

"No, just shipped back to the internment camp with barbed wire and armed guards—I'm not sure what the difference was." Pulling another peanut from the bag, he held it up and contemplated it. "Those sayings I mentioned, *shikata ga nai* and *gaman suru*, they mean that *it can't be helped* or *just endure it*, both of which are seen as Japanese virtues."

He threw the peanut, and we watched as the red squirrel attempted to make off with the latest offering but was intercepted by the two others, and then a third, which led to a tangling of bushy-tailed rodents until one of them distracted him long enough for one of the others to get away with it.

"I think, in cowboy parlance, we refer to that as *the nail that sticks up gets hammered first.*"

"Exactly." He folded up the end of the bag of peanuts, placed it in his briefcase, and closed it, standing and patting me on the shoulder as he passed while walking toward the back door of the courthouse.

I called after him as he pulled one of the heavy glass doors at the rear of the building and started inside toward the steps that led to the courtroom upstairs. "Just for the record, we're still talking about squirrels, right?"

SUNDAY, MAY 24, 1964

The brakes on the old ranch truck were never that great, but when I slammed them down, the wheel locked to the right and we once again found ourselves in a ditch.

Henry's head bounced off the dash, but he caught his cap and sat there looking around, the cloud of dust enveloping us. "That was quick, are we there?"

"Very funny." Climbing out, I looked back at the road, but the kid in the demon mask was nowhere to be seen.

The Bear joined me on the road and glanced around. "Another coyote?"

"I know you don't want to hear this, but it was the girl in the mask."

He stared at me. "And you missed her?"

"I think so."

He looked back at the truck and peered under the vehicle. "She is not under there."

"Oh, good."

He moved around the front. "But you have a flat tire."

I joined him. "You're kidding."

"I am afraid not." He walked over and booted the deflated tire on the passenger side front. "Do you have a spare?"

"I do."

"That is good."

"It's flat too."

"That is not good."

"Yeah, I ran over a nail on the Pacific Coast Highway last week and never got around to getting it patched." Circling back, I walked up onto the road and studied the main entrance of the abandoned and haunted camp. "She doesn't want us to leave."

Henry's face rose above the fender where he'd been studying the flat. "What?"

I turned toward him. "The kid, the demon, whatever she is—she doesn't want us to leave."

"Are you losing your mind?"

"Henry, I'm telling you that something is going on around here, and she knows what it is."

"We do not even know who *she* is."

"Does it matter?" Moving toward the back of the truck, I watched as he lowered himself and slid under the rear where the spare tire hung. "You're going to need a wrench for the nut that holds that carrier."

He grunted. "No, I am not."

"You're angry."

"No, I am not, but it is interesting that every time we make to leave, this mysterious demon child of yours appears." There was more cranking and grunting and soon the deflated spare was being pushed from underneath the truck.

Picking it up, I pressed on the deflated rubber, verifying that it wasn't roadworthy. "I didn't veer us into the ditch to keep us here, Henry."

He scooted out, grabbing the bumper and rising to face me. "That is not what I said."

"It's what you intimated."

"You agree that it is strange that no one else has seen this demon child?"

"Other people have seen her; both Parker and Noriko."

"Noriko said there are no children in the town and that is all she said, while Parker stated that it is not good fortune to see the demon child but nothing about seeing her himself."

"Well, he was right about that." I started rolling the wheel toward town. "But it was the way they both said it."

He shook his head, walking alongside me as we made the top of the hill.

"What?"

"There appears to be a lot of interpretation going on here."

I stopped, turning to look at him. "Well, since you've changed your mind, just go."

He stared at me, making a face. "What?"

"If you're all-fired sure that we need to leave, just go."

"Without you?"

"Without me."

He stuffed his hands into the pockets of his jean jacket. "Who would look after you?"

"I can look after myself."

He smiled a grin as sharp as a paper cut. "Where is your spare tire right now?"

I turned in the gathering gloom to see the wheel and tire gaining speed as it rolled down the hill toward the tiny town. "Oh, shit . . ."

We both ran after it, me perhaps trying a little harder as it went through the intersection, aimed squarely for the rear end of Mike Tanaka's Corvette, still parked in front of the bar/café.

We'd just gotten past the service station when the thing hit the rear bumper with a loud thump, climbed the rear deck, and slammed into the windshield frame, hopping up and then falling into the passenger seat as if settling in for a ride.

We both stopped in the middle of the road, staring at the partial disaster as the private investigator pushed open the door of the establishment and stepped onto the walkway, plying his teeth with a toothpick.

We approached, examining the damage to the sports car. "Sorry."

He kicked his head sideways, looking at the bent bumper, the scuff marks on the trunk lid, and the bent chrome of the windshield edge. "You two are a one-man wrecking crew."

"It kind of got away from me."

He came down the steps as Noriko came out of the café to survey the damage. "I can see that." He glanced at me. "Where were you headed with it?"

"Over to Pickens's place. Our spare there is flat." I threw a thumb over my shoulder. "You're going to find this hard to believe, but um . . . We ran off the road."

"Again?"

"Again. Yes, sir."

He continued working on his teeth and examining both the Bear and me. "You know, I'm beginning to think the two of you might be better served taking a bus back east."

"You could be right, but in the meantime, do you mind if I get my tire?"

He walked toward the front, turning the spare in the passenger seat and patting it like an old friend. "Why bother?"

"What do you mean?"

"Pickens is gone." He patted the near-bald tire. "I can run it up to Iron Springs or down to Wilhoit, but I doubt any of them will be open till the morning."

"We'll just wait for Mr. Pickens."

"You're in for a long wait; he left town to go fishing this weekend and won't be back till Wednesday."

Henry turned to me. "You know, our luck just keeps getting better and better."

"Does anybody have keys to the service station? I believe I can probably patch the tire myself if I have the tools and supplies."

Tanaka once again ran his hand over the smooth surface of the tread. "And how far do you figure you'll get on this tire before you're walking back in here again?"

I had to admit that the thing didn't look too roadworthy. "Any suggestions?"

"I'm sure Everson's got the tools and a tire that'll probably fit it up at his place. I could drive you there . . ."

"Yep, I don't think, even as eager as the judge is to get us out of here, that he's going to want to help us much."

The private investigator thought about it. "As I recall, there's a full-blown ranch shop off Route 89, and I bet they've got a tire that'll fit this rim, but there won't be anybody there until tomorrow morning either."

"After what we've done to your car, I don't think we can add to your burden by . . ."

He waved me off. "I wasn't going to make it back to Phoenix this late anyway. I'll just stay in the little roadside motel that's near there, get up first thing in the morning and get it fixed, and run it back here to you."

"That's a lot of driving."

"Ah, it's a fun car to drive." He examined his vehicle. "Or used to be."

"I'll be happy to pay for the damages."

"I'm glad to hear that." He circled around, opening the door and climbing in before waving at Noriko. "Thanks for dinner, kiddo. See you next month?"

She smiled down at him as he turned the key and fired up the V-8, it's throaty exhaust settling into an idle as he turned to look at us. "I'll be back early, but if I don't catch you, I'll leave it over on the stoop of Pickens's place."

"Can I give you some money?"

He waved me off again. "Oh, you're going to owe me more than that."

Shifting into gear, he pulled out, chasing his headlights over the hill and out of town, the small block growling away like a caged cat.

We watched him go, and then Henry smiled at the girl. "Hi."

She folded her arms, looking down at him. "Hello."

As disasters go, this one was working out because we were lucky enough to hit the Astoria on chili and cornbread night. So we sat at the bar, wolfing down the food and sipping cold A-1 beer. Henry was flirting with Noriko when I got up from the barstool and walked over to the Seeburg jukebox that was playing Charlie Feathers's "That Certain Female."

The Bear had dumped a couple of quarters in but had only selected a few songs, leaving the rest to me. I scanned the offerings and chose some Charles Mingus, and even found some Art Blakey and Bill Evans. "Who's the jazz fan?"

"Me."

I turned to look at her. "You're kidding."

"No, the guy who rents us that thing and serviced it also changes out the 45s, and he stuck a few jazz singles in there. I liked them, so he always brings me more." She sighed. "He hasn't been here in the last year, and I'm not sure if he went out of business or just forgot about us."

The Bear grinned his most appealing smile. "I do not see anybody forgetting about you."

I turned back to the jukebox so that neither of them would see me rolling my eyes and watched the mechanism glide across the one-hundred records and snatch Dave Brubeck's "Take Five."

I moved around the room, studying the photographs and finally finding the US Navy portrait of the late Andrew, who, at the time it was taken, would've been about the same age as me. Lieutenant JG, Junior Grade, Everson was wearing his dress blues and a white officer hat, and he had been a handsome kid—smart, you could just tell, but there was a touch of worry on his face.

What was running through that head at that point in his young life? Was it possible that they were the same things that were running through mine at roughly the same age?

"They tell me he was very kind."

I turned to find Noriko standing beside me. "You look like him."

"You think?" She leaned in, studying the photo of her father. "Most people say I look more like my mother."

"The only female member of the Tokyo Twelve?"

"Yes." She glanced up at me and then turned and moved back toward the bar where Henry watched us, especially me, with a wary eye. "They say she was a real hell-raiser back in the day—I guess once she got her license, she drove like a bat out of hell."

The Bear gave Noriko his full attention as I walked toward the front windows and looked out onto the dark street.

"Do you like working here at the bar?"

She leaned on the other side, replacing his empty bottle with a full one. "Most of the time."

His voice had a funny sound to it. "I could see owning a bar, sometime."

I laughed.

I studied his reflection as he turned to look at me. "What?"

"You don't have the temperament for running a bar."

I listened to his stool squeak as he turned back to her. "Do not pay him any mind, he is just upset about his truck."

I continued to stare at the church. "Hey Noriko, have you ever seen that kid in the devil mask?"

I heard the squeak again as he turned, his voice warning. "Walt . . . ?"

I stared at him. "I'm just asking a question."

She came around the bar, carrying a fresh beer to me, in an attempt to laugh and dilute the tension. "No, I've never seen a child in a mask around here, but I've heard tales . . ."

"Thank you." I took the beer and glanced at her. "What kind of tales?"

She leaned against the glass and placed a hand on the cold surface. "Some people say it's a ghost."

"Of whom?"

"Of the people who died here."

"What people?"

"The Japanese, like me."

"People in the internment camp?"

"That's what they say."

I turned and sat on the sill to sip my beer. "Who says it, and what exactly do they say?"

"Just stories . . . I mean, I wasn't here so I can't really say, but the story is that somebody, maybe more than one somebody, died here, and the Hannya mask worn in Noh theater and Shinto kagura is a demonic and vengeful spirit that seeks revenge on those who betrayed her."

Henry joined us. "Hannya means wisdom, does it not?"

Noriko looked at him, a little shocked. "Yes, it does."

I studied her. "Noriko, I hope you don't mind me asking but how did you learn Japanese? Your mother was gone, and I assume that by the time you were of age that all the internees were gone from here?"

She took a long time to answer, and when she did her voice was flat and emotionless. "There was a man, Pat Fujita, who they used to take me to visit. He was Japanese, and I got him to teach me."

"Was he an internee who remained here after the war?"

"I don't know."

"Why else would someone who was of Japanese descent be here?"

She finally smiled a sad smile. "I think he was stranded, like me."

I glanced at Henry. "What happened to him?"

"I don't know."

I found it hard to keep the disbelief from my voice. "You don't know?"

"People leave here all the time." She pulled her hand from the glass and held it to her chest to rewarm it. "Everybody but me."

"Noriko, was your mother Mae Mayko Oda?"

She turned to look at me, her eyes wide. "How do you know that name?"

I glanced at Henry again as he continued to give me the warning look. "When we were poking around over at the camp yesterday, when you and I talked, we found a Buddhist shrine in one of the bunkhouses and it had an identification card for her. Was that your mother?"

She began walking away.

"Noriko?"

She turned, and she was mad. "What right do you have poking around here in other people's business?"

I raised my hands in surrender. "None, I'm just trying to find out what's going on around here."

"Why?"

Henry took a few steps toward her. "Noriko, we are afraid that something terrible has happened here, and if something has . . ." He looked at me, widening his dark eyes in reproach. "Well, my friend here has a difficult time letting these types of things go."

"It is my shrine to my mother." She gestured around the bar, her arms falling to her sides in defeat. "And this bar is a shrine to my father—I'm surrounded by shrines."

He took another step toward her, holding out a hand. "We do not mean to pry . . ."

"Why is there a .32 shell casing on the altar in the bunkhouse?"

Henry gave me another hard look as they both stood there.

"And why is the church locked up?" I took a deep breath. "If we're not allowed to ask any questions after this, then that's my last one."

Henry held the handout to me, but with a very different meaning in it. "Walt."

Noriko glared at me for a good, long time. "I think you better go."

"Where?" I walked over to the bar, put down my mostly full beer, and slipped on my hat as I pulled on a sleeve. "'Cause if you throw us out of here, my next move is to go over there and yank those chains off and sleep in that church."

Her eyes became panicked as they flitted between me and the structure across the intersection. "You . . . you can't do that."

"Why not?"

She swallowed. "It would be breaking and entering."

"Just looking for a place to sleep." Putting my jacket on the rest of the way, I walked toward the door and adjusted my hat. "What's in that church that everybody's so scared of, Noriko?" I placed a hand on the knob. "A perfectly salvageable church in a community that services what, about fifty square miles? There's a shortage of just about everything in this world, but there's never a shortage of preachers— where's the one for that church?"

"Father Pietro, he left too."

"When?"

"I think before I was born."

I couldn't help but give out with a grim smile. "Everything around here appears to have happened before you were born."

"Yes."

"Don't you want to know these things, or do you know already and just aren't sharing like the rest of them?"

She said nothing, so I turned the knob and stepped into the cold, clear air, closing the door behind me and then flipping the collar up on my jacket, wishing I'd brought the beer with me.

Making good on my threat, I started toward the church and was about halfway across the road when I heard the door behind me open and close and a familiar voice. "Walt!"

I ignored him and kept walking, only to feel a strong hand on my shoulder, spinning me around. Swinging an arm at him, I missed as he stepped back, the hands now open and spread. "Easy."

Cocking my right, I spread my boots in a fighting stance. "She's not being honest with us, Henry."

"So?"

I stared at him, incredulous. "So?"

"Did you ever stop to think that perhaps she cannot?" He circled to my right the way he always did, shortening your lead and jamming you up, a trick I'd seen him use many times on other opponents. "You do not know what it is like to be a minority; to always be outnumbered."

I stood there looking at him, finally thinking of something to say. "I'm trying to help."

"Who?" He continued circling, his back now to the church. "And how, by making every decent individual in this town uncomfortable?"

"This town stinks to high heaven, Henry."

"It is not our town, Walt. It is not even our state."

I took a deep breath and then slowly lowered my fists. "I don't get you."

"In what way?"

"We're going off to war, and yet to you it's this philosophical construct, some kind of moral allegory—and it's not, it's life and death." I pointed back at the bar. "Do you think Andrew Everson knew what he was getting into?"

"If he did, do you think he would've gotten on that ship?"

"Yep, Henry, I do." I took a step away. "A third of the way across the country is a very inconvenient time for you to have a crisis of conscience."

"A time of consciousness is never inconvenient."

I growled. "You know, it's statements like that that make me want to punch you in the teeth."

He smiled the smile, and I could feel my anger rising even further. "And stop grinning."

"I am sorry I am being inconvenient, but it is our lives we are talking about."

I whirled on him. "You think I don't know that? You don't think that it crosses my mind as I'm punching buttons on a jukebox that it might be the last time in my life that I'll be doing it?"

"The USOs have jukeboxes."

I raised my fists again in utter frustration. "Shut up."

"I am just—"

"Shut up!"

"Do you want to hit me, because if you think it will make you feel better, I give you permission."

I hit him.

It was a right jab that planted squarely on his jaw and took him completely by surprise. Stepping back, he raised his hands to catch the brief exhale of blood and to flex his face to feel if anything was broken as he crouched forward and attempted to not bleed on his shirt.

Reaching up, he felt his jaw and, satisfied, pulled a folded bandanna from his back pocket, then dabbed at the blood at the corner of his mouth again. "I did not think you would do it."

"Neither did I, but then you gave me permission."

He flexed his jaw, and a fresh amount of blood trickled out before he folded the bandanna up and patted his mouth some more. "Can I punch you now?"

"No."

He nodded. "Then we are done?"

"Yep."

I stepped toward him in hopes that we would shake hands, and had to admit that even though I was leery, I never saw it coming—a left hook that turned my head with a snap as I stumbled sideways, trying to stay on my feet as my hat hit the ground.

Shaking my head, I refocused my eyes, trying to get things settled. Stretching my own jaw muscles that were still sore from the last battle with the oil-rig worker Lester, I felt my chin and looked at the Bear. "I didn't give you permission to do that."

He continued to wipe his mouth. "I figured I owed you."

Reaching down, I picked up my hat, placing it on my head with a tug. "Are we done now? I mean, really done?"

"Sure."

I stuck out a hand. "Pax?"

We shook. "Pax."

I glanced around, still feeling the effects of his punch. "So, where are we sleeping tonight?"

"I have made arrangements to sleep on Noriko's sofa in her home."

I made a face, and it hurt too. "What about me?"

"I suppose you could go sleep in your truck."

I gazed at the bar's warm lights. "You're not going to intercede for me?"

"No."

"Can I punch you again?"

"No." He walked past me toward the Astoria.

"Thanks a lot." I glanced around the desolate town. "I'll meet you at the service station in the morning?"

"Sure."

I stood there watching him go, the severed wingman set adrift. "Don't worry about me."

He called over his shoulder as he dabbed his mouth some more. "I will not."

Pulling my collar up, I looked back at the church and thought about making good with my threat, but Henry was right in that all I'd be doing would be making things harder on the people who had been kind to us, or to him at least.

I'd just started to walk off toward the truck, a little better than a mile away, when I thought I caught some movement around back in the graveyard.

Moving to my right, I saw that the gate had been left open, and I could hear the noise that the slight breeze had caused when opening and closing it. So, I walked around the building and kneeled to secure the gate with the metal latch, at which point I saw another bundle of wildflowers lying by the fence. I picked up the bouquet and sniffed at the lupine and poppies, both of them very fresh.

Carefully placing the flowers where they had been, I straightened and noticed that the back door of the church was now hanging open. I quickly glanced around, figuring I should at least close the thing.

Reopening the gate, I stepped inside and walked on the path toward the center of the grave markers, mostly stone, but then becoming older and wooden the closer I got to the structure.

The door was actually only open a bit, perhaps a third of the way.

There were no lights on inside or any indication that the church had been broken into. For all intents and purposes, it looked as if the door had simply come unlatched and swung open.

There were five steps leading to a small porch surrounded by a railing. The church windows were narrow and tall, with leaded, artistic designs, even though the glass was only a few colors. The spire had a bell tower that cast a shadow in the moonlight. It cut across a portion of the cemetery and the building where I now stood like some kind of dividing line between good and evil.

I eased up the steps, stayed to one side, and peered in, still seeing nothing unusual.

I stepped forward and saw something lying on the floor, something white: a candle, similar to the ones on Noriko's family shrine back at the camp.

Pushing the door open to an anteroom, I crouched and picked up the candle, unlit with an unburned wick. Peering through the darkness, I could see that there were more candles scattered across the floor and a box lying nearby from which they must've fallen and rolled away.

I picked up a few more and wished I had some matches or a lighter so I could make use of the things. In the trapezoid of light from the open door, I took the box and began replacing the candles in there to avoid somebody stepping on them and taking a Brodie.

I'd just finished repackaging the candles when I heard a noise from inside the church, a noise like the kind I'd heard before.

Singing.

It was the same wavering song I'd heard coming from the bunkhouse yesterday. Plaintive and poignant, the pitch was very high—a female voice—and I was certain it was Japanese.

I tucked the box of candles into the crook of my arm and moved toward another door, this time with a priest's cassock hanging on a hook. The door was partially open, leading to the sanctuary where the singing was coming from.

Peeking through the open space, I could see past the chancel, the light from a single candle on the floor in the aisle between the pews.

There was someone kneeling there, her face turned upward, and I could see that she was wearing the demon, or Hannya mask, frighteningly lit by the single candle.

The entire scene seemed so surreal, but also sad and rending with the song she was singing, and with the movement of the mask, the shadows on it by turns chilling and then melancholy.

I'd just started to gently push the door open and at least let the singer know I was there, when I heard a noise behind me. Then I felt something crash into the back of my head, and then . . . I didn't feel anything at all.

"Alone, Sheriff?"

I glanced at Whinstone. "Excuse me?"

"I'm sorry, are we boring you, Sheriff?"

I cleared my throat, straightened the tie that was strangling the life out of me, and noticed the sunshine lazily drifting through the slats of the venetian blinds, which were casting bar-like patterns onto the courtroom's threadbare carpet. "Excuse me, but I'm not sure I understand the question?"

"You say in your deposition that you felt as if your life was being threatened by these men."

"Well, they had drugged me, handcuffed me to a chair, and were pointing guns at me. So, yep, I felt as if my life was endangered." I watched as he walked over to the railing where a trial jury might sit, and I couldn't help but think he was rehearsing for when he hoped it would be. I used to be entertained by watching lawyers attempt to be Raymond Burr in *Perry Mason*, Andy Griffith in *Matlock,* or James Whitmore in *The Law and Mister Jones*. Right now, I had an idea that Whinstone was channeling some kind of fictional character. I hadn't watched TV in twenty years, however, so I felt I was at a disadvantage.

His hand came up and palmed his chin as he gave the impression he was thinking. "And yet there you were alone."

"Yep."

"Well, since your life was endangered, did it ever occur to you to enlist some of your staff as backup?"

"There was a lot going on at that time . . ."

"Such as?"

"Personal issues, and we're somewhat shorthanded."

Whinstone adjusted his glasses, even going so far as to remove them and polish them with his tie. "What sort of personal issues?"

"Personal ones."

He glanced at me. "*Your* personal issues?"

"Some, yep."

He guided the glasses back onto his face. "I understand you just got engaged, is that true, Sheriff?"

"Yep."

"To your undersheriff, am I correct?"

"Yep."

"Objection." Judi Cole flipped her pen with a clatter onto the hard wooden surface of the defense table and stood, shaking her head. "Your Honor? Once again, is this going somewhere?"

Whinstone pushed off the railing and turned toward the bench where Judge Snowden looked genuinely interested in what he was going to say next. "Counselor?"

"I'm just trying to get a clear picture of the working environment of the Absaroka County Sheriff's Department at the time of these events."

"To what purpose, Mr. Whinstone?"

"Well, it's already been established that Deputy Saizarbitoria worked exclusively with Mike Regis and, until the unfortunate outcome, really didn't have any problem with him."

Snowden looked down at the papers on his desk, probably wondering if he was ever going to get back to his home in California. "Would you like to depose Deputy Saizarbitoria, Counselor?"

The prosecutor smiled. "I don't think that will be necessary,

Your Honor, but I would like to depose the undersheriff, Victoria Moretti."

Boy howdy.

MONDAY, MAY 25, 1964

Being kissed isn't the worst way to wake up unless it's a thousand-pound mule with the foulest breath you've ever smelled.

Fluttering my hands up to my face, I pushed the elongated head away from mine and sputtered, feeling the effects of a skull-splitting headache. Pulling my elbows up behind me and looking at the pie-bald creature, I could now see she was loaded with a packsaddle, a bedroll, pickax, shovels, tin sluice pans, screens, and a wooden box that had the words DANGER EXPLOSIVE stenciled in red on the leather-strapped lid.

"Over-Jenny likes you."

Stretching my eyelids, I looked between the mule's legs and could see the shadow of a small man squatting easily at her left. "Howdy."

He smiled with crooked teeth. "You're going to have to crawl out from underneath her—Over-Jenny doesn't back up."

I started to move but then stopped. "I'm not so sure I can."

"Need a shot of water?"

"That might help, and a pound of aspirin if you've got some."

I watched as he swung an old canvas-covered Boy Scout canteen from his side, slipping the strap from his shoulder and loosening the cap before handing it to me. "Here you go, I haven't got any aspirin."

Tipping the thing up, I took a sip and handed it back to him before struggling on my elbows until I was out from under the mule, glancing around to find myself lying in the cactus-strewn desert, with the sun just starting to rise into the cool, gray morning skies.

I shuddered.

"Are you cold?" He'd come around and was now crouching

beside me in his jodhpurs and laced high-top leather boots, examining the back of my head.

"I guess so."

He stood up and took a cotton blanket from the mule and handed it down to me as I sat up. "Lucky Over-Jenny here found you. I didn't see you until she stopped and was standing on top of you."

I felt the back of my head and could feel a loose flap of skin along with the oozing and crusted blood there. "Are you sure she didn't step on me?"

"Oh, I think you would've felt it." He examined me. "Actually, I'm pretty sure that you were already beaten up by the time you got here."

Struggling to my feet, I stood, holding the blanket around me. "And where exactly is here?"

He swiped off his shapeless hat and glanced around, thinking about it. "Contreras, maybe Juniper Wells . . . I don't think we're far enough east to be near the Derby Mine or far enough west for it to be Bagdad or Colby. Why, are you particular?"

"No, I just like to know where I am on a regular basis."

He laughed. "I hardly ever know where I am."

I got my first good look at him, and, for all intents and purposes, he looked like a desert rat that stepped out of the history books. The sunbaked wrinkles in his face were so numerous that if he had eyes, I certainly couldn't see them. And his mouth was just a straight slit framed in wispy silver hair and a pointed beard that stretched to his naval. "Any idea how I got here?"

Pulling himself up to a less than towering five and a half feet, he pointed a bony finger at the tracks in the sand where we stood. "I would say that was a Studebaker Transtar one-ton stake bed, probably light blue."

I stared at him, thinking some of my brains might've leaked out. "How do you know it was light blue?"

The pointed finger rose to a nearby hill. "I saw it drive over that way." Turning back to look at me he smiled and shrugged. "It could have also been gray; my eyes aren't what they used to be." He picked up the mule's reins and turned her toward us. "Folks usually dump garbage or junk out here and Over-Jenny's gotten used to nosing 'em out. I just let her have her head, and she brought us to you." He smiled with the thin mouth, revealing more of the crooked teeth. "Somebody throw you out?"

"Something like that." I looked around but couldn't see any landmarks. "Which way is Bone Valley from here?"

"Bone Valley? Why would you want to go there?"

"My truck broke down, and I've got a buddy who might be in trouble."

"If he's in Bone Valley, then he's definitely in trouble."

"Which direction?"

He raised the same finger, pointing south. "That way."

I started off. "Thanks, Mr. . . . ?"

"It's more than sixty miles, and there's nothing between here and there—without food or, more important, water, you'll die in three days."

I stopped. "Can I borrow your canteen?"

"Nope, I need it for Over-Jenny and me."

I started off again. "Well, I've got to try it."

He called out. "You need to get that head of yours sewn up!"

"I'll manage."

He called out again. "I can take you to the next spring, but you'd do better to travel by night and avoid the heat—that's the only way you'll make it."

I pulled his blanket a little tighter. "It's not hot."

"It's gonna be." He led the mule toward me. "Where are you from, *danshi*?"

"Wyoming."

"Don't they have deserts up there?"

"Not like this."

"Oh." He slapped his hat against his leg, raising a cloud of dust. "I can get you over to Alto Wells, east of here, and give you water and food."

"I need a car."

"I don't have a car."

"A truck?"

"Nope."

"Is there anybody else around here who can help me?"

"There isn't anybody around here but me for about fifty square miles." He glanced at the horizon. "And whoever it was who dropped you off."

I looked south and then east at the rising sun, but figured he was right, and I'd just die out there. "Looks like I'm going to Alto Wells."

We walked for a few hours angling southeast, where there was a mesquite or ironwood tree that afforded a little shade because somebody had dragged a piece of corrugated steel and leaned it against the trunk, filling the side areas with stacked rocks. "Who built this?"

"I did." He tied the mule off in the shade and poured her some water from an old Ames Neville Desert Water Bag into one of the pans. He pulled the cork attached with rope and then handed it to me and gestured for me to take a drink.

I did and then studied him. "You've got these little way stations hidden all around?"

As if knowing what I was thinking, he responded by shaking his head. "Not south."

"Why not south?"

"No gold there."

"This what you do, Pop, prospect?"

He took the water bag back and took a great swallow. "For a very long time now."

"You rich?"

What I could make of the glimmer of his eyes grew sharp, and he studied me. "Define rich, *danshi*."

"Lots of money."

"Well then, no." He shook his head, disappointed in me. "But I've got the desert for a home, the sky for a ceiling, and no man to tell me where to go or what to do."

"Sounds pretty great." I sat in the shade and looked up at him. "I'd rather not be called *boy*—my name is Walt Longmire. Do you mind if I ask yours?"

"You speak Japanese?"

"A few words."

"Fujita, my name is Patrick Fujita."

I continued to scrutinize him, long enough for him to turn and examine me back. "You've got friends in Bone Valley, Mr. Fujita."

He took his time responding. "Do I now?"

"Yes, sir. You taught Noriko how to speak Japanese, didn't you?"

He said nothing, stepping away and taking another sip from the Desert Water Bag.

"She speaks very highly of you."

"Is her grandfather dead?" he asked. "Because that is the only way I would ever go back to Bone Valley."

I leaned against a rock and felt my head. "No, I'm afraid Judge Everson is very much alive."

"That is too bad."

"I take it the two of you didn't part amicably?"

"No, as a matter of fact we did not part at all. I simply walked away."

"You walked away from Bone Valley to here?"

"In a way, I had some help . . . To Iron Springs first, where I met a man and bought his trappings."

"And you've been out here in the desert ever since?"

"Yes, and I guess that probably says something about my relationship with my fellow man." He turned to look at me, smiling as he crossed his legs, and then sat. "By the way, who won the war?"

I considered an answer. "Well, from the amount of electronics and compact cars flooding the country, I'd say the Japanese." He attempted to hand me the water bag again, but I waved him off. "Mr. Fujita, what happened back in Bone Valley?"

"Pat." He placed the cork back into the bag's spout and reached up to hang it on a rusted nail on the inside of the makeshift structure. "Why do you want to know?"

"I think something bad happened there and the repercussions of it are still having an effect on people's lives—people like Noriko."

"And you think bringing these things to light will make them better?"

"For the living, yep."

"And what about the dead?" He nodded toward a rock shelf in the distance, near the foothills of the mountains. "Do you see that ridge there?"

"Yep."

"There used to be a spring in that place." He reached into a shirt pocket and handed me some terra-cotta shards with geometric patterns painted on them. "I found these in that spot from a tribe that attempted to live there a couple thousand years ago. There are also some collapsed structures and the remains of a garden and an old, rusty metal rake where a group of Mormons tried to settle." He stood, moving in that direction, and then placing a hand on the mule's stout neck, he stroked it. "Now me, you, and Over-Jenny are here . . . But how long do you think we'll last?"

"Bone Valley still very much exists."

"But for how long? When that cursed old man dies, do you think anybody will actually want to stay in that God-forsaken place?"

"What did Everson do?" I sat there, waiting. "Were you one of the internees, Pat?"

"*Internees* . . ." He glanced at me. "What do you think that word means?"

"I'm not sure I understand the question."

"*Intern*, what do you think that word means? Sounds like we were sent there to be trainees or to learn something. Well we did: imprison, confine, detain, hold, jail . . . Words are important, young man, they define our world. *Internment camps* sounds a lot better than *prison* or *concentration camp*, doesn't it?"

"Yep, it does."

He stared out at the ridge that led to the mountains. "I was a linguist and a teacher in my youth, but it took a very long time for me to understand the power of words—designed to make lies sound truthful and murder respectable."

"George Orwell."

"Very good." He turned to consider me. "They labeled us as *enemy aliens* and called for an *evacuation*, sent us to *assembly centers* and then *relocation centers*—a very careful use of language?"

"You'll excuse me for saying, but it doesn't sound like you're completely ready to give it up."

"It doesn't matter what I'm ready to do."

"I think it does." I pushed off the rock and stood. "What do you know about the Tokyo Twelve, Pat?"

He breathed a laugh and then looked at the ground as the waves of humor shook him like an earthquake, his back heaving until he raised his head and wiped the tears from the folds of his eyes. "*Danshi*, I am one of the Tokyo Twelve."

It was the middle of the day, and the blistering sun was at its highest, the three of us trudging along avoiding the cactus and the odd rattlesnakes and Gila monsters. Fujita spoke gently, as if trying to not disturb an abandoned world with his words. "I guess the government thought they were doing us a favor, putting us there rather than sending us off to a maximum-security prison or letting us become victims of vigilante riots."

"How could they do that to American citizens?"

"You had to understand the times; besides, I wasn't an American citizen—I'm still not."

"You're not?"

"No, and to understand that you have to understand what was going on in Japan at the time." He tipped his hat back. "I am from the northernmost island, Hokkaido, and there was a period of drought and famine before the war and many Japanese had no choice but to leave or starve. As a teacher I signed an agreement that I would work the Canadian rail service teaching the workers English, but they abandoned that and I spent a year breaking rocks and laying track, back-breaking work for very little money—about a dollar a day." He stopped, looked around, and then continued to lead his mule. "We were in British Columbia and working near the American border, so I decided to make a run for it and ended up in Spokane, where I worked in a laundry for a number of years and gave language lessons before moving to Sacramento, where I got a job translating Japanese books and poetry for a small publisher. When Pearl Harbor was struck, I remember thinking that it must be some kind of joke, but then the FBI came banging on my door in the middle of the night and they hauled me away." He laughed. "I kept thinking that they must want me for my language skills, reading transcripts or break-ing codes. I was very naive." He reached back and rubbed Over-Jenny's nose. "Then they put me in a horse stall in Santa Anita."

We followed a dry creek bed and suddenly came up on a rock structure that led down into the ground and a small shed with a cov-ered stall and a singular ironwood tree, where he deposited the mule. Slipping off her pack and all the supplies, he stacked them next to the opening and then pulled off her harness.

Trailing some poles across, we watched as she drank deeply from a basin in the corner. "Home sweet home."

Walking past me, Fujita headed for the other structure, leading me down the short ramp where he pushed open a rough-hewn door and went inside, pausing to light an oil lamp on the table. The floors were handlaid stone and so were the walls up to ground level where rough-hewn timbers took their place. There was a bunk against one of the partial walls and an old coal cookstove that looked as if it had seen better days. There was also a gigantic Christmas cactus by the one window to which he paused to introduce me. "This is Riku, he's over a hundred years old."

I waved at the plant. "Howdy, Riku."

He took off his boots, so I did the same.

He lit another lamp on the table and then crossed to one end of the room, where he uncoiled a rope from one of the low rafters and pulled on it, lifting a section of the roof made of corrugated metal and letting in a slight breeze and a little more light. "I have one of these on each side, according to which way the wind is blowing or the sun happens to be."

There were two chairs at the table, so I took one.

He stood there for a moment and then went over to a box that was mounted on the wall, where he pulled out a small bottle and two earthenware cups. "Drink?"

"Sure."

He sat, pouring a little into a cup, slid one toward me, and then went back to the makeshift cabinet to pull out medical supplies, including a needle and thread. "Sake, I make it myself."

"Out of what?"

"Fermented rice."

I picked up the small cup. "You're not having any?"

"You must pour for me; it is tradition to allow both conversation and the sake to flow."

"Oh." I did as he had requested and then watched as he set the medical supplies on the table, slugged his drink down, and smiled at me. "Steady my nerves."

"Have another." He was having trouble finding the eye of the needle, so I poured him one more and took the tools of the trade from him and threaded the thing the first time out, handing it back to him. "Are you going to sterilize that?"

"Sure." He held the needle out over the globe of the oil lamp and then went about arranging the scalp on my head from behind. "So, who hit you?"

"Well, I'd be guessing, but I'd say a fellow called Lester?"

"Lester Cobb?"

I felt the needle going into my skin but all in all it didn't feel so bad. "We weren't formally introduced, but he seems to have taken a genuine dislike for my person."

Pat continued working. "That could be genuinely hazardous to your health."

"You know him?"

"He was one of the guards at Bone Valley." He continued looping the thread and manipulating my skin in an attempt to patch it together. "A strange man."

"You can say that again. I'd never met him, but he tried to take me on twice and I was able to hold him off, but this time he got behind me . . . If it was him."

I felt a tug at the back of my head, and Pat tossed a long, uneven splinter onto the table in front of me. "With a stout piece of lumber, it looks like."

"I guess he decided to up the ante."

"You're lucky he didn't kill you."

I carefully sipped the sake and found it truly wonderful. "You don't think hitting me in the back of the head with a two-by-four and dumping me out here in the middle of the desert isn't tantamount to killing me?"

"*Tantamount*, I have not heard that word in ages." Fujita swung around to look at me. "You went to school?"

"Did."

He looked puzzled and then added. "What now?"

"The United States Marine Corps in less than a week."

His face grew very serious as his eyes widened. "There is a war?"

I glanced at him. "Vietnam." He continued to stare at me, and I started to get a little concerned as I thought back on my history of Southeast Asia. "I guess you would've called it French Indochina?"

He continued to look puzzled. "There is a war there now?"

"Yep, the country is divided into two parts, North and South, and the northern part is communist and being assisted by the Chinese and the Russians."

"The Russians and the Chinese, but they are our allies."

It took me a moment to form my next words. "Pat, how long have you been out here in the desert?"

He continued working on my head. "I can't honestly say, but I am assuming it has been at least twenty years."

"You don't have a radio or any kind of contact with the outside world?"

"Only when I go into Iron Springs for supplies and to trade in my findings from out here, including the gold. Mr. Mayfield Dixon is one of the only people I've spoken to regularly for quite some time and he doesn't talk politics, but for that matter neither do I. Then there are my gifts of the divine providence . . ." I felt a tug as he finished up and came around to look at me. "There, not too lopsided." He gestured toward the bottle. "Pour me another."

"Gladly." I did as he asked and then handed it to him.

He took it and once again knocked it back. "This new war, it's a continuation of the old war?"

"Well, as much as all of them are continuations of the previous wars . . ." I watched as he poured me another. "No, and there was one in-between in Korea, or Chōsin, I guess you would've called it."

He considered my words. "This country has a lot of wars."

I sipped the sake. "Yep, I guess we do."

"And you have enlisted for the latest one?"

"Yep."

He sat in the chair opposite me, folding his hands in his lap. "Don't go."

"What?"

"Don't go. When you are young it all seems like some great lark, but it is not—it is humankind at its absolute worst. You're young, and think you'll live forever but you won't, I can assure you." He smiled a sad smile.

"My friend Henry, the one back in Bone Valley? I think he might be having second thoughts along those lines."

"He enlisted too?"

"Yep, but he's beginning to wonder about what he's doing. He's Northern Cheyenne, an Indian." I took another sip of the sake and then reached out and picked up the bloody splinter from the surface of his table, hoping to change the subject. "Pat, do you know that Bone Valley is haunted?"

He shook his head in dismissal. "This land is haunted by many things."

"This is the story of the ghost of somebody, maybe more than one somebody, who died here, and that this Hannya, a demonic and vengeful spirit, is out there seeking revenge on those who betrayed her."

His eyes stayed steady on mine. "A very old wives' tale concocted by a vengeful wife."

"Noriko also referred to her as Hannya, which means wisdom?"

Fujita shrugged in response.

Finishing off the tiny cup, I sat it back on the table. "You don't know anything about that, a child wearing a theatrical mask back in Bone Valley?"

"A child?"

"I'm assuming, because whoever it was, they were very small, so a child, yes."

"I don't know anything about that."

"Noriko does."

He stared at the table, and I noticed every time I mentioned her a sadness crept into his expression. "She is a young woman with an overly active imagination."

Pouring him another, I sat the bottle down and then nudged the cup toward him with my fingertips. "I've seen this demon too."

He stayed still for a moment and then reached across and poured another for me. "What does it look like, this devil of yours?"

"A horned demon, but sad." I picked up my cup and took another sip. "I think, whoever it is, that they tend a shrine for Mae Mayko Oda in the old camp. Noriko says it's her that does it, but I think she's lying. Now, why would she do that?"

"Mae Mayko Oda."

"Did you know her?"

He knocked the sake back in his fashion, his eyes watering from the alcohol content—at least I think that's what it was. "Why do you care?"

"I have this thing about the truth, and I think it's running low in this valley."

"I would have a hard time arguing that." He actually laughed. "Have you ever heard of the Yuki-onna?"

"The what?"

He nodded his head and then spoke in a low voice. "The Yuki-onna is a *yokai*, or snow spirit, who lives in the frozen lands of the mountains, taking the lives of those foolish enough to wander into her domain." He nudged his tiny cup toward me again, and I obliged him, watching as he tipped the cup up and drank the entirety again. "In the thirteenth century there was once a young samurai who went into the world to seek his fortune but was retained by a great daimyo, a feudal landowner. The young samurai was dispatched to deliver a message of dire military importance to another daimyo in an adjacent kingdom but, after days of traveling, found his way blocked by armies of the invading Mongols."

I reached across and primed the pump by filling his cup once more.

He picked it up, but this time he sipped. "Realizing that there was no way for him to fight so many, he was forced to traverse a snow-covered mountain pass. The young samurai had almost made it to the precipice when a sudden storm struck, causing him to lose his way. Trapped in the crevasse of a small canyon that was rapidly filling with snow, he drew his sword and prepared to commit hara-kiri rather than slowly freeze to death. Just as he was getting ready to plunge the blade into himself, he thought he saw something in the snow: an outline of a woman."

Raising his face, he imitated the character in his story, seeming to look past me, his eyes searching for something before leaping up and grabbing the needle from the surface of the table and holding it like a sword. "Turning the savage blade, he pointed it at the figure and said—Stay away, I am Kamakura shoganate, in procession of the kiri-sute gomen, and will kill you if you draw nearer!"

He turned his face to deliver an aside, his beard swaying as he continued in a more conversational tone. "The figure did not go away, but it did not come closer, and rapidly, the young samurai began freezing to death. He had just given up hope and started to turn the sword on himself again when the figure moved in close. He started to turn the sword back but discovered that his arm was frozen and would no longer move. Horrified, he watched as the figure pressed against him. It was a woman, a strange woman as pale as snow and covered in a fine sheen of frost, who placed her arms around him, holding him very close."

Hugging himself, Fujita continued with the story. "Her eyes captured his, and she spoke in a haunting, whispering voice—You are so very young."

Pat nodded as the character, acting out the shivering and dying man. "Y-y-y-yes."

He turned back to me. "It was the Yuki-onna and she took pity on him because he was so young, telling him to close his eyes and she would save him. But he did not believe her and said that if he closed his eyes, she would take him away. She told him—No, I will save you, but under one condition: you must never tell anyone of our meeting. The young samurai promised and closed his eyes." Fujita took the needle and stuck it into the table.

"The next morning, he awoke and discovered that the snow was gone and in its place wildflowers blanketed the mountainside and the breeze was warm and caressing. Continuing on his way, he delivered the message to the daimyo and an epic battle was won. Years later, the samurai was a man of great importance who had won many campaigns but was ready to retire and lead a life of leisure. He had always remembered the mountain pass of his youth and what had happened to him there, so he returned to that place to find a small cabin in the canyon, the exact spot where he had almost lost his life."

Picking up his cup, he took another sip. "Standing there, he watched as a beautiful woman came from the tiny structure and called out to him, asking if he was tired and would he like food and drink and to rest in her home. He agreed and as the months passed, he would return there and visit with her, finally making her his wife."

He set the cup back down. "They lived happily together for many years, when one evening, the aged samurai sat by the open window, looking out at a lovely summer evening, and began telling his wife the story of what had happened to him all those years ago when the mysterious Yuki-onna saved his life. As he finished the story, he sensed her hand on his shoulder, and it felt very cold. He turned to watch as his wife's face grew pale, paler than any person he had ever seen, and a luster of frost crept over her entire body."

He placed a hand on the table, pulling out the needle and once again holding it like an undrawn sword. "His wife's eyes met his as he stumbled back, overturning his stool and falling against the wall, clutching at his sword as she screamed a sound like the splitting of great trees with the volume of a typhoon. Try as he might, he could not draw the weapon from its scabbard, almost as if it were frozen there. She drew closer and enveloped him in her arms and forced his eyes shut."

I poured him another and watched as he picked up the tiny cup, holding it before him like a sacrament. "The aged samurai blinked open his eyes in that last moment of his life and could see that his wife and the summer cabin were gone, and, in their place, he was once more frozen in the crevasse, covered in snow and ice—dead."

He lifted the cup with a great deal more ceremony, raising it to his lips and sipping.

In the face of such a performance, I wasn't sure of what to say. "You're quite the storyteller."

He drank some more, finishing it off. "Thank you, I don't get many opportunities." He refilled my cup and then went back to the door and began putting on his boots. As I rose, he waved for me to sit. "Rest, you have a great deal of traveling to do tonight." He gestured toward the one bunk. "Sleep. I have work to do, but I will be back late in the afternoon to help you get ready."

I sipped some more sake, holding the warm liquid in my mouth and then swallowing. "Is it really going to take me three nights?"

He finished lacing the tall boots and stood, reaching a hand out to stroke the petals of the Christmas cactus. "You look to be in good shape, so perhaps less."

"I don't have three nights."

He grinned. "Then perhaps we will find a way to speed you up."

"But you said you didn't have a car or truck."

Resetting his hat, he thumbed the latch and pushed open the door, allowing the glare of the mid-day sun to strike at the threshold. "No, I don't."

"I'm not taking Over-Jenny."

"I would not allow you to." He stepped through the door as I stopped him with my words.

"So, Pat . . . What's that story of yours supposed to mean, anyway?"

Fujita stood there, backlit by the blinding light just before he closed the door. "Be very careful in your dealings with demons, my friend."

9

"Victoria Moretti."

"And your occupation?"

"Undersheriff of Absaroka County."

The prosecuting attorney's voice took on a different tone. "And you work under Sheriff Walt Longmire?"

The Terror shrugged. "Under, on top, whatever."

It was at this particular moment that Judi Cole lowered her head onto the surface of the defense table and Judge Snowden chose to cough into his hand and take a moment to compose himself. "Excuse me. Continue, please."

"Undersheriff Moretti, how long have you been working . . . um, *with* Sheriff Longmire?"

"Five years."

"I see, and in those five years would you say he is a competent law enforcement official?"

"The best."

"How would you describe the last five years in his employ?"

She stared at him with intent—I knew that stare. "Swell, it's been swell."

"Swell?"

"I believe that's what I said, Counselor. Twice."

He walked back over to his table and collected a sheaf of papers.

"Do you know how many times this department has resorted to deadly force in the last five years, Undersheriff?"

"Suppose you tell me?"

"Over a dozen times." He looked up at her. "Do you think that's normal for the county with the lowest population in the lowest populated state in the country?"

"Define *normal*."

He ignored her and continued. "And would you be surprised to know that the majority of these acts can be laid at the feet of Sheriff Walt Longmire?"

"He's got big feet." She smiled at him. "He's also got big hands, and you know what that means . . ."

"Suppose you tell us?"

She eased back in her chair. "Big boots and gloves."

Laying the papers back on the table, he sat with his arms folded, looking at the threadbare carpet. "Undersheriff Moretti, I'm getting the feeling that you're not taking this independent hearing very seriously."

"You're kidding, right?"

"Excuse me?"

She gestured toward me, sitting at the defense table. "He just saved the state a couple of billion dollars—I'm thinking you should be having a fucking parade for him."

"Undersheriff," Snowden's low voice intoned.

She folded her arms, once again staring at Whinstone.

"You'll excuse me for saying so, but it seems to me that the department and particularly Sheriff Longmire are pretty quick on the trigger."

She swiveled her eyes and crossed her legs. "Yeah, no."

"No, what?"

The tarnished-gold eyes unloaded on him. "No, I don't excuse you for saying so."

He stared back at her, probably unaware that he wasn't going to make a dent. "Undersheriff Moretti, are you in a relationship with Sheriff Longmire?"

Judi rose. "Objection, Your Honor."

Snowden leaned back in his chair. "Mr. Whinstone, we're on thin ice here."

"I'm just trying to get a clear picture of the somewhat curious business practices of the Absaroka County Department and Sheriff Longmire."

Vic leaned forward, placing her hands on the railing that divided her from the open courtroom, and only I knew how quickly she could leap over the thing and strangle the attorney. "This is such bullshit."

The judge sighed. "Undersheriff."

"No, I mean it. He gets drugged, handcuffed to a chair, shot at, and who knows what, and you assholes want to go after him? This is all because the family of that rich son of a bitch raised a fuss and has connections."

"Undersheriff."

"No, really . . . I love how you guys second-guess what real people who are out there on the streets are doing, making split-second decisions affecting life and death, and then having to come in here and answer to you Monday-morning quarterbacks."

"Undersheriff."

"I've got only one thing to say to you, all of you . . ."

MONDAY, MAY 25, 1964

"What is it?"

"Chicken."

I stared at my fork. "It doesn't taste like chicken."

"Sure it does."

"Where did you get a chicken out here?"

Fujita leaned forward, forking in more of the rice and strange meat. "It's like a roadrunner."

"So, it's roadrunner?"

"Sure."

I stared at the very pale meat. "It doesn't look like any kind of bird."

He ate another bite and chewed. "Then it's pork."

I'd inadvertently fallen asleep in the chair after Pat had left and was only awakened when I heard scuttling in the kitchen and a plate containing the mystery meat was slid under my nose.

"You're not being very convincing."

He nodded, taking another bite. "If I told you what it was you wouldn't eat it."

I went ahead and took the bite; it tasted a little like pork but was chewy, and I tried to settle my mind and not hypothesize about what it could be. Looking out the makeshift skylight, I tried to judge what time it might be, but my pocket watch had been broken and without it, it was difficult.

I took another bite and found that the taste was actually growing on me. "Any idea what time it is, Pat?"

He looked at the skylight too. "Probably about seven."

"Is it dark enough for me to go after we finish . . ." I glanced down at my plate. "Whatever this is?"

"Sure."

"Do you think you can map out some stops for me, so that I know where to rest?"

He gestured toward the food. "I can do better than that but eat your food. There isn't much between here and Bone Valley."

I took another bite with some rice. "I've asked you a couple of times, but you keep avoiding answering—what happened in Bone Valley? There's a private investigator there asking questions not only about that but also concerning a missing reporter who was digging around."

He scraped together another morsel and shoveled it into his mouth, chewing silently.

"Bone Valley, the Tokyo Twelve . . . What happened?"

Fujita swallowed, reaching out and taking a mug of water in his hand, then took a sip. "I haven't been in that place for twenty years . . ."

"Then what happened when you were there?"

"They were hanged."

I sat there, staring at him. "Excuse me?"

"You heard me, they were hanged. They were executed—hanged."

"The internees, they hung them? The federal government?"

"In a sense. The guys they left there to take care of those people . . . They murdered them."

"The judge, Everson."

"Yes."

"How many?"

"Eleven."

"Of the twelve . . ." I sat my fork down. "Pat, of the original Tokyo Twelve, you're the only survivor?"

"Yes."

I pushed my chair back, the scraping on the stone floor almost as bad as that in my soul. "We have to go tell somebody."

He shook his head. "Who?"

"The authorities, the police . . ."

"They're the ones who put us there."

"More than twenty years ago."

He smiled a sad smile, shaking his head. "And you think they're going to care about it now?"

"I don't know much about the law, but I know there's no statute of limitations on murder, let alone mass murder."

"Where's your proof?" He continued to smile at me. "Where are the bodies? The official story is that they just ran off, at least that's what I've heard."

"You, you're the proof."

"And you think they're going to take the word twenty years after the fact of some crazy desert rat who's not even a US citizen?" Fujita finished up his dinner and then took the remains over to the dry sink and sat the plate in there, then went over to the cactus by the window, stroking its petals fondly. "Do you know how Riku here got to be over a hundred years old?"

"I've got the feeling you're going to tell me it's from minding his own business."

"That is correct." Pouring the remainder of the water in his mug on the plant, he crossed back to the sink and deposited the mug. "In case you haven't noticed, my interactions with my fellow man have led me to living alone in the desert with a mule and a cactus."

"Don't you feel any responsibility to those people who died?"

"You are too young to understand, but we the living have no responsibilities to the dead, our accountabilities to them have passed and they no longer have any more use for us than we have for them—our duties are to the living, and that should occupy us enough." He walked to the door and began putting on and lacing up his boots. "Come with me, and we will see about getting you back to your friend to whom you have responsibilities."

With that, he reached up and took his Desert Water Bag from the nail on the doorjamb and then pushed open the door and went out, leaving me no choice but to follow. Pulling on my boots, I hopped after him as he appeared to be walking out into the desert. "At least tell me how it happened."

"Why would you wish to know such things?"

Adjusting my hat, I stopped and looked at him, hands on hips. "So I can understand it better."

"Understand? What leads you to believe that you could ever understand? Do you know what a lynching is?"

"I think I do."

"I don't think you do, and I hope you never learn." He started to turn again but then stopped. "It was mid-August in 1942 immediately following the Guadalcanal campaign that Everson's son Andrew died on the *Astoria* when it was shelled and sunk. The next night they attempted to kill all of us—do I need to draw you a picture as to why?"

"Everson was in charge of the camp?"

"He was in charge, yes."

"So, in revenge he murdered the Tokyo Twelve."

"All . . . all but one."

"How did you escape?"

"I had a friend who helped me." His eyes came up, looking at the desolate horizon. "I will never forget the sounds the others made . . ."

He moved toward another tarp covering something leaning against the ironwood tree.

"And you ended up here?"

He slung the rope that was attached to the water pouch over his shoulder. "Yes."

"And never looked back."

"No." He took the final steps toward the tarp, fingering a discolored, brass grommet with a rope, and tied it off to the trunk of the tree. "We owe the dead nothing, young man, because they know better than we do the only thing of any importance—that it is better to live." He untied the rope on the tarp and dragged it to one side, revealing an old military motorcycle painted a desert tan. Pulling the tarp the rest of the way off, he flapped the dust and turned to look at me. "Every once in a while, something shows up out here in the desert. I'm not sure how it happens but things just arrive out here. I call them my gifts of the divine providence." He glanced at the motorcycle again. "Do you know how to ride one of these things?"

"No."

"That is unfortunate in that neither do I." He regarded the contraption. "I got it started once, years ago, but I'm not sure if I remember how. I attempted to ride it only one time, broke my leg, and decided I would never try again."

There was a Saint Christopher Protect Us badge stuck at the center of the handlebars, for whatever good that had done the most recent operator, and a small, scraped, metal plate on the dented gas tank, identifying the old bike as a 1942 WLA Harley-Davidson. "It's never going to start with the original fuel in it, which by this time has become vintage lacquer."

"I cleaned it out and have a container of fuel that I've scavenged, and it started before."

I studied the thing rather dubiously, even though there appeared to be air in the tires. "Where did you find it?"

"Lying out here in the desert. I guess it did not want to be in the army anymore. There was a base where they trained with these and jeeps."

"I wish you'd found a Jeep."

"Me too, but it'll get you there in one night as opposed to three." Fujita stared at the thing, hung the water pouch off the saddlebag on the back, and then turned to look at me. "You are sure you wish to do this, that you truly want to go back there?"

"He's my friend, maybe my only one . . . I can't just leave him there, in that place."

"Very well." I watched as he reached behind the contraption and fetched out an old galvanized-steel oilcan, shaking it to his ear. "Yes, this is full and should be enough to get you there or near enough there so that you can walk the rest of the way."

"If I don't break my leg."

"Yes, that is always an option with these things." He pulled the handlebars, walking it out from under the tree and into the open, where I could see Over-Jenny watching us from her paddock, obviously curious as to what it is we were up to.

Pat lowered the kickstand and reared the bike back, setting it upright as he unscrewed the cap on the gas tank, filling it up with the foul-smelling fuel. Fingering a rubber knob adjacent to the speedometer on the tank, he turned it, and then pushed what I assumed was the choke on the carburetor. "You should watch all this carefully."

"I thought you were going to start it."

"I am, but that does not necessarily mean that it will stay running."

"Right."

He pushed the grip on the left all the way forward and then reached over to the right side and flipped out an engine kick-start lever. He stepped back, gesturing for me to straddle the thing. "Your turn."

"What?"

"You have to kick it to start it."

"I thought you were going to do that?"

"No, that is how it broke my leg the last time."

I eyed the contraption with distrust. "It kicks back?"

"Yes, but not the first three kicks, which will push fuel into the carburetor."

I threw a leg over and did as he asked, cranking it with my boot the requisite three times, and then watched as he adjusted the choke. He then turned a switch on the gas tank, causing a green light to flicker.

"That's probably a good sign."

"Yes, I do not know how the battery has stayed charged enough for this length of time, but it has." He gestured toward the grip in my right hand. "Twist that back toward you, once."

I did as he said and then watched as he took a few steps back and to the side.

"What?"

"This is the part that broke my leg."

I swallowed. "So, kick it?"

"Yes."

I lifted my weight and straightened my leg, figuring that if I was going to get only one chance before retribution, I was going to make it count. There was a brief grumble from the motor, a sputter, and then nothing. I glanced at Fujita as he took another step back and then enjoined me to try again. Repeating the procedure with the same results, I glanced at him once more.

He moved forward cautiously, reached down in front of my leg, and adjusted the choke again before stepping back even farther as if the thing might explode at any moment.

He gestured again, and I kicked the thing to life—sputtering, rumbling, and then sounding as if it were going to die.

Pat gestured toward the grip on the left, yelling to be heard above the sound of the motor. "Turn that one back all the way!"

I did, and it sputtered and spit.

He gestured to my other hand as he stepped forward and adjusted the choke a third time. "Give it some gas!"

I did, and it sputtered a bit more before settling into an uneven idle. "Sounds good considering!"

He nodded and then switched on the headlamp before opening the lid of a metal box attached to the front fork and pulling something from it wrapped in wax paper and cloth. "If you are going back to that place, then you should also take this." Unwrapping it the rest of the way, I watched as he pulled out a green parkerized-barrel .45-caliber semiautomatic pistol.

"Whoa . . ."

"I have taken care of it over the years but have never used it." He checked it quickly and then started to hand it to me. "Do you know how it works?"

"No, I've never handled one like it before!"

He leaned in close and then expertly went through the motions of dropping the magazine, showing me the glistening brass rounds, reinserting it, sliding the action, and then punching a small button on the side. "It is loaded with seven rounds, but the safety is on. To fire it you must only push this button. I will wrap it again and put it back in the box so that if you crash, you will not shoot yourself."

"Pat, I don't need it!"

He rewrapped and placed the firearm back into the metal box, adding another package from his pocket. "Jerky, for the road!" He then pulled out a pair of vintage goggles and a leather helmet before closing the clasp on the lid, finally standing and looking at me.

I stuck a hand out to him. "Thank you!"

He shook the hand and then handed me the goggles and helmet before stepping far back.

"I'm going to look like the Galloping Ghost." I pulled the leather helmet and goggles on and glanced down at the thundering machine. "Now what?"

He shrugged. "I do not know; I have never gotten this far!"

I glanced at the accelerator grip, which seemed self-explanatory, then the gear-shift knob on the left side of the tank and a large toggle lever above the left running board, a simpler peg on the right. "I think that one is the brake, so this other side must be the clutch, and it must be in neutral in that I'm not crashing through the cactus yet!"

He nodded. "Yet!"

"Thanks for the vote of confidence!" I looked up into the desert twilight. "Which way do I go?"

"Straight past my place, there will be only one path heading south—at the mesa, stay to the right and then take the path to the right. Stay on that path until you hit the two-track and then follow it to the left. There will be a bridge over a wash, and you take a left on the other side. Whatever you do, don't go over the bridge and go straight, because that will take you into the middle of the basin, where you will most certainly run out of gas and die!"

"Right!" I blipped the throttle.

"After you take the left on the other side of the wash, it's a straight shot south for more than thirty miles, but keep an eye out, because the road splits. And if you're not careful, you'll accidentally take the right fork, which will lead you to Hillside rather than Bone Valley! If you stay to the left, you'll travel along a ridge where there will be a number of hills before you come over the last one, and you'll see the town before you get there because it'll be morning!"

"Right!" I blipped the throttle again. "I think!"

He fumbled in his pocket and pulled out a piece of folded paper. "I have made a map of all the things I have told you."

He stretched it out to me, and I took it, unfolding and giving it a quick look. "Thank you!"

"Good luck!" He stepped back so far that I could hardly see him in the looming darkness.

"Say, how fast is this?"

"Faster than walking!"

Giving him a quick salute, I pushed the thing forward, coming off the center stand, and looked down at the most baffling part, the paddle lever at my left boot. I figured I was in neutral, and if I pushed the front of the thing down, it would engage.

I tried that, but nothing happened.

I looked up at Pat, who raised his hands to admit that he didn't know either.

Rocking the paddle lever back with my boot, I reached down and peered at the gearshift, one notch forward and two behind where it sat now—first, neutral, second, and third. At least that's what I figured.

Nudging the shifter forward, I was satisfied it wasn't going anywhere until I pushed the front of the pedal down, which I did, suddenly engaged, and I found myself rocketing across the open space past the paddock, where Over-Jenny reared back behind the gate to get out of the way.

The last I saw of Pat Fujita he was running in the other direction toward one of the trees for cover as I blasted by. I turned right to miss the house and then back left to avoid a patch of cactus where I finally saw the path ahead in the yellowish light of the headlamp and steered toward it like the steel ball in a pinball machine.

I bounced off a rock but kept the bike upright by trailing my boots out to the side. After striking a few things, I came to the conclusion that placing them on the running boards might be a safer option.

Running the directions through my head, I spotted the mesa in the distance and slightly to my right, so I was pretty sure I was headed in the right direction. The path stayed about the same width and was flat and straight, and I started getting gutsy, thinking I could shift into second to gain a little speed and conserve some gas.

Something, however, told me to wait until I was a little more certain of myself. Besides, I appeared to be traveling at a good ten miles per hour, and even with the limited visibility of the single headlamp, it was possible I could overrun the thing and this little adventure could come to a sudden end.

As the mesa approached, I thought about what Pat said about what happened at the internment camp in Bone Valley. How was it possible that no one had followed up on the deaths or disappearances of nearly a dozen people? It was wartime, and I guess I could see how something like that in the ass-end of the country could be forgotten and swept away.

But not completely forgotten.

Slowing down over the rough ground, I thought about the girl in the mask and wondered how she could know about any of what had happened. Had someone told her, the way Fujita must've told Noriko? If that was the case, then someone was protecting her, and maybe that was the person who had hit me in the back of the head.

Whoever it was hadn't wanted to kill me or lacked the nerve. The question was whether they thought they would kill me or just get me out of the way. If it was someone who hadn't wanted to kill me, then dropping me off near Fujita's realm of influence meant that it was somebody who not only knew Pat but also knew where he was, and I couldn't help but think that all these people were the same person.

Noriko.

But was she strong enough to knock me out cold, and if she was, then how the heck could she get me in the back of the truck the way I'd done Lester?

Could the child in the mask be hers? The age was hard to judge, but from the size, I had presumed it to be improbable, unless she'd had the kid when she was twelve. I'd estimated the demon child to be maybe ten or twelve years old.

The son, Parker? After my initial dealings with him, I'd kind of started feeling sorry for the man who only seemed to want one thing from Bone Valley: out.

And what about the private investigator, Mike Tanaka? Where did he fit into all of this, if anywhere? And what about the reporter, Yoshida?

A mule deer sprang from a roadside bed and leaped in front of me, causing me to run off the road and brake, but not enough to kill the motor as I puttered back onto the trail and concentrated on what I was doing.

The mesa loomed large to my left, and I watched as it stretched miles to the south. Whatever road the truck had taken must've been much better than this trail, and it was possible that when I got to the two-track I would rejoin it.

Any way you cut it, I had hours of unfamiliar riding to do on a very uncomfortable conveyance and felt glad I'd gotten a long nap in this afternoon.

The path split at the tail end of the mesa, and I took the fork to the right, pretty sure of the instructions till I got to the two-track and followed it to the left and got across the bridge. I hoped to pull to a stop, if I could negotiate it, and then consult the map that Fujita had given me.

The dirt road came up fast, and I wallowed the bike into the deep sand, almost turning it over, but I postholed a leg and veered to the left, keeping it upright.

Four times as wide as the previous trail, I was feeling a little easier, but the tracks were deep washes of sand, and I had to try to keep the motorcycle in the center berm or risk falling over. A more experienced rider would've probably had no problems negotiating the road, but a more experienced rider didn't appear to be holding onto the handlebars.

I was getting the hang of it, though, when I saw the road rise and level out before noticing the timbers that buttressed one end of the bridge. Slowing, I got to the structure and pushed down on the back of the paddle lever at my left boot and applied a little brake with my other.

I was feeling pretty proud of myself as I coasted to a smooth stop—until the motor quit.

Sitting there, straddling the thing, in the otherworldly quiet of the desert night, I pulled the goggles from my face and let them hang about my neck. "Well, hell."

Gripping the handlebars, I stepped down on the center stand and heaved back, setting it upright before dismounting and looking around. The bridge, if you could call it that, was a number of planks loosely arranged on some timbers, none of them looking sturdy.

I walked out on one and watched as it bowed like a diving board. Stepping over to another one, I bounced on it and figured the bike probably outweighed me by a good fifty pounds and that there wasn't a board here that would support the two of us at the same time.

Looking at the spread, I figured I could walk on one and wheel the bike on another and maybe make it across, but not with it running.

I tried to find the water pouch, but it was gone, perhaps having fallen off on one of my near misses along the way. Unfortunate, but this would be even more so if I passed the turnoff and ended up out in the middle of the desert.

Pulling the map from my pocket, I struggled to see it in the dark, carefully tracing the tip of my finger along the pencil marks and trying to recall Pat's words, remembering that I needed to take a left as soon as I crossed the bridge. I stared into the darkness in that direction but could only see the main track that went straight into the endless landscape, but first I had to get across.

Taking the bull by the horns, I pushed the bike off the stand and then slowly rolled it forward, thinking that perhaps it had been a blessing that the thing had died before I'd gotten to the span and broke through to the wash below.

There was no water that I could see reflected in the gully, and the drop was only about ten feet, but if the boards broke and we fell, that would probably be the end of the line for the two of us.

Nudging the front wheel onto the board, I leaned to a side, placed my feet on one of the other boards, and started across. The boards bowed to a remarkable degree at the middle, making it harder to push the motorcycle uphill, but I felt like I was going to make it— except it was about then that I heard a loud cracking noise.

I stopped and tried to get a read on which board had made the sound and wasn't sure.

I stood there for a moment but figured whichever one it was, that they weren't getting any stronger and started pushing again. The wood cracked, and this time I was pretty sure it was the one the two wheels of the motorcycle were on.

I pushed forward and rolled the bike quicker just as the board let go.

Grabbing it at the back of the seat, I hoisted the motorcycle up onto the timber buttress on the other side, effectively balancing it on the edge as the board clattered down to the wash.

I tried to roll the motorcycle forward, but it wouldn't budge, so there I stood, holding it on the precipice at the other side, both of us on the verge of plummeting back over the edge. There were only two options left: either give it one good hoist or just let the damn thing go.

The thought of walking across the desert made my decision for me, so I yanked.

Summersaulting, the motorcycle leaped forward but then fell toward me, barking my shins as it landed on the hard-pack dirt on the other side.

I took a breath, stepped forward, and picked it up, then balancing it on its wheels, I straddled it, and thought about how I had started it in the first place. I figured it was as warmed up as it was ever going to be, so I didn't bother with the choke or the advance and made sure she was in neutral and then toed out the starter lever and gave it a good stiff kick—and that's when she kicked me back.

I guessed the three preliminary kicks not only advanced the fuel but made sure the rotation of the big twin was ready to turn over rather than turn back, sending me partially over the handlebars before falling over on my other leg.

Lying there for a moment, I then dragged myself out from under and tried to stand. I was sore, but it didn't feel as if anything was broken, and for a moment I thought about tossing the thing off the bridge into the wash.

Then I thought about walking twelve hours on my sore legs.

Picking the machine up again, we had a civilized chat, and I straddled the seat, slowly kicking the lever until I met resistance at the top of the action. Looking at the handlebars, I leaned in and could see that Saint Christopher had abandoned me, or at least the medallion had, perhaps reminding me that I was coming to the numerical end of my nine lives.

I prepared myself, then kicked, and was rewarded with a jolt, a shudder, and a lopsided idle, the headlamp glowing to light the road ahead.

Adjusting the handlebars, I sat there looking for the road to the left but couldn't see anything. Pat had been adamant about taking the left at this point or I'd be headed for the middle of nowhere.

Pulling out the map, I unfolded it and held it out in front of the headlight. Just as he'd said, the arrowed line turned left immediately after the bridge.

Thinking that maybe I just couldn't see it from here or that maybe the scale of the map was off, I shifted into first and nudged the clutch pedal and idled forward, scanning the brush to my left as best I could.

Nothing.

Nothing except the outline of a towering saguaro in the starry night that appeared, with its two arms, to be giving directions.

"That way, huh?"

Engaging the clutch, I coasted to a stop.

"So, how old are you?"

Predictably, it didn't respond.

"Not trying to turn me into fertilizer, are you?"

The cactus remained as stoic as ever, and I decided to play out my string with a wary eye to the left in hopes that the cutoff would appear. Looking up at the star-splayed sky, I thought about how the ancient mariners had plied the seas with only the heavenly bodies and lead line, sandglass, cross-staff, nocturnal, quadrant, astrolabe, or sextant—and here I was without even a compass.

Shifting my eyes to the cactus, I smiled, figuring I had a captive audience and decided to swap stories with the plant. "You know, there was this woman who used to cross the US-Mexico border every day on a motorcycle." I blipped the throttle. "The border patrol guys knew she was smuggling something but couldn't figure out what; dogs couldn't sniff anything, metal detectors were useless, and even taking the motorcycles apart didn't help. After a few years the head guard was getting ready to retire, saw the old lady one last time, and told her he had to know what she was smuggling, promising not to do anything to her. The old lady asked him if he was serious, and he said yes—what are you smuggling?" I blipped the throttle one last time. "Motorcycles, she said."

Nudging the pedal, I tootled off, shifting from first to second and into the darkness, following the feeble beam of the headlamp as the night closed in. I was already missing the company of the cactus after a mile or two, but figured I'd see more of them before the trip was over.

10

I stared at my undersheriff, who was reclining on a bunk, sipping a glass of wine and reading a copy of *Peyton Place* she had gotten from the jail library. "I can't believe they locked me up."

I scooted the visitor chair in and leaned against the bars. "What did you think they were going to do after what you said?"

"I thought they would take the act as constructive criticism."

"Well, they didn't."

She dropped the paperback onto her chest. "The people in charge of this hearing have no fucking sense of humor."

"I think that's been established, yep."

She rolled over, careful to not spill her wine. "What's for dinner?"

"Dog and I thought we would order a pizza."

"From where?"

My Philadelphia born, of Italian heritage undersheriff, was a connoisseur on the subject of pies and had strong opinions concerning which ones in the state of Wyoming were at all edible. "Pie Zanos on Main Street."

"That'll do."

"You mind if I ask where you got the wine?"

She sat up, turned, and picked up the bottle in order to refill her stemware. "Ruby brought it down to me before she left." Vic tapped the edge of the stemware on the metal frame of the cot, where it made an unnatural sound. "Plastic—evidently she's afraid I may take my life."

"You seem to be holding up."

She sipped her wine. "Civil unrest has a terrible price."

"You told the prosecutor to go fuck himself."

"Yes, I did."

"Then you told a federal judge to go fuck himself."

"Yes, I did." She lowered her glass, the picture of unrepentance.

"How's your book?"

She picked up the paperback and flapped the pages at me. "Hey, these people were up to some lascivious shit in the town. Did you put this in the library?"

"I don't think so; what's the publication date?"

She tracked it down with a forefinger. "1957."

"Before my time, it must've been Lucian, or maybe Ruby."

"Pretty racy stuff for the Rubster."

I shrugged. "She had her moments back in the day . . ."

"Why don't you go get another glass and join me."

I did as she suggested, then stepped over Dog and retreated to the communal bathroom where I called in the pizza and then boosted a shaving mug from the sink, rinsing it out and returning with it between the bars.

She poured as she talked. "I don't think I've helped your cause."

"Maybe, but I don't think you did much damage either."

She sipped her own wine. "So, this hearing is just to feel you out and see if Rondelle's or Regis's families want to waste their money coming after you?"

I sipped my wine, and it tasted a little funny. "They've got a lot of money to waste."

"So, which one is richer, the Rondelle family or Regis?"

"Regis, by far."

"So, they're the ones funding all this?"

"I guess, but it's Tom Rondelle's wife who's spearheading it in an attempt to clear his name."

She leaned back against the concrete wall. "That's going to take some doing."

"Yep, I think at first she wanted to throw Regis under the bus, but when his family came forth with the funding, I guess she started seeing a mutual interest."

"Don't they know this is all going to fail?"

"They're not particularly quick thinkers, at least not in broad daylight."

"Hence the hearing?"

"Hence the hearing." I took another sip of my wine and then reached down and petted Dog as he quasi-slept. "I guess I need to go get a pizza."

"They don't deliver?"

"Nope."

"Well, I'll be here in this literary bed of salacious iniquity." She picked up her paperback and began reading and sipping wine. "Hey, what if I need to go to the bathroom?"

I pushed on the cell door and nudged the bars open. "It's not locked."

"Oh."

I stood along with Dog, who took advantage of the open door, pushed the bars the rest of the way, and then leaped up to join Vic on the cot. "I guess I'm going alone."

Without looking up, she waved. "Ta."

Climbing the stairs, I went the rest of the way up and was confronted by Barrett, my part-time dispatcher, who covered weekends and evenings whenever we had a lodger.

He lowered his textbook, *Rising Through the Ranks: Leadership Tools and Techniques for Law Enforcement.* "Do I really have to stay here with her?"

"Yep, it's the law."

"The cell isn't even locked, and you're here."

"Not for long, I'm headed over to pick up a pizza. Do you want anything?"

"A pay-toll slice."

"Gotcha." I turned and started down the steps of the old Carnegie Library, saluting the painting of Andrew and the photographs of all the previous sheriffs of Absaroka County. "Anything else?"

"Nope, I've got a power drink."

I mumbled as I pushed open the door and stepped outside. "Gotta keep your strength up."

It was a beautiful July night, one of our better months in Wyoming when it hardly snowed at all, and I decided to just walk the half block to the local Italian place. Circling around the courthouse, I took the long steps leading down to Main and crossed, going in and picking up the pizza and heading back, using another route up the hill to the crosswalk and the straight shot to the old Carnegie Library that was my office.

The light was red but turning green as I stopped on the corner waiting for the black Mercedes with Teton County plates to pull out, but it sat there idling at the green light. It was one of those shoebox types, squarish and anything but utilitarian looking.

The windows were darkly tinted, but I raised an arm to indicate that the driver could go ahead, but it just sat there, unmoving, and, after a moment, the rear passenger window whirred down.

I stood there for a moment more as the light changed back to red, then walked into the crosswalk and veered over to the open window where a stately older woman sat in a dark dress and pearls. "Sheriff Longmire?"

Balancing the pizza box in my left hand, I glanced at the driver, who didn't turn, and then back to the woman. "Can I help you?"

She removed an expensive pair of eyeglasses and smiled at me with flawless teeth as she extended a perfectly manicured hand. "I'm Beverly Rondelle."

TUESDAY, MAY 26, 1964

It was a town, but it wasn't the town I was looking for. It was more of a ghost town, really.

I coasted the Harley to a stop in the middle of the street, where it predictably died.

Screwing off the gas cap, I rocked the thing back and forth but didn't hear much sloshing, which didn't give me much hope in getting very much farther. Replacing the cap, I looked around at the vacant falling-down buildings pressed hard between two buttes and tried to remember the towns that Fujita had mentioned when I'd first met him . . . "Contreras, Juniper Wells but not far enough east to be Derby Mine. I've been traveling south and then west, so the only other towns he mentioned were Bagdad and Colby, which means I'm farther west than I should be." I glanced around and could see the mountains to the west, which wasn't good. How could I have gotten east of the mountains, or maybe those were different mountains.

Turning south, I could barely see a two-track heading in that direction.

Stretching my shoulders, I stepped off the bike for a moment to give my ass a rest and flipped the stand down, pulling it up and setting it upright. Taking a few steps, I almost tripped and fell over before remembering to take off the goggles.

Sleepy.

The porch of one of the dilapidated buildings looked inviting, but I knew that if I went over there I might sit down, and if I sat down, I might lie down, and if I did that, I might fall asleep and wake up next week.

I kicked a piece of wood, revealing a hand-painted sign lying on the ground that read COLBY.

Well, that settled that.

Pulling the map from my pocket, I held it up in the moonlight and traced the spot just past the bridge where the left was supposed to have been, and then traced my fingertip westward, where there was nothing but a blank expanse of paper—looking kind of like where I now stood.

I knew I needed to go south and that the road out of Colby appeared to be the only option.

The private investigator, Mike Tanaka, had mentioned a partial settlement just off Route 89, where he was going to go to get the truck tire fixed, but that would have been yesterday morning, not the one coming up. If I could get there, it's possible I could get a ride back to Bone Valley.

All I could do now, however, was head south until I hit 89 and then take a guess which way to go toward civilization—if the gas held out that long.

I folded the map back up, leaned over, stretched my back in utter fatigue, and felt guilty about taking a moment. But if I didn't, I might end up riding off into a ditch or a rock, which would end the trip right there. I reached up to finger the damage to my head and was glad that the stitches appeared to be holding. I was about to climb back on when I remembered the jerky Pat had put in the fork box.

Undoing the clasp, I opened it and pulled out the parcel of dried meat, taking a strip and biting off a piece that tasted a lot like teriyaki. It was good or I was starving, I wasn't sure which, but I stood there chewing and looking at the other bundle in the metal box.

I carefully pulled out the bundle and unwrapped the pistol.

We had firearms at the family ranches back in Wyoming, but my family's tastes tended to run toward revolvers, or what we called wheel guns. I'd never even held a semiautomatic, something I was sure the US Marines were likely to remedy.

Unwrapping and palming the thing, I studied it, the chromate, military sheen looking grave and detached. I thought about punching the safety off and taking a shot, but wasn't sure if I might need all the rounds later, never mind what I'd said to Pat.

I was about to rewrap the wheel gun when I heard a noise behind me and turned east, peering into the rocky pass where I'd come through. The moon was well off its peak and the shadows were black, but I could've sworn I'd heard something in there.

Feeling tough, I switched off the safety and aimed it into the darkness. "Come out, come out, whoever you are."

There was a snort.

"Over-Jenny?" There was another snort, and I could see something out there but nothing nearly as large as a mule.

Taking another step in that direction, I chewed on a different bite of jerky and then tossed a piece out just to see if I could lure whatever it was. There was a snuffling noise, and I could definitely see something moving in the darkness.

Not moving, I waited, and then watched as a piglike creature sniffed in the direction of the bit of jerky, the pink of its snout in contrast with the rest of its furry, black body that seemed to dissolve into the dark. It stared at me with its tiny eyes and then snuffled some more before reaching the jerky and snatching it from the ground. He backed away about a step and then stood there looking at me and chewing.

"Javelina." I lowered the pistol. "Pretty good, huh?"

I was about to throw him another piece when there was a sudden flash and he disappeared, screaming in the darkness. Stunned, I took a few steps in that direction and listened as the squealing and screaming continued.

Raising the .45 again, I took another step, listening to whatever it was that had gotten the javelina kind of grunt-roar with a sickening crunching sound until all went silent.

Unable to help myself, I took another step and could now see a massive cat crouched over the still struggling javelina, with its teeth buried into the back of its prey's neck. It looked up at me, making the guttural noise intermixed with a hissing. I'd never heard noises that low from a cat and figured its lung size must've been enormous.

I'd been around mountain lions my whole life, but none of them compared with this one, which was easily twice the size of normal, approaching a good three hundred pounds.

Holding the pistol on it, I stepped back, but when I did, it advanced with the pig still in its teeth, dragging it forward.

"Huh-uh . . ." I aimed the big semiautomatic between the golden eyes and held it there, steady. "I think you've got enough to eat for one night."

Continuing to back away, I bumped into the rear of the motorcycle but then stood there as still as I could. There was more shuffling as the big cat turned and circled back into the canyon between the buttes and disappeared, but not before displaying his colors; a tawny golden hue splashed with black rosettes.

A jaguar.

I'd never actually seen a jaguar before, but that most certainly was what he was—I wondered how many of them were in Arizona.

I took a deep breath, maybe the first I'd taken in moments, and glanced down at the motorcycle.

I was wide-awake now.

I'd gotten to the point where I wished the thing would run out of gas just so I could fall over and catch a few winks and had finally gotten my wish as it sputtered to a stop and died with finality. No amount of kicking seemed to have an effect, so I lowered the kickstand at the side of the road in hopes that somebody would find the bike or might recognize it as Pat's and get it back to him—though I doubted he wanted it.

Pulling open the fork box, I tucked the remainder of the jerky into my shirt pocket and unwrapped the big Colt, wondering what I was going to do with it. For lack of anything else, I made sure the safety was on and stuffed it into the back of my pants, covering it with my jacket and praying to God that it wouldn't go off.

Closing the box, I took one last look for the Desert Water Bag on the back of the Harley, and it once again disappointed me by not being there. I turned and started walking, aware of a faint glow on the horizon to the east, indicating the morning was coming in the next hour or so.

Hopefully I'd get to some water by then.

It was a slight uphill grade that veered to the left as I walked along. There was nothing in sight, but the road looked more traveled, a few others having joined it from either side as it wound its way south.

I couldn't help but glance around every once in a while. I didn't think the jaguar could've kept up with the motorcycle, especially after eating an entire pig, but you never know.

Reaching the top of a rise, I looked down at a sweeping valley and could see a long concrete strip that must've been Route 89, stretching both ways to the horizon.

There was a small cluster of buildings where the dirt road I was on split into two roads and cojoined the state route in two directions. The assemblage was smaller than Bone Valley's and with what looked to be a couple of utility sheds for the road department, an abandoned gift shop, and of all things, a squarish stone church—Wilhoit, maybe.

Picking up my pace, I made my way down the hill and actually saw a truck go by, the first sign of human life I'd seen all night. I thought about running after it in that there didn't appear to be any activity in the small hamlet, but my legs just wouldn't go for it, and I watched as its stacks billowed black exhaust as it continued east.

Getting closer, I could see that the utility buildings were locked up and looked like they hadn't been used for quite some time. The stone church with three front doors and a small steeple and bell, on the other hand, looked to be in good shape, and I was pleasantly surprised to see a metallic-blue Corvette convertible parked along the opposite side, my spare still sitting in the passenger seat.

I walked over and checked, making out the scuff on the rear deck of the sports car and the dent in the back edge of the windshield. Reaching in, I squeezed the tire and could feel it had been repaired.

Strangely, I noticed that the keys were still dangling from the ignition as I leaned back with my hands on my hips.

"Can I help you, my son?"

I looked up to find a dark-haired young priest with his hands on a chain railing as he looked down at me from on high. "Good morning, you wouldn't happen to have a glass of water, would you, Father?"

He glanced around. "Is this your car?"

"My borrowed motorcycle ran out of gas about four miles north of here."

"Oh, my . . . Well, let's get you something to drink." He disappeared into the church, and I circled around, climbing the steps and pushing my way inside. Pausing in the vestibule, I waited as the priest reappeared with a glass of water and a ceramic pitcher, handing the glass to me. "Welcome to Our Lady Queen of the Desert Catholic Church, I'm Father Kinnell."

"Walt Longmire." I took a swallow and then another before studying him and figuring he was in his midthirties. "How old is this place?"

"It was built in 1883 but was closed two years ago."

"What are you doing here?"

He took the glass, refilling it from the pitcher. "Once a month I come here and celebrate Mass on a given Sunday." He stared at me. "It's Sunday, by the way."

I glanced around the empty sanctuary. "Doesn't look like much of a turnout."

"I was hoping that was why you were here."

Taking another sip, I moved toward the pews. "I'm afraid not." I gestured through the doors. "You wouldn't happen to know where the owner of that convertible outside might be, would you?"

"Actually, when you showed up, I thought it was yours."

"No, it belongs to a private investigator by the name of Mike Tanaka. Have you seen him?"

The priest shook his head. "No, I got here this morning, and it was there."

"That's my spare tire in his passenger seat. He was going to get it patched and run it back to me in Bone Valley."

His face took on a different expression. "Bone Valley. I haven't heard that name in a number of years." He refilled my glass again. "I take it, it still exists?"

"It does."

"The previous priest who used to come out here for the monthly Mass had connections there."

I took another drink and thought about what Noriko had said. "Father . . . Pietro?"

He stared at me. "Are you from around here?"

"No, but I've been getting a crash course." Crossing to the closest pew, I sat on the end as he moved forward and sat in the one ahead of me before turning.

"Did you know Father Pietro?"

"No."

"I did, very well. I am the one who gave him his final rights."

I stared at the water remaining in my glass. "He's dead?"

"Yes, a number of years ago, he passed away in Idaho."

"Did he ever talk about Bone Valley, the internment camp there?"

He studied me a moment more in that special quiet that a sanctuary has and then stood. "Would you like something to eat?"

"What I need to do is get back to Bone Valley."

"You came from there?"

"Yesterday." I rubbed my head delicately. "And I've got a friend back there I've got to make sure is all right."

He reached out and refilled my glass. "I don't have much to offer, but I have a chicken sandwich and some carrots."

I stood again and drank down the glass. "Sold."

Following him into a back room with a small table and chairs, I sat as he opened a paper bag and took out his lunch, a sandwich, and some carrots in a plastic bag, which we shared between us. "It's not much of a rectory, but I make do once a month."

"From what I understand, Father Pietro was the priest in Bone Valley?" I took a bite and chewed the sandwich, and it tasted like the best thing I'd eaten in years.

"He was, much like I am the part-time priest here. He used to go up there the same way I come here, once a month. From what I am to understand he used to be the regular priest in Bone Valley, but when the diocese closed that one, he moved here. This used to be more of a going concern with a number of ranches in the area, but things have changed, the population shrank, and the congregation can't support a full-time church. He left, and I took over his duties here."

"When did they close the church in Bone Valley?"

He took a bite of half of the sandwich and chewed. "Years ago."

I laughed a hollow laugh that rang in the empty church like a blasphemy. "Can you be more specific?"

"When the, um . . . instance happened at the camp, he left and never went back."

"The instance?"

Father Kinnell ate some more of his sandwich and poured himself some water. "There was a fire, I understand, and a number of people were killed."

"The internees at the camp?"

"Yes."

"I heard it wasn't a fire."

Saying nothing, he swallowed some water and studied me.

"Father, have you heard of a man by the name of Pat Fujita, a prospector who lives north of here?"

"No."

"Well, he's one of the survivors of that disaster, and he says that those people, including himself before he escaped, were lynched."

He sat his sandwich down and stood, trailing his fingers across the table before walking to the small window in the back door of the building. "The seal of confession does not allow me to reveal anything that Father Pietro may or may not have said during his last rites."

I finished my sandwich and reached for a carrot. "That statement alone tells me everything I need to know, but if those people were murdered, don't you think you have a responsibility to them, even if Father Pietro didn't?"

"Who says he didn't?" He placed a hand on the door. "You know, a priest may be tortured, maimed, killed, fined, imprisoned, but he may not disclose the knowledge he has acquired in the confessional. He may not reveal anything under this seal to anyone, not even to the penitent himself unless the penitent permits him. Under no conditions may this be qualified; the seal of confession is inviolate for this is true confession to the Lord himself as a matter of *de fide* dogma."

Crunching the carrot, I studied him. "But you're saying he did tell someone?"

"I am saying that the information Father Pietro acquired was not through the means of confession—my information was obtained through confession with him." He turned to look at me. "His experiences in Bone Valley were acquired firsthand."

"He was there when those people were murdered?"

"That, I cannot say."

"He reported them?"

The priest said nothing.

Having finished the carrot, I got up and walked over to him. "To whom?"

"The diocesan bishop."

"And what happened?"

"I don't know, but I assume it was covered by the priest-penitent privilege and nothing was done." He shook his head, looking up at me. "I do know that Father Pietro was transferred and spent the rest of his life in penance at a monastery in Idaho where he slowly lost his mind. It was there in a moment of lucidity that he asked for me to come to him and administer last rites."

"So, it was there that he told you what happened."

"Yes."

"And you're *not* going to tell me."

"You don't understand, I can't."

"Eleven people." I walked back over to the table and drank down the rest of my glass of water. "Thanks for lunch."

"May I ask where you are going?"

"Back to Bone Valley." I walked into the sanctuary and past the rows of pews as he came after me, grabbing my shoulder and partially turning me.

"What good would it do?"

I turned the rest of the way and looked down at him. "Witnesses. Witnesses to what happened all those years ago. At least Father Pietro tried to do something, tried to report it—you haven't even got the guts for that."

Looking at me sadly, he shook his head. "Hearsay evidence, the dying statements of an old man who has lost his faculties during the ministrations of his faith . . . That's what you would have me report on and to whom?"

"Anybody. You say you have a higher responsibility to the church, but I say you have a greater responsibility to your fellow man." I gestured behind me. "What they did back there was gruesome, an affront to all of us, and no one believes that their singular, small voice can bring justice to this situation." I looked around the sanctuary, at all the empty seats. "Back when this church meant something, when these pews were full and all these people were singing, all those voices combined to make something. Well, the same thing goes for the truth: if enough people tell it, then it becomes something; something important, something honest."

Pushing the door open, I turned and walked down the steps as he came through and continued to follow me. Opening the door of the sports car, I slid the seat back and climbed in. Father Kinnell appeared at the driver's side door. "So, you're stealing your friend's car?"

"I'm returning it." I glanced up at him. "If he's not here, he's in Bone Valley."

"Stealing it." He took a deep breath and continued looking at me. "I will have to report it to the authorities."

Cranking the starter, I jammed the car into reverse. "You do me a favor and do that."

I was about to pull out when a massive jade-green Cadillac De-Ville pulled in smoothly from the highway and parked behind me, blocking my way.

I glared back at three Asian men who were getting out of the car—one of them, a bald guy almost as big as me opening the rear door and holding it as another hard-looking older man in a suit and porkpie hat got out and slipped on sunglasses before looking around. He approached, straightening his thin tie as the others stayed at his flank. "Hello, there."

"Would you mind moving the Green Hornet, here? I'm trying to get out."

The priest raised a hand. "Excuse me, but this man is attempting to steal this car."

"Really?" He glanced at me as he drew up alongside the sports car. "Are you really stealing this car?"

"I'm taking it back to a friend."

"And who's that?"

"Mike Tanaka."

He glanced back at the others, a skinny one in a dark suit and one with a wispy goatee and a colorful floral shirt. "That's funny; we know a Mike Tanaka." He turned back to me, slipping down his sunglasses, and I noticed he was missing the pinkie finger on his left hand. "Out of Phoenix?"

"The guy I know is a private investigator."

"That's him, used to be with the San Francisco Police Department?" He glanced at the others again and smiled an ingratiating grin. "We're supposed to meet Mike around here, somewhere."

"You're friends of his?"

"More . . . business associates. Do you know where he is?"

Getting tired of craning my neck, I switched off the car and opened the door, climbing out to face the guy with the keys in my hand. "I think he's in a place called Bone Valley, a little ways away from here."

He thought about it for a moment and then started back for his car. "C'mon, we'll give you a ride."

I stood still. "I'd rather drive myself."

He stopped with his back to me and just stood there.

The other men didn't move either as he turned to look at the big one. "Now, you say you're a friend of Mike's and we're all friends of Mike's . . . What kind of friends would we be if we were to just let you take Mike's car?" He turned a bit, reaching out and tapping the quarter panel on the Corvette. "This is one fast car, and what if you were to just take off up the road? I don't know if this big boat of ours would ever be able to catch you." He looked back at me. "And then what do we tell Mike—that we had his car and let some guy . . . What'd you say your name was?"

"Walt Longmire."

"And we let this guy, Walt Longmire, drive off with it? That wouldn't be very friendly, now, would it?"

By the time I glanced at the two other guys at the front of the

Caddy, the skinny one had his hand folded up inside his jacket while the goatee had his draped at the small of his back.

The boss gestured toward the one with the hand folded within his jacket. "C'mon, Kazuo here can drive the race car in the heat, and you and I can sit in the back of my air-conditioned car and head over to Bone Valley and see what we can dig up—give us a chance to talk and get acquainted."

The skinny guy, Kazuo, dropped his hand and came around the front of their car to the back of the Vette and waited.

With one last glance at the guy in the hat, I tossed Kazuo the keys and he caught them right in front of his face before I pointed at the wheel in the passenger seat. "That's my spare, don't lose it."

With one last look at the priest, I moved forward to where the big guy held the door open to the sedan. The guy in the hat was about to climb in when he nodded toward the big guy. "This is Nomu and he'll take that gun you've got at your back, if you don't mind." He started climbing in but then added. "I don't like guns."

Nomu and I stood there studying each other, both of us thinking the same thing, but I wasn't ready to shoot or wrestle anybody just yet. Pulling the Colt from under my jacket, I held it up to him with two fingers. "The safety's on."

He nodded and placed his hands around the barrel, taking the weapon from me.

Climbing in after the older man, I settled in the seat and watched as the other two climbed in the front, Nomu starting the DeVille and pulling it out of the way, and Kazuo following us in the sports car.

The older man removed his hat and sat it on his crossed knee, then extended a hand with a little finger missing. "Tadashi Sato."

I shook the hand. "Under different circumstance I'd be happy to meet you."

He shrugged. "These are the best of circumstances, a mutual interest—any friend of Mike's is a friend of ours." I watched as he lowered a compartment in the seat in front of him and took out a vintage bottle of scotch and two glasses. "How did you make his acquaintance?"

"We were in Bone Valley when he showed up there. I guess he's got a friend who disappeared, and he's been looking for him . . ."

"Alan Yoshida?"

"You know him too?"

Sato poured himself a glass and gestured toward me, but I declined. "I do, we all do."

"He was a cop too."

Tadashi sipped the liquor. "He was."

"I don't suppose you guys are cops?"

The big guy, Nomu, laughed as Sato reached up and touched his shoulder, upon which he grew absolutely silent. Leaning back, the older man pulled off his sunglasses and folded them, placing them into the pocket of his blazer behind a decorative pocket square. "No, no, we are not with the police."

"Then how did you get to know Mike?"

"I met him in a previous occupation, as a soldier."

"You were with him in the army?"

"Not yours, no."

I turned to look at the man, studying the lines at the corners of his eyes as he smiled at me. "You fought for the Japanese?"

"I did."

"But Mike told me he fought in the European theater in the war?"

"I may have underestimated you, Walt Longmire." He swirled his glass. "Mike did fight in the European conflict, then after the war he was still with the military and one of the few who spoke fluent Japanese. You see, I didn't speak English all those years ago."

"He was your interpreter?"

He studied the amber liquid. "More of an interrogator, really. I was debriefed by Mike when he worked for army intelligence in San Francisco at the Presidio many, many years ago." He smiled again and chuckled to himself. "Here we are discussing me when all I want is to know about you."

"Just one more question?"

"Certainly."

"Why haven't you asked me for directions to Bone Valley?"

He sipped the rest of his drink and examined me as we took the cutoff from the main road. Sato's interest was seemingly drawn through the window and into the passing desert landscape. He tasted my name, along with the scotch. "Walt Longmire, I have definitely underestimated you."

11

I gently took the hand and kept my eyes on hers. "Mrs. Rondelle."

Continuing to smile, she scooched over, motioning for me to enter. "Have a seat?"

I gestured with the pizza box. "I'm afraid I can't, I'm on a delivery."

"To that spitfire of an undersheriff of yours?" She laughed, patting the seat beside her. "As you can see, I keep abreast of the hearing on a daily basis. Please join me. I won't take up too much of your time, honest."

I stood there.

She shook her head but continued smiling. "We can give you a ride to make up time."

I pointed my chin over the top of the Mercedes and past the courthouse. "It's only half a block."

She reached out and pulled the handle, partially opening the door. "I promise not to kidnap you, Sheriff."

Seeing few options, I opened the door and climbed in with the pizza, then leveled it in my lap. "What brings you to Absaroka County, Mrs. Rondelle?"

"Beverly, please."

I nodded and waited for her to continue as the light changed and the driver took a left, navigating slowly toward the mountains. "Beverly."

She glanced at the boxes that filled the cargo area behind us. "Oh, picking up my husband's belongings from his office down in Cheyenne."

"Long trip, both ways."

"Yes, but I like driving across the rest of the state, if nothing else it reminds me that it exists." She looked toward the front where the driver sat. "Besides, Bennett is good company."

As we approached the corner that led to the parking area, I spoke to him. "Take a left, here."

He ignored me and continued straight.

I turned to her. "So, you *are* kidnapping me?"

"Bennett is deaf."

"Oh."

She tapped the back of his seat and then signed to the bald man in the rearview mirror before turning back to me. "We'll just drive to the edge of town and then turn around and deliver you to your office."

"Okay."

She placed an elbow on the armrest, supporting her stylish gray hair, the smile fading. "You're not going to say it?"

"Say, what?"

"That you're sorry for killing my husband?"

"Of course, I am."

"Of course, you're going to say it or of course you are?"

"Both." I turned a little toward her, the weight of what I had to say lying heavily on my conscience. "Lethal force is one of the things I take most seriously in my line of work, Beverly."

"But you felt as though you had to kill Tom?"

"At that time I felt I had to defend myself—he had shot through a door at me twice. Killing him was a possible outcome, but one never desired."

"What if I were to tell you that Mike Regis had a gun on Tom and had forced him to go to that door and fire those shots?"

"I wouldn't be surprised at all."

She looked genuinely shocked. "You wouldn't?"

"No. Regis made it clear that he felt your husband should be invested if they were going to kill me, but I could tell from the amount of nervousness that Tom's heart wasn't really in it."

She nodded, looking at her lap. "You think my husband was a good man?"

"Not particularly, but I don't think he was a hands-on killer like Regis and the others were that night."

"No, no he wasn't . . . In a boardroom, in a power lunch, he was a gladiator, but not out here in the real and violent world, which is something I'm learning—we're not very much removed from the animals as we think, are we?"

"Sometimes not, but some of us more than others."

She reached up and patted the driver on the shoulder as he wheeled into the Forest Service offices and then drifted the SUV around, turning right, heading back for town. "You know that all I am is a front for the Regis family who are attempting to rebuild the reputation of their son at your expense, right?"

"Actually, no, I didn't."

"They have another son, Phillip, whom they are grooming for public office, but there isn't much hope for that with the cloud of discomfiture or scandal that this distasteful episode has attached to the illustrious Regis name."

"I see."

"They're going to try and depict you as some sort of cowboy sheriff, completely out of control in this little fiefdom of yours in their beloved Wyoming."

"Their beloved Wyoming? They're not even from here, are they?"

"Is anybody in Jackson? The family is actually from Wisconsin, but the important part is that they're after you."

"Yep, I kind of figured that."

She studied my face as I examined the lid of the pizza box. "They have a lot of money and a lot of political connections with which to do that."

"So I keep hearing."

She leaned back in her seat and waited, but I didn't say anything else. "I just want you to know that I don't blame you for my husband's death."

"I appreciate that."

"But I do blame Mike Regis."

I smiled. "Well, I blame him for a lot of things, but he paid a terrible price for his actions."

She leaned forward, lacing her fingers and resting them in her lap. "I'm going to approach you with an idea that I've been warned not to."

"Warned by whom?"

"Legal counsel."

"Then take my word for it, you shouldn't do it."

She took a deep breath and slowly let it out, giving herself time to think. "We're both in a lot of trouble here, you more than me, so I'm thinking we can help each other."

"In what way?"

"I was hoping we could form something of a partnership."

I made a face to indicate that I honestly didn't know what she was talking about. "Partnering to do what?"

"Pool our resources against the Regis family?"

"Mrs. Rondelle . . ."

"Beverly."

"Beverly, I don't think you understand what it is I do for a living." She laughed. "Oh, I think I do . . ."

"No, you don't, just by asking me to take a side indicates to me that you don't understand the nature of what it is I do. I'm not a gang member, I'm an officer of the law. I uphold and defend the rule of law. There are no sides other than truth and untruth. My official job is to protect the people and belongings of the residents of Absaroka

County, although sometimes I get drawn out into a larger scale." I turned my head to look at her. "I'm just a sheriff, but I have the weight and power of the county, the state, and the nation at my back, so if those people want to come at me, they can . . . I'm easy to find."

We turned at the corner and this time, without bidding, the driver pulled into our parking area, slowed to a stop before getting out, and walked around to open the door for me.

I climbed out and got a look at him, a handsome young man, although maybe older than I thought, with pale-blue eyes, muscularly built in a tailored blue suit and silver tie. I nodded to him, at which point we both looked back inside as Beverly Rondelle leaned down to look up at me.

"And you don't think wealth and power can warp that truth?"

I thought about it. "Not in my county."

"Oh, Sheriff—you've got a lot to learn." She looked at me with an emotion that could be described only as pity. "And school is in session."

TUESDAY, MAY 26, 1964

"So, you just finished your college degree in Los Angeles?"

"Yep."

Tadashi Sato continued sipping his scotch and watched the desolate landscape as the DeVille cruised along. "A magnificent city—a man can find anything he wants there."

"I guess."

"You don't agree?"

"Oh, I enjoyed it, but I'm not sure I'd want to live the rest of my life there."

He shrugged. "Perhaps I am biased—it has a wonderful Asian community, and the resources are plentiful . . . Besides, I like the ocean. Do you?"

"Yep. I was a landlocked kid from Wyoming who hadn't even seen an ocean until I got to California."

"And this was after the football?"

"No, before, during, and after. I had a girl I knew who got me and this friend of mine into surfing."

"Surfing?"

"Yep."

He glanced at me, incredulous. "You are too big to surf."

"That's what everybody keeps telling me."

He nodded, smiling as he took out a cigarette case and offered me one, which I declined. "I have never tried it; I was born into a fishing family and even now it is a passion with me. Did you know that there are 6,582 islands in my native country?"

"No, I didn't."

Putting away the case, he pulled a metal lighter from his pocket and lit a cigarette. "I am originally from Rebun, a small island, mountainous, with many fishing villages along its inlets." Studying the lighter, he pushed a small button, which amazingly enough played music. "Do you know this tune?"

I listened but couldn't make it out. "I'm afraid not."

He pushed the button again, silencing it. "Ringo No Uta," or the apple song. It was very popular in the postwar period." He returned it to his pocket. "Surfing . . ."

"Yep."

"Not much of that around here."

"No."

He smoked his cigarette, then cracked the window and blew the smoke toward the space at the top. "So, why are you here, if you don't mind my asking?"

"Just passing through."

"On the way to . . . ?"

"Reporting for duty, we've been drafted."

"Vietnam?"

"In all likelihood."

"Also a beautiful country with a very strong French influence . . . War-torn now, though, the result of centuries of colonialism."

I studied him. "Are you a communist, Mr. Sato?"

He laughed. "Far from it, about as far as you can get . . . Actually, I am a firm proponent of the capitalistic system . . . Trust me."

"And why is that?"

"Of all the facets of humanity, young man, the one inalienable motivation you can count on most is greed."

We rode along, and I finally had to ask. "If you don't mind, what did you do that would require you to be held and interrogated after the war?"

He smoked some more and thought about it. "Are you sure you want to hear that story?"

"I think so."

"Well, I'm not sure I want to tell it." He studied me, taking another drag from the cigarette. "Young people can be so very judgmental. Are you?"

"I don't think so."

"Let's test that, shall we?" His eyes went back to the window. "Have you ever heard of Manshu Detachment 731?"

"I have not."

"I am not surprised in that it was a secret project during the war and something of an embarrassment to both sides afterward. Unit 731 was used for biological weapon research . . ."

"That's against the Geneva convention."

"Yes, and exactly why the Japanese military decided to proceed with it—if it was illegal, then it must work." He smiled as he finished his cigarette and then flipped the butt out the window. "I was a medical student at the beginning of the war and was conscripted. But instead of placing me in the infantry, I was selected to report to the Epidemic Prevention and Water Purification Department of the

Kwantung Army, Kamo Detachment, or Ishii Unit, which seemed innocent enough although odd, and which I was to discover later was actually a facility for human experimentation that had been in operation since the midthirties. You know of the Japanese invasion of Manchuria?"

"I do."

"Since this part of China was under the control of Japan, it was decided that it would be used for the research in that it would provide a deniability if it should be discovered. But more importantly, it could provide a much-needed natural resource in bulk—the Chinese people." He cleared his throat, lit another cigarette, and continued. "I was assigned to a special project called Maruta. Do you know this word?"

"No."

"Logs, the word means logs. I was later to learn that it had been translated from the word *holzklotz*, which means the same thing—interesting to think that the initial research was done in Germany. I still remember superior officers asking how many logs fell in the last experiment."

I mumbled to myself. "My God."

He dismissed my response with a wave of cigarette smoke. "There was no God in Unit 731." He turned to look at me. "In hindsight, the methods were remarkably primitive. If there was a need for a specific body organ, say a brain, the order would go out and soon the guards would drag in a subject, or log. They would hold the log down and break open his living head with an axe. They would then take the brain off to pathology and the rest of this log would be incinerated. Prisoners were routinely injected with diseases and told they were vaccinations, pathogens such as syphilis, gonorrhea, cholera, smallpox, and botulism."

I shook my head in disbelief. "But surely the effects of these diseases were already known?"

"Of course, that's why they were used. It's extraordinarily foolish for mankind to think that he can kill with the lethality of nature, as she has been at the game much, much longer. No, Unit 731 was more concerned with the delivery of these deadly pathogens, how they could be used as weapons. It was only a question of time before the tide would turn on Japan, but we had neither the natural resources nor the manpower to fight an extended war, so we needed an advantage, such as the defoliation bacilli bombs that carried anthrax, typhoid, and bubonic plague—infected fleas."

"Fleas?"

"Oh, yes. A lesson taught to us by the decimation of one third of the human inhabitants of Europe in the Middle Ages. Fleas are remarkably indestructible and, when released on an unsuspecting populace, spread like wildfire into areas of China not occupied by Japanese forces. If I were to estimate, I would say that these experiments were responsible for close to a half million deaths."

I leaned back in my seat and stared at him. "Why don't I know about this? Why didn't people talk?"

"You mean survivors? There were no survivors of Unit 731, and of course all the, uh . . . logs . . . were destroyed."

"And no one found out?"

"You mean the authorities?" He shook his head. "There was great concern when the Red Army of Russia began descending through Mongolia in August of 1945, so the Japanese ministry had over a thousand prisoners and workers shot and the compound destroyed."

"August of '45?"

"Yes." Sato turned to look out the window again. "This date means something to you? By that time the Americans had refined their own particular weapons to obliterate 226,000 people in two quick flashes of atomic light."

"But how did they keep us from finding out about Unit 731?"

"The Japanese government simply denied it, but after they were threatened with the Soviets, they conceded the information to the supreme commander of the Allied forces and the man responsible for rebuilding Japan during the occupation. He secretly granted immunity to all of the physicians involved with Unit 731 to garner the research information and keep it out of the hands of the Chinese, and more importantly the Russians."

"Douglas MacArthur?"

"Yes." He tapped his fingers on the window as we drove by the Bone Valley Internment Camp, the swooping chain-link fence and guard tower becoming more evident. "You find it hard to believe that your government could have been involved in something so immoral?"

We pulled up to where my truck sat on the side of the road, looking like some kind of wounded animal. "That's mine, there."

Sato tapped Nomu on the shoulder and the giant pulled in alongside my truck, with the Corvette tucking in behind. I started to climb out, but the older man placed a hand on my arm. "No, Kenji and Kazuo will take care of it." He reached out again, this time tapping the shoulder of the goateed individual in the passenger seat. "You don't mind, do you, Kenji?"

Without a word, the man climbed out, slipping off his blazer along with the narrow tie that he unthreaded from his neck. Then, tossing them both onto the seat, he closed the door, walked back toward the spare in the passenger seat of the Vette, and rolled up his sleeves.

I had a feeling that if Sato had asked him to climb out and wrestle a crocodile, he would've done it with the same aplomb.

"Are your keys in the truck?"

"They are."

"We will continue then."

Without a word, Nomu put the car into gear and continued over the rise toward town, leaving the others to deal with my disabled truck.

"If you don't mind me asking, what is it you do now, Mr. Sato?"

He placed the glasses and bottle of scotch in the form-fitting compartment in the back of the seat and folded it up before turning the clasp and lacing his fingers on one knee. "Now?"

"I'm assuming you're no longer in the medical field?"

"In a sense, but no. I found my wartime experiences to be somewhat disheartening." He thought about the next words as we pulled up to the pumps at Everson's Last Chance Service Station. "In answer to your question I am in the fixing business, I am in the finding business, and I am in the removal business—and business is very, very good."

Nomu switched off the Cadillac and lumbered out, coming around and opening the door for Sato as the older man reached into the sleeve behind the seat and pulled out a newspaper before climbing out as I followed. The town was very much as I'd left it, maybe more desolate, if it was possible, and the CLOSED sign still hung on the glass door indicating Pickens was still fishing.

I glanced around, wondering where Henry could be, and then took a few steps, staring at the sign and thinking that it was a pretty good analogy for my life right now. Turning, I shoved my hands into my pockets and confronted the men standing by the green car, this time wondering why it had taken me so long to put two and two together. "Sounds far reaching, this business of yours."

"It is." He pulled out his cigarette case, then opened it, lodging a cigarette into the corner of his mouth, then lighting it with the musical lighter that played the bittersweet melody. "Now . . ." He repocketed both and then took a deep drag before tipping his hat back and pulling the *Los Angeles Times* from under his arm. He opened it and studied one of the pages before folding it back and handing it to me. He smiled the cold smile and then tapped the grainy photograph above the article on the sinking of the *El Espectro*—Henry, Rachael, and me standing on the beach talking to the sheriff of Los Angeles County in what seemed like a lifetime ago. "Let's talk about the last time you and your friends went surfing."

———

"We didn't take any of the stuff out on Point Dume, how could we? My friend was unconscious, and I was close to it after dragging the crew out of the water, and by then the sheriff's department was already there."

Sato sat on the bench outside the service station and adjusted his sunglasses as Nomu stood a short distance away, clutching one elbow and looking at me as though I were a lamb chop. "Is that the timing of things?"

"What do you mean?"

"The boat struck the rocks; you and your friend went into the water to save the crew and the shipments were only discovered on the beach after the authorities had arrived?"

"Yep—that alone was almost enough to drown us."

"Tell me about the girl."

"There's nothing to tell; she didn't go into the water because by that time the surf had become too strong. Hell, we shouldn't have been out there ourselves."

"Then why were you?"

I whirled around to look at him. "They were drowning."

Nomu took his hand from his elbow, but Sato waved him off. "But you did not know them."

"No."

"And you did not know what was on the boat?"

"The drugs, no."

He nodded. "A great deal of the shipment of *El Espectro* has come up missing."

"It's probably at the bottom of the Pacific Ocean."

He waited a moment before responding. "Possibly."

"You don't honestly think that we took it." He continued to stare at me through the dark lenses. "Do you?"

He glanced around. "Where is your friend?"

"I don't know, but I'd like to find him and that's my next order of business."

"And ours." He smiled.

"So, you guys tracked us all the way from Los Angeles?"

"There were questions as to why you had left town so suddenly . . ."

"We were drafted!"

He spread his hands, gesturing to our desolate surroundings. "And yet, here you are in the middle of nowhere, and only you."

"How did you find us if even we didn't know where we were?"

He cocked his head. "I told you; it is my business."

"Was it Mike Tanaka, the PI out of Phoenix?"

"I am afraid, like newspapers, I do not divulge my sources." He stood, pushing his porkpie hat back on his head and stuffing his hands into his pockets; he came toward me, angling, like a snake. "The wounds on your head, you say that someone struck you and left you for dead in the desert?"

"Yep."

"And yet, you were stitched up, able to borrow a motorcycle and even a weapon?"

"It's a long story."

"We have plenty of time."

"I don't. I want to find my friend and get back out on the road."

"How long have you been here?"

"Two days."

He gave me a questioning look. "Two days to get your truck fixed?"

"The guy who owns the place—Pickens—he couldn't get the parts."

He turned and looked up the road where my truck came over the rise and approached us, the Corvette coming along behind. "And the tire that Mike had fixed?"

"We were on our way out of town when I swerved to avoid something . . . something on the road and blew out the tire."

He watched as his cohorts parked behind the Cadillac. "What?"

"What, what?"

"You said you avoided something on the road. What was it?"

I sighed, thinking about how if I kept talking, I wasn't going to end up believing me either. "A kid, a kid in a mask."

"A mask?"

"Yep."

"A Halloween mask?"

"No, one of those theatrical Japanese masks like you see—not Kabuki but Noh theater. Hannya mask—'angry woman face,' is I think what my friend Henry said."

"He is Japanese, your friend Henry?"

"No, he's Northern Cheyenne, but he notices those kinds of things, cultural ethnicities are of special interest to him."

Sato nodded, walking past me as the others joined Nomu, who now leaned on the grille of the big car. "A child in a traditional mask roaming the streets of a ghost town?"

"I thought it was odd too."

"Are you lying to me, Mr. Longmire?"

"No."

He nodded for a moment and then without looking, pointed toward the thin guy and the big guy. "Kazuo, Nomu, show him what is in the trunk."

They moved in that direction, but I stood still, listening to the desert wind as it scoured the landscape. "I don't think I care to see what's in your trunk."

Pursing his lips as if kissing a thought, he stared at the ground.

"I don't know what you guys do for a living or why you're here, and to be honest, I don't want to know. It wasn't any of my business back in Malibu, and it's none of my business now."

"I still want you to see what is in the trunk of my car." He pointed at Nomu. "Give him the keys."

In a flash they were thrown in my face, and I barely caught them before they bounced off my nose. Standing there holding them, I waited a long while and then took a deep breath and started around the other side, where Kenji stood.

He stepped out of the way and extended a hand, allowing me to pass as I continued by and came around the rear of the DeVille. Sticking the key in, I turned it, lifted the trunk lid, and stared into the cavernous interior.

I stood like that, thinking about what I was looking at, a million questions racing through my head as I tried to not let my imagination overrun my rational thought.

Gently closing the trunk lid like a coffin, I pulled out the key and then threw it at Nomu, who wasn't quite as quick as I had been, and watched as the keys smacked him in the face and fell through his hands as he bent and scooped them up, dropping them into his pocket before considering me without a shred of emotion.

I stared back at him, then passed Kenji and came around the front of the car before sitting on the front of the hood and staring at the pavement myself. "Any reason why it is I had to see that?"

Sato came over and sat on the hood beside me. "I thought it best for you to understand the severity of our business."

"Did he do anything to warrant that?"

"When we visited him, we discovered two packets of the shipment in the floor of the closet in his apartment."

"Before or after you killed him?"

"Does it matter?"

I thought about the last time I'd seen Deputy Reeves alive on the sidewalk in L.A., swapping football stories. "He played strong safety with the Cal Poly Mustangs in San Luis Obispo in '58; they were 9-1."

"Strange, the things you remember about people when they are dead." He pushed off, stretching his back and then turned. "He worked for the people who hired me."

"Unfortunate."

"For him, yes." He glanced back at my truck. "We have searched your vehicle."

"I figured."

"And found nothing."

"I figured that too."

"So, now we need to speak with your friend. Henry, is it?"

"Yep."

"Any idea where we should start?"

"I'd say over at the bar/café across the street."

"The Astoria?"

"Yep."

He turned and walked in that direction, studying the building as he continued. "How urbane."

I glanced around and could see that the others had pushed off the big four-door and were moving toward me, slowly, like herding dogs. Waiting a moment, I shrugged, turned, and followed Sato as he paused at the corner, taking the time to look both ways. "There isn't much traffic."

"One can never be too sure." We crossed the street and then he paused to look up at the sign above the door. "Why the Astoria?"

"Judge Everson, the guy who owns the town? His son died on-board that ship during the war when it was sunk by a Japanese torpedo."

"Oh, my."

He continued up the steps as the others followed behind me, Nomu raising a hand to push my shoulder. "You touch me again, Oddjob, and I'm going to break off your arm and beat you to death with it."

Without turning, I climbed the steps and caught the door as it swung after Sato's entrance, finding him standing in the middle of the room, taking in the shrine.

He gazed at each photograph and piece of memorabilia. "Amazing."

"His father is somewhat fixated."

He crossed toward the bar and looked at the painting, the others joining us, fanning out a little behind me; Nomu standing by the door in sentry duty. "What does this Everson do?"

"Oil, I think, but he used to be a circuit judge."

He sat on the same stool Henry had the night I'd been removed from town. "Does anyone work here?"

"Everson's granddaughter; she's half Japanese."

"Truly?" He continued glancing around. "More forbearing than I would've thought."

I picked up the book that was lying there and sat on the stool at the other end of the bar, taking a moment to turn it over and look at the cover. "Not really."

There was a noise from the kitchen as Noriko appeared between the swinging doors, surprised to see us there.

Sato stood, sweeping off his hat and subtly bowing. "Kon'nichiwa."

She also bowed, ever so slightly. "Ohayō gozaimasu."

"Your accent is Hokkaido, northernmost prefecture . . ." He smiled, shaking his head. "I have not heard it in years."

She placed a hand over her mouth in embarrassment. "The man who taught me was from the forty-seventh prefecture."

"Pat Fujita says hello." She turned to look at me as I leafed through the paperback, her eyes wide. "I met him, in the desert, yesterday."

Sato glanced at me and then returned his eyes to her. "By any chance would you have some food? My friends and I are famished."

She looked at me again and then came over and stood in front of him on the other side of the bar. "I'm afraid it's American food."

"That's fine, we're all citizens here." He smiled, placed his hat on the seat beside him, and dropped his sunglasses in there before taking a seat. "First off, do you have any coffee?"

"Certainly." She started to go but then turned and spoke to me. "And you?"

"Coffee, please."

We watched her go and then he turned on the stool to study me as I rested the book face down on the counter. "She does not look happy to see you again."

"No, she doesn't." I watched as the other two moved to the table nearest the bar, Nomu staying at his post by the door.

"She looked genuinely surprised to see you."

"Yep, she did, didn't she?"

Reappearing with a tray of mugs and the a silver coffeepot, she started to serve the two men at the table, filling their cups and then noticing the giant by the door, who looked at her impassively. Going behind the bar to fill Sato's mug, she moved to fill mine as well, and I watched as she sat the mug on the bar.

She'd just started to pour when I placed my hand over the mug in order to meet her eyes.

"Where's Henry?"

She stared at me, the pot suspended above my flattened hand, her eyes completely still. "Henry, who?"

12

"She wanted to make a deal."

"What kind of deal?"

We sat there on the floor of the cell, eating pizza and drinking wine, even though I'd cheated and gotten a can of Rainier from the downstairs refrigerator. I picked up the can and swizzled it a bit, taking another swig. "Does beer go bad?"

"In a can, generally, no." She leaned forward to get my attention. "What kind of deal?"

"Beverly Rondelle seems to think we need to team up against the Regis family, whom she's pretty sure is coming after me."

"Does somebody need to remind them that you aren't the one who killed their son?"

I sat the beer down. "Maybe I need to get in touch with Ruth One Heart."

"Auntie Ruthless?" Leaning back against the concrete-block wall, she sipped her wine. "Where is she these days?"

"On her way back to DC."

"So, Rondelle says this is not only personal but political?"

"I guess they've got another son they're grooming for political office, so they need somebody to wipe the bad taste out of the voting public's collective consciousness here in the state."

She raised her glass. "And that's you?"

"Cheers." We touched the rim of her wineglass to my can, and she sipped. "Easier to go after some bumpkin sheriff in Wyoming than pick a fight with the United States Department of Justice?"

"Something like that." I picked up a piece of pizza and considered. "The thing I don't understand is that they've got a recording of the entire time Regis and his bunch had me tied up at my grandfather's place, and as far as I know that's admissible."

"With a federal court order, but those generally last only thirty days and aren't necessarily public record . . . They might be sealed." She picked up a slice for herself. "Got any pals at the DOJ?"

"None that I can think of."

She sunk the extended canine tooth of hers into the pizza and started to chew. "Might be good to know."

I took a bite and thought about it. "I'll wait and see if we go to trial."

"Do it now. I happen to know that you have in-house counsel."

"I'm trying to keep her out of this."

She took another bite and chewed. "Why?"

"She's in the running for AG."

That got her to stop chewing. "Your daughter, attorney general for the state of Wyoming?"

"Let me emphasize the phrase, *in the running*."

"Shit, we'll be able to get away with a lot more than we did with Joe Meyer."

"I don't think that's the idea."

"Joe's retiring?"

"From what I am to understand."

She continued eating and eyeing me as a smile crept across her face. "How long was Meyer the AG?"

"Coming up on ten years."

"Gotta be a record."

"It is."

The smile grew broader. "How are you going to like having your daughter for a boss?"

"Well enough to not let her get involved in this prelim-hearing mess."

"All she would be doing is making a phone call."

"No."

"Then call Ruthless yourself."

Having lost my appetite, I tossed the piece of pizza back in the box. "I'll just wait till we find out if there's a holding order—no sense stirring up a hornet's nest until we need to." When I looked back up, she was smiling a melancholy smile. "What?"

"I like it when you say *we*."

TUESDAY, MAY 26, 1964

I said the words slowly. "My friend Henry."

She stared at me. "I don't know what you're talking about."

"Are you crazy?" I glanced at Sato and then back to her. "Henry Standing Bear, Northern Cheyenne, about six-foot-four and two hundred and thirty pounds, built like a running back because he was one, goofy John Lennon Greek fisherman's cap, disgustingly handsome with jet-black hair down to his shoulders, because they made him cut it to play football? *That* Henry."

She stared at the floor. "I don't know who you're talking about; I've never seen anybody like that."

"Really?"

She nodded and began backing away. "Yes."

I reached over and flipped open the book next to my hand, *The Complete Poems of François Villon*. "This is his book. He got it from one of the classrooms at the internment camp the other day—the day I met you on the steps of one of the barrack bunkhouses."

She glanced at the others and then back to me. "I think you better leave."

I stood. "I'm not leaving until I find out what happened to my friend."

Noriko moved back to the wall where a phone hung and picked up the receiver. "I'll call the police."

"Please do."

"No, don't." Sato gestured for her to put it down and then sipped his coffee. "Our friend here is a little excitable and may have gotten confused about some things." He turned to the two sitting at the table. "Kazuo, when you searched the truck was there enough luggage for two men?"

He flipped off his sunglasses and slid them onto the table. "No, only one suitcase and a bedroll—enough for only one and the clothes seemed to be this one's size."

"You went through my suitcase?"

The skinny one smiled at me. "We went through everything."

Noriko hung up the phone and approached Sato. "Are you the police?"

"Something like that—more lost and found." He sat his mug down and then turned and gestured toward the sports car parked on the corner near the service station. "Perhaps you know our friend Mike Tanaka? We have his car and would like to get it back to him."

"I don't know anyone by that name."

He paused just a moment too long. "Really?"

"Yes."

"Well, we must have the wrong town."

"What?"

He turned to look at me. "We should drink our coffee and move on."

"I'm not going anywhere." I turned to Noriko. "Look, I don't know what kind of game you're playing here . . ."

"Mr. Longmire, we should go." He sipped his coffee one last time and then stood, picking up his hat and placing a small card on the counter. "This is an exchange number; if you should see either of these two men, would you call it, please?"

Noriko took the card and examined it, giving him a curt nod before returning her eyes to the floor. "Certainly."

I turned, figuring there wasn't anything else to do, following Sato to the door and then turning to look at her. Her eyes were still on the floor as Nomu opened the door and held it. I started to say something more, but then just let the words die in my mouth as I turned and walked out.

Standing on the boardwalk, I looked around trying to figure out what I was going to do just as Sato came and stood beside me. "She's lying."

He lit a cigarette, and we listened to the musical lighter for a moment before he closed it. "How do you explain the missing suitcase?"

"Whoever took Henry took his suitcase."

"You don't think he could've just left, gone on?"

"He wouldn't do that. Besides, she said she'd never met him." I nodded back inside. "Did you see her face when I mentioned Pat Fujita."

"Yes, I did." He took a drag on the cigarette. "I believe that was before she composed herself." He turned to look at me through the dark lenses. "Who is Pat Fujita?"

"A desert rat, the one who saved my life and loaned me the motorcycle."

"And the gun?"

"Yep."

He nodded. "And how does she know him?"

"He was interned in the camp down the road, and he taught her, Everson's granddaughter, Japanese." I took a step off the curb and out into the street. "Look, I don't know what you guys are going to do, but I need to find my friend."

"And we need to find Mike Tanaka."

"Why?"

"The less you know about our business, the better."

I watched as the other three came down the steps and stood with him. "Why didn't you tell me about the suitcase missing from my truck?"

He stepped off the curb and walked toward me. "In my experience it is sometimes better to allow people who are lying to continue lying—they become more confident in their lies and then they make mistakes. An excellent example would be Deputy Reeves in the trunk of my car . . ." He turned to his men. "Speaking of, we should be doing something with the body before it becomes truly offensive."

"Well, you can do whatever you want, but I'm going to look for my friend."

"No, I am afraid that you will have to come with us."

"And if I don't?"

He shrugged and grinned a smile without the slightest bit of warmth in it. "We are already digging one hole."

Nomu and I were just about done digging the grave when I leaned on the shovel handle and looked up at Sato, squatting by the edge. "Explain again why it is that I had to help dig the hole?"

"You are young and in miraculous shape like Nomu; it only made sense that the two of you should dig the hole."

I glanced over at the bald man, not quite as tall as me but every bit as wide. "He doesn't sweat?"

The head man studied his hireling. "He doesn't appear to."

"What's his story?" I wiped the copious amounts of sweat from my face with a sleeve and began digging, the two of us continuing to bump into each other. "Is he some kind of athlete?"

"Sumo."

I stared up at him. "Really, wrestling?"

"Used to be, but as you can see, he has retired."

"Why can I see?"

"Sumo wrestlers are not allowed to drive cars and if they do, they can receive a lifetime ban from the sport."

I thought about it. "All right, I have to ask, why?"

"Any modern technology is seen as impure or a distraction. Besides, at his wrestling weight he didn't fit behind the wheel."

The giant continued to silently dig. "Does he ever talk?"

"Not unless it is something genuinely important."

I nodded as my partner in crime climbed from the hole and turned to look down at me along with the other three, giving me a distinct and niggling feeling that my life span was drawing shorter. "Is this where you guys kill me?"

Sato made a face. "Why would we do that?"

I glanced around to indicate the ridiculousness of that question. "Because I know you killed a guy and are burying him out here in the middle of the desert?"

He began counting off on his fingers. "One: how do you know we are the ones who killed him?"

"Well . . ."

"Two: are you not helping us to bury him?"

"Yep, but . . ."

"Three: don't we need you if there is any hope of retrieving any portion of the shipment for which we are looking?"

"Okay . . ."

"Four: doesn't that make you an accomplice to the crime?"

"I suppose, but I could still talk."

"Five: I would advise against that since you will soon be in a war in Southeast Asia, and it would be very easy to arrange your disappearance there."

"Okay." I reached the handle of my shovel out to Nomu, who gripped it and easily pulled me out of the hole with one hand, where we stood, almost nose to nose. "For now."

Nomu and I watched as the other two men took over and unlocked the trunk of the big sedan and carried the body, wrapped in a sheet and plastic, unceremoniously tossing it into the makeshift grave with a resounding *thump*.

I watched as they removed their jackets and ties and began shoveling sand into the hole, spelling us out. "So, Reeves was involved with the drug smuggling?"

Sato raised an eyebrow over his sunglasses. "The shipment, yes. It would appear that the working wage for Los Angeles County deputies is not very high these days."

"Don't you guys worry about some kind of backlash from all this?"

"Possibly, if we were discovered, but doubtful since we are only subcontracted—we have no personal connection to any of this business and the police will be solely looking for that." He took a few steps and turned to me. "So, speaking of suspects, who do you believe might have abducted your friend?"

"Judge Everson."

"The man who owns the town?"

"Yep."

"Then we should go talk with him."

I snorted as I walked around the hole. "That might be easier said than done."

"And why is that?"

I looked over the grave at the man. "He's not the talkative type, and he hates everything Japanese."

"And yet his granddaughter is at least part Japanese?"

"Half."

He folded his arms. "Interesting."

"Had you ever heard of the Bone Valley Internment Camp before?"

"No."

"How about the Tokyo Twelve?"

"No."

"Neither had I, but doesn't that make you curious?"

"No." He glanced down into the grave that was slowly filling. "For me, young man, the past is the past—nothing good can come from digging around in it."

"What if I were to tell you those stories; enable you to hear those voices?"

Unfolding his arms, he stuffed his hands into the pockets of his slacks, then turned and walked away. "I have made a life of ignoring those voices."

I watched him go and saw Nomu slipping on his suit jacket and sunglasses, assuming the fig-leaf position, gripping his hands over his crotch. "How about you, Oddjob?"

Predictably, he said nothing.

Walking around the grave, I moved over to the big car where Sato sat and had flipped down the back of the driver's side rear and was talking on what I assumed was a radiophone. Not wanting to overhear, I continued toward the rear and sat on the trunk lid, waiting for him to finish.

Unrolling the sleeves of my shirt, I unbuttoned the second button at my collar and waited. After a moment, Nomu walked past me and then looked back at the other two, watching as they finished filling the hole with dirt and sand, his eyes finally returning to me. At least I thought they were, in that it was hard to tell with the sunglasses.

We stood there looking at each other, but I didn't see any reason to try to start another ill-fated conversation. It was about then that he surprised me by speaking in a lung-vibrating bass. "He will not kill you."

"Really?" I stared at him for a few seconds, and then slipped on my Ray-Bans in a sunglass-duel. "How do you know?"

"He is an honorable man."

I laughed. "He poisoned and murdered people wholesale in China . . ."

"That was during wartime."

I stared at him for a moment and then gestured toward the grave. "And what about our friend, Deputy Reeves over here—what do you think he has to say about it?"

He stared at me for another long while and then started to walk past but paused. "For your information, the character Oddjob you mentioned from *Goldfinger*, the seventh novel in the James Bond series by Ian Fleming, is Korean, not Japanese."

I watched him go as he returned to the grave and took off his jacket, carefully folding it and placing it on the ground with his sunglasses. Then he grabbed the shovel from one of his comrades, evidently unhappy with the progress they were making

"He likes you."

I turned to find Sato who, sitting halfway out of the car, had hung up the phone and was looking at me. "How can you tell?"

He stood, stretching his back. "There has been a change in plans."

"Nifty phone in the car there."

"It has its advantages." He tipped his hat back and turned to look at me, and I could see the .45 Colt stuffed into the front of his pants. "Our work here, for all intents and purposes, is over. The people we work for are satisfied that no one here had anything to do with the missing product, and we can now return to San Francisco."

"And that's it?"

"Yes."

"What about me?"

"What *about* you?"

I patted the quarter panel of the Cadillac. "So, you guys just drive off and leave me here in the desert, that's it?"

He smiled the cold smile. "That depends on whether I can count on your discretion."

I took a deep breath and let it out slowly, shaking my head at the absurdity of my situation. "I'm not so sure you can."

"You have no idea how sorry I am to hear that."

"I could lie to you."

"You could, but that would be beneath you."

"Well then, let's get this over with . . ." I pushed off the Caddy and stepped toward him a little faster than he was prepared for, grabbing his arm and pulling him toward me, slipping my hand to his beltline and snatching the semiautomatic. Spinning him around, I held the muzzle to the side of his head. "Don't move. I haven't ever killed anybody, and it'd be a shame if I had to start with you."

He said nothing, and I moved him forward to where two of them were shoveling and the driver, Kenji, was mopping his forehead with a handkerchief. Having finished wiping his face, he turned to me, froze, and then slowly reached for his armpit.

"Don't."

The other two stopped shoveling and now also watched me.

Sato raised a hand, and they appeared to relax.

I cleared my throat. "Yep, welcome to the Not-Okay Corral." Releasing the boss, I stepped away just in case he tried to duplicate my actions. "You guys need to get out of here, and I'm not going to stop you, but I also don't intend to get shot doing it, okay?"

Sato glanced at the others and then back to me. "You are sure this is what you want to do?"

"No, I'm not really sure of anything right now except that I need to go find my friend." I glanced over their shoulders. "Town is that way?"

"A couple of miles." He smiled again. "We can give you a ride?"

"Thanks, but no thanks."

"As you wish . . ." He moved toward the jade-colored sedan as the others drifted behind him. "What makes you think we won't simply wait for you in town?"

"It'd be beneath you." I gestured with the gun, moving the others toward the Caddy. "I need the keys to my truck."

Kenji stopped and then reached into his pocket slowly, perhaps realizing the opportunity to be shot by an amateur is much greater than that of a professional. He tossed the keys to me along with my rabbit-foot. "I hope it brings you luck."

"Me too." I let him take a step before calling out to him. "I need the keys to Mike's car."

He smiled and shrugged, regarding Sato, who gestured for him to do as I said. "You can't blame a guy for trying."

I caught the keys to the sports car and looked at the head man. "I'll see that he or his wife gets them."

They all started to climb into the Cadillac as their boss shut the door and nudged to one side, pulling out *The Complete Poems of François Villon* and handing the book through the window to me. "Your friend, he might want his reading material when you find him."

I waited until the others had climbed in and closed the doors before approaching the open window and holding out my hand. "He might at that."

Sato handed me the book and then paused. "One more thing?"

"Yep."

"When you catch up with whoever has your friend." He extended a fist, palm down. "You might need these."

I shoved the book under my arm and spread my hand out under his, whereupon he dumped a handful of .45 ACP ammunition into it. I stared at my reflection in his sunglasses as Nomu started the engine and slipped it into gear. "I think you and I will meet again, Mr. Longmire."

I lowered the empty weapon and backed away from the car, a little sheepish as I watched them go. "Not if I have anything to say about it, Mr. Sato."

It was a short walk into town, but I had plenty of time to eat humble pie along the way with a side of extreme humility and plenty of self-effacement to wash it down.

From the distance, through the heat waves undulating from the dirt road, I could see my truck and Mike's Corvette still parked in their respective spots.

When came upon the boardwalk, I could see from the sign that the Astoria was closed and there were not many signs of life anywhere else either. I kept moving toward the Last Chance Service Station but paused for a moment when I saw some movement under the church porch.

Reaching up, I rubbed the knotted ridge on the crown of my head. "Not again."

I stopped, there in the middle of the road, and stared into the gloom of shadow, finally turning and walking in that direction, crouching down and peering under the porch. "Howdy. If you're under there, I'm looking for my buddy—and even though nobody seems to see you in this town, I bet you see everything."

I squatted there for a moment longer and then started to stand when a stag-handled Bowie knife a little over a foot long was tossed from under the porch to land at my boots in the dusty street.

I picked it up, looking at the signature turquoise bear-paw design in the elk bone.

Raising my face, I could see the demon mask looking back at me from under the porch. After a moment, she gestured toward the back of the church, so I assumed she wanted me to come in that way.

I stood with the knife and glanced around before circling the building, straddling the short fence and cutting through the grave-yard and up the steps, where I found the back door hanging open just a bit.

Pushing it fully open, I stepped inside, allowing my eyes to adjust to the darkness.

There were no candles this time, and with only the painted windows there wasn't too much I could make out. Glancing to my right, I could see the doorway I'd been looking through when somebody had cracked my head, and as I moved forward, I kicked something, and the noise it made sliding across the floor convinced me that it was the piece of wood that had done that deed.

I carefully pulled the opened door toward me, staying against the facing to look inside. Once again there were no candles burning, but a few slivers of light brightened the room just enough for me to see the center aisle where the girl had been kneeling just the other night.

The rug she had been kneeling on was pushed, and there was a trapdoor open, the lid thrown back.

Looking around, I crept forward, moving past the altar and

scanning the pews and walls. As near as I could tell I was alone and, other than the open trapdoor, nothing in the place had changed.

I got to the altar and looked down the center aisle and could see candlelight flickering in the room below. Stepping forward, I looked the rest of the way in and could make out that there was a rickety ladder propped up in the hole. What light there was flickered from out of sight, but I could still see some old milk crates against a wall and a dirt floor.

I stuffed the knife into my belt, pulled the .45 from my waistband, and circled the opening but couldn't see much else, finally figuring the only way I could was to step onto the ladder and climb down. Doing just that, I would've traded the Colt for a flashlight in a heartbeat.

The ladder shifted with my weight but held, and I started making my way into what looked to be a hand-dug cellar, at which point I glanced around as I descended in hopes that I wouldn't get hit in the head again.

Reaching the floor, I stepped back and turned the boxes lining the walls, finding they were canned goods and preserves. There were a few pieces of broken furniture and a table in the center of the room with a person lying on it.

Stepping forward, I laid the gun on the table and reached over to pick up a candleholder, lifting it so I could see who it was.

It didn't take long to figure out it was Mike Tanaka. Someone had patched him up fairly well, stitching and cleaning his wounds, but he was still in pretty bad shape. There was even a makeshift splint on his left arm with a couple of pieces of wood and some cloth wrapped around them to hold his wounded arm in place.

My inspection had made its way up to his face when I saw his one eye looking up at me. "Are you really here?"

"Mike?"

The breath halted in his throat and then he forced the words out. "Are you real?"

"Yep, I'm real." I leaned in, turning his face toward me a bit. "What happened?"

"Everson's thugs got me as I was trying to get your tire fixed. They brought me back to town and we got into an argument . . ."

"I figured, but how did you get down here?"

His eye cast about. "The girl, the one in the mask."

"I saw her . . ."

"They left me on the street, and she pulled me under the porch of the church."

"Yep, we're in the cellar of the church right now, but I've got to get you out of here and get you some medical attention."

"No, no . . . I don't want to draw attention to her." He looked up at me. "Or you."

"Who is she, Mike?"

"I don't know, but she's strong." He smiled, glancing back over his head toward the part of the room that fronted the main street. "She dragged me under the porch and down through a crawlspace and even lifted me onto this table."

"She's the one who doctored you up?"

"Yeah."

"Well, she got my attention out front, but she doesn't seem to be here now." I held his head, trying to make him more comfortable. "Do you know where Henry is?"

"No, but I need to tell you something."

"About Tadashi Sato?"

The one eye stared at me.

"I met him, out in the desert."

He leaned his head to one side and coughed. "How? What were you . . . ?"

"I got clobbered here in the church and then dumped out there where I met Pat Fujita, the sole survivor of the Tokyo Twelve, who helped me get back. So, Tadashi Sato is a friend of yours?"

"Not exactly a friend . . ."

"Employer?"

He shook his head in my hand. "More of a co-employee."

"So, whoever hired him hired you?"

"Yes. Look, something you should know . . ."

"Rest. I know a lot of it already. They seem to be satisfied that Henry and I didn't have anything to do with the missing drugs."

"Where are they now?"

"On their way back to the coast."

He nodded, even though his energy was fading. "It was a business opportunity. I didn't think you had anything to do with that stuff, but they were looking for the two of you and I didn't think they would harm you—just dumb luck that they found you while looking for me."

"Sato, his men, and I stopped in over at the Astoria, and Noriko pretended she didn't even know who Henry was."

"She's just trying to protect herself."

"Well, we've got to get you out of here and I need an ally."

"No . . ."

I pulled one of the set of keys from my pocket and sat it on the table beside him. "Your car is out front and I'm not taking responsibility in getting the keys back to you. Now, if I can get Noriko to take you to the nearest hospital in my truck, where would that be?"

"Prescott."

"Then you can contact the authorities and get them back here while I look for Henry."

"You're going to get yourself killed."

"He's my friend, Mike."

"He may already be dead."

"I hope not, for their sake." I lowered his head back onto the surface of the rustic table, sat the candle back down, and then picked up the gun and stuffed it into the back of my pants. Just as I started to leave I saw some movement at the other end of the room and the dug-out ramp that led under the porch.

The effect of the flickering candle on the mask was dramatic as she raised her face to look at me, the teeth on the disguise a golden color, different from the other parts and more metallic looking.

Afraid that I was once again talking to a mask hanging on the dirt wall, I took a step forward, but then watched as it receded into the darkness. I stopped, raising my hands to show that I meant no harm as the flickering light of the candle slowly revealed the hideous face again.

I watched as it tilted forward, and just as Henry had shown me in the barrack, the emotion of the mask changed, now looking so sad.

I didn't want to scare her, especially after she'd confided in me, but I wanted her to know that I was going for help and that I'd be back.

I gestured toward the wounded man. "Thank you."

The demon mask nodded a curt response, and I was tempted to go over to her or pull the knife and ask her specifically about Henry, but I was afraid she might run away.

I started up the ladder and had made it only two rungs when I felt a hand on my leg and stopped, then turned to look down. She was there, her hand on my calf as she looked up at me through the eye-holes of the mask.

"I'll be back."

Gently slipping from her grasp, I got to the top of the ladder and stepped out onto the floor, then reached over, taking ahold of the trap to shut it when she reached up toward me and the light from above.

I stared at her hand for a long moment and then began lowering the door.

"I promise."

Closing it, I started to pull the rug over when I noticed the twine attached to the other side of the door and watched as it was pulled through a hole in the floor from below, further disguising the trap-door from outside view.

Who could she possibly be? Who could live like this for years, like a ghost?

I stood and walked back toward the altar, taking a right and heading for the doorway to the antechamber, but then stopped to look back at the threadbare rug that covered the trapdoor as if it wasn't there—and thought about the hand that had reached up to me in the darkness like a flower breaking from the dark earth.

It had been a small hand.

But it hadn't been a young hand.

13

Instead of heading out to the courthouse first thing the next morning, I made a call to the Department of Justice Treasury Task Force and was told that Agent Ruth One Heart was on leave. "I figured that, after the shooting, but I'm in a preliminary hearing and was hoping I could speak with her?"

The woman on the other end rustled through some papers, and I was strangely comforted by the fact that the federal government still had such things. "As far as I know, she hasn't been here at the office at all."

"You mean, in the last few days?"

"That's what I mean."

"Well, where did she go? She was supposedly on her way there a couple of days ago."

"That would be hard to say—once we have an agent go on leave, they go on leave. Aruba, maybe? I know she's gone there before."

"Aruba?"

The woman on the phone sounded distracted. "Yeah, they tell me it's nice."

I clutched my forehead in an attempt to dissuade the headache that was erupting there. "Is there any way I can contact her?"

"You can leave a message on her voicemail, but I don't know if she's checking it."

"Thanks." I waited as she transferred me, and I listened as the familiar voice told me to leave a message after the tone. "Hey, it's your older and favorite nephew calling . . . As far as I know, I'm your only nephew. Anyway, I'm wondering if the recording you did the night of my abduction is sealed or available, because I'm struggling through a preliminary hearing and could use that information possibly before I go to trial. Anyway, the office manager at the DOJ just said you were on leave and might be, in of all places, Aruba? Call me back, please?"

After leaving the number, I hung up the office phone and thought about where I wanted to sleep tonight. Vic was in my usual holding cell, so I could take the other and figured that was where Dog and I would end up.

Walking out of my office, I looked around for my backup but remembered that the beast was sharing the bunk with Vic because she was smaller and could allow for such things.

It looked like I was on my own, but I wasn't really sleepy, so I walked down the steps, opened the door, stepped out onto the concrete landing, and leaned on the iron rail. It was a beautiful night, and I always enjoyed my town when it was asleep like this.

Hearing a noise, I turned and saw Dog sitting on the other side of the glass door.

I opened it and watched as he passed me, trotting across the sidewalk and onto the lawn of the county courthouse. He lifted his leg on one of the pine trees there and I waited, but when he was done and lowered his leg, he took a few steps toward Main Street.

"Hey."

He ignored me and crept forward toward the front of the courthouse.

"Hey. Don't go off after squirrels, okay?" He kept going, so I followed just to make sure he didn't disappear into the silent town.

As I turned the corner, I saw him trotting around the front of the building to the far side. Hustling to keep up, I got there and could see he was sitting by a bench, having his head scratched. I preferred to err on the side of caution, however, so I slipped my hand down, un-strapped my .45, and placed my hand on it. I figured it was somebody just heading home after a late night at one of the bars, or a part-time insomniac just out for a walk in the warm night air, but then why had Dog gone right over?

Keeping to the right, I circled the bench and came up from behind.

I noticed the person there had long hair, wore a leather jacket, and was pretty good sized. At first, I thought it might be Henry, but there was something that told me it wasn't my best friend—first off, he would've known I was there, and second, he would've already made some kind of smart-ass remark.

As I got closer, I could see the individual was tall but not Henry big.

I stood there and watched Dog being petted, aware that my backup was usually a better judge of character than me.

I reattached the leather strap and walked behind the bench, then circling around I sat and turned to the individual sitting there pet-ting my dog. She gave his head one last scrub and then looked at me, pulling the curtain of silver-laced black hair from her special-agent face. "You rang?"

TUESDAY, MAY 26, 1964

Circling behind the church, I stopped when I saw the two Everson trucks setting outside the Astoria, the local work crews having come in for lunch—which meant I had a choice.

First, I had to get assistance for PI Mike and the only hope of that was Noriko. She may have pretended to not know who Henry was in the face of the friendly neighborhood yakuza, but she couldn't turn down trying to help the private investigator unless I'd dreadfully overestimated her.

So, go in, confront the others, and hold them there, then send her on her way to Prescott?

And who was going to help her get the wounded man from under the church without letting everyone know the exact location of the demon-masked individual?

I was suddenly missing the San Francisco mob.

The equation—how do you subtract one Japanese waitress from a half dozen oil-rig workers and leave one Wyoming cowboy?

Distraction. But what kind of distraction?

It was about then that I heard a throaty motor fire up, the throttle blipping a few times. I listened as the vehicle, whatever it was, engaged the clutch and roared from the other side of the church. After a moment it came into view, and I was stunned to see Mike Tanaka's Corvette blasting into the crossroads of Bone Valley and then swerve to the right toward the parked trucks and then peel off to the left in a power-sliding donut, spraying dust and gravel in a monumental cloud.

Incredulous, I could see the tiny person in the driver's seat, which had been pushed all the way forward, her thin arms flailing at the steering wheel, the demon mask cocked back, giving the impression that Satan was behind the wheel and having the time of her life.

The sports car went full circle before shooting straight ahead and vrooming away, hitting third gear and blistering north.

I stood there at the corner of the church and was partially concealed in the dust, watching as the men poured from the Astoria, scrambling for their trucks and clamoring in hot pursuit, or as hot of a pursuit as the sluggish work vehicles could muster.

They headed north, buried in the dust of the Vette, and disappeared as I stepped out onto the road. I waited a moment to be sure they were actually gone before crossing the street, clomping up the steps, and swinging the door wide to find Noriko standing behind the bar in utter surprise.

"C'mon, we don't have much time."

She stood there, staring at me. "Look, I don't know why you said you didn't know Henry, but I've got a wounded man in the basement of the church, and he needs medical attention."

"Who?"

"Mike Tanaka."

"That can't be. Mike just drove by."

"That wasn't Mike, that was whoever the crazy person in the demon mask happens to be." I moved back toward the window and looked after the rapidly disappearing vehicles. "Look, Mike is hurt, and we've got to get him to a hospital, a real hospital like the one in Prescott. You drive, right?"

"I do."

I reached out a hand. "Then come on before they get back."

She came around the bar, untying her apron and throwing it on the countertop. "There's no way she could've been driving that car."

"All I know is that she was wearing that mask."

We scrambled through the door. "I need to lock up."

"We don't have time for that."

I started for the back, but she broke off and headed toward the front of the church and the porch. "It'll be faster this way."

I paused for only an instant and then followed as she led me to the other side of the porch. I watched her as she removed a section there that covered the foundation, revealing a portion from which the blocks had been removed, and I could see that there was a tunnel leading down into the room where I'd been.

"You knew this was here?"

She said nothing but gave me a glance before crawling down the dirt chute.

I followed, even though I wasn't sure that I would fit.

I did, but just barely, and could see Noriko scrambling out the other end. Following, I shrugged my way down to find Mike standing by the table. She held him up. "Where the hell am I?"

I took his right arm and glanced at the ladder but immediately dismissed the idea. "Under the church, but we've got to get you out of here before Judge Everson's men get back."

"Where are they?"

"You wouldn't believe me if I told you." Half carrying him toward the chute, I watched as Noriko climbed in, turning to reach her arms out to take Mike's as I fed him into the tunnel and then pushed him up as she pulled. He groaned a few times and cried out only once when she pulled his injured arm a little too hard, but I was amazed at the progress we made as we got him to the outside and then propped him against the steps of the church. "Wait here, and I'll go get my truck."

Running across the street, I pulled the keys with the rabbit-foot fob from my pocket and jumped into the half-ton. Firing up the truck, I pulled through the pump island at the service station and then wheeled around in front of the church where Noriko already had Mike up and on his feet.

Setting the emergency brake, I opened the door and came around to help her get him into the passenger side of the bench seat, then shut the door. I escorted her around the truck, put her in, and trailed my eyes north, where every other vehicle in town had gone. "Get him to the hospital and then get the authorities: Prescott PD, Sheriff's Department, its Highway Patrol—I don't care who, just anybody."

She stared at the dash as if she hadn't ever seen one.

"Where's Henry?"

She turned to look at me. "I don't know, honestly, I don't."

I glanced north but still couldn't see anybody. "Why did you say you'd never seen him?"

"Those men you were with, I didn't like them, they looked dangerous."

"Well, you're right about that."

She continued staring at the instruments on the dash, then at the oversize wheel and the stick shift.

"You're sure you can drive this thing?"

She reached over and pulled the door away from me, slamming it shut and turning and releasing the emergency brake as she pushed in the clutch pedal, shifted into gear, and popped it. Like a bull pawing the dirt in granny gear, the half-ton barked a start in granny gear and then veered off south as she called out to me, lurching away. "Sure I can, my mother taught me."

Last man standing, I stood there in the middle of the deserted street and wondered where my friend was and how I was going to find him. The only place I could think to look for him would be at Everson's, but how was I going to get there? It would take all day to walk, and chances were that Everson's men would see me somewhere along the way.

Not for the first time in the American Southwest, I was a man in need of a ride.

I was beginning to miss Over-Jenny.

At the Last Chance Service Station there was a monstrous tow truck parked in one of the bays. It would mean breaking and entering, and it would also mean hoping that the keys were in it or in a place where I could find them.

I found my feet moving in that direction.

Working my way around the outside of the building, I found a back door with a singular pane that would be the easiest to replace. I found a rock about the size of a softball and crashed it into the wire-reinforced glass, breaking it, but the wire still held.

Reaching back, I slammed the rock into the wire and bent it inward enough to chip the remaining shards away, then peeled it back with my hand far enough to where I could reach down and feel the handle, releasing the knob and then turning it from the outside.

Extracting my arm, I saw it was bleeding a bit where I'd scratched the underside, but not enough to bother with bandaging. Pushing the door open, I stepped into the room where we'd first met the mechanic what seemed ages ago.

I moved through it quickly and went into the front of the shop to look around, and there, hanging on a nail, was a key on a fob.

Snatching it from the nail, I entered the first bay and spotted the loop of rope on the right that opened the garage door. Pulling the thing, I raised the door and stuck my head out to see if there were six guys waiting for me, but the street was empty.

Wherever the desert demon was, they were leading the Everson roustabouts on a merry chase.

Returning to the slowest vehicle in Bone Valley, I slipped inside and stared at the confounding multitude of buttons, levers, and other assorted instruments. Spotting the ignition switch, I slipped the key in and pumped the gas one time, hoping that I wouldn't flood the thing, and hit the starter.

"C'mon . . ."

The V-8 sputtered once and then rumbled to life with an off-sided idle.

Grinding the gears on the first try, I noticed the gas gauge was at half a tank. Backing it out, I swung around and hit the brakes, shifting into first and letting out the clutch as the tires, propelling me forward, bit into the dirt.

I was getting used to the stiff clutch, so wheeled past the pumps and turned right, up the road toward Everson's place. The one-ton had a suspension like a Conestoga wagon, but I figured I'd still have kidneys by the time I got there.

Wrapping a fist around the suicide knob, I directed the big truck east and thought about what, exactly, I was going to do.

Pulling the Colt from the back of my pants, I lodged it into the seat beside me and thought about how far I was willing to go to get my friend, and try as I might, I couldn't see that distance at all. If the judge and his men had taken Henry, then they'd made their own bed and now had to sleep in it.

Making the foothills, I shifted down into second to climb the hill leading to the expansive house, although listening to the free exhaust, I figured I wasn't going to sneak up on anybody.

I turned into the driveway, circled around, and then stopped in the exact spot where we had parked the unconscious Lester. I hoped I wasn't headed for a Round Three, because if there was, I wasn't going to be easy on him. Killing the engine, I opened the door, stepped out, and looked up at the deck to see if anybody was looking down at me. The coast appeared to be clear, so I reached back in, pulling the semiautomatic out with me.

Moving toward the house, I figured I'd start with the part I knew and climbed the stairs to the deck, then keeping to the left and looking through the space in the drapes. The place seemed the same, but I couldn't see anyone.

Moving to the right, I found the handle, slid the glass door open, and surveyed the room. Everson's glass was still on the side table where he'd left it, and even mine was sitting on the mantel underneath the noose. I could see two doors, one leading to the left with stairs and possibly the garages below, and one to the right, which hung open, that I assumed led to the inner sanctum. Heading in that direction, I spotted something interesting sticking out from the shelf underneath the bar—the butt of a shotgun stock.

Backtracking, I stuck the .45 into my pants and pulled out a J. Stevens 520A 12-gauge trench gun not unlike one I'd seen in the hands of Lucian Connally, the sheriff back home in Wyoming at one time. The bluing was a little worn, and there was a crack at the base of the stock, but it handled more like what I was used to, and I needed a little familiarity.

I noticed the safety was on, and it was indeed charged and ready for action, even against a small multitude.

I thought I could hear voices from somewhere inside the house. Creeping up to the doorway on the right, I paused and listened but couldn't hear them anymore.

I wasn't too concerned if someone saw Pickens's tow truck out front, figuring they'd assume it was him.

Easing around the jamb, I looked down a hallway that opened into what seemed to be a kitchen. I listened some more and then started that way, leading with the trench gun—even going so far as to push off the safety.

Pictures hung on the wall, and I glanced at them as I made my way; photos of Everson in his judicial robes, shaking hands with state dignitaries, including Barry Goldwater, as well as pictures of his two sons—Andrew, the one in uniform, and the other, Parker, not. There were also older photos of a woman who I assumed was his wife and I couldn't help but wonder what the story could be there, assuming she must've run off—and I didn't blame her.

I heard the voices again, but this time they were farther away.

Edging into the end of the hall, I looked around in the kitchen and a dining room to my right. There was another hallway across the room, which I assumed led to the bedrooms, but I figured they probably didn't have Henry in there.

Backing up, I thought I'd look in the other direction when I heard the voices again, this time much closer. Ducking back, I waited—it sounded like a couple of individuals had entered the kitchen and then stopped, although continuing their conversation.

The one voice was younger and a little whiny with what sounded like something wrong with his mouth. "I don't like this."

There was a pause and then another voice, muffled and nasal. "Well, I'm not crazy about it either."

"Why do we have to do it?"

"Because we were told to." There was some shuffling and what sounded like somebody pulling out a chair or stool. "Look, the quicker we get this done the better."

"Who's going to do it?"

"We'll flip a coin."

"I'm serious."

"So am I."

"You were in Korea, so you've done this kind of thing."

"Not like this."

"But you did it, right?"

There was a pause and then an agonized noise before the nasal voice continued. "I was a cook, what do you want me to do, poison him with shit on a shingle?"

"How are we supposed to do it?"

"I think we're supposed to shoot him."

"With what?"

"Judge's got a shotgun in the living room, under the bar." There was a longer pause. "Personally, I'm never going anywhere near that guy."

"You can say that again. If Lester hadn't slipped him a mickey at the bar and then hit him over the head, I think he would've killed us all."

"Well, he's chained to a radiator now."

"This is going to be a hell of a mess to have to clean up."

"We have to clean up after we do it?"

"You can't just leave a dead body and all that gore down there." There was another extended pause. "Well, which would you rather do, shoot or clean up?"

"Neither."

"Well, you have to do one 'cause I'm not doing it all."

The chair scooted back. "I'll clean up."

"You're sure? 'Cause I'm not helping, especially if you end up puking your guts out."

There was another long pause. "Maybe I should shoot?"

Having had about as much as I could take, I stepped into the kitchen, trailing the 12-gauge trench gun like a howitzer in the direction of the voices.

Trying to adopt a more serious expression, I stared at the two men who looked as if they'd gone all ten rounds with a half-dozen heavyweight champions of the world. In as bad shape as they were, they still raised their bandaged hands and stared back at me with black eyes, each of them a mass of broken bones, bruises, and contusions.

I angled the Stevens away, figuring they weren't much of a threat in the condition they were in. "How does the other guy look?"

Neither of them answered.

"Where is he?"

Neither of them answered some more.

"Guys, I know you can talk; I've been listening to you for the last five minutes."

The older one with the bandage across most of his bruised face was the first to speak. "We didn't have anything to do with this."

"Yep, you look and sounded pretty innocent." I glanced at the younger one whose hands were almost completely wrapped and splinted. "What were you going to do, beat him to death with this shotgun—you don't even have a trigger finger."

As he spoke, I could see he was missing a few teeth as well. "He like to kill us."

"I'm amazed he didn't. Where is he, downstairs?"

They nodded in unison.

I gestured with the gun. "Let's go."

Herding them along in front of me, we made our way back down the hallway and into the living room, where we made a right and moved toward the stairwell. I saw the older one thinking about closing the door behind him. "Don't. I think you guys have had enough, and, if not, this riot gun will make a hell of a mess that I'll make the other one of you clean up."

The older flipped on the lights in an impressive garage lodging a number of Everson's trucks and equipment parked in stalls as long as the house itself. The older one kept moving as we approached a steel door along the back wall before stopping. "In there."

We stood, looking at each other, the younger one's face turning back and forth between us like a tennis match.

I broke the silence. "Well?"

"I'm not opening it."

"What were you going to do, shoot through the door?"

"Yeah."

Pushing the two of them aside, I knocked.

Nothing.

"Just so you know, if he's dead, it's not going to end well for either of you." I rapped my knuckles on the door again. "Henry, it's Walt."

The door snatched open, and we all fell back as a pipe was swung at our heads. It dented the metal doorjamb instead—the pipe being attached to the hand of a very large and vengeful Northern Cheyenne Indian, while the wrist of his other was cuffed to a radiator.

He towered over the two men who had fallen and were now covering themselves in fetal positions, then glanced at me and rubbed his head. "It took you long enough."

I turned to the other two on the floor. "I think the two of you are lucky I came along."

Henry dropped the pipe and dragged the radiator out to stand in front of us like he was taking the thing for a walk. He looked a little worse for wear but still game as he turned to the older one, speaking down at him. "Do you have the key to these handcuffs?"

He peered at the Cheyenne Nation through his fingers. "Um, no."

The Bear rubbed his jaw and then reached for the pipe on the floor again. "Then I am going to kill you."

I put a hand out, gesturing toward our surroundings. "It's a shop, I'm sure we can find something that'll cut them off."

He seemed disappointed, and I noticed he didn't have any skin left on the knuckles of either hand. "Very well . . . *Then* I will kill them."

"The demon stole the Corvette?"

We watched as the younger one, Del, continued to try to hacksaw the cuff from Henry's wrist. "Yep."

The Bear nodded his head, sage-like. "It is a very strange demon."

"Agreed." I lowered my head so Del could see my face. "If you could quicken it up a bit? We're kind of in a hurry here."

He redoubled his efforts as the Cheyenne Nation glanced at Will, the older one, and then back at me. "Pat Fujita is alive and living in the desert?"

"Yep, and he was one of the Tokyo Twelve, the one who loaned me the motorcycle and the gun. I used that to get to another town— but I don't remember what its name was—that has the church where Father Pietro was after the incident here."

"And Pietro is still alive?"

"No, he died up in Idaho, and Father Kinnell, the younger priest, is the one I met who told me the story."

He shook his head in amazement or perhaps attempting to clear it after being drugged. "Where does the yakuza come into this?"

"There, when I found Mike Tanaka's car, they pulled up and I got grilled about the missing drugs back in California."

"And they are the ones who had the deputy's body in the back of the car."

I nodded. "The one we buried out in the desert."

"And then they drove off and left you?"

"At gunpoint, yep."

"They are confident we are innocent?"

"I think so."

"And Mike?"

"I think he's the one who got wind of the situation and told them where we were."

"And who beat him?"

I shrugged, and we both looked at Will and Del, the older man the first to speak. "Not us, you're the only one we beat up."

"And the demon was nursing him?" Henry asked.

"Yep and provided the distraction to get rid of Everson's men so that I could loan my truck to Noriko, so that she could get Mike to a hospital."

"And then you came looking for me."

"Yep."

"You have been very busy."

The chain on the cuffs was proving to be more than a little difficult to saw through when I spotted a key hanging on a hook above one of the tool boards and reached up to pluck it off, shouldering the oil-rig worker out of the way and then unlocking Henry.

"Convenient."

"Yep." I pocketed both the cuffs and key in my jacket, then turned to the other two. "Where is the judge?"

"I don't know."

"He wasn't with the others, at least I didn't see him." I turned to Henry. "Did you hear anything?"

"No."

Will looked over the fleet. "His truck is gone."

"Where would he go?"

"Couldn't really say. He sometimes goes to Prescott or other places."

I was incredulous. "With a man chained up in his garage?" They didn't seem to have an answer for that, so I turned back to Henry. "C'mon, let's go."

He walked over and picked up the pipe. "You two, come over here."

They froze, and I didn't blame them.

"Now." Reluctantly, they went, and I followed as the Bear opened the door to the room where he'd been imprisoned. "Get in there."

If possible, they were even more reluctant now. Filing in, they looked at him as he lifted the pipe, bringing it down with all his force and annihilating the knob on the inside of the door, sending it skittering over the concrete floor. Slamming the door, he bashed the outside knob in the same manner and then tested the door by trying to pull it open through the gaping hole. It didn't move, and he turned to me, satisfied.

"They thought you were going to kill them."

"I might have if you had not been here."

"Tough guy." I led us to the door that opened by the stairs to the carport and looked out to see the two Everson trucks that had been in town chasing the demon-driven Corvette. "Crap."

"What?"

"They're out there, at least their trucks are."

"Give me the shotgun."

"No."

"Give it to me."

Giving up, I handed it to him but pulled out the Colt. "Keep in mind that if we go to the authorities, it would be best if we haven't killed anyone."

Nudging me out of the way, he braced himself against the door. "Why would we go to the authorities?"

"Do you see this going any other way?"

"Certainly."

"With us shooting everyone?"

He placed a shoulder against the door and a hand on the knob. "The possibilities, as they say, are endless." Throwing his weight into it, I watched as it flew open and, firing the shotgun, he stepped onto the concrete.

As I followed with the .45 in my hand, I was relieved to see he had unloaded on one of the rear tires of the nearest Everson truck and then weaved to the side before firing it into the tire of the second. Then he hurried toward the tow truck on the far side.

I placed a hand on his shoulder as we ran. "Not that one, it's our ride."

We scrambled for the big truck, keeping an eye on the balcony above, but no one had arrived yet. Climbing in, I handed Henry the Colt and then hit the starter, pumping the gas.

It turned over but didn't catch.

"Oh, hell . . ." Grinding it again, I didn't pump this time, remembering what Pickens had said about flooding the thing. I continued grinding the starter and listened as the power began running down.

We heard some noise from above, and I was pretty sure that we were assembling a crowd when a bullet shattered the back glass in the tow truck.

Without a thought, Henry opened the door and swung out, levering the trench gun on the balcony above and scattering double-aught buckshot in that direction. The sound was tremendous, and there were a few shouts as the Bear fired again before ducking back down and looking at me. "This position is indefensible, so either we get this truck started or we run for it!"

I hit the starter again, but this time it caught for a second.

Another rifle slug shot through the roof and broke the driver's side window to add impetus to our escape. So I was pleasantly surprised when the V-8 roared to a sputtering start, belching black smoke from the rear.

Henry dove in, and I made a sweeping turn to the left, circling around the work trucks and directly below the balcony in hopes that they would have trouble shooting at us through the redwood deck.

Blasting out of the carport, I headed for the road as more shots were fired, glancing off the heavy equipment on the flatbed section at the rear of the truck.

I'd just turned onto the main road when another truck appeared, coming in another direction, and I made a swerve to the right to miss hitting it. I'd pulled up almost beside them when I saw Judge Everson's surprised look.

Turning left, I slammed into the rear quarter panel of his truck, almost knocking him from the road, and watched as he veered to the left, burying the thing in the ditch, skinning a lodgepole pine and sliding to a stop in a cloud of dust.

Pulling back and centered on the road, I hit the gas, taking the big truck up to about as fast as it would go, considering its low gearing.

Henry turned his head for a moment to look through the shattered rear glass. "We are fortunate in that the shotgun had only four rounds in it."

"Is anybody following us?"

Placing the butt of the scattergun alongside the transmission hump with the action open, he hunkered down to look at the side mirror and then shook his head. "Nothing. I cannot help but imagine that until they get another truck out of their garage and get assembled that they will be able to follow us."

"They'll need Everson for that."

He slumped back in the seat. "Yes."

Keeping the accelerator floored, we cleared the trees at the base of the foothills and looked straight ahead where the road disappeared at the horizon toward town. "So, now what?"

"I am not sure."

"We go to the authorities."

"And say what."

"I don't know much, but I know that there's no statute of limitations for murder, especially mass murder—ten people were hanged in this place twenty years ago."

"I thought it was the Tokyo Twelve?" He stared straight down the road, shaking his head.

"What?"

"I cannot believe you came to rescue me in a tow truck."

14

"So, not so great-aunt?"

She continued petting Dog. "Nope, a half aunt to be exact but nobody really says that anymore."

"So, just aunt?"

"Yeah."

"Which means you'd be Cady's great-aunt One Heart."

"Yeah."

"And Lola's great-great-aunt One Heart."

"Yeah." She sat back in the bench and tugged on Dog's ear. "And what am I to you, monster?" He stared up at her with unadulterated love as she looked out onto the silent street, the traffic lights having switched over to a blinking yellow. "Nice time of night."

"Yep, quiet. My favorite."

"In answer to your question, yes, the recordings of the confrontation the night out at your grandfather's place are sealed."

"Why?"

"I would imagine because the IRS is all over this fraudulent mineral fund like salsa on an Indian taco."

"And billions of dollars to the Internal Revenue Service takes precedence over some sheriff in Wyoming?"

"Pretty much."

I nodded. "Well, you're not the first meeting I've had tonight."

She laughed. "I heard your undersheriff is sleeping in the brig?"

"After drinking wine and eating pizza."

She held out her wrists, the ribbed cuffs of her flight jacket riding up her arms. "Geez, take me in, Sheriff."

"Beverly Rondelle stopped by to tell me she wasn't taking me killing her husband too seriously."

She dropped her arms with a shrug. "Big of her."

"And that she thought we should team up against our mutual enemy."

"What, the IRS?"

"No, the Regis clan, who she thinks are after me in an attempt to whitewash the family image."

"But I'm the one who shot Mike, not you."

"And that's why I'm telling you, because if they're after me they're most certainly after you."

"Legally or physically?"

"I don't know, and it's possible that Beverly Rondelle is simply overreacting, but she doesn't strike me as the overreacting type."

She nodded. "I'll have my connections at the DOJ give them the once-over."

"It might just be a state thing in that they're positioning their other son, Phillip, for a political career here, and I quote, in *their* beloved Wyoming."

"They're from here?"

"Wisconsin."

"Maybe it's an honest mistake, they're both W states." She reached out and pulled Dog's ear again. "When is your preliminary hearing over?"

"Excluding any earthshaking revelations, my guess is by the end of the week."

"I'll head back to DC and put in a good word to get the recording released."

"Thank you." I sighed, the fatigue of the day getting to me but feeling the conversation should be longer. "Are you flying that bumblebee of yours all the way back east?"

"I am."

I stared at her.

"What?"

"I was kidding." I shook my head. "I mean, you mentioned it, but I didn't think . . ."

"It'll take about three days with the fuel stops, but I've done the flight plan so many times I've got it memorized." She smiled. "I'd invite you along, but they might see that as a flight risk."

"I better stick around."

She stood, popping the leather collar of her jacket up. "So, do I get to see my great-great-niece when I get back?"

Following her lead, I also stood. "I'll make arrangements with the assistant attorney general to get you on the calendar of the assistant to the assistant attorney general."

"The AAAG?" We walked around the front of the courthouse. "I hear she's not going to be assisting for very much longer?"

I shook my head. "You want to know the difference between a Wyoming state secret and common knowledge?"

"Common knowledge is harder to come by?"

"You got it." We stopped at the base of the stairs of the old Carnegie Library I called an office as I turned to look at her. "Please be careful."

She reached out and took my hand. "That's sweet . . ."

"I'm not kidding."

She studied me and then placed a hand on my shoulder. "You're not, are you?"

"No, I'm not.

She nodded and then reached down and scrubbed the top of Dog's head. "You look after him, you hear?" She turned and started for the street. "And you look out for him, you hear?"

I watched her go and couldn't help but feel a slight sense of unease as I listened to her footfalls echo on the sidewalk in the empty town. Maybe I was just getting nervous in my old age, or maybe I just enjoyed her company, or maybe I was right.

I ran a hand over Dog's head just to get his attention before starting up the steps, but then stopped when he didn't follow. "Hey?"

He glanced back at me with his big, bucket head, then sat there before turning to look in the direction where Ruthless One Heart had disappeared.

TUESDAY, MAY 26, 1964

"It would appear that the demon has come home to rest."

Indeed, Mike Tanaka's metallic-blue Corvette was parked under the awning at the Last Chance Service Station. "I guess she got tired of lapping them all over the Arizona desert."

I pulled in front of the garage door and parked, then got out and watched as Henry, still holding the shotgun, shut his door. I went over and tugged the loop of rope and waited until the glass-paned door was all the way up before he asked. "What are you doing?"

I gestured toward the tow truck. "I think we should return the borrowed vehicle before we leave."

"And then what?"

I glanced at the sports car, and then back at the tow truck, and finally at him again. "Which, pray tell, do you consider to be the better getaway car?"

He conceded the point. "So, we drive to Prescott, grab the truck and our bags, check on PI Mike and Noriko, report everything to the authorities, and then hit the road?"

"I doubt it will be all that easy, but yes."

I climbed back into the tow truck, pulled it into the stall, and gathered my things, hanging the key back on the nail before exiting and allowing Henry to lower the garage door. I handed him *The*

Complete Poems of François Villon he'd become so attached to, and we started toward the Chevy when Henry stopped. "There is only one problem."

"What?"

"The keys are missing."

Shoving the .45 into the back of my jeans, I peered at the dash and saw that he was, as usual, right. "Well, hell."

We both glanced around the empty streets, me looking toward the church and the Bear looking toward the camp. "Do you think you can hot-wire it?"

Looking at the newfangled contraption that bore a striking resemblance to a Mercury space capsule, I shook my head. "I wouldn't even know where to start."

He took a step toward the street. "Then we need to find the demon."

"That may prove to be a problem in that she's avoided capture around here for who knows how long." I took a step into the street. "This is all so weird . . ."

He looked up the road leading back to Everson's place and then walked back over to lift the garage door. "We are running out of time."

"I know. What are you doing?"

"Getting the box of shotgun shells Pickens has in his storeroom."

I stood there, wondering how many rounds I had in the Colt, finally pulling it from the small of my back and dropping the magazine—five.

Henry reappeared, stuffing his jean jacket pockets with ammunition and lowering the garage door as he crammed the book under his jacket. "You do not wish to leave the demon."

I turned and stared at him. "No, I don't. She's made a concentrated effort in trying to help Mike and us—exposing herself to a great deal of danger."

"There are only two places she could be."

"That we know of."

"You take the church, and I will take the camp."

"Okay, but what do we do if they show up here?"

"Avoid them until we can get to the car with the keys. If they arrive, stay hidden, and I will too. If they are here, and you are not, I will come and find you in the church."

"Under the church, there's a rug in the middle aisle on the sanctuary—just pull it back and you'll see a trapdoor that leads to the basement."

"Got it." He turned and started trotting off, the shotgun in hand as I called after him.

"Be careful!" He raised a hand in response and soon disappeared over the rise that led to the internment camp as I turned to the church, muttering to myself. "Time to get religion."

I crossed the street and thought about crawling through the foreshortened tunnel under the porch, but then decided I should do a sweep through the church before dropping into the basement.

Rounding the church, I stared at the flowers that appeared alongside the picket fence that surrounded the tiny graveyard, wondering who could be buried there. Hopefully, we'd finally get a chance to talk with the demon, but who knew if she even had a voice or was in any way sane?

After what I thought she'd been through, I had my doubts.

Circling behind, I came up on the small porch only to find the door shut this time. I turned the knob and felt relieved when it nudged open. The place looked much as I'd left it, but I wasn't sure of what to do, because roaming around calling for a demon didn't seem prudent.

I checked all the anterooms, but there wasn't anyone there or any signs there had been. I'd just started into the sanctuary when I saw something at the edge of the platform where the altar sat, a tinfoil something.

Drawing closer, I could see it was a small plastic tray covered with foil.

I reached a hand down and could feel the heat coming off the thing and could only surmise that it was hot food.

Who could possibly be responsible for keeping the demon fed other than Noriko, who I knew at this point was somewhere in Prescott, miles away.

Peeling back the covering, I could see it was meatloaf, mashed potatoes, green beans, a slice of white bread, and a small carton of milk.

"Someone had to take care of her." I turned to find, of all people, the slouching figure of service station manager Donnie Pickens lodged in the doorway.

"How was the fishing?"

Ignoring my remark, he came the rest of the way in and glanced about. "Where is she?"

I watched as he moved down the side, looking through the pews. "So, when you clubbed me here in the church, you were just trying to protect her?"

He straightened, looking across the sanctuary at me. "Why aren't you gone?"

"You mean, why am I not dead out in the middle of the desert where you left me?"

"I knew Pat would find you, I just didn't figure you were stupid enough to come back."

"So, just abandon my friend and my truck?" He didn't answer. "So you know about Pat Fujita out there?"

He nodded. "I deliver him supplies too."

"His gifts of the divine providence? Like the motorcycle?"

He actually smiled. "Yeah, I didn't take into consideration that he'd kill himself on it . . . Tools, equipment, sometimes food I drop off. I think he knows it's me, but we have a mutual agreement about ignoring each other."

I nodded and then studied my boots, planted on the hardwood floor. "To answer your question, Henry and I didn't want to leave the demon unprotected here."

"She's protected. She's been protected for more than twenty years now."

I let the dust settle on that one before volunteering my suspicion. "It's Mae, isn't it? Mae Mayko Oda, Noriko's mother, the one who was married to Everson's son Andrew."

Pickens came around the back and up the center aisle, then stood on the rug that covered the trap door. "How did you know?"

"A feeling. She didn't move like a child, and when I saw her hands, they weren't the hands of a child. Besides, Noriko slipped and told me that her mother had taught her how to drive, and how would she have been able to do that unless she was still here when Noriko came of age?"

"She always liked to drive . . ." Pickens grouped his stained, knotty hands together. "We would go out in the dark after Andrew died, but she was crazy and wanted to drive around out there with the headlights turned off, like she used to with him. I don't know how many things we ran into."

"So, Noriko and you were the only ones who knew she was here?"

"She slowly began losing her mind, and hell, who can blame her?" He nodded, reaching up and pushing his welding cap back on his head. "At first just me, but I knew she wanted to see her daughter and I knew her daughter missed her—it just wasn't natural."

"It couldn't have been easy."

"No, no, it wasn't."

"Donnie . . ." I took a step toward him. "What happened?"

"What do you mean?"

"That night in '43 with the Tokyo Twelve, what was it that happened?"

He looked away from me and at the floor, but finding no comfort there he gazed up at the vaulted ceiling. "Horror, that's what happened . . . a damnable horror."

"Tell me about it?"

He retreated and sat on the edge of the platform. "Everybody lost their minds around here for a while. There was always animosity between the camp and the town. Everson didn't want it here, especially after Mae and Andrew took a shine to each other, but I thought things were calming down. But then Andrew was killed, and things just spun out of control."

"Meaning?"

"The government was stretched pretty thin at that time and after making the mistake of building the camp, they discovered that they couldn't spare the staff and support for keeping it open—I mean, really, an internment camp for a couple of dozen people? It was asinine . . ."

"Why didn't they just return them to the regular camps?"

He shook his head. "They'd already made examples of them, and I think they were thinking about just shipping them off to federal penitentiaries, but before they could do that, Everson saw it as his patriotic duty to volunteer and take care of the place." He shook his head. "Can you imagine? Hating it as much as he did—the government came in and gave a few of them some training and then just handed them the keys and walked away."

He stood and crossed in front of the altar, trying not to pace but pacing nonetheless.

"It worked for a while, hell, they even had dances and softball games . . . That's how Andrew and Mae met; the dances, discussing books, and he'd take her out for long drives in the desert . . ."

"What happened?"

"She got pregnant with Noriko, and I think things changed for Everson."

"In what way?"

"He started to soften a bit, certainly toward Mae and definitely after Noriko was born." He shook his head. "After Andrew was killed, things went all to hell. Everson decided he didn't want his granddaughter being brought up in an internment camp, so he came down here and offered to buy Noriko from Mae."

"Buy her?"

"Maybe not in so many words, but yeah. He told her that the bunch of them were going to end up in prison and that they'd take the child away and put her up for adoption, and did she really want her daughter brought up by strangers when she could at least be with blood relatives?"

"So she gave Noriko up?"

"What other choice did she have?" Pickens turned and crossed in front of the platform again. "I thought it was over with, but I guess Andrew's death kept preying upon his mind and pretty soon Everson decided that those people had to go; that he couldn't have them down here reminding him of his dead son." He looked at me, and I could see the welling tears in his eyes. "There were a couple dozen of them that had been thrown in with the malcontents, so Everson put in to have them transferred back into the general population camps. Hell, for all I know he did the paperwork to get the Twelve shipped off too." He stared at the ground. "But they didn't ship off that last dozen . . . I wasn't there, but they hanged all of them at once, from the rafters of the barrack, kicking chairs out from beneath 'em. They didn't do a very professional job and most of 'em strangled to death before being shot. I'd heard that they were kicking, screaming, and choking . . . It was a mess. They hung from the legs of some of them to kill 'em and then set the place on fire."

He breathed a deep sigh.

"In the confusion with all the smoke, I was able to get into the building and get Pat down without killing him and just carried him out of the place on my shoulder."

"And Mae?"

"When I got back inside, I could see that the rope they hanged Mae with broke or burned and she was still lying there on the floor, alive." He sobbed and then swallowed. "They were drunk and didn't see me stuff Mae in a coal chute in the floor—she was small and fit. I stayed there until the fire was going good and then went outside and got her out of there. I dragged her under the next building and the next until I finally ran out of buildings and carried her over here to the church and Father Pietro. We hid her under the church and built her a place . . ."

"Why didn't you just get her out of here?"

"You don't know what kind of condition she was in; her neck was broken, third-degree burns all over her body, and she'd half lost her sensibilities. By the time she'd gotten herself together, her mind was almost completely gone. Now, where do you suppose you take a person like that, not now but in wartime?"

"Where did the mask come from?"

"I guess back in her other life in Seattle, Mae used it in them damn plays she was in. I think she retrieved a couple of 'em from one of the barrack bunkhouses that are still standing and started wearing one and never stopped." His voice cracked. "Nobody ever came out here to check on what happened until that reporter from Phoenix showed up a few years back and started nosing around."

"Alan Yoshida."

"Yeah."

"And what happened to him?"

"I don't know. Then that PI, Tanaka, showed up and started asking questions."

"Were you involved with that?"

"No."

I made a noise in my throat. "Do you seriously expect me to believe that you weren't involved with any of this?"

"Believe what you want."

"You honestly don't know what happened to the reporter, Alan Yoshida?"

"Oh, I'm sure he's dead out there somewhere buried in the sand,

and I've got suspicions about who did it—probably the same one who almost killed Mike." He continued pacing. "When I found Tanaka after they'd beaten on him, I told them I'd finish the job and brought him down here. I get those jobs every once in a while—that's how I got that desert rat, Pat, out of here. They think I'm some kind of grim reaper who finishes the job, but all I do is try to get people out of this town alive, when I can—like you."

"Everson hung his own daughter-in-law?"

He ignored my statement and went on. "They don't trust me any-more; they know I know too much, and I might tell what I know, but first I've gotta get them out of here."

"Who?"

"Noriko and Mae."

"Well, we'll help you."

He laughed. "You can't even get yourself out of here."

"We might surprise you." I glanced down at the trapdoor. "In the meantime, you don't know where she is?"

"No, but she hasn't touched her dinner." He looked back at me. "Do you know where Noriko is?"

I thought about whether I believed all the things he'd just told me and decided I did—nothing else really made sense. "She's driving Mike to Prescott in my truck to get him tended to, which is why we need to find Mae and get the keys to his car—at least that was our plan."

"And where's your friend?"

"Henry's at the camp, searching for her."

"Then we should go there, because that's the first place they'll be looking for you."

We'd just started to move toward the back door when we heard a car pull up in front of the church, and Pickens stopped, listening. "I don't know that vehicle."

Changing directions, we moved down the main aisle and toward the front doors that faced the service station. Once there, Pickens pushed one of the doors open a bit to where he could see through the crack and out onto the main street. "It's a group of guys in a Cadillac."

"Let me see." Crouching down, I could see Tadashi Sato standing in front of the big sedan and leaning to talk to someone in the back of the Caddy while two others fanned out in a bodyguard fashion. "I know these guys."

He turned to me, incredulous. "You know these guys?"

"Yep, I just don't know what they're doing back here again."

"Again?"

"Yep, things happen when you go fishing."

He glanced through the crack in the door as Sato raised up and lay an arm on the roof of the car, tipping his porkpie hat back and then taking off his sunglasses and massaging the bridge of his nose. "They don't look like reasonable individuals."

"They're not; the last time I saw them they had a body in the trunk, and I had to help them bury it out in the desert."

"What?"

Pulling back, I stood. "How about I go out there and talk with them?"

He watched as the large man, Nomu, walked into the street, all the while staring at the church. "They don't particularly look like talkers either."

I pulled the .45 from my pants and handed it to him. "Maybe they just need more help burying bodies."

He stared at the big Colt. "This is Pat's?"

"Yep, he loaned it to me." I nodded toward the street. "They took it away from me last time, and I don't see any reason in letting them do it again."

"And what if they stuff you in the trunk this time?"

Turning and moving down the aisle between the pews, I yanked open the door to the anteroom and started out the back. "Feel free to throw a few shots into them."

Hopping over the graveyard fence, I rounded the building with my hands in the air and wondered what I was going to do and say, but my mind was made up for me when the two gunmen's hands went for the insides of their coats.

"Don't shoot."

They looked back at Sato as he rose up from the open door pulling his hat back down and turning to see me. "My friend, you're still here?"

Keeping my hands up, I stopped in the middle of the street and shrugged. "Not of my own volition." I glanced at Nomu and the other one. "You're missing a man."

Sato spoke to someone and then moved around the car and approached me, waving his hands at the others to indicate that they could relax. "Where is your friend?"

"Um . . . Doing some investigating."

He met me in the middle of the street. "Us too—and what have you discovered?

Stuffing my hands into my jeans, I stared at him. "Absolutely nothing that could be of any interest to you."

He grinned the enigmatic smile. "How about you let me be the judge of that?"

"I don't know what you mean, none of it has anything to do with the stuff you're looking for."

He folded his arms, walked past me toward the church, and then stared at the spire and then the door. "What an amazing structure." He drew a deep breath and then slowly let it out. "You know, religion is a funny thing. It can bring solace to so many, but I have also seen it rob them of so much. Perhaps it was my experiences in Manchuria, but I have never been able to exercise the certainty of mindset that religious people seem to achieve."

"I think they refer to it as faith, but I'm afraid I don't understand . . ."

"And neither do I." He turned back to look at me. "I am not en-lightened enough to know what is going on a great deal of the time but am insightful to know when something is wrong. My very survival has depended on this ability, and I have honed this perception into a business acumen."

I shook my head, more than a little uncomfortable as to where this conversation might be leading. "Meaning . . . ?"

"You have told me that you and your friend had nothing to do with the incident back on Point Dume."

"That's right."

"And yet, in the small time I have spent here, I seem to feel that something is wrong in this place, something terribly wrong, and this triggers my suspicions that there may be more to what is going on here than meets the eye."

I moved forward where I could once again see his face. "Oh, there's something rotten here in Denmark, but it doesn't have anything to do with you or the incident back in California."

"Why don't you tell me, and then let me be the judge of that?"

"You keep saying that, but it's, uh . . . a long story."

"We appear to have plenty of time on our hands." He glanced around the all but empty street. "And why don't you tell me by starting with our friend, Mike Tanaka. Where is he?"

I cleared my throat. "He was headed to a hospital in Prescott the last time I saw him."

"The hospital, oh my . . ." Even with the response, he didn't seem surprised. "And when was that?"

"This morning."

"What happened to him?"

"He was beaten up."

Sato took another step forward and turned to gaze at the church. "By whom, might I ask?"

"I don't actually know. I mean, I've got some theories."

"Why?"

I stared at the side of his head. "Why do I have theories?"

"No, why was he beaten?"

"I think he was asking too many questions."

He turned toward me and took a step sideways, placing himself directly between the church and me. "Ah, like us."

"I'm pretty sure he was asking about other things."

He leaned in closely, pulling his sunglasses down to reveal his eyes. "Do you know about Mike's service record?"

"Excuse me?"

"His war record. Mike is a very courageous man."

"Yep, he told me about . . ."

"May I see your hands?"

"What?"

"Show me your hands."

"Why?"

"Whoever it was who beat Mike must've been a very capable individual, and I am simply wanting to ascertain if that person might've been you."

Keeping my hands in my pockets, I shook my head. "Why would I beat up Mike?"

"You may not have but let me see your hands and we'll know for sure."

"You know my hands are skinned up from previous fights, digging and riding the motorcycle."

"Let's have a look and see if they are in worse shape than before."

I pulled my hands from my pockets and held them out to him. "Mike is the closest thing we've got to a friend in this place; as you know, he ran my tire over to another town to get it patched up. We aren't responsible for beating on him."

He took my hands and held them like the medical man he was, studying them, noting the collection of bruises, cuts, abrasions, and skinned spots across the knuckles. His eyes came up above the sunglasses again, dark, like swirling drains.

"You did not do it."

"No."

"But your friend might have."

"He didn't."

He studied me a bit more before dropping my hands. "You are hiding something, and that concerns me."

"It has nothing to do with you. What I'm dealing with here is ancient history."

He turned a bit, looking down the road. "Like the camp."

"Yes."

"And the Tokyo Twelve?"

I stared back at him for a long while. "You know about that?"

He didn't smile this time. "As I said, I have also been doing some investigating."

"Then you know it doesn't have anything to do with you."

"How can you say that?"

"Because it has nothing to do with Point Dume, or the drugs, or anything you're involved with."

"We are now beyond that. I told you, I am in the finding and fixing business and the situation here has caught my attention—I think it needs fixing."

"Well, we're in agreement on that. I just think our methods are going to be different, unless you're willing to go to the authorities?"

He pursed his lips, studying the ground between us and maybe more. "An interesting word, *authorities* . . . Who is to say that I am not the authority in this situation?"

"The law."

"Another interesting word. Whose law? Theirs? Yours? Mine?" He took the cigarette case from his jacket and pulled one out, lodging it into the corner of his mouth, then removing the musical lighter, igniting it. As the tune played, he took a drag and then slowly exhaled, plucking a piece of tobacco from his tongue and flicking it aside. "Do you know what law is, Mr. Longmire?"

"A set of rules enforced to regulate behavior—the art of justice."

"The art of justice." He put away the case and the lighter. "I like that, but who does the enforcing?"

"A social or governmental institution."

"You mean like the camp just down the road?" When I ignored him he slowly turned in a circle, smoked his cigarette, and looked at the endless desert. "I don't see any of those government institutions around anymore, do you?"

"Just because you can't see them doesn't mean they're not here."

"Oh, I think it does . . . You see, in the absence of law there is power, and power in that instance becomes the law."

"That's just force."

"And even with all its ceremony and claptrap, that is all the law is, trust me." He abruptly turned and began walking back toward the big Cadillac. "Come with me."

I stood still.

"Come." He called over his shoulder. "I wish to show you something."

"Look, if it's another body in the trunk, I don't want to see it."

He stopped, taking the cigarette from his mouth and turned, finally waving a hand for me to follow. "Come."

"And if you need help burying it, why don't you try the next town?"

He waved the impatient hand some more.

Reluctantly, I started in that direction as he circled around the car, stopped at the back seat, and indicated I should look inside, where I found Noriko Everson.

"Hi."

She seemed a little worried, and so was I.

15

"You really think a different tie will help?"

Ruby tightened the relic around my neck as I stooped down to her, maybe tightening it a little tighter than need be. "It can't hurt, Walter."

"Right."

"How old is this jacket?" She picked up my other tweed blazer that I kept in my locker downstairs for emergency purposes, examining the end of one of the sleeves. "The moths that made these holes have been dead a quarter of a century."

I took a look for myself. "It's not that bad."

"You can afford a new one."

"This one is fine."

"Walter, what we're attempting to do at this late date in the hearing is establish an impression, and the impression we're striving to *not* give is one of stewbum."

As my dispatcher held it out, I shucked on the offending item and stood back to let her have a look at me. "Well?"

"You have some natural attributes that help mollify the stewbum impression."

Both Ruby and I turned to find Vic leaning in the doorway of my office and sipping from a mug. "Fashion advice from a felon . . . What are you doing out of jail?"

She gestured with the mug. "I came out to get a cup of coffee—is that okay? A person could die from neglect back there in the holding cells." She glanced behind her into the communal office and yawned. "We got any doughnuts?"

Ruby walked past and stood with my undersheriff as they both studied me. "Yesterday's, but I think they're on the verge."

"So is that blazer." She took another sip of her coffee. "Did Royal Horse Guards give you a pair of riding pants that matched?"

"Okay, I think I've had about as much hilarity as I can stand from the two of you for one morning." I walked toward them and forced them to make way as I continued into the outer office. Saizarbitoria stood at Ruby's counter and was leafing through some papers. "Verdict?"

He straightened, nodding his head and tossing the papers back in the pile. "I think your jacket looks fine."

"The Department of Justice, please?"

"Ruthless is right. They sealed it, and I don't think there's anything anybody can do other than her. And you say she's flying her own plane back to DC?"

"I guess it's something she does all the time."

He stared at me.

"What?"

"I think this is the third time I've ever seen you in a tie."

"Take a good look. It might be the last." I glanced down at the sheaf of papers Sancho had printed out from the DOJ. "So, I'm in a holding pattern for the next three days."

"When is the hearing over with?"

"I guess that'll be up to the judge, but I'm betting that one way or another he'd just as soon go home this weekend."

"How do you think it's going?"

"In all honesty, I think the Regis family has it in for me, and it's just a question as to how much financial force they can muster."

"You wouldn't be in this mess if it wasn't for me."

I waited a moment, then sidled over to the other side of the counter and leaned there, across from him. "That's not particularly true. I was the one they were going to be gunning for all along."

He stared at the floor. "Yeah, but me partnering up with Regis didn't help."

"Well, did you learn something?"

After a moment he spoke. "I think I did."

"Then it's not a loss now, is it?"

When he raised his face, he was smiling to himself with a little left for me. "Somehow, I knew you were going to say something like that."

I nodded, pushing off and coming around the counter and heading toward the door and the courthouse as I popped a fist into his shoulder. "I don't know about you, but I've never made it without a few mistakes along the way—that's the part of life you learn from."

He called after me. "You've made mistakes?"

"Why do you think I'm wearing this tie?" Continuing on, I clomped down the stairwell and pushed open the front door, walking through and listening to the low hiss as it closed behind me like the burning of a slow fuse.

TUESDAY, MAY 26, 1964

"What happened?"

"I got Mike to the hospital but then they started asking me a lot of questions. I was able to get out of there before the police showed up, but just barely. I got in your truck when these guys came over and put me in their car and drove me here."

I turned to Sato. "Why?"

"She was about to be taken for questioning and I didn't think that would be advantageous to any of us, so we interceded."

"Again, why?"

"We've taken an interest in this situation, and do not ask why again. Think of it as a pro bono case—in my line of work I rarely get the opportunity to do good." He stubbed out a cigarette butt on the heal of his polished shoe and dropped it on the concrete as one of his men appeared, driving my truck over the rise and gliding into the service station and parking alongside the Caddy. "Where is your friend?"

"Looking for somebody."

He glanced at Noriko. "Her?"

"No, somebody else."

"Who?"

"You wouldn't believe me if I told you."

"But this friend of yours, you're sure he exists?"

"Sometimes I wonder, but yep, I'm pretty sure." I held a hand out to Noriko and helped her from the Caddy, then turned back to Sato. "Look, I don't mean to be unappreciative, but I think you guys should get out of here."

He continued studying me, a look of bemusement on his face. "My turn to ask why."

"You remember the guy I was telling you about, her grandfather? Well, he's looking for her and us . . ."

"And would that be him in one of those vehicles that are parking over there?"

I looked over my shoulder to where three of the Everson work trucks had pulled to a stop in the crossroads. "Yep, that would be them."

The three men, Kenji, Kazuo, and Nomu, moved from the Cadillac and automatically spread out in anticipation as the larger group, carrying hunting rifles, baseball bats, and even shovels, poured out of the vehicle. Parker Everson stood alongside the cab of his father's truck and held a rifle, with Lester standing a little away from him holding another, and with Del and Will and a couple of others I hadn't been introduced to in attendance.

Sato adjusted his sunglasses. "They don't look friendly."

"No, they don't." I watched as Judge Everson himself opened the door and then lingered in the opening of his dented truck, using the door as a shield.

Sato squared off with the assembling group as his own men continued to spread out farther, making for an even wider target, whereas Nomu paused at the trunk of the Cadillac and then moved away. "Maybe they are planning on digging our graves after they shoot us?"

"You know, they say one of the biggest mistakes you can make is thinking that everybody thinks the way you think." I released Noriko and continued past him into the no-man's-land between the two parties. "Judge."

Everson the Elder leaned into the space between the cab and the open door. "Is that my granddaughter you have there?"

I glanced back at Noriko. "Yep, sir. It is, but I'm not so sure we *have* her."

"Come here, honey."

She didn't move.

I turned back to him. "It would appear that she doesn't want to come with you."

He cocked his head. "Well, I don't give two hoots in hell what you or anybody else wants. If you don't give her to me, I'll just have to take her."

Sato stepped up beside me. "That may prove to be more difficult than you think."

Everson turned his head and spat. "And just who the hell are you?"

"Simply an interested party."

"You better get disinterested and get the hell out of here," Everson said. "Where's that redskin buddy of yours?"

"Oh, he's around here . . . somewhere."

"Well, you should gather him up and get out of here too. I've had about as much of all of you as I can stand."

"Just walk off and leave this situation as is?"

He dropped his head, looking into the cab at something, and then slowly raised his face again, pushing his hat up. "Best offer you're gonna get."

Parker gestured toward his father. "Poppa . . . ?"

"We're not leaving your granddaughter here if she doesn't want that."

"She doesn't know what she wants." He produced a large .357 revolver from the truck, draping it in his hand through the open window and over the side mirror. "You're not leaving me many choices."

"You've got one."

Parker tried to get his father's attention again. "Poppa . . . ?"

"Shut up, Parker." Judge Everson stared at the ground between us and then reached into the cab of his truck. "No, I've got two choices."

He dragged what appeared to be a human form from it and dropped it onto the ground. Still standing beside the door of his truck, he reached into the cab again, lifted something up, and held it near his own face—the demon mask of Mae Mayko Oda.

Her arms lay at her sides, and it seemed that she was unconscious if not dead. Everson stooped to lower the muzzle of the pistol to the side of her head.

I took an involuntary step forward. "Haven't you done enough to her already?"

"I was satisfied to let her run around out here with her mind gone, but now she's become useful. Now, here's the deal . . ." He adjusted the muzzle to the temple of her head. "On the count of three you give me my granddaughter."

"So, do you have to hold a gun to the head of everybody you want to keep around?"

He pulled the hammer back on the .357. "One."

"She's your daughter-in-law, for God's sake."

He jammed the muzzle into her lifeless ear. "Two."

"Don't do it."

"Th—"

There are very few things in life that will throw a pause into you like the jacking action of a Stevens 520A 12-gauge trench gun in proximity, and that was what Everson was dealing with right now.

"I am impressed." Even from the distance, I could hear the Cheyenne Nation's voice. "I did not think you could count that high."

There are few individuals as stealthy as the Cheyenne, and even fewer Cheyenne who are as stealthy as Henry Standing Bear. His focus was entirely on the back of the judge's head as he prodded the older man's crown with the big barrel. "Raise the revolver and then lower the hammer—do it carefully or you lose your head."

I watched as Everson hesitated for the briefest of instances but then slowly lifted the barrel of the .357 and carefully dropped the hammer.

"Hand it back to me."

As the others in the group began turning, the Bear reached up and took the revolver, still holding the shotgun to the back of the man's head with one hand. "Now ease back and have a seat in the footwell of your truck, keeping your hands to your sides where I can see them."

I watched Everson, who did as he was told. "What do you think you're going to accomplish with all this, Chief?"

The Bear shoved the revolver into his belt but kept the barrel of the shotgun in Everson's face as he reached down, taking the crumpled woman in one arm and effortlessly lifting her onto his shoulder. "You talk bravely for a man who handcuffed me to a radiator."

"Once is usually enough for most."

"How do you think you are going to sound without teeth?"

"You don't dare—"

The movement was so fast you wouldn't have seen it if you hadn't known it was coming, but I knew it was coming and still barely saw it at that. The butt of the shotgun swiveled around and caught the man in the side of his face, causing his head to snap to the side and bounce off the open door as he fell forward onto the pavement, a tooth skittering across the concrete.

Spinning the trench gun in his one hand, the Cheyenne Nation leveled it at the crowd of men who had edged toward him. "Anyone else?"

No one volunteered, and I watched as he stepped over the judge, went around the door, and picked up the mask, carefully placing it back over Mae's face. Then he walked toward us, Everson's men making room as the Cheyenne Nation slowly turned toward them and backed up to where I stood.

Reaching out, I took the incapacitated woman from his shoulder and cradled her in my arms, her head lolling against my chest as the inexplicable mask looked up at me, revealing the mottled flesh at the side of her face where she'd been burned all those years ago. "'Bout time you showed up."

"I like planning my entrances."

"Uh huh." We began slowly backing away as Nomu moved forward holding what looked to be some kind of small, boxy gun in his hands. "What the hell is that?"

"Israeli. They call it an Uzi; the Secret Service uses them."

We'd almost made it to the front of the Cadillac when we were met by Noriko, walking past us in the other direction. "What are you doing?"

She turned to look at me as she reached up to touch her mother's limp arm. "I'll go with my grandfather. I have to keep her safe."

I stared at her for a moment and then at her grandfather. "We can't leave you here."

"You have to."

Sato stepped toward her. "No, we can take the two of you with us."

"Where?"

"San Francisco, or anywhere else you would like to go—anywhere away from here."

"He would just follow us or find us."

"I can keep that from happening too."

She stared at him. "Who are you?"

He started to speak but then stopped to breathe a laugh. "Up until twenty-four hours ago I had an answer to that question, but it appears to have left me. I suppose I am a man looking for some form of redemption."

Noriko looked over her shoulder to where Judge Everson had moved forward, unarmed. "No, it will only make things worse."

"May we take your mother? I'm sure we can find a better place for her."

"No, she belongs here, with us."

"No one deserves that."

She held her arms out for the crumpled body I had cradled in my arms. "Yes, some of us do."

Rather than handing Mae over to her, I took a few steps and handed her to Everson as Noriko joined him and then watched as he walked back toward his truck, to place the masked woman inside. Holding a handkerchief to his jaw and mumbling, the judge circled back around. "This isn't over."

Sato buried his hands into his pockets and stepped toward him. "Yes, it is—or I can make it so."

The judge stared at him.

"I have killed more people than you have ever known." He glanced back at his men, fully armed and ready to fire. "And at this moment, with a simple wave of my hand I can kill you all."

Noriko turned toward him. "Go, just go . . . Please."

Henry spoke to her, and her eyes turned toward him. "Come with us."

"Where? And what would we do with my mother?"

"We will figure something out."

"No, we've both been here so long I don't know if we're even capable of being somewhere else."

The Bear glanced at the judge, still standing in front of the truck. "That's what he wants you to think."

"Then, maybe for once, he's right."

"No." We all turned as Donnie Pickens approached from the church, holding the .45 at arm's length and pointing it at Parker. "This has got to stop." He pulled up a few steps away, still holding the gun on Parker. "Don't you see, with Mike in the hospital up in Prescott this whole thing is going to blow open . . . Alan Yoshida, the Tokyo Twelve, all of it. I'm amazed there isn't somebody here already."

"There isn't, and there isn't going to be." Everson took a step forward and then stopped. "They called me and asked about Mike, and I told them that he'd been down here and got into it with some of the boys and that things had gotten a little out of hand, but that I'd be happy to take care of any of his hospital bills." He dabbed a little more blood from his mouth and then folded his arms. "So, if you're waiting on the cavalry, you two-timing sonofabitch, they aren't coming."

Pickens's hand trembled, holding the semiautomatic. "Just . . . let them go."

"They're family, Donnie. I can't believe you would ask me to do that, but I'll tell you what I can do . . ."

The explosion of the rifle shot wasn't what any of us expected, least of all Pickens, who dropped to the ground, the .45 skittering across the pavement to my feet as we all watched the pool of blood flow from his head.

I was unsure if he was the one who had shot Pickens, but Lester took a step toward him and then the large man turned his hunting rifle on me.

Judge Everson, looking a little shaken, pushed off the hood and walked toward us, gesturing for Parker to take Noriko to his truck. "The negotiations for what's going to happen with the women here are over—we're now in negotiations as to what's going to happen with the rest of you." He dabbed at his mouth some more. "A bunch of Nip gangsters from out California way and a couple of draft dodgers . . . Do you honestly think that anybody is going to care where all of you disappeared to?" He glanced at Sato. "We'll shoot them and file it under A-Favor-To-Society, and if anybody asks about you and your friend here, we just say the last we heard of you two chickenshits, you were headed to Nogales."

"I should have shot you."

"Yeah, you probably should have, but you didn't." He walked out in front us and then past toward the road leading back to the high-way, and he paused to toe the body of Donnie Pickens with his boot. "Now let me be clear, things have gotten way out of control around here, but that's okay because I'm pretty good at getting things back under control. Now, what's going to happen is this—you gentlemen are going to go back to that pestilential freak show in California, and you other two are just going to continue on your way." He turned to look at us. "And that's as good a deal as it's going to get."

"You know we're going to talk." I glanced at Sato and then Henry. "At least we are."

"What good will it do? A couple more might come in here asking questions, but we'll just tell them we have no idea what you're talk-ing about, damned drugged-up college kooks dodging the draft."

"What about Mike Tanaka?"

He took a step back to avoid the blood still pooling from Pickens's wound. "People die in hospitals all the time, son."

"You are truly a piece of work, old man."

"Thank you." He turned and walked past us back toward his truck, and then gestured to a couple of his men to fetch the body lying in the street. "Now, is there anything else?"

"Don't you feel any remorse, any shame in the things you do?"

He turned, looked at me, and pointed to where they had loaded the lifeless body of the Last Chance Service Station manager into the back of the truck with the rolled tarps and other refuse. "That's what you get when you interfere in other people's business." We watched as he and Parker continued on, the judge climbing into the driver's seat, the two women crammed in between them. Everson turned the wheel and pulled out, only to stop and call over to us through the open window. "Especially family business."

He pulled away and waited as the others gathered up in the remaining vehicles and motored out, Lester giving me a particularly hard look as they drove away with Judge Everson taking the rear.

Sato walked past us, gazed after the cavalcade, and then looked down at his shiny loafers and the pool of blood on the pavement. After a moment, he took a cigarette from the case and then struck the lighter that played the gay tune.

"You know, I'm getting really tired of that song."

He smiled and nodded, taking a deep drag and then exhaling through his nostrils like twin stacks as he clicked the lighter closed. "I can give you a piece of advice, if you'd like?"

"I'm listening."

"You can only help people as much as they wish to be helped."

"So, that's it?"

"I am afraid so," Sato said. "Not the ending any of us wanted, but so be it. True violence is limited in its imagination—other than to kill them all, there was very little else to do. We offered the young woman every available option, and she turned us away. It's possible she knows more about the situation than we do, and if so then we must yield to her decision—it was hers to make all along. What cannot change must be endured."

"So, you'll just head back to San Francisco?"

"We will."

"Aren't you worried that Everson might turn you in?"

"Not particularly . . . He has, as they say, enough skeletons roaming around in his closets."

"And what about us?"

"That is another question." He took a drag on the cigarette, his words flowing out with the smoke. "The two of you are innocents, and innocence is the greatest of wild cards. I find the most difficult of individuals are those who want for nothing. How do you deal with a person like that? There is no leverage, no way to influence them." He turned to look at me. "But how do you know what I have told you is true? Our names, our past, where we are from . . . ? Why, in the position we are in, would I have ever told you the truth?"

"It sure sounded like the truth."

"That is crucial in a good lie: that it bare at least a passing resemblance to the truth."

"So, I can tell everything to the authorities?"

"Or we can kill you."

"You make it sound like there isn't any difference."

"Oh, there is. I have grown to like you and even your friend here . . ." He looked around. "By the way, where is he?"

I looked over to where Henry had been standing and then around the canopy of the service station, then circled and saw only Sato, his men, and me. "Oh, shit."

He took a step past me and looked back up the road where the trucks had retreated. "You don't think . . . ?"

"Yep, I do."

He smiled, the way alligators smile. "Then we must go after them."

I moved toward my truck, which was parked alongside the Cadillac. "This really isn't your fight anymore."

"You would go by yourself?"

I opened the door of my truck and began climbing in. "It's still my fight, and I can't leave Henry to face them alone." Noticing the keys weren't in the switch, I held out my hand.

Sato stared at me for a moment and then extended his own hand to Kazuo, who deposited the fob there, his boss turning to look at me. "You will die."

"Maybe."

"You don't even have a gun."

Hitting the ignition, I pulled the door closed and held up the .45 I'd acquired. "I thought you didn't like guns?"

"That doesn't mean I don't see the need for them."

"Okay . . ."

I stuffed the Colt into the seat beside me and he stepped away, still smiling. "I don't approve of you or the things you've done, but I think I have to thank you."

The smile faded. "You think you do."

"Yep."

He stepped back, shaking his head. "For sending you to your death?"

I hit the ignition and depressed the clutch, putting the old girl in gear. "Well, let's hope for something better than that, shall we?"

He extended his three-fingered hand through the window. "We will not be here if you should make it back."

I shook the hand, but then retrieved it, watching as the smile returned. "I wouldn't expect you to." I started to let the clutch out and drive away when I had to ask. "Is anything you've told me the truth?"

"Every single word, young man. Every single word."

I pulled out and cut through the portico, taking a right onto the road that led to Everson's place and trying to think of what I was going to do. What was Henry thinking, taking them all on by himself, and what was he going to do with the two women if he could convince Noriko and actually get them out of there?

And this was all providing we made it out alive, any of us.

Driving up the lonely road, I tried to convince myself that I'd done the right thing, sending Sato and his crew on their way, but now, as I faced the odds, I wasn't so sure. I'd never been involved in anything like this, and the chances of success seemed pretty remote.

In the distance, I could see a vehicle coming back down the road—Everson's truck. Slowing, I could see Henry at the wheel and the two women and the son Parker in the cab.

Braking to a stop, I waited as they pulled up. "What happened?"

Henry shook his head, looking at the assembled group. "When I climbed out of the bed and held the shotgun to his head, the judge pulled over. The others didn't see us stop and the last we saw of the old man he was standing on the side of the road." He glanced at Everson's son. "He decided to come with us."

Parker was sitting on the far side of the cab looking through the windshield as if the rest of us weren't even there. "Hey?"

His face turned to me, and I could see he was crying.

"You did the right thing."

He swallowed and then spoke, looking down at the unconscious woman under his arm, the demon mask having slid to the side to reveal even more of her burned face. "Maybe not, but it was all I had left to do."

Noriko turned and looked back up the road. "We better get moving, yes?"

"Yep." I couldn't see Everson or the trucks, but it was only a matter of time. "We better get going if we're going to get out of here before they figure out what happened and double back."

Henry nodded. "Agreed."

I could see Pickens's body still rolled up in a tarp in the back of their truck. "We need to get to a city; someplace with a police department or authorities where we can get these two to safety."

"And us?"

"Yep, us too." I glanced down at the gauge. "I'm almost out of gas. What about you?"

"This one has got a half a tank."

"We're going to need fuel." My eyes drifted back to the body again. "I don't think Pickens would mind."

Wheeling my truck around, I followed them as we made our way back to town in a cloud of dust as I continually glanced out the rearview to see if we were being pursued.

We made it back to town, and as good as his word, Sato, the others, and the Cadillac were gone. Pulling around in the opposite direction so that I could fill my truck from the other side, I joined Henry in fueling the trucks as Parker, with Noriko joining him, got out and looked back up the road.

"Do you see anything?"

Noriko was the one who answered. "No."

I turned back to Henry. "We've got the body and two eyewitnesses, that should be enough, don't you think?"

"I certainly hope so." Snatching Everson's .357 from the dash, he shoved it into his jeans and stared at the mechanical numbers rolling within the pump, clicking with each second that passed. "The Japanese gangsters left?"

"I told them to. I figured what this town needed was fewer itchy trigger fingers." Hanging an arm in my open window, I couldn't help but bring up the subject. "If you don't mind my asking, and even if you do, what were you thinking?"

He sighed. "I just could not let her go away with them."

"Could you have let me in on the plan?"

"I would have if there had been one." He finished filling up his tank first and hung the handle back on the pump. "So, do you suppose the Vietnam War will be more orderly than this?"

"We can hope."

He wandered out toward the others, joining them in looking up the road, and I wasn't surprised when he spoke first. "They are coming."

Letting off the handle, I hung the thing up, satisfied that at least I had enough gas to get the truck to Prescott. "C'mon, let's go!"

The others ran back, jumping into the open doors of the truck and firing it up as I did the same. I had just put the shifter in gear, turned the wheel and begun pulling out, when I looked at the seat beside me and saw, lying there—the grinning demon mask.

16

Freshly scrubbed and dressed in a different suit jacket and tie, I walked down the sidewalk, turned through the glass doors of the courthouse, and began climbing the stairs on the left, an old habit.

The vintage wooden banisters and steps were on both sides of the hall, and I remembered asking my old boss, Lucian Connally, why it was that they'd gone to such an expense when building the court-house since one set of stairs would've been perfectly suitable. The previous sheriff of Absaroka County had said that back in the day, they'd had many a confrontation on the single set of stairs both before and after court dates, sometimes resulting in individuals being thrown one story to the marble floor below.

Another set on the left side seemed like a small price to pay.

Checking my pocket watch, I could see it was 8:57 a.m., and unless I hustled, I was going to be late. It was odd, but there wasn't anybody milling about in the hallways or anterooms the way there usually was, and I was feeling a little nervous about the whole thing when I noticed that the large, wooden double doors leading into the courtroom hung open, and nobody was inside.

Poking my head in, I could see that Judge Snowden was at the bench, packing his papers into a well-worn leather satchel. "Anybody home?"

He looked up and smiled. "Well, the star of the show."

Entering, I glanced around at the all but empty room. "Am I missing something?"

"You didn't get the email?"

"I don't get any emails."

"Text?"

"Nope, I don't get those either." Standing next to the corner of the plaintiff's table, I took off my hat and rolled the brim in my hands. "How about we do it old school, and you just tell me what's going on?"

He finished stuffing the satchel, stepped down from the platform and around the clerk's table to sit on the corner of the defendant's table, then placed the luggage beside him along with his ivory-colored hat. "The state has dropped the case against you."

Sitting on the corner of the table, I had to laugh, and then asked. "Just like that?"

He nodded with a matinee smile. "Just like that."

"Mind if I ask why?"

"I got a phone call this morning at about 5:00 a.m. from the Department of Justice, informing me that they had unsealed the One Heart recordings from that evening at your grandfather's house with Rondelle and the rest."

"Ruthless."

"Yes. Anyway, I contacted Mr. Whinstone and advised him that it would behoove him to be in my chambers the first thing this morning along with Ms. Cole, and we would listen to the recording and see what would be in the best interests of the state."

"And how did that go?"

"We didn't make it all the way through. When we got about five minutes in and they started talking about getting rid of your body, Mr. Whinstone began losing interest in pursuing the case against you."

"Too bad, I would've enjoyed listening to that recording."

"I'm sure the jury would have too." He stood, picking up his satchel and slipping on his hat. "I think with the right studio musicians and backup singers we could've gone platinum."

I stood and followed him out. "So, you're headed back to California?"

"I am."

He followed me down the stairs on the right, another old habit, and we pushed the glass doors I'd just entered through to step outside into a gorgeous, high-plains morning. "Can I buy you breakfast at the Busy Bee?"

"I'm tempted, but I can still make the 10:37 a.m. flight over in Sheridan if I get a move on."

"Need a lift?"

He gestured toward a maroon Oldsmobuick parked in the lot. "Nope, I've got a rental I need to return."

"Well, is there anything I can do for you?"

He stuck out a hand. "Shake and say goodbye, Walt Longmire."

"Goodbye, Walt Longmire."

We shook, and he gave me a dubious look. "That gag is so old it's got whiskers."

I watched as he started for his car but then turned, his grin fading. "I don't think this is over, Walt. You cost some people an awful lot of money, and they're the kind of people who aren't used to losing much of anything."

I stood there as he climbed into the car, backed out, and then circled around my office and the courthouse, heading for the airport twenty-eight miles away.

I thought about what he'd said and then about Ruthless One Heart and wondered where she was in her three-leg flight to DC, possibly somewhere over Nebraska in her little Bumble Bee aircraft or maybe not that far if she'd only gotten started this morning. I'd need to have Ruby find the treasury agent's phone number for me again and give her a call of thanks for getting the recordings unsealed.

I wondered how she'd done it?

TUESDAY, MAY 26, 1964

"Where could she have gone?"

I picked up both the demon mask and the Colt .45, then took a few steps toward the street while looking at the building across the way. "Possibly the church?"

He started to hurry past me. "I will look."

"No." I threw out an arm and stopped him. "I know the place. You take them and go ahead. I'll check there and if I find her, I'll be right behind you."

He looked at me, shaking his head. "And if you do not?"

I was now hurrying across the street and shouting back. "I'll be right behind you."

I ran around the church, leaped over the makeshift grave, and clamored up the steps, kicking in the back door and hurrying into the sanctuary.

The rug was covering the trapdoor in the aisle, but that didn't mean she wasn't down there. I heard the truck with Henry and the others roaring away as I snatched the rug back and flipped the trapdoor. Then I scrambled down the ladder into the cellar. "Mae!"

I wasn't sure if she'd answer, and I wasn't sure if she wouldn't just hide from me, but if that was the case, then why leave the mask on the seat of my truck?

"Mae!" There wasn't anybody in the main room of the cellar, but who knew if there were other places where she could be hiding. In the decades-long game of hide-and-seek, Mae Mayko Oda was world champion. "Mae!"

Listening, I heard a couple of vehicles pulling up on the main street, and I could only guess that it was Everson's men if not the judge himself.

I hadn't been fast enough, so what to do now?

There was shouting out there, and I listened as it sounded like one of the trucks was driving off, probably chasing the others.

Climbing up the chute where we'd pushed PI Mike up from out of the cellar, I emerged under the porch of the church and could see six of Everson's men poking around my truck at the Last Chance Service Station across the street.

I could crawl back down into the cellar and hide, but it was only a question of time before they found me, and besides, my friends needed my help. Standing there with the mask in my hand and trying to ignore the chorus of voices in my head telling me this was the stupidest thing I'd ever even thought of doing in my entire life—I climbed out from under the porch.

"Trick or treat."

The group turned from the truck to see me sitting on the steps of the church, then looked at one another and fanned out as they crossed the street, more than a little wary.

Along with the comic duo of Del and Will, two other guys looked familiar, and there was Lester, in the front, with the hunting rifle aimed directly at my chest. "Where are the others, asshole?"

I pushed the mask up on top of my head. "Gone, long gone."

The giant drew closer, still keeping the muzzle leveled on me. "They left you here?"

"No, I chose to stay."

He glanced at the others. "And why is that?"

I stood, carefully hanging the mask with the .45 inside on the railing and watching as the wind caused it to sway back and forth in a taunting fashion. "I figured you and I had unfinished business."

Lester barked a laugh and then smirked at the others. "How about I just shoot you where you stand?"

"Maybe you should, you chickenshit—seeing as how I've kicked your ass twice now."

There was a lengthy pause as he considered his options. "I wouldn't push my luck if I was you."

"What's the matter, Lester, afraid the third isn't a charm?" I stepped off the first tread and took another stride toward him, then took off my jacket and laid it on the steps. "How 'bout you put that rifle down and we show these boys what you are made of?"

"Kick his ass, Lester." Will growled, or maybe it was Del—who the hell could tell them apart?

I took another step toward him—almost there. "C'mon, Lester. Now's your chance, why don't you try and kick my ass again?"

"You better shut up."

I leaned in a little. "Shut me up."

He swung with the rifle, just like I knew he would, and I was just able to pull back out of the way as the butt passed my face. Then I planted the best uppercut I'd ever thrown in my life into his guts.

His knees crumpled, and I couldn't see how he could possibly still be standing when he swung around again, clipping the wooden stock first off my shoulder and then the crown of my head.

I lurched back, acting as if he'd caught my eye, pawing at it, and stumbling a little. The ruse worked in that through my one eye I watched as he tossed the rifle to one of the morons and moved in for the kill. Lester reared back for a full-body swing, but when he did, I used the hand covering my eye to deliver a jab into his face that caused him to lose his balance a bit before I slipped my arm in to block his punch with a parry and then responded with a lead hook.

I felt something strange in my left shoulder where the defenseman from Wisconsin had torqued it and where the boat off Point Dume had slammed it, but luckily my right fist caught him in the chin. His momentum kept it from landing with as much force as it could have, but his elbow came around to clip me in the same shoulder, which wasn't a strategic hit, but powerful enough to stun the muscles on my left arm as it hung to my side, partially useless.

Staggering back, I watched as he rose up from a stooped position and kicked me in the midsection. Surprised, I doubled over and tried to pull some air back into my lungs but wasn't having much luck.

Sensing the advantage, the giant staggered forward and kicked at me again, but this time I grabbed his steel-toed boot with the hand that worked and yanked, causing him to lose his footing and land on the pavement with a sickening thud.

Before he could move again, I clambered onto his chest and punched him hard in the face. His head bounced off the pavement but then he rolled to the right, pitching me off. I staggered to my feet and backed away as he lumbered up again. "Are you the one that killed Alan Yoshida?"

"Who?" He stretched his jaw, feeling at a tooth there. "I don't know who the hell you're talking about." He swung the big right I knew was coming and it clipped my chin even as I ducked back. But the momentum was too much for him as he kept going, tripping over his own feet and then having to catch his balance with one hand, which I kicked out from under him and watched as he hit the pavement.

"The reporter from *The Arizona Republic*?" Rolling him over with my one good hand, I placed a knee at the center of his chest and rested all two hundred and fifty pounds there. He tried to reach up and push me off, but he didn't have the energy and I slapped his hands away. "Alan Yoshida."

He wheezed a response. "Never heard of him."

I drew back to hit him again, but he raised a hand to stop me. "Wait! Wait, honestly, I don't know who you're talking about."

"The guy who was Mike Tanaka's partner back in San Francisco, the newspaper reporter that disappeared?"

"It wasn't me." He wiped some of the blood from his face as he fought to breathe. "Honest."

I waited there for a moment, looking at him, wanting to believe he was lying, but I couldn't. I slowly stood and extended my good arm out to the guy holding Lester's rifle. "Hand me that." He hesitated, and I growled at him. "Give it to me or I'll shove it up your ass and pull the trigger."

He handed it to me, and I sniffed the end of the barrel. Then I turned back to Lester. "You didn't shoot Pickens either, did you?"

He lay there breathing on the cement. "No."

"Then who did?" When he didn't answer, I turned to the others. "Then who did?"

They didn't answer. I was getting tired of the whole thing, so I took the few steps over to my jacket and picked it up, collecting the mask from the railing along with the .45 turned to face them. Rolling my shoulder in a spark of agony, I could feel a hitch and the void where my shoulder should've connected to the socket but didn't.

I stared at Lester a moment more and then did what I had to do, trying not to cry out from the shards of pain that were shooting through my left side like chain lightning.

"Okay . . ." Turning to look at the other four, I knew that if I didn't start talking soon, I was going to pass out. "Who's next?"

Though they were still pointing their guns at me, nobody answered, so I sat the mask on my head again, stuffed the .45 under my good arm, and, reaching down, grabbed the wrist of my disabled one. I extended it and turned it with a jerk just as the medical guy on the sidelines of the Rose Bowl had taught me.

The crunching noise was disgusting, but I didn't collapse and instead stood there, staring at the four of them all steely-eyed. Taking the Colt with my good hand, I glanced at them in turn. "Now, as far as I know, none of you four idiots have killed anybody, is that right?"

They stared at me.

"Is that right?"

They came back this time with a barbershop quartet in the affirmative.

"I'd say this unholy mess around here is about to come crashing down, and the more the bunch of you help, the better it's going to look when the cops get here, you read me?"

They nodded.

I looked down at Lester. "Take this piece of shit to the station over there, and everybody put your weapons in the back of my truck."

They did as I said, and I pulled the keys and pocketed them. Then I made hard eye contact with each of them as I stuffed the .45 into my jeans. "You do anything else than what I'm telling you, it's not going to end well for any of you."

Walking between them and making sure I had all the weapons, I climbed into my truck, then carefully placed the mask in the seat beside me, thanking God that all I had to do with my left hand was hang on to the steering wheel, leaving the shifting and driving to my right.

Taking a deep breath, I turned the switch, slipped the truck in gear, and motored onto the main road leading out of town, watching the four of them help Lester get seated under the portico where they all sat.

I didn't get far before seeing something I wasn't prepared for near the same place in front of the internment camp where we'd first spotted PI Mike. It was the truck Henry had been driving, now pulled over into a barrow ditch with both doors hanging open and Judge Everson's truck parked behind it.

One of Everson's men was standing in the road with his lever-action carbine, looking at me as I approached.

I slowed the half-ton down but kept moving until I pulled to a stop directly in front of him as he continued to aim the rifle at me. I pushed in the clutch but left the truck in granny low as I raised my hands. "What's going on?"

Making a show of it, he pushed his chest against the grille and stared at me over the sight of the carbine, shouting to be heard above the motor. "When we got here the truck was run in the ditch and the others went in after them. My job is to stop you if you came along."

I made a show of glancing toward the camp. "Doesn't look like we're going to have to wait much longer."

When he looked to the right, I popped the clutch.

Say what you want about these ranch trucks—but that low gear that you use to start a heavy pull or even leave engaged so that you can climb out and trail along behind them and throw bales into the bed? It moves out when you drop the clutch.

As I figured, his .30-30 Winchester went off, but I'd already ducked behind the truck's firewall.

Pushing the clutch back in so as not to run over him completely, and not hearing anything, I slowly raised up to look out the windshield and could see nothing but a large dent cleaving the front edge of my hood and the rifle setting at the base of my windshield. Slipping the mask onto my arm, I pulled on the emergency brake and cut the ignition, then I climbed out.

Carefully peering around the front of my truck, I could see the guy lying there on his back, halfway underneath, with a massive knot growing at the center of his forehead where he must've dented my hood with his head. "Well, that worked better than I thought."

Hurrying forward, I snugged the .45 in the back of my jeans, picked up the Winchester carbine from the hood of my truck, and then stooped to grab him by the scruff of his jacket. I dragged him from under my truck and deposited him in the ditch by the parked vehicles.

Then I walked up a slight embankment and stepped over the collapsed fence to look around at the compound of a dozen bunkhouses. Why would they have stopped, and where could they have gone?

There was a scream in the distance, and I started jogging that way, getting back to the open area where the baseball field had been and where Noriko had been sitting on the steps.

On the right, I could see the last bunkhouse where I'd found the shrine to Mae and figured that must be where they were. Running between the buildings, I could hear shouting and what sounded like bodies hitting either the walls or the floor.

Swinging around to the open side where I'd kicked down the door, I charged up the steps only to be met by another one of Everson's men. He had the J. Stevens trench gun that Henry had been carrying aimed at my stomach.

It was going to be tight for me to bring the Winchester around, and all he had to do was be in the vicinity with the shotgun—besides, I had the .45 at my back—so I raised the barrel.

He stared at me. "Where's Harv?"

"Who?"

"The guy out on the road who was supposed to stop you."

"There wasn't anybody out there." I figured telling him I'd run over his buddy wasn't likely to get me any points.

He gestured with the shotgun. "That's his gun."

"It was just lying out there on the hood of your truck."

"Drop the rifle and come with me; you're just in time for the party."

I leaned the .30-30 against a railing and started past him. Carefully making sure that my jacket hung over the Colt at my back, I entered the building and he followed.

About halfway down the barrack where we'd first found the altar, I could see there was something going on with Judge Everson, his son Parker, and three other men as they gathered around a burn barrel, the flames licking the cool air of the long, empty building.

As we got closer, I could see Henry on the ground with Noriko beside him, cradling his bleeding head. Mae was lying motionless on the floor near the altar with the candles, the sword, the photographs, and the cartridge. Parker stood to the side with his head down.

The guy behind me called out as we grew closer. "Hey, I got the other one here."

When they turned, I could see that Everson was holding a rope. He played the loop out from the knot, and I could see it was a noose, just like the other one that hung from the rafters of the barrack in the still air, like dead weight. "Well, you're just in time."

"For the lynching?"

He shook his head. "This is no lynching, son. This is justice, pure and simple."

"Funny, I don't see any jury."

"You're looking at it." He fingered the rope. "At the hands of persons unknown . . . In history that's what the official transcripts of such activities recorded; at the hands of persons unknown." He glanced around. "Well, here we are—persons unknown."

"We're all known here." I noticed Henry's hands were tied. "What'd you do to my friend?"

Noriko interrupted. "We saw Mae running between the buildings and Henry pulled over to try to get her, then they showed up."

The judge crossed to her, reaching down and stroking her hair before turning back to me. "After the last time we knew we had to take more severe measures; we had to restrain your friend here." He looked past me. "Where's Lester and the others?"

"What, are you going to hang them too?"

"They'll be dealt with."

"You know you're insane, right?"

He tightened the noose. "You be careful of the words you throw around here."

"There's no other excuse for your action—you've lost your mind."

He stared into the flames of the fifty-five-gallon drum. "They said that when I was disbarred through judicial misconduct. That I no longer had the ability to tell right from wrong after Andrew died . . . Me, they said that about me, a man who upheld the rule of law in this territory longer than anyone alive."

"Mr. Everson . . ."

He held a hand out to the flames as if warming it. "*Judge* Everson."

"Look, I don't know how you started out, but you don't get to kill whoever you want."

He slowly began shaking his head. "You don't get to judge me."

"Yes, I do. Two of them survived, did you know that? Mae here is one . . ." I gestured toward the woman lying on the floor in the shadows by the altar. She looked up at me at the sound of her name, the mottled surface of her burned skin carrying an unearthly sheen, her hairline pulled back far from the scar tissue, one eye blind with cataract. "And Pat Fujita, who Donnie Pickens had been taking care of all these years—he's still out there alive in the desert."

"Another situation to be dealt with."

"Alan Yoshida, was he another situation to be dealt with? It's his body that's buried outside the church cemetery, isn't it?" I moved to the left, keeping my back away from them and angling it away from the one who had brought me in. "Is that how things happened back in '43, when you hung everybody in a barrack much like this one and then burned the place to the ground to erase all evidence of it ever happening?"

He turned and walked away from the fire, his back to all of us. "You don't know what happened that night."

"That's right, I don't, but I can make some guesses . . . But I'd rather you tell me, Judge."

There was a long pause, and then he spoke in a voice you could barely hear. "I can't."

"What do you mean you can't?"

He turned and yelled, the spittle flying from his mouth in strings. "I can't because I wasn't there!"

I stared at him, no one else saying anything.

"Did you hear me; I wasn't there that night." He took a step toward me, gesturing with his arms at the entire building, the camp, maybe the world. "I wasn't here when it . . . when all this was happening." He circled the barrel, the lower part of his face lit from below by the orange flames, looking something like the demon mask on my arm. "I don't suppose poor Donnie included that part, huh?"

"No."

"Or Pat Fujita? You think I didn't know where Pat was for twenty years?" He gestured toward Mae. "Or that we couldn't have caught this poor, pathetic thing in all that time?" He reached out a hand. "Gimme that mask." When I didn't move, he gestured again. "Gimme that mask, please?"

Sliding it down my arm, I handed it to him and watched as he kneeled by the altar and carefully placed the mask over the woman's face as she brought a hand up and touched his hand.

He patted the hand, slipped his jacket off, and gently placed it around her. "I never would've hurt her, but I couldn't let you take my granddaughter. Don't you see, this place is like a house of cards and all you need to do to bring it down is to just remove one."

"What happened that night all those years ago?"

He made a noise in his throat. "Does it matter?"

"Yep, to those ten people who died it most certainly does."

He stood, handling the rope a bit more. "I figured maybe we could scare you off . . ."

"What happened?" A different voice spoke, slurred with a thick Japanese accent, and it took a moment for me to realize it had been Mae, the mask muffling her voice. "I can't . . . I can't remember what happened."

He swallowed and kneeled down to her again. "It doesn't matter, Mae. It doesn't matter." His face came up and he glanced around the room at all of us. "There had been drinking that night, too much drinking . . . I'd been in Prescott verifying the details of the telegram on how exactly Andrew had been killed."

Parker stepped forward. "Poppa?"

Everson ignored him. "When I got here, I saw the fire . . . I was afraid that something like this was going to happen. So I'd been working to get as many of the internees out and get this godforsaken camp shut down for good." He looked at Noriko. "I remember stumbling through that burning building, exactly like this one, looking for you."

"Poppa . . ."

"The bodies were hanging from the rafters like in a slaughter-

house." His voice caught in his throat. "Even with all that, I remember counting them, counting the bodies in hopes that some of them,
any of them, might've survived . . . My God, I'm the one who taught
him how to tie that knot."

"Poppa."

"It wasn't enough that you hung them, but you had to shoot them
too?" He made the same agonizing sound in his throat as he stood.
"Mae was nowhere to be seen, and neither was the baby." His eyes
were watering, and I watched as he scrubbed a thumb and forefinger
into them. "I was choking to death from all the smoke as I fell down
those steps and they were all out there drinking and laughing like it
was some great thing they'd done, like it meant something after
what had happened to Andrew." He tossed the noose into the fire. "I
remember hitting you; I don't know how many times." He glanced
at Noriko again. "Then I saw you rolled up in a blanket out there on
the bare earth and it drew me away, possibly the only thing that ever
could."

"Poppa."

Everson looked at his son. "And then you killed that reporter,
Yoshida . . . How could I have ever raised you?"

Parker reached his hands out to his father, circling the barrel as
the other man backed away. "I did it for you, Poppa. I did it for
Andrew."

"Innocent people, innocent people who didn't have a damned
thing to do with the death of your brother, Parker."

"No, Poppa, no."

The older man reached out and snatched the rifle away from his
son and tossed it to me. "Well, it's over. I can't do it anymore . . . I
won't do it anymore." He stared at his son, the two of them looking
at each other over the burn barrel. "I'm sorry, son."

Parker glanced first at me and then the others. "We can just clean
it up, Dad, the same way we always have . . ."

"We . . . We?" The judge gestured toward me. "Check that rifle and tell me if it's been fired recently? Tell me if that isn't the weapon that killed Donnie Pickens?"

Parker ignored him, caught up in the excitement of his plan. "We just do what has to be done and then we tip this barrel over and the fire takes care of the rest, just the way it always has. You don't even have to be here, just leave and I'll take care of it all." He actually laughed. "You don't even have to know it happened, okay?"

The judge turned back to his only remaining son. "But I do, Parker. I know all of it. I'm sorry, I thought I was protecting you, but I wasn't; I was just protecting our lives, shielding us from what I knew would come in time." He turned his face away, biting a lip. "And now it's here, and it's that time."

He was about to speak again when there was a shot, and I thought for sure it had been the old man himself, but it wasn't. I watched as Parker raised the small semiautomatic up and continued to point it at his father.

The judge didn't move, but just stood there as the blood blossomed on his white shirt in the V-opening of his coat. Everson's expression didn't change as he slowly began sinking to the floor until another man and I caught him and tried to hold him up.

Crouching there, we held him as he looked up at his son's face, lit up from the burn barrel as he kept the muzzle of the .32 trained on us.

His face was blank as he began speaking. "I've always been the strong one, the one that did what had to be done . . ."

I'd just started to make a move for the .45 at my back when, beyond them, about twenty yards away I could see a flare of light illuminating another face in the distance, sheltered by a porkpie hat that faded to the pointed ember of a lit cigarette and the faint tune of "Ringo No Uta," or the apple song.

Parker continued talking, unaware of anything going on around him. "My brother, my father, they all underestimated me, thinking I was weak, but I was the one that did what had to be done, okay?" He raised the pistol until it was pointed directly at my chest. "I'm sorry . . ."

He shuddered, at least I thought that's what it was, and then suddenly stopped speaking, the expression on his face changing to one of wonderment as he looked down at the kissaki point of the Yo-mashiro school katana blade that protruded from his chest a good ten inches.

Noriko screamed as Parker dropped the pistol, blood drooling from his mouth as he grabbed the point of the sword with both hands and then slowly bent forward in an agonizing bow until his head entered the flames from the barrel, the only thing visible behind him, the kagura Hannya mask—the demon face of the woman done wrong.

EPILOGUE

I leaned back in my chair and listened to it squeal along with my daughter on the long-distance line to Cheyenne. "What do you mean you can't make it?"

"I'm just trying to get caught up from all that time I lost during this hearing."

There was a long silence as I listened to her breathe, building up a huff on the other end of the state. "It's a reception for the appointed posts in case he gets elected governor."

I picked up my coffee mug and took a sip, having to admit that the newfangled machine did a pretty good job. "Tell him he's got my vote."

"He'd better."

I sat my mug back down and repositioned the phone as Vic entered and stood in the doorway of my office. "When is it?"

"Saturday night."

She came in, sat in my visitor chair, and propped her boots up on the edge of my desk as I winked at her. "You've got a place I, my betrothed, and Dog can stay?"

"I do."

"All right, we'll be there."

Vic leaned forward. "Is that Cady?"

"Yep."

"I need to speak with her." I handed my undersheriff the phone and then leaned back in my chair again as my undersheriff placed a hand over the receiver and stared at me. "Do you mind?"

"Excuse me?"

"Us girls need to talk."

I stared back at her. "Oh." I stood and then vacated my space and moved out into the main office, wondering what exactly the girls needed to talk about.

Ruby was seated at her desk chatting with Saizarbitoria, the Basque contingency of our deputy staff, as Sancho reached down and petted Dog. "What's going on, Boss?"

I glanced back toward the now-closed door of my office as I rested my mug on the counter. "Evidently something to which I'm not supposed to be party." I reached into my pocket, pulled out the skinny tie, and handed it to him. "Here, take this for the first time you're charged with a homicide, whenever that may be."

He examined the skinny artifact. "It looks like a shoelace."

"They were all the rage in the fifties." I thought about it. "And the early sixties."

"Were the early sixties very different from the late fifties?"

"No, decades tend to go like that; it takes a few years for them to exert their individuality." I stared at him. "What decade were you born, the eighties?"

He continued to stare at me.

"Nineties?"

He stared at me some more.

I sipped my coffee. "Never mind."

The phone began ringing, and Ruby smirked at us as she picked up the receiver and began talking to whoever was on the other end.

Sancho leaned in confidentially. "So does this mean this crap with the Regis clan is pretty much over?"

I leaned my back against the counter and looked down the stairs at the golden light of the late summer morning and thought about calling Henry to see if he wanted to go fishing this weekend—then I remembered my command attendance at the reception in Cheyenne. "Oh, I'd imagine it'll blow over now that the legal aspect has been settled. They may try to come at me from another direction, but it'd be dangerous for them to work out in the open like that. So, I suppose yep, it's over."

"Walt?"

I turned to look at Ruby, who held the receiver out to me. "Department of Justice in DC."

"Probably Ruthless."

She had a strange look on her face. "No, I don't think so."

I took the thing, holding it to my ear. "Sheriff Walt Longmire speaking."

"Sheriff, this is Deputy Director Shawn Noble, and I was wondering if I could ask you a few questions concerning Treasury Agent Ruth One Heart?"

"Yep?"

"When was the last time you saw her?"

"About four days ago; Thursday night I believe."

"And she was preparing to fly back here to DC?"

"As far as I know, yes." There was a long pause. "Do you mind telling me what this is concerning?"

"Did she seem upset or emotional the last time you saw her?"

"Deputy Director, do you mind telling me what's going on here?"

"One Heart's flight plan filed with the FAA gives a first reporting point in Omaha but failed to arrive there on Tuesday."

"You mean she's missing?"

"That's exactly what I mean—the controller in Omaha reported her overdue and now missing."

"Do you think she had engine trouble and just landed somewhere?"

"That's exactly what we're trying to ascertain, but you've had no contact with her since Thursday night?"

"None."

"Well, it's probably just as you said, engine trouble or something and she's sitting at some Nebraska farmer's kitchen table having breakfast and trying to figure out how to get her plane out of a cornfield."

"I hope you're right." I took his number, and we both promised to contact each other if either of us heard anything.

Handing the phone back to Ruby, I sighed as the two of them continued to study me. "Um . . . Ruth One Heart is missing."

WEDNESDAY, MAY 27, 1964

It was dark in more ways than one as the two of us stood there attempting to keep warm. Snapping the lighter shut, he adjusted his ridiculous sunglasses and smoked, looking into the burn barrel that we'd dragged from the building in an attempt to keep it from burning the place down. "So, do you sleep with those things on?"

He straightened his narrow tie and ignored my question and asked one of his own. "What would you like to do, Walt Longmire?"

I glanced at the steps of the building where Sato's men had the judge's men rounded up and sitting on the barrack steps like prisoners of war. "To be honest, I don't know."

"There is one, very simple answer."

"Yep, I knew that was the one you'd be lobbying for."

He shrugged, picking a speck of tobacco from his tongue and flicking it toward the pebbled sand at our feet. "It is the one option that has the benefit of being foolproof."

"Yep, but there's something about killing nine men who might've done nothing but exercise bad judgment and then burying them in a hole in the desert."

He grinned a grim smile at the flicker of the flames. "'Exercising bad judgment,' is that what you would call it?"

"What would you call it?"

"Just desserts."

"Well, you would know all about that now, wouldn't you?"

He studied me, but the smile held. "Careful, I have told you how indiscriminate those holes in the desert can be."

I glanced at the two bodies wrapped in the sheets, lying in the open bed of one of the trucks. "You don't have any reason to kill us, this problem has solved itself." I gestured toward the group of men on the steps. "They don't have anything to gain by telling any of this to anybody."

"Perhaps, but some of them are stupid."

I stepped away from the barrel and then turned like a rotisserie chicken. "You can't go around killing everybody who's stupid, first of all because you can't afford the ammunition and second because there won't be anybody left."

"What about you?"

"What about me? I'm not stupid . . . mostly."

"No, you're not, you figured it out before the judge told us."

"I did."

"You have a knack for this kind of thing. Have you ever considered a life of crime?"

"Not really."

"Then perhaps the other side." Sato continued to study me, there in the half-light. "Will you speak of this to anyone?"

"I don't know." His eyes widened. "I'm just trying to be honest here. I mean, Parker was responsible for it all: the killing of the Tokyo . . . the Tokyo Ten, the murder of Alan Yoshida, getting the others to beat the shit out of Mike Katana, shooting Donnie Pickens, and then finally killing his father. And correct me if I'm wrong, but if the judge and his son are dead, then shouldn't Noriko inherit all the money and property?"

"Yes." Succumbing to the burn barrel heat, he stepped out past me. "We can arrange it so that it looks as if the son killed the service station manager and then the father killed the son."

"With a sword?"

He shrugged, but I could tell he was already thinking about it. "It will be tricky, but it can be done."

I glanced back at the group, still seated on the barrack steps. "And these guys?"

He gestured, opening his hands to the obvious. "The offer of the hole still stands."

"I can't allow for that."

He tilted his head in a look of absolute incredulity. "Allow?"

"They didn't kill anybody . . ."

He took a few steps past me. "The Tokyo Ten, as you referred to them, did not hang and shoot themselves."

"That was Parker."

Turning away, he smoked his cigarette. "He had help."

"But we don't know which ones."

"There are ways of finding out."

"Look, haven't you seen enough of that for one lifetime?" I stuffed my hands into my coat and discovered that the handcuffs were there, so I took them out and tossed them to him. "If you're going to kill them, then you're going to have to kill me."

He studied the cuffs, the soft shine of the metal reflecting the fire. "You mean that?"

"I do."

"It would be a shame." He walked out a bit farther to where I could see Noriko attending to Henry in the cab of one of the trucks. "Do you speak for them?"

"I believe I do."

"Then she, like you and your friend, must keep your mouths shut."

"Well, I'll have to talk to them about that."

He turned, now very serious as he walked past me toward his men, then tossed the butt into the barrel. "Perhaps you should ask them?"

I stood there for a moment more, then did as he said, approaching my truck and standing there by the door as Noriko sat on the edge of the seat. She was wearing Henry's Greek fishing cap and looked up at me as she cleaned the wound on the Cheyenne Nation's head. "Hi, kids."

The Bear looked up. "How goes the parley?"

"Complicated."

"Not so complicated—he wants to kill everyone?"

"Pretty much." I nodded my head toward Noriko. "Except for this one and her mother . . . Speaking of, where is Mae?"

Noriko continued working on Henry. "Gone."

I glanced around in the collected gloom of the abandoned camp. "Gone?"

She nodded. "It's what she does."

"Well, our friendly neighborhood yakuza want to kill all of Everson's men because some or all of them may or may not have been involved in the killing of ten of the Tokyo Twelve—he has a point."

The Bear tweaked his neck. "But you will not allow that?"

"No, and neither will you."

"I won't?"

"No."

"Why?"

"Because once the killing starts it's going to be hard to see where it's going to end, old buddy. For that and numerous other ethical reasons . . ." I looked into the bed of the other truck parked in front of us and at the pair of wrapped bodies looking like mummies. "Let's just let the dead bury the dead, shall we."

"So, we must bargain with them."

"In case you haven't noticed, we're not in much of a bargaining position."

The three of us remained there in the silence of deliberation until Noriko finally spoke. "Our silence, we will trade our silence for their lives. I have grown up with those men, most of them are like family to me. I don't think they are truly evil, and if they did something terrible long ago, even partially, then I feel as though they have paid enough of a price." She stood, handing me the bloody cotton swab and straightening her blouse and the letterman's jacket that had belonged to her father. "I will speak with him and win all our freedoms." She started to go but then turned to look back at us. "Besides, he will not kill me."

We watched her, Henry gingerly pulling himself through the door and then standing.

"How's your head?"

"Fine, and yours?"

"Looking to stay on my shoulders."

Noriko approached Sato, even going so far as to bow just a bit as they stood by the barrel, and they began speaking in Japanese.

Henry gazed after her. "I could stay."

I turned to look at him. "Excuse me?"

"Here, I could just stay here in Bone Valley, and you could go on."

"Henry, you can't hide here forever."

"Why not? Mae has."

I let the dust on that one settle. "Look, if you want, I'll drive you down to Nogales so you can run off into Mexico and dodge the draft properly."

He felt his head. "No, I will go with you; I have family to visit in Oklahoma . . . hopefully." The conversation by the burn barrel continued and Noriko and Sato seemed to be talking in a convivial manner. The Bear leaned toward me. "I have the shotgun under the seat. Do you have anything?"

"The .45 at the small of my back."

He nodded. "Good. If we go down it will not be without a fight."

We watched as Noriko broke off from Sato and started toward us. "He has taken us up on our offer."

I glanced at Henry and then back to her. "You mean he won't kill the others, and we can go?"

"Yes."

Henry took her hand. "What are you going to do?"

"I suppose stay here, it's all I've ever known—besides, there's my mother."

The Bear tugged at her hand. "Come with us and bring your mother."

"I couldn't do that to her—I think this is the only place in the world where she can survive." Noriko took a deep breath and stepped back from him. "There is a favor, though."

"There always is."

"You must give me a ride home."

"We're happy to."

She nodded toward the piles of weapons in the back of our truck. "And you must drop all of those off and lock them up in the service station after we leave." She glanced back at the group on the steps, who were now standing as Sato's men moved off toward the Cadillac. "Mr. Sato thinks it would be best if they were not armed while he and his men are here, arranging things."

"Agreed."

As we finished unloading the guns, I turned to Henry. "Your bags are at the Astoria?"

"Yes."

"Well, why don't you head over there, get them, and say goodbye to her, and we'll hit the road."

"You do not wish to spend the night?"

"No, I don't—just in case anybody changes their minds."

He shrugged and walked away as I picked up the last two rifles and placed them in the back office, thinking about the man we'd met here only a couple of nights ago. Donnie Pickens had devoted his life to both Noriko and Mae, and for that kindness he'd been killed.

It still didn't feel right walking away from this mess and allowing Sato and his group to clean it all up with a nice bow, but anything else might mean more hardship for the two women, and I couldn't enable that.

Coming back out front, I locked the door and then watched as a jade-green Cadillac drove slowly up the road, like a shark in search of a meal. It stopped at the corner, and I heard the electric window in the rear whir down, Sato's cigarette glowing in the cavernous interior like a bad intention. "It will be daylight in six hours."

I looked east toward the mountains as I approached but couldn't see any sign. "I'd say you're right, and you guys have some work ahead of you before you contact the authorities."

"Yes, we do."

"How, exactly, are you going to make it look as if father and son had killed each other?"

"You doubt our skill in such things?"

"No, it's not that—I'm just curious."

"It is sometimes better to not know the answer."

I stuck a hand out to him. "No offense, but I hope we never meet again."

"As do I, but one never knows." We shook hands, and he handed me a card. "Take this, and if you get into trouble over there, call this exchange number."

"And then I can get in more trouble?"

"One never knows."

I stepped back and watched them motor away into the desert, all four of them, not including the two bodies I was sure were in the trunk. I looked across the road at the church and then found myself walking into the street.

I figured Noriko was right: that the men here had taken care of her and her mother in their own fashion, that there was always PI Mike Tanaka to keep an eye on things, and that through his connections with Sato he could keep track of the story they made up. It wasn't honest, but it served a common good.

I stood there breathing in the keen night air and then finally kneeled in the street, peering under the porch of the church. "Are you there?

There was no answer, not that I expected there to be.

"I can't imagine the things you've been through, Mae." I glanced at the warm lights on at the bar/café down the street. "But Noriko is a fine woman, and of all the things you should be proud of, I think I'd start with her. She's going to need your help, and you might need some too."

Talked out, I stood and started to go to my truck but then stopped and looked into the darkness for a long while. "Mae . . . I guess what I'm saying is that I think you can stop hiding now."

I turned, walked across the street, and climbed into the truck before starting it and pulling it through the crossroads, where I stopped in front of the Astoria to toot the horn.

Henry and Noriko came out and shared a lengthy kiss as I looked the other way, spinning the massive garnet of a suicide knob like a roulette wheel.

After a moment the Bear threw his bags into the back with mine, alongside the surfboard, and then climbed in, shutting the door behind him.

Noriko stood on the wooden walkway in the Bear's fisherman's cap and raised a hand to me in a silent goodbye, but then shouted. "I've been meaning to ask, whose surfboard?"

I thumbed my chest. "Mine."

She shook her head and then laughed. "You're too big to surf." With that, she turned and went back into the Astoria where, after a moment, the lights were turned off.

Putting the half-ton in gear, I reached up, gripped the knob, circled around, and headed out of town, only to spot something lying in the road. Slowing to a stop, I ignored Henry's questioning look and climbed out.

Walking to the front of the truck, between the headlights, I glanced about but could see no one.

I took a knee and picked the thing up. Then I smiled as it grinned in affirmation, walked back to the old ranch truck, climbed in, tossed the item into the Cheyenne Nation's lap, and closed the door, forever driving out of Bone Valley.

After a few moments I watched as he joined the two of us in smiling as he carefully placed the Hannya mask over his face and slumped against the door, not saying another word for 657.4 miles.